THE
GOOK
LOVER

THE
GOOK
LOVER

Ron Wulkan

Putnam, St. Clair & Wyeth
Publisher

ISBN 978-0-615-15455-8

LIBRARY OF CONGRESS CONTROL NUMBER: 2007933317

Published by Putnam, St .Clair & Wyeth

Original art and cover design by Jill Joli Wulkan

Printed in the United States of America

This is a work of fiction. Names, characters, places and incidents are products of the author's imagination or are used fictitiously and are not to be construed as real. Any resemblance to actual events, locales, organizations or persons, living or dead, is entirely coincidental.

Dedicated to Jill, my best buddy, 24-7 business partner, editor, art director, artist and loving wife. Meeting over the North Pole was the start of a perfect friendship.

*"The stupid neither forgive nor forget;
the naive forgive and forget;
the wise forgive but do not forget."*

From 'The Second Sin' by Dr. Thomas Stephen Szasz, Professor
Emeritus of Psychiatry, State University of New York

The Rape of Nanking, Unit 731 war crimes, World War II and
the Korean War are all grim truths. Of the estimated 72
million people killed during the time frame of this fictional
story, more than half were innocent civilians.

ACKNOWLEDGMENTS

I am grateful for the encouragement of the late Iris Chang, journalist and award-winning author of 'The Rape of Nanking,' © 1997 (published by BasicBooks, a subsidiary of Perseus Books, L.L.C.) whom I met at the Rape of Nanking Conference at the Woodrow Wilson School of Public and International Studies, Princeton University. Her book had just been released as I was revising my fictional version of the event that she had so superbly written about with historical accuracy.

Deep appreciation to Catherine Wright and Dr. Raphael Haddock of Sarasota, who pointed out a near-fatal personality flaw in Tomi Tomigawa that my wife Jill had known from the outset; but one that I had stubbornly denied. To have such bright, perceptive and honest friends is a rare blessing.

Any errors in Japanese vocabulary and syntax in this novel are mine. They are dredged from a sincere but dusty memory after six busy decades.

PROLOGUE

Streams of shoppers and office workers impatiently brushed past the limping old man, unaware that he was the 'Henry Ford of modern Japan.' No one knew what he had done in 'Double U Double U Two,' a quirky name the winners gave a war started by the losers.

He smiled as the crowd smoothly flowed around a yellow taxi that brazenly blocked the Fifth Avenue intersection. Manhattan traffic misbehaved like American English, an illogical pudding that somehow worked well despite its oddities. A language that didn't take itself seriously was needed in a world of unintended consequences. No wonder the once-rigid *Nihongo*, Japanese, soaked up American slang.

A book store window became his vanity mirror. He saw himself as younger and ignored his sagging jowls and arthritic stoop. Self-admiration vanished when he read the title on a book display: *The Rape of Nanking, The Forgotten Holocaust of World War II*.

On the dark red and black front cover was the photo of a Japanese officer holding the familiar flag. An Imperial Army cameraman had posed him on that stinking riverbank. Cropped out of the original shot had been the obscene raft of floating flesh. He remembered how bodies of women and children quivered from feeding swarms of Yangtze River black fish.

He peered at the author's portrait. How did this much-too-young Iris Chang discover his sixty-year-old photo and write a book about Matters Best Left Unsaid?

The old man, whose chromed name now glittered on millions of cars, inhaled acrid traffic fumes and thought of the centuries-old lament of *Kamo no Chomei*: "Because I was born in a world of foulness and evil I was forced to witness such heartbreaking sights."

Like the gentle monk, he had witnessed heartbreaking sights. But some of the foulness and evil were his. He limped into the store to buy a new book of past sins denied.

CHAPTER ONE
TOKYO, 1932-1936

The boy was the newest link in the unbroken chain of legendary Tomigawa warriors who had fought on the winning side of Japan's many wars. When his father returned from duty in Manchuria, the Tomigawa household gained a servant, Taiko. Two years older than the boy, she taught him many things and they shared secrets.

At night, after she cuddled and pressed on him, she whispered her inside thoughts. He learned that Japan was hurt by poor rice harvests and something called the Depression. Like many starving farm families, Taiko's parents sadly did the *Zassoo o Nuku Wakai,* 'Weeding Out the Young.' Her older brother was sent to the Army to earn food and rent money for the family.

The next harvest was worse and Taiko's reluctant parents were about to contract her to a brothel when Taiko's brother died saving Major Tomigawa's life. The grateful officer hired Taiko as a family servant with wages that kept her family from disaster.

In time, their secret pleasures increased. After every climax, he kissed Taiko's tears of happiness that inspired his first haiku:

> *The tears of Taiko*
> *Diamonds from inside her soul*
> *Sparkle through the night.*

"I will pay for the poem by giving you a new name," she teased. "Tomi fits you better than Tomoyki." The boy vowed that whenever he heard the name, he would think of her. But at military prep school, Tomi was called 'The Memory' by envious classmates. He wasn't the top scholar, but he remembered everything. While others wasted time sleeping, he reviewed the day's lessons. He required only three hours of sleep, a habit born of his Taiko nights.

When Tomi was named Outstanding Cadet at the Imperial Military Academy, his proud father declared, "Now you are a true Tomigawa warrior! Your destiny is to follow in my path."

But on February 28, 1936 Tomi was told to report to the academy commandant. When he entered General Inukai's office, the senior staff rose from their chairs as if he were the superior. Confused, he barely managed a proper salute.

"Cadet Tomigawa," General Inukai said in a too-kind voice from beneath his white walrus moustache, "your honorable father single-handedly averted a national crisis. To remove the shame of the First Regiment's symbolic mutiny, Major Tomigawa committed *Seppuku* outside the Army Club at dawn. His ritual death shocked the hotheads. They dismantled the checkpoints and marched their troops back to camp."

Tomi was sent home in a staff car whose engine was as familiar as his textbooks. He spent his free time at the motor pool working with mechanics. He ignored the sedan's smooth purr and fought back tears as they merged into the traffic flow of vehicles and rickshaws.

At home, some of his father's fellow officers attended his mother. Her eyes were red but Lady Tomigawa behaved as expected of a noble woman. Tomi imitated her outward calmness until they left. Then she allowed her inside to vent.

"You don't have a father anymore, Tomoyki!" she cried. Taiko scurried in with a cold compress and made her lie down. The wet cloth over Lady Tomigawa's face didn't muffle her bitter rage. "Why him? Among all officers, why was he selected? Your father refused to join the comic opera mutiny started by foolish officers trying to embarrass the Army into a 'Strike North' strategy. The secret Imperial Wish is to 'Strike South' against the colonial powers. War is harsh, but rotten Army politics are worse!"

Tomi patted his mother's balled fist. She sat up and moaned, "He did it the ancient way, but he was alone. No one helped him!"

She bent forward as if the *kana*, sword, had entered her belly, and she beat her forehead against the tatami mat. Mother and son knew how it went: Bow to the Imperial Palace. Kneel. Expose belly. Unsheathe heirloom Tomigawa sword. Wrap new silk tightly around blade's middle and grasp with both hands. Plunge steel deep inside and yank blade across belly. The hot, slippery mass emerges reeking, steaming. Unbearable agony.

In ancient times, a trusted companion with a bared sword stood behind the kneeling noble for the merciful beheading. But no one released Tomi's father from a slow painful death. His suffering was a lesson to the rebels about an officer's ultimate loyalty to the Emperor.

***

Standing before his father's ashes at the household shrine, Tomi's mother presented him with the Tomigawa sword. "Your ancestors achieved great honor with this *kana*. Now it is yours. Do no less."

Tomi, the only Tomigawa warrior left, returned his mother's low bow with a slightly higher one that reflected his new status. He hooked the heavy scabbard to his dress uniform belt clip, donned the broad white sash attached to the box containing his father's ashes. A waiting Army limousine took them to the Yasukuni Shrine, a half mile from the Academy.

Lady Tomigawa walked slightly behind her son as they slowly moved between the ranks of officers at the Shrine. General Inukai intoned, "The spirits of the 126,363 warrior heroes who dwell within our military shrine greet Major Tomigawa as their worthy companion. Though he did not die in battle, his sacrifice is accepted with favor by the God-Emperor. Tomigawa-Sama's death serves as a reminder to all officers of their absolute loyalty to the Imperial Wish. The Army recognizes his son, who continues the Tomigawa tradition." The General's rows of medals jingled faintly like fragile wind chimes as he bowed to the white box of ashes Tomi carried.

During the drive home, Tomi's mother uncharacteristically snapped a loud, course order through the glass partition to the limousine driver, who failed to hear her. Assured of privacy, Tomi's mother turned to her son, "Well, what did you learn from the ceremony?"

"Why, Father was honored as a hero."

"Think of what you saw, Tomoyki" she snapped. "The mutiny leaders of the First Regiment were the rear rank, but they attended. It means they will not be punished except for slow promotions. Why was General Inukai chosen to greet your Honorable Father's ashes, instead of one of his superiors on the General Staff?"

"Because he is my commanding general at the Academy?"

She sighed, "Tomoyki, your father had scant political sense but hoped you would be better at it. The Imperial Palace political generals didn't attend because they suspect, with good reason, that other old generals had encouraged the mutiny. It was a subtle warning. Study little details as you would enemy tactics. Your father wasn't awarded a medal despite his terrible sacrifice. Why?"

Tomi stammered ignorance. His mother frowned. "Because it would rub salt in the wounds of the rebels. The Palace clique wants to smooth over the feud between the 'Strike North' and 'Strike South' factions in the Officer Corps. The political generals need total Army support for their grand plans. Understand?"

Tomi waved a negative hand and his mother explained, "The generals in the Palace are ambitious and impatient, a bad military combination. They would expand the empire southward while old generals like Inukai want to attack our traditional northern enemy, Russia.

"Your father was uneasy about the Palace's thirst for military adventures, but his loyalty came first. The ceremony revealed something important that few noticed: Today's world is fading and tomorrow's world has yet to reveal itself."

***

Everything changed after his father's death. The Academy demanded scholastic perfection from Tomi. Although he mastered *Eigo*, English, with ease, he almost failed Mandarin Chinese. He was tone deaf and Chinese tonal accents changed the meaning of identical words. The word for 'mother' and 'horse' was the same, but pronounced differently. His classmates laughed when he once recited, "Order the troops to saddle their mothers."

On weekend leave, he was Lady Tomigawa's student of politics by day and Taiko's erotic master at night. To teach him political nuances, his mother recounted complex court intrigues of her clever Fujiwara family ancestors. She compared them to the Tomigawas, who won battles but lost to the politics of the less than astute Imperial Court. Her blasphemy worried him.

"The rightful place of the Tomigawa-Fujiwara family is on the other side of the Palace Moat, not here. The blood in your veins is as noble as those whom you revere. Your ancestors served selflessly in many wars while palace cowards gained wealth and power. Even today we remain poor but proud *Samurai* because we refused to money-grub with the common opportunists when Japan modernized. Frankly, I'm not sure we were right."

His mother revealed what others dared not speak. On his final weekend home, his mother explained that, contrary to current news stories, Japan's China Incident began with a piss.

"A Japanese sentry at Peking's Marco Polo Bridge walked off to empty his bladder when accidental shots rang out from a nearby Chinese Army unit. In the confusion, the Japanese officer assumed that the absent soldier had been captured. After trading insults with a Chinese captain, the angry officer attempted a rescue and the shooting started. Other Japanese units joined in and the accidental skirmish became a firefight with heavy casualties on both sides.

"It was the excuse the Army wanted," Mother said. "Claiming the Chinese had attacked first, our elite divisions in Shanghai began the offensive. Tokyo's weak civilian government was powerless. The Army knew the secret Imperial Wish and was ready, having been stationed in China with European and American troops since the Boxer Rebellion thirty-six years ago.

"The Chinese were unprepared and the West failed to act. In four months, General Matsui's army has pushed up the Yangtze despite growing resistence. Our army will capture the southern capital city of Nanking and the short war will end. The Palace war-lovers' gamble is succeeding."

Tomi was confused. "Mother, if the Imperial Wish is to strike south at the European colonies, why did the Army start the China

Incident?"

"Japan needs China's resources to finance military expansion into Southeast Asia, and the Chinese Army is weak from competing warlords, corruption, and local Communists."

"What about the Soviets?"

"Also weak, but the Palace thinks the rewards are much greater in the South."

Tomi asked, "What was Father's opinion, and yours?"

She smiled. "At last you are thinking instead of swallowing everything you're taught, even by me. What was Napoleon's blunder in Russia?"

"He attacked a feeble Russia and was so confident of quick victory that his troops wore summer uniforms. Long supply lines, Russia's defensive depth and winter defeated the biggest, best army of Europe."

"Exactly. Your father and I talked much about this. He was a realist who knew Japan could only win short wars launched with surprise attacks. Despite grandiose talk, Japan cannot sustain a long war. Your father believed *Nippon* would be better served through trade policies backed by military strength. He hoped the Europeans could be eased out of Asia without war.

"Foreign adventures often carry more risk than their planners anticipate. But he warned that *gaijin*, westerners, were an unpredictable race. Like others, he feared America might impose a naval blockade to strangle our economy, forcing us into a premature war that we cannot win."

Tomi frowned, "If Honorable Father didn't agree with his superiors, why ...?"

His mother interrupted, "He was trained to obey unto death, just as you are. But loyalty should not stop you from thinking. Keep such thoughts locked deep inside even as you perform your combat duties in the approved outward manner."

"I have no secret thoughts. Besides, the fighting will be over long before I'm commissioned."

"No, my son," she said sadly. "Your cadet days are over. Last evening I was told you are being sent to China to continue the Tomigawa tradition for propaganda purposes."

"What? Before graduation next year?"

"Yes. We don't know who arranged it, but it carries a nasty price. You are assigned to the 16th, the division with the worst reputation in the Army."

CHAPTER TWO
NANKING CHINA, NOVEMBER 1937

Cold morning mist blurred the muddy countryside, softening everything except the screams of the two Chinese women and the girl-child. They reminded Tomi of his big mistake on his first combat patrol. He had neglected to include the girl-child in the sex break and First Lieutenant Harada mercilessly scolded him in a loud voice heard by the men.

"A soldier has two minutes to off-load his gear and outer uniform, grab quick sex comfort, eat, drink and return to battle-ready. Using two females takes the patrol 45 minutes."

"I understand, Sir."

Harada ignored him. "Adding the girl-child allows everyone to take sex comfort and eat their rations in a half-hour. A precious 15 minutes is gained." Harada's snarl exaggerated his lower-class accent, "Unlike you, my men didn't have breakfast or hot tea served to them this morning. So watch how we do our duty and learn, Probationary Officer Tomigawa!"

Tomi bowed low. *Hai!* "Yes Sir! " Harada walked away in disgust. Tomi was in the awkward twilight between Academy cadet and commissioned officer. His bad luck to be assigned to the 16th was worsened by having the bully Harada as his superior. He was called *Kuma*, 'The Bear,' behind his back, as much for his vile temper as his thick body and face.

The pig farmyard was filled with soldiers, some eating and a few impatiently waiting their turn with the women. Warm in his new greatcoat, Tomi watched the females battered into cold mud on their naked backs. Only lowly second-class privates were still in line. When the next soldier eclipsed the girl-child's body, she screamed as he dug his hobnail boots into the ground for leverage.

The men were as oblivious to her shrieks as they were to the distant rumble of artillery and the noisy crows circling overhead in hungry excitement.

Tomi thought, *"Does the girl-child's pain say more about us than China?"* He tasted self-doubt and gripped the hard scabbard in his gloved left hand. In this miserable place without a name, was he the only one bothered by gang rape? Gloom, black as the noisy crows, trapped him. Sadly, he looked away from the rapes into the scowling face of First Lieutenant Harada.

The Bear sneered, "Too delicate to serve with real men in the field?" He turned and deliberately broke wind at Tomi. Beatings were part of Army discipline, but not this crude insult; not even to an 18-year-old probationary officer. Harada growled, "Paper soldiers don't belong here!" The insult was worse than the fart of disrespect Harada left behind as he stalked off.

Tomi forced himself to look. A recruit named Sato was the last to finish. He wiped himself with straw in an exaggerated gesture and hitched up his pants. He reclaimed his ammo belt, overcoat and pack from a comrade. Sato disengaged the tripod of rifles, passed two to comrades and almost dropped his own. Allowing a rifle to fall was as bad as a poor bayonet stroke.

Harada shouted, "Attention! Form ranks!" Tomi took his position behind the last squad and saw Sato drop his rifle in the mud while fumbling with a trouser button. Lieutenant Harada followed Tomi's startled glance and knew Sato's sin.

The Bear and his senior sergeant shoved their way to the trembling recruit. In a practiced east-west, west-east double blow that sounded like a single slap, the Bear split open Sato's lip. Harada said, "Tonight you'll lick pig shit off your rifle!" The Bear spat in Sato's terrified face. Harada's wet mark of damnation turned a soldier into *eta*, a subhuman.

Back at camp, Sato knew he'd be punched, kicked and worked eighteen hours a day at hard labor. In a sleep-deprived haze, his mistakes would earn more beatings. Food and water would be withheld. If he fainted, non-coms would revive him by urinating on his face.

Tomi's father had told him that such hazing was brutality, not training. But Army doctrine held that severe punishment made superior warriors. The recruit suicide rate was higher than other armies but it did produce tough, remorseless fighters.

Harada shouted, "Probationary officer! Supervise bayonet execution. Use worthless Sato."

"Sir, is the girl-child to be included?" Tomi asked, worried about his earlier mistake.

"Forget her. What are you, a gook lover? Get to it!"

As Tomi did a smart about-face despite the mud, he noticed several men smirking at the insult. "Master steel and you master men," his father had taught him.

"I am not a paper soldier! I'm not a gook-lover. I will be master of men," Tomi swore to himself as he pointed to Sato and the next man. In his deepest parade ground voice, Tomi shouted, "You and you, fix bayonets! Prepare to execute the two women!"

The soldiers approached, pointing their weapons at the naked women. They clutched the limp girl-child between them and begged for their lives in hoarse wails. Sato said, "You dumb sows, the child ain't gonna get hurt."

Harada ordered the patrol to stand at ease and watch. He expected Tomi to botch his first killing assignment. The more witnesses, the greater Tomi's loss of face.

On Tomi's orders, a corporal pried the girl from the frantic women and dragged the sobbing child by her long hair across the barnyard. Her naked back left a smooth, narrow path in the mud.

Tomi barked, "Use bayonets!" The old woman begged on her knees until a single downward thrust made her meat for the crows. Sato's target, the one he had just used for sex comfort, painfully limped toward her daughter, trying to call her name. But only hoarse animal sounds came from a throat ruined by ceaseless screaming. She croaked, "Oooo Ahg! Oooo Ahg!"

Dark mud laced with streaks of bright blood covered her back and buttocks in contrast to her front, scraped clean by rapists' uniforms and metal buttons. Crescent marks dotted her upper body. Tooth bites.

Laughing soldiers mimicked her. "Oooo Ahg, Oooo Ahg!"

One man yelled, "Looks like a crippled monkey!"

"No! Too big!" shouted another. "That thing is Oooo Ahg, The Crippled Chimpanzee of Nanking!"

Sato chased the terrified woman and slipped in pig shit. The men howled and Tomi yelled curses at the recruit. Lieutenant Harada grinned. The young probationary officer was, as Harada had expected, an inept fop.

"Whore!" Sato snarled and awkwardly jabbed the rifle's 20-inch bayonet at the woman. The blade entered Oooo Ahg's scrawny side, caught on a splintered rib and stopped. Bayonets were for groin, gut, stomach or throat. Hit bone and the blade stuck. The impaled Oooo Ahg groaned. With each heave of her thin body, the embedded bayonet and rifle wobbled in Sato's loosened grip. His face twisted in boyish confusion.

Knowing Lieutenant Harada would blame him for the fiasco, Tomi grabbed the rifle stock from Sato's flaccid hands. "Cockroach! That's not how to use a bayonet." He yanked out the blade and the woman squealed like a hog being slaughtered.

Tomi bellowed, "Pay attention to this lesson." Timing his words to his motions in a poetic beat, he chanted, "Hit high into the stomach. Thrust up and up. The blade seeks the heart."

As Tomi uttered *shinzoo*, heart, he withdrew and the target crumpled.

"Continue the attack," he said and spun around. The bayonet became a glint-edged arc circling the whirling flaps of his greatcoat. Before his coattails returned to vertical, he lunged and deftly sliced open Sato's nose tip. Blood welled down the recruit's split lip as he fell backward over the low sty rail, spread-eagled in churned mud. Tomi leaned over and aimed the bloody blade tip at Sato's eyes. The recruit squawked as much in terror as in pain.

"Remember this well, Second Class Private Sato of the 16th Division! Someday you will be a good soldier and this lesson may save your life," Tomi said with more politeness than required as he carefully leaned the dirty rifle upright against the fence. He took Sato's hand and lifted him out of the mud-shit. Never before had the soldiers witnessed a recruit treated with consideration; or an officer who wielded the bayonet with such graceful skill.

The Bear grunted amiably, "Not a bad bayonet lesson, Probationary Officer. Lead the patrol."

***

-11-

Tomi fought the thick, rich mud that sucked his boots with each step. Their patrol, far behind the fighting front, was a terror sweep designed to stampede the remaining civilians toward Nanking's defenders and spread confusion. Harada had left the girl-child alive to add to the panic.

Months earlier, the rich fields had yielded bountiful harvests of barley, cotton, millet, soybean and tobacco. The heavily-laden infantrymen marveled at the river plain's dark fertility and ached to farm it. They were sons of poor rice farmers who tilled tiny plots of overused land rented at usurious rates. The lower ranks seethed with bitterness at the selling of their sisters to brothels and were told to blame the West rather than the landlords and money-lenders who gouged them.

The officer corps was angry because weak politicians pandered to colonial powers who had thwarted the expansion of Asia's only modern, industrialized nation. After key pro-western politicians were assassinated by right-wingers, the Army was free to follow the Imperial Wish.

A group of unarmed Chinese were flushed out by the patrol but many escaped in a hail of hasty shots. Harada blamed Tomi. "Dammit, Tomigawa! From now on, no more than one bullet will be fired for every five gooks captured and bayoneted."

Despite the impossible order, Tomi couldn't fault Harada. The army was low on ammunition, food and everything else because of its vainglorious tradition that insisted fighting spirit overcame an archaic supply system staffed by officers not considered true warriors.

Fighting spirit had nothing to do with it. A terrified, half-naked Chinese running for his life across a muddy field was faster than a Japanese soldier who wore a steel helmet and carried a 9- pound rifle with sixty rounds of ammunition; plus blanket, cold rice rations, canvas shelter-half, a 2 -1/2-pint water canteen, gas mask, poncho and bayonet with scabbard.

The 115-pound soldier was squat and bowlegged from generations of poor peasant diet and overwork. On a daily field ration of 4 ounces of rice and a small hunk of dried fish, the tough Japanese soldier easily outmarched the bigger European. It was Japan's 2,597th year of training its warriors for hardship and self-sacrifice.

Grateful for a whispered suggestion from Senior Sergeant Otake, Tomi carried out Harada's demand. Five of the fastest soldiers gave their 45-pound packs and rifles to comrades and, armed only with unsheathed bayonets, formed a skirmish line ahead of the patrol to run down prey.

Sergeant Otake drew Tomi aside and murmured, "Sir, what if the Chinese have guns?" Tomi hid his embarrassment and armed one of the soldiers with his own pistol.

Long before the winter light began to fade, 38 Chinese civilians had been captured without a shot. A satisfied Harada had them all quickly bayoneted.

Sergeant Otake muttered to Tomi. "Sir, the men are exhausted. If we catch any more gooks, can we use them as mules to carry gear instead of killing them right away? First Lieutenant Harada might agree if you proposed it." To Tomi's surprise, The Bear grunted approval.

The only sounds heard for the next half hour were panting men and the squish-splat of hobnail boots in mud. Suddenly, Sergeant Otake hand-signaled the patrol to halt and assume firing position. Tomi scanned the field ahead but saw nothing except a winter-dormant orchard dotted with huge piles of pruned deadwood.

Sergeant Otake crawled over to Tomi and silently jabbed his finger at a large mound of tree cuttings. Annoyed that a non-com, old enough to be his father, saw an enemy that he couldn't, Tomi impulsively snaked head-first into the nearest huge pile that blocked their view. Halfway in, his face was punctured by sharp, pointed branches. One barely missed his eye. Despite severe pain Tomi continued burrowing to the far side, where he saw a squatting man, cigaret dangling from his lips, trying to relieve himself. Other Chinese were resting against tree trunks, smoking and talking. Tomi reversed his snaking motion and rejoined the patrol.

Lieutenant Harada and Sergeant Otake ignored the young officer's bloody face when he whispered to the Bear, "Gooks. Far side of mound. Twelve bunched together. No weapons in sight. No sentries. Probably deserters."

Harada whispered, "Sergeant Otake, take one squad around the right flank. Tomigawa, lead another squad around the left. I'll take the center. Fixed bayonets. Charge in exactly four minutes. Let no one escape."

The simple trap worked and the surprised Chinese were caught in a ring of steel. Their hands tied, each captive was loaded with several full field packs and equipment. Freed from the weight, the men joked as they kicked the prisoners into a line.

Sato discovered another Chinese hidden in a nearby ditch and loaded the man with his pack. Sergeant Otake remarked to Tomi, "Sir, see how Sato's prisoner stands. That man is not used to physical work."

Tomi ordered Sato to bring over his newly-caught mule. Sato gave Tomi an unnecessary salute and shoved the Chinese forward. The prisoner affected a theatrical cowering pose.

"He looks different, Sir. Maybe he wasn't with the others. Best we check him," Sergeant Otake said.

Tomi trotted over to Harada. "Sato's prisoner looks suspicious, Sir. With your ability to speak Chinese, would you care to interrogate him?"

The Bear shrugged indifferently. In ungrammatical Cantonese, Harada ordered the prisoner to unload. As the man squirmed out of the shoulder straps, Harada kicked him in the groin. The prisoner fell into a fetal position. With careful aim, Harada smashed the man's arm with his boot. The prisoner uttered an upper-class Mandarin curse that even Tomi understood.

"Permission to search the prisoner, Sir?"

Harada snorted, "Be quick about it; then bayonet the fucking landlord bastard. Let the dogshit recruit carry his own damn pack." Harada walked off with his binoculars to look for more civilians.

Sergeant Otake lifted the groaning man to his feet by his uninjured arm. When Otake's hands moved past the bound hands, the prisoner tensed. "He's hiding something!" The senior sergeant yanked down the prisoner's pants.

Slung below the prisoner's narrow hips was a pouch the sergeant handed to Tomi. Inside the body-warmed oilskin packet

were several folded sheets of rice paper. Tomi ran to Lieut[e]
Harada and presented the packet to him with a formal bow.

The Bear unfolded the first sheet and gasped when he saw
the elegant characters and official chops that signified
importance. Harada carefully folded the papers, placed the packet
in his blouse pocket and buttoned the flap. He roared, "This is a
special prisoner! He must not escape or be injured. We return to
camp immediately!"

Sergeant Otake bound the prisoner's hands, made a noose
from tent cord and tightened it around his neck. The patrol
moved out with the prisoner in the center. Trailing behind was
Sato. Despite his swollen nose, split lip and heavy pack, he strutted
like a victor.

At camp, the mule-prisoners were knocked to the ground
and left under guard until tomorrow's sword and bayonet drill.
Harada personally tugged the special prisoner toward Division
Headquarters, a cluster of large tents.

Sergeant Otake and Tomi check the men before turning in.
Rewarded with hot bean curd soup in addition to their usual dried
fish ration, the men cheerfully bragged about the bayonet lesson
on Oooh Agh, the Crippled Chimpanzee of Nanking, and remarked
how decent the new officer was.

Sato's punishment was reduced to a single beating by a
disinterested corporal.

Too weary to trek across camp to the first aid tent, Tomi
invited Sergeant Otake to rest and sip hot sake with him. The
veteran non-com grinned when Tomi thanked him for his many
suggestions. Otake explained, "This is how we did it in the old
Army, Sir. Assisting new officers is part of our job."

"I'm curious, Sergeant, how did you know there were Chinese
in the orchard?"

"Tobacco stink. That reminds me. I told Lieutentant Harada
that you detected the Chinese courier."

"Why? You deserve the credit."

"Once you have the right officer, take care of him and he'll
take care of the men. You will do more good for us than any
personal credit I could get. It's the Army way, Sir."

A messenger appeared, ghostlike, out of the darkness.

)fficer Tomigawa? You are to report to Division
nmediately."

te, Tomi splashed canteen water on his face,
nds bleed again.

command tent were First Lieutenant Harada,
___.ı officers and two staff colonels. Their shadows
were exaggerated by flickering kerosene lanterns. The colonels
stood behind an empty campaign chair as if it were a throne still
warm from a ruler's bottom.

They scowled at his filthy uniform and blood as Tomi saluted
and bowed. The shorter of the two colonels, his round face
accented by baldness, said, "First Lieutenant Harada reports you
identified the spy. How did you know?"

"Honorable Sirs, First Lieutenant Harada's skillful
interrogation in Chinese revealed the true identity of the prisoner,
who had not behaved like the others."

"But how did you know there were Chinese hidden out of
sight in the orchard?"

"Cigaret smoke, Sir." Tomi tried not to blink. The puncture
wound next to his eye won the fight as the dominant pain.

The other colonel said, "The prisoner culled from the herd of
gooks is a rare catch. For someone with Academy blackboard
chalk dust on his hands, you did well on your first patrol."

From the tent entrance behind him Tomi heard a deep
cultured voice purr, "Chalk dust or not, you did better than well,
Tomigawa. I am most pleased with you." An immaculately dressed
general walked in and posed as if for an official photograph. "How
remarkable the man wasn't killed on the spot and his papers
undetected."

With his full cape and beautiful uniform, the lean general
was a golden crane among barnyard fowl. The high gloss of his
polished boots reflected lantern light when he crossed his legs.
Tomi wondered how the orderlies kept the general's boots free of
China's mud.

The tall colonel said that the official papers had been
translated and that the prisoner disgorged added information. "A
successful interrogation, General Suzuki Sir," he preened. "We in
the 16th Division are experienced in such matters."

This elegant crane was the Imperial Palace Suzuki Tomi had heard so much about.

The general nodded, "Now that you have drained the Chinese officer, clean him up and bring him here in a condition that allows him to respond coherently to my questions. Now gentlemen, I wish to speak to young Tomigawa alone."

The shocked officers tried to hide their curiosity as they left in order of rank. When Harada passed Tomi, the Bear worried if his fart would ruin his career.

Heavy eyebrows and steel-rimmed glasses dominated General Suzuki's narrow face. Tomi's father had said that General Suzuki was an intellectual with a great personal fortune. He was very political and a leader of the 'Strike South' expansionist clique. In English class, Tomi had learned that the name Smith was as common as Suzuki. However this general was called 'The Number One, Most Honorable Smith Of All.'

In formal Imperial Court style out of place in a field tent, he said, "Your prisoner is an aide of Generalissimo Chiang Kai-shek. Indeed, you are the son of that brave warrior who died for the Emperor. The Tomigawas continue to serve Nippon well."

Tomi bowed low, accepting praise for all of his ancestors. "Stand at ease," Suzuki ordered. Tomi snapped his left foot in front, bent the knee slightly, with his left hand on the hilt of the Tomigawa sword. Despite a bloody face and filthy uniform, he was impressive.

General Suzuki shifted his own sword between his legs and smoothed his tunic. He looked like a hawk when he removed his eyeglasses and polished them with a handkerchief monogrammed with an English letter.

"I had the honor of informing *Showa Sama,* The God Emperor, about your father's sacrifice. It served a most useful imperial purpose at a critical time. But look at you! Did you have to spill precious Tomigawa blood in your first day in the field? Are you so anxious to die young?" He scowled at Tomi, "There are many ways to serve The God Emperor. Not all are in battle.

"Effective immediately you will be posted as a junior liaison officer between General Nakajima of the 16th Division, and Army Commander General Matsui's staff. You'll be in a lowly but critical position, able to keep me informed of events in the coming occupation of Nanking. Our Army, rich in rigid, opinionated officers, lacks objective, flexible observers. It is our weakness. Your inexperience will be to my advantage because you lack bias."

Annoyed by Tomi's look of disappointment, General Suzuki snapped, "You must show the same loyalty as did your father. This is why I had you assigned here. Understand?"

Tomi didn't, but barked, "Yes, Sir!"

"Congratulations on your battlefield promotion, *Second Lieutenant* Tomigawa!"

Tomi had killed a woman, witnessed a gang rape and captured unarmed civilians for execution. His sword was unbloodied and his aching face wounds were inflicted by a farmer's rubbish pile. Now he was going to be an errand boy for the rest of the very short war. He was a failure.

"You will be awarded the Exceptional Service Medal. The reasons are complex. Think of it in terms of the Nanking Sword Contest."

Lieutenants Mukai and Noda were vying to be the first to cut down a hundred Chinese with his sword. The score, 89 to 78, was highly publicized because the Army wanted to show the nation how well the war was progressing in China.

The general inserted a cigaret in his holder and lit it. He bragged, "When I learned that Major Tomigawa's only son had captured an important Chinese officer, I saw a rare opportunity to add a new chapter to the Tomigawa legend. Fresh from the Academy, you killed hundreds of heavily-armed Chinese soldiers and single-handedly captured a high-ranking courier with vital secrets that will hasten the fall of Nanking. If one officer can do this, imagine what our entire Army can do!"

General Suzuki aimed his cigaret holder at Tomi. "Your heritage, heroics and dramatic face wounds are proof of our racial superiority!

A logical language, Japanese has one word, *eiyuu*, for battle hero, and another, *shujinkoo*, for fictional book hero. Tomi knew which he was.

"Tomorrow," said the general, "You'll be flown back to Japan for a five-day leave and receive your medal at a Headquarters ceremony. Do not quibble over any minor variations you mistakenly think that you recall from the heat of battle. We have no choice. Equally important ..."

Events were happening too fast for Tomi. Confused, he missed General Suzuki's next comment. Did the general mention *kekkon,* marriage?

"... For these political and family reasons, the Suzuki-Tomigawa *kekkon* will be in accordance with a secret vow your late father and I made. The Suzuki-Tomigawa marriage will be held during your furlough. You will meet your betrothed at the medal awarding ceremony."

Suzuki ignored Tomi's astonishment and continued, "She is the daughter of my late older brother. A fine maiden, only a year older than you. The bloodlines of both our families are without flaw, save for your family's unfortunate habit of marrying women who cannot produce enough heirs. Our family has strong, wide-hipped women. My niece will give us many sons."

The general rubbed his hands and said awkwardly, "The future of the Tomigawa blood line must be assured in these perilous times. Yet to preserve tradition, a Tomigawa must be present when Nanking falls and China becomes our vassal state. For these conflicting reasons, certain unusual events must precede the ceremony. There isn't time for a proper honeymoon."

The general coughed. "Military expediency overrules social custom. A discreet meeting with your future bride is highly unconventional, but necessary. Your mother will be approached with proper ceremony and protocol, but on an accelerated schedule."

Tomi swayed as much from shock as fatigue. Openly embarrassed, the general continued, "We have no other choice. The Tomigawa line must not end with your premature death by accident or in battle. It is important to the nation.

"After the wedding, you'll be flown back in time for the final battle. A word of warning: If you fail to cooperate fully, or if you repeat this conversation to anyone, you will be made a comfort woman brothel inspector and later discharged from the Army in disgrace. And the Lady Tomigawa will also be affected."

Tomi lowered his eyes and bowed, hiding his scorn. The

crass threat showed weakness.

"Beware of General Nakajima. Your division commander is a dangerous man with powerful patrons. He will order you to tell him all my requests and questions. Do so. Obey him to the fullest. Serve him well, but keep me informed."

Suzuki looked up and saw insolence and disillusionment in the tall youth's direct stare. To spy on one's superior officer violated Tomi's code of honor.

"Good!" General Suzuki smiled broadly to hide his irritation. "I want an intelligence bound to me by unshakable family loyalty and honor, not by fear or threats that wear thin with time. Not all of our enemies are outside Japan. Some are in the army. By birth, you are in the Emperor's most loyal faction. Do your duty diligently and stay alive. You must produce more Tomigawas."

Tomi's unpatriotic thoughts were erased when the general intoned, "Your loyalty binds you to this..." Suzuki whispered, "... personal Imperial Wish." Tomi folded his torso to the lowest bow of obedience. To be one step removed from the Emperor's Wish was a sacred duty, despite Suzuki's stratagems. This was what Tomi was born to do.

"There are countless young officers ready to lead their men and die for the Emperor, but there is only one Tomigawa left alive. Your father's destiny is now yours."

Tomi choked out an emotional, "I obey."

"Now, Second Lieutenant Tomigawa, tell my aide to have Yu Hsu-ch'en brought to me."

"Sir?"

"The officer you captured. His name is Yu Hsu-ch'en."

Fifteen minutes later, the guards dragged a bloody heap into the tent, accompanied by the two staff colonels. Stench filled the tent and the taller colonel spat, "Shit-stinking gook."

Frowning, General Suzuki stood up and gestured the Chinese prisoner be placed in his own chair. Captain Yu was lowered into the seat and the black, blue, and bright red flesh of his destroyed manhood showed. There were bleeding wounds where his fingernails and toenails had been. But for luck, Tomi thought, he could be a prisoner interrogated by Captain Yu.

In fluent Mandarin, General Suzuki asked a question.

Corkscrewed by torture, Captain Yu turned his head toward the voice before answering. Using Tomi's new rank, the general told him to have an orderly fetch his flask. The two colonels' raised eyebrows followed the newly-promoted lieutenant out the tent.

When Tomi returned, General Suzuki and the Chinese officer were chatting in Mandarin. The two colonels glowered and Tomi edged into a dark corner that smelled of mildewed canvas and the prisoner's odor. Interrogators had avoided the tongue and brain. Prisoners usually broke when a lit cigaret was pressed into an eyeball. Captain Yu Hsu-che'n had been more than brave. Both eyeballs were destroyed.

During a pause in the conversation between General Suzuki and Captain Yu, the bald-headed colonel politely asked, "Sir, General Nakajima's personal interpreter is outside. Shall I call him in? We don't understand Chinese."

General Suzuki stared at the colonel and quietly asked, "Didn't you tell me that your people drained the prisoner of all pertinent information?"

The taller colonel responded, "Yes, General! We've confirmed earlier intelligence reports about troop strength and we now have fresh estimates of their ammunition and food supply. By the time we finished, this gook was begging to tell us details of his mother's sexual union with a pack of dogs," the colonel smirked.

General Suzuki coldly replied, "This is not so. Your men failed. They were so busy enjoying their work, they neglected to ask the right questions. I'm now correcting your interrogation team's mistakes. I have no use for incompetent fools."

The tall colonel flinched as if slapped. He would punish his interrogation team and they, in turn, would make the prisoners suffer much before tomorrow's executions.

General Suzuki said, "The Honorable Captain Yu is from a prominent family friendly with Generalissimo Chiang Kai-shek. We've been gossiping about the old days ... not military matters. My old friend Chiang Kai-shek hasn't changed a bit since Tokyo, when Sun Yat-sen and he were our honored guests.

"In those days Chiang would rather fuck than eat, and Captain Yu informs me that the Generalissimo is still the randy goat. When his concubines aren't on their knees or backs, they're busy packing his prize collection of ancient scrolls."

Glaring at the colonels, Suzuki snapped, "Don't you realize the significance of this? Chiang never relocates without his precious collection. This means that he intends an orderly retreat from Nanking and will take the cream of the army with him. He doesn't intend to surrender! Your interrogators failed to learn that Chiang and his elite divisions will be gone before we grind down the forces covering his retreat. If my assumption is correct, Nanking will not be the final battle."

General Suzuki switched to formal Imperial Court language. "So! The enemy will spurn favorable surrender terms following the fall of his southern capital. Instead of the decisive battle we planned, China will retreat and fight, fight and retreat. It will become a long war of attrition that we hoped to avoid.

"My compliments to Honorable Generals Matsui and Nakajima. Tell them I suspect Chiang will retreat with his main force and with sufficient supplies for long-term resistance. I will personally inform the General Staff of this unpleasant but distinct possibility."

The colonels responded in unison, "Yes, Sir!"

"Captain Yu said Chiang's German advisor, General von Falkenhausen, received orders from Berlin to stay behind in Nanking with the European civilians instead of accompanying Chiang's army to the interior. Nazi Germany no longer supports Chiang. That's the only good news to report."

General Suzuki paused as if expecting a response. When the colonels remained silent, he patiently said, "Captain Yu's exact word was 'interior.' If the Chinese retreat beyond Hankow to Chungking, it is beyond our bomber range and worse, our supply lines will be stretched thin."

General Suzuki shook his head, "So like the Chinese! Just when you think you have them cornered, they surprise you. A crafty race."

The orderly arrived with a brandy flask and the general motioned him to serve the Chinese officer. The aide carefully poured brandy into the cap and held it to the prisoner's mouth. Yu gulped the liquid, coughed and nodded gratitude.

Suzuki removed the lit cigaret from his holder and placed it between the Chinese officer's lips. After several puffs, Captain Yu Hsu-che'n took a deep drag and exhaled smoke with solemn finality. General Suzuki dropped the butt and said, "Second Lieutenant Tomigawa! Escort Honorable Staff Captain Yu Hsu-che'n to the central campfire, where you will behead him." Turning to the two colonels, Suzuki said, "General Matsui's officers are invited to witness the execution but no one is to interfere."

Tomi, the most junior officer in China, was ordered to perform the execution instead of a higher ranking officer as Army protocol demanded. Tomi had never seen an execution. His only guide was a scene from an old *Samurai* movie and common sense. The guards lifted Captain Yu from the filthy chair. General Suzuki murmured in Mandarin and Captain Yu answered in the soft tones of friends saying farewell.

Captain Yu was dragged the final seventy yards of his life to the campfire. There he waited in silent pain until a sufficient number of high ranking officers gathered. Only then was Captain Yu forced to his knees with head bent. Tomi felt Captain Yu's rapid breath on his wrist when he finger-combed the soil beneath sightless eyes. A handful of large pebbles were removed from the soft dirt pile where sharp steel hopefully would end its journey in a single, clean stroke. If the prisoner moved as the blade fell, or if Tomi's aim was flawed, several hacks would be needed, and blood-splattered witnesses would curse Tomi as a butcher.

Captain Yu flinched at the metallic whisper of the sword as it left its scabbard. Tomi raised the blade above and behind his head, widened his stance and calmly looked down. The crowd hushed and the only sound was the cheerful crackling of the campfire.

Tomi was grateful when he saw two vertebrae bumps on the exposed neck enlarge. Captain Yu had pressed his chin deeper into his chest to help. The sword's downward travel was swift and Tomi felt the crunch. The severed head rolled and landed on one cheek. The mouth and lips moved as if talking.

Only Tomi heard Captain Yu say the half-word, *'tzi'* to him as the blade severed his neck. *Tzi-tzi* was 'thank you' in Mandarin.

Tomi was congratulated as he used his good handkerchief to wipe Captain Yu's blood from the Tomigawa blade. He tossed the blood-smeared cloth into the campfire and watched it flare upward for a brief moment. He sheathed his sword, relieved its edge was undamaged.

A dapper captain gingerly picked up the dripping head by its ears. Holding it away from his spotless uniform, he shouted, "This is the fate of all Chinese cowards in Nanking!"

In a low growl Tomi commanded, "This brave warrior has earned our respect." Chastened, the officer carefully placed the head on the ground and retreated into the crowd. So evenly cut was the neck that Captain Yu's head remained upright. The flicking campfire illuminated Captain Yu's open mouth as if he were silently screaming at his fate. Tomi surrendered to a sudden impulse and recited to the head:

Farewell to this world, and to the night farewell.
We who walk the road to death, to what should we be likened?
To the frost by the road that leads to the graveyard,
Vanishing with each step we take ahead.
How sad is this dream of a dream.

With his punctured face and mud-caked uniform, Tomi looked like an oversized demon. He bowed to the silent officers and disappeared out of the circle of light.

***

The next morning at reveille, Tomi's infected face was a deep orange from antiseptic liberally applied by a medical officer. Bandages covered his eyebrows, cheeks and chin. He wore a borrowed pair of collar flashes; the double red horizontal bars on yellow background with a single silver star that designated his new rank.

When he was told to report to the headquarters duty officer, he expected travel orders. Instead, a major with the shoulder braid of a general's aide-de-camp led him into the command tent. The major saluted the bent back of an extremely short general, who was studying a street map of Nanking. "Sir, as you requested, Second Lieutenant Tomigawa of the 16th."

The little general slowly turned and Tomi faced Matsui Iwane, Army Commander of the nine divisions that had fought from Shanghai to Nanking. Tomi saluted and bowed. His view of the floor was bordered by white bandages.

"Ah," General Matsui said mildly, "the young swordsman who recited the Chikamatsu poem last night. Tell me, do you agree with the revered Chikamatsu that an essential conflict exists between sense of duty and the human feeling of compassion? And if you do, how is an officer to deal with this contradiction as we prepare for Nanking's fall and occupation?"

Surprised, Tomi looked up and met soft brown eyes studying him. Who but the scholarly Matsui would test a new officer with a philosophy question? Tomi didn't know if General Matsui wanted an honest answer or the customary polite lie. Tomi gambled on honesty.

"Honorable G-g-g-general, S-s-s-sir," he stuttered, then tried again. "Honorable General, it is this lowly one's inadequate understanding that the revered Chikamatsu-Sama wrote poems and plays about real emotions, as did the barbarian Shakespeare, his inferior contemporary." Tomi hesitated, but General Matsui gently nodded encouragement and Tomi remembered the little general was a noted scholar of Chinese culture.

"With the General's permission, Sir, this lowly one was taught that Chikamatsu-Sama agreed with the ancient Chinese concept that contradictions are all around us. Thus, a Japanese Imperial officer, being a superior person, can perform his duties and experience the contradictory emotion of compassion."

Gasps of indignation from the staff were ignored by General Matsui, who said, "An interesting response. Give me an example of such a major contradiction here in China." General Matsui was testing Tomi's *honne*, 'inside,' more than his intellect.

He replied as his mother would. "Honorable General, we fight Chiang Kai-shek because his actions proved that he is without honor. Yet this same Chiang was a friend and disciple of the Japanese Army only three years ago. This unworthy one recalls that Sun Tzu wrote, 'the only constant in war is change.' Change creates contradictions. Is it possible that compassion is an element of change?"

Realizing he had gone too far and could be shot for heresy, Tomi chattered the orthodox credo, "By following *Bushido*, the

'Way of the Warrior,' an officer cannot stray from the correct path of duty regardless of change, contradictions or involuntary compassion."

The tall colonel shamed by General Suzuki hissed, "Insolent ass! What do human feelings have to do with our duty? There is no place for compassion in *Bushido*. What are they shitting forth from the Academy these days?"

Tomi thought he was doomed until General Matsui quietly said, "The lieutenant answers honestly in accordance with his modern training at the Military Academy. He is a product of his times. The Empire needs this new type of thinking officer."

General Matsui turned and openly searched Tomi's bandaged face. "The new generation will cope with a different world than the one we know." The general had a coughing spasm and spat into a red-stained handkerchief. Only Tomi was unaware that General Matsui was tubercular.

"Gentlemen, consider how we plan to re-equip the army next year. The future is almost upon us and new thinking is demanded of us." Coughing in his fist, the tubercular general tapped his finger on the map. "Here at the gates of Nanking, dramatic change may transmute Japanese history in ways that we cannot imagine. Empire-building contains the seeds of contradiction and Japan still has an opportunity to accept the Chinese as our wayward brothers instead of enemies."

There were murmurs of agreement from staff officers, who scribbled General Matsui's remarks in their official diaries. He had accepted Tomi's clumsy response, yet deflected the colonel's anger without anyone losing face.

General Matsui said, "You bear the name of a renowned warrior family, Lieutenant To-Mi-Ga-Wa." He stressed each syllable as a separate word, giving the literal meaning of the name: *To-Mi-Ga-Wa*: 'A Door to One's Side.'

"In time," the general continued, "we may discover the many side doors of Lieutenant Tomigawa." Everyone laughed at the general's pun on Tomi's family name. Only Tomi understood the general's message. He knew Tomi was General Suzuki's spy.

General Matsui told his aide-de-camp to assign Tomi as a liaison officer-courier between the 16th Division and the general's headquarters. "And put him on a Tokyo flight immediately." The general turned his back to study the map. Tomi had been dismissed.

Three hours later, Tomi was led to an unarmed observation bi-plane with two open cockpits. The pilot was surprised by Tomi's lowly rank but handed him goggles and a small paper bag.

After a bouncing takeoff, they gained altitude and Tomi caught a glimpse of the battle lines before they flew into a low cloud. Tomi prayed Nanking wouldn't fall before he returned.

They banked tightly to the southeast and followed the Yangtze River Valley at fifty miles an hour. Tomi hated the noise, bone-shaking vibrations and the taste of engine oil that sprayed his bandaged face. He quickly filled the vomit bag. Flying wasn't as glamorous as it appeared.

At the busy Shanghai Airport, he had to wait for the next passenger plane to Tokyo. He declined a visit to the officers' brothel and instead got fresh bandages and enjoyed a hot soak. He read a week-old newspaper. An editorial strongly warned the U.S. Government not to enact a threatened boycott against Japan, despite pro-Chinese sympathies among Americans.

When the passenger plane climbed above the Bund waterfront, he saw many freighters being loaded with China's wealth. Over the East China Sea, Tomi fell asleep to the monotonous drone of the engines.

CHAPTER THREE
TOKYO, NOVEMBER 1937

Lady Tomigawa fainted when he emerged from the taxi. An Army wife was accustomed to surprise visits, but not to seeing her only child disfigured with thick bandages on his face.

He carried his mother inside and Taiko wailed, "Why didn't you write us that you were shot?"

"These are scratches, not war wounds," Tomi said. His mother revived and with practiced skill, cleaned the puncture wounds and replaced the clumsy bandages with smaller, neater ones. She had been a medical volunteer during the 1923 earthquake.

Lady Tomigawa waited until Tomi finished eating before she said, "Imagine my surprise when Tokyo's prestige matchmaker came here and announced he represented the Suzuki Family."

"When was this, Mother?"

"Yesterday." After repeating the entire conversation she asked, "Is this suddenness an Army political matter?" Her penetrating stare belied the delicate tone.

"Yes, Mother. General Suzuki claims he was close to Honorable Father and had me sent to China. By the way, the Suzuki woman, what's her name?"

"Why it's Taiko, the same as our maid. Odd coincidence, isn't it?" She pulled a sepia photograph from her kimono sleeve and gave it to her son. In most betrothal photographs, the maiden posed demurely with downcast eyes of genteel subservience. This woman stared at the lens as if daring the camera to hide her independent spirit and thick body. Tomi wondered if she was one of those modern women. But she wore a flowered kimono, indicating a virgin.

"What did the matchmaker say about her?"

His mother pursed her lips, "Suzuki Taiko attended the best schools, although I heard that she had western friends. Her family is far from venerable, but General Suzuki is an ascending star and she has a significant inheritance from her late father's estate."

She gently touched a flower arrangement. "The matchmaker stressed the young lady's health and intelligence. That's usually said when a girl isn't good looking. But she isn't homely. One suspects that her flaw may be the lack of a docile personality."

When Tomi asked her opinion, she said, "You spoke with Suzuki; what do you think?"

He took several sips of green tea before giving the reluctant answer, "I have no choice. General Suzuki demands a Tomigawa-Suzuki joining. It is an order to be obeyed."

They were startled by a crash from the kitchen. Taiko, always careful and meticulous, had dropped something. His mother sighed, "These times are not ideal for the Tomigawas."

***

Chimpo-San, 'Mr. Penis,' stiffened when Taiko slid open his bedroom door and slipped into their sleeping quilt. Their frantic kissing made his face wounds ache. When they paused to catch their breath, she touched his face. "It hurts much?"

"No," he lied. "I will remove the bandages in the morning."

"Good. Now I'll welcome home *Chimpo-San.*" With slow, teasing familiarity, Taiko kissed his entire body. His fingertips gently touched where her lips joined his flesh amid the gentle aftershocks. Drained, he lifted her head and kissed her, tasting both of them.

Now it was Tomi's turn. He was a starving hummingbird sipping nectar from silky folds. She writhed and twisted, finally whispering, "No more." He knew better and reached her again. When she was beyond hummingbird pleasures, he slid on top. She was unaware that her head pressed painfully against his bandaged wounds. But he didn't stop until exhaustion forced them back to the cold night. He kissed the tears from her eyes and cheeks. They cuddled and she clutched *Chimpo-San* – the ritual that began their pillow talk.

In the slurred accent of her village background, she complained bluntly, "That Suzuki Taiko ... even the name she steals from me." Unknowing, her grip tightened and hurt his shriveled member. "Everything's changed. We'll never have this again," she said.

"No, we will ..."

She interrupted his protest with carefully rehearsed words in the softer Tokyo accent she painstakingly acquired. "You live in a man's world and have responsibilities. I have always dreaded the day when you would marry a highborn lady to breed many sons. That day is here. My only wish is to be near you always, but I don't see how such a thing is possible. Yet I accept what is to come."

"We'll be together, Taichan. I promise."

She shrugged. "If the gods are pleased with us, perhaps. Even if we are destined to be separated, Tomi, I request a promise from you that I never had the courage to ask before. But time races away from us."

"I'll do anything for you, Taiko. What is it?"

"When you become powerful, promise me you'll end the shame of the 'Weeding of the Young.' No one cares that the poor are forced to sell their daughters. This cannot be right."

Taiko, who had never asked him for anything, wanted him to change society. He could never keep such a vow. "I expect to die in battle and then our spirits will be joined forever. But should I survive, I promise to try to end the 'Weeding of the Young.'"

She sobbed, "Such horrible matters crack my heart. We must accept our fate, but some things are too evil to be allowed. Now please sleep. Tomorrow is your important day and I must clean and iron your dress uniform." She left behind their scent.

***

The next morning, he stood in the wide plaza and bowed toward the western wall of the Imperial Palace, then briskly strode into Army General Headquarters. An orderly escorted him through a maze of offices and hallways. Knowing this would be the only time he'd be in the heart of the Imperial Army, he tried to absorb everything.

He was led into a second floor reception room where six officers lounged in chairs. Against the opposite wall a sergeant-major as tall as Tomi stood ramrod straight. Tomi was the only one without a medal on his dress tunic. The officers glanced at his red streaked face, then resumed their conversation, snubbing him.

Tomi joined the sergeant-major, who wore the collar insignia of the Second Infantry Division, the elite Northern Honshu unit. Tomi politely introduced himself to the soldier, who boomed out, "Tomigawa? Forgive my boldness, Sir. Are you the son of Major Tomigawa?"

"Yes, Sergeant-Major."

He grinned, exposing two gold front teeth. "Hah! I thought so. You look like him. This is a profound honor, Sir. I'm Muranaka. Your father was my captain at the *Tsutsujigaoka* Barracks in Sendai. He was the finest officer I ever had the privilege to serve." The sergeant-major's accent revealed the tight-lipped, staccato delivery of the Miyagi Prefecture, famous for producing Japan's biggest, toughest soldiers and marines.

Muranaka bellowed, "Allow me to offer my congratulations, Second Lieutenant Tomigawa."

The other officers stared. The sergeant-major whispered, "Your honorable father treated us fairly and never punished without just cause. I try to follow his example but it is very difficult." Tomi nodded, thinking of Sato and Oooo Ahg's pig farm.

A cavalry captain sauntered over and haughtily interrupted, "You're Tomigawa? Well, well, well. You must be an afterthought, because your name wasn't on the orders. No matter. You are in all the newspapers. Such publicity won't hurt your career." Sergeant-Major Muranaka backed away with a bow that was ignored.

"I apologize, Captain. I haven't seen today's newspaper."

"Really?" he drawled in an affected accent. "Your first patrol was quite something, capturing an important spy with papers. You singlehandedly hacked through an enemy unit. You got a battlefield promotion plus the honor of beheading the spy."

Captain Yu's final *'tzi-tzi'* echoed in Tomi's head.

"Nice face wounds," the captain said. "Wish I had some."

Everyone snapped to attention when General Suzuki walked in with a retinue of officers. In full dress uniform, Suzuki wore a monocle instead of glasses.

After introductions, General Suzuki lead the group down a flight of stairs and they marched across the parade ground, taking the salute of an honor guard. Despite the cold morning, there was a large crowd of military and civilians. Many were government ministers clad in English-style morning coats, striped pants and top hats. Their somber clothing contrasted with the colorful kimonos and coats worn by the women. Only the reporters and photographers wore shabby Western-style clothing. Tomi saw his mother in the crowd with Taiko standing behind her. Taiko looked small and out of place in his mother's second-best coat.

Other citations were announced by an adjutant, but Tomi's was read by General Suzuki, a singularity not lost on the politically-sensitive crowd. Tomi blocked out the lies and stared at Suzuki's monocle, glinting in the morning sun. When the ceremony ended with three 'Long live the Emperor' *Banzai* cheers, Tomi noticed his mother raise her arms in silence.

The ceremony dissolved into congratulatory confusion as press photographers posed the heroes with bureaucrats seeking reflected glory. General Suzuki preened when General Inukai, commandant of the Military Academy, bragged, "Tomigawa was our best cadet ever! He's the only one who memorized the entire Infantry Officer's manual. A fantastic brain!"

With mock severity, the general barked, "Second Lieutenant Tomigawa! Recite something from the Infantry Tactics Manual. Let's see, make it Chapter Seven."

Tomi visualized the manual page and began reciting in a low drone carefully barren of pride. After several sentences, General Inukai boasted, "Stop! See what I mean? I can't remember what I had for breakfast, but this lad doesn't forget anything!" He put his arm around Tomi and said, " Now if you'll excuse us, General Suzuki, I want to introduce our young hero to many who are anxious to meet him."

When they were a safe distance away, General Inukai muttered, "Be careful Tomigawa. Having *Ichiban* Suzuki as your patron is like wielding a sword without a haft. It cuts the hand of its holder. Too bad we can't teach political infighting at the Academy."

"Sir, what should I do?"

"Damned if I know," General Inukai sighed. "You are dealing with politicians in uniform, not warriors. Unless you learn how to survive by their rules, you may end up like your father. Ah, here we are. Nobles and officers of the Imperial General Staff! I present you Second Lieutenant Tomigawa, one of the finest the Academy has ever produced."

Later, the old general showed displeasure as General Suzuki approached them with reporters and photographers in tow. Tomi posed with the two generals in a photograph that became an icon of Japan's military achievements. Old General Inukai stood in the center, his round glasses gleaming over an old-fashioned curved white mustache. His chestful of decorations were earned during the 1905 defeat of Czarist Russia, the first time an Asian nation defeated a European empire.

The monocled General Suzuki was proud of his Great War Allied Victory medal and the French Croix de Guerre. He had spent the war behind a desk and in the fleshpots of Paris, but he looked very much the Imperial Household representative.

Tomi was more than a head taller than the generals. The low winter sun cast shadows on his puncture wounds and long cuts over his left eye, cheekbone, upper lip and chin. When Tomi saw the published photo some days later, he was proud to look like a battle-scarred warrior who had survived bullets and sword slashes. Memories of the farmer's brush pile were fading.

Despite his mother's protests, General Suzuki insisted the press interview her. "Lady Tomigawa, your proud day must be recorded." He turned to the scribbling reporters and intoned in formal Imperial Court syntax, "The noble Lady Tomigawa proclaims to Japan how she regrets having only one son to serve the God-Emperor instead of one thousand sons. The Tomigawa tradition of victory in every war continues."

'The Number One Suzuki of Them All' dismissed the press and herded the Tomigawas toward his family for introductions. Polite bows were exchanged and Tomi had his first glimpse of Suzuki's Taiko.

Tomi thought that his own Taiko, standing with the other servants and chauffeurs, was far more beautiful than this Taiko.

The Suzuki's Taiko was thick-waisted and the top of her exquisite pile of pomaded hair didn't reach Tomi's new medal. The fullness of her dark, lustrous hair was repeated on heavy eyebrows that emphasized her small eyes in a fleshy wall of wide cheeks and chins. Her kimono failed to conceal breasts of *gaijin* proportions.

General Suzuki squinted through his monocle, measuring Tomi's initial reaction to the niece. As if the invitation hadn't been pre-arranged, General Suzuki said, "Lady Tomigawa, may the Suzuki family have the honor of your presence and that of your hero son this afternoon?"

Lady Tomigawa replied, "We are deeply honored by the gracious invitation."

At home, a downcast Taiko silently served mother and son a cold lunch. His mother ignored Taiko's rare sullenness by cheerfully recounting the names and bloodlines of every personage at the morning ceremony. *Kankei,* family connections past and present, were Japan's social glue and her memory was prodigious.

When their taxi arrived that afternoon at the sprawling Suzuki compound with its many houses, the Tomigawas were impressed. His mother murmured, "Even political generals can't afford such palatial residences." The impolite soldier at the gate, an assassination guard, didn't salute until he scrutinized them. Tokyo's elite of all political persuasions posted these guards after the recent murders of pro-Western officials.

Classic in design but oversized, the Suzuki tea house comfortably held all the principal Suzukis and several lesser relatives. Suzuki Taiko performed the classical tea ceremony with grace. The marriage broker hadn't had time to finalize dowry negotiations, making the genteel conversation a cut-throat battle of money and social dominance.

Lady Tomigawa subtly moved the conversation to her only bargaining point. Her soft, musical words were daggers hidden in velvet and honey. Eyes downcast, she began the attack. "I am so sorry to be unworthy of this lavish hospitality from you important personages. Such honor is undeserved." With polite noises of appreciation from a fragile ancient cup that cost more than her monthly widow's pension, she sipped the thick green tea.

"I so admire the excellent taste of the Suzuki Family in duplicating the tea house of the *Shogun Yoshimasa*," she said. "And on such a grander scale! The original was built six centuries ago. I cannot recall the exact date, but ..." She interrupted herself with another sip of tea, certain that everyone awaited her next words. "Oh dear, I apologize to all of you for my ignorance. I really should know every date of the *Yoshimasa Shogunate*, because the Tomigawa family still refers to him, in the privacy of our humble home, as the greatest general our family ever had to the privilege to serve."

General Suzuki shifted uneasily at the insult and was chagrined that the conversation had become a comparison of family backgrounds.

"My son Tomoyki's ancestors," she said, "on both maternal and paternal sides, had the honor to serve *Shogun Yoshimasa*, a most remarkable man. The records show that several Tomigawa knights fought alongside him in his biggest victories."

As if he had died last night, she lamented, "What a brave warrior and scholar was our *Yoshimasa-Sama*. Imagine, he fought all those important wars, yet found time to study classical literature and bring Buddhism to our sacred land from China ... as well as such cherished rituals as the tea ceremony your lovely Taiko performed so well."

Lady Tomigawa looked around with exaggerated admiration. "My scatterbrain cannot help thinking such thoughts as I admire this magnificent tea house and the memory it evokes of the famous *Shogun* that our family continues to revere." Her sigh echoed centuries of social superiority. She had reminded General Suzuki that his ancestors were nameless peasants when the Tomigawa knights were making history.

General Suzuki bowed and smiled at Lady Tomigawa as he gloomily thought, "This stuck-up bitch is an unscrupulous bandit! The dowry contract has yet to be signed but the marriage has been announced. Now at the last moment, the She-Devil-Bitch blackmails me! How big a dowry must I pay for her big-headed, oversized son?"

Lady Tomigawa wasn't finished savaging the Suzukis. "Please excuse this one's foolishness and bad manners, but I do so admire the Priest Sesshu's black ink on white paper scroll on your wall. I remember its last owners well, a most distinguished family. I hope my flawed memory does not embarrass me again. Ah yes! I remember now! Priest Sesshu painted it in the 15th Century when he mastered the Chinese *Sumi-e* technique."

She lowered her voice as if to reveal a family secret and said, "We once had similar temple art of the *Nara* and *Heian* eras, but one's possessions change with time, *neh*? My foolish mind wanders so. Please forgive an old widow's silly thoughts, but the scroll painting reminds me that *Nippon* now fights a glorious war, just as it did when this painting was created." She looked around and smiled at the stunned Suzuki faces.

"Ah, isn't this a most remarkable coincidence! We lowly women are honored to sit here with two warriors, the distinguished general and my son, so recently back from the land where the art originated. We pray Japan climbs to new, glorious cultural heights in the next three centuries."

The Suzukis thought the onslaught had ended and murmured relieved agreement when Lady Tomigawa resumed her attack. "May there continue to be great families, like the illustrious Suzukis, who show their appreciation with tasteful and most generous acquisitions. We Tomigawas, without regret, have scant treasure to display to guests except the memories of our honorable ancestors. We lack tangibles such as this rare *Sesshu* scroll. Instead, we look upon our ancestors' heroic deeds as our art collection. A warrior family's material sacrifice in serving the God-Emperor is a light burden we bear, yet its value surpasses the heaviest gold. Is this not so?"

She bowed and didn't raise her slim torso until polite responses were made by the reluctant Suzukis. His mother's face was impassive, but her glittering eyes revealed all to General Suzuki: mother and son descended from nobles who outranked the new money upstarts.

General Suzuki nodded and smiled benevolently. The only outside display of emotion was his vigorous polishing of the monocle. His insides seethed at being forced to increase an already generous dowry sum. But the general knew when to retreat. He could force her son into marriage with threats, but

Lady Tomigawa had linked prestige against the dowry amount without the marriage broker present to act as a bargaining buffer.

The general realized that the bigger the dowry, the more prestige the Suzukis gained from the marriage. When Lady Tomigawa informed the marriage broker of the new dowry amount, General Suzuki would lose face if he haggled. Whatever amount she said would be final. Suzuki's strategy of a speedy marriage was about to cost him a much larger fortune than he had planned. He damned Lady Tomigawa inwardly but smiled and responded courteously, "Your ladyship's presence reminds us of the legendary knights who brought glory to Japan. Having a Tomigawa warrior join the Suzuki family is an event we treasure."

General Suzuki had surrendered to Lady Tomigawa. By nightfall, the puzzled matchmaker would be informed of the much larger dowry and the contract would be signed. Lady Tomigawa, the easy victor, sat demurely with eyes downcast, when General Suzuki asked her, "Have I your permission to show our young hero the gardens that one day will be his?" The general and hero rose and bowed to Lady Tomigawa, who responded with a queenly bow that reminded the General he was superior in Army rank only and that she belonged with those who strolled inside the Imperial Palace's Fukiage Gardens.

Mother and son locked eyes and both knew how proud he was of her warrior spirit; how she used etiquette, charm and wit as weapons. No one could outmaneuver or keep a secret from her. She knew his thoughts because his *honne*, 'inside,' came from her, while his *tamae*, 'outside' appearance, was his father's.

She had always had known about his nights with Taiko! The thought was like a kick to the head. Tomi followed the general out of the tea house while fighting for self-control. He barely heard the general brag, "The Suzuki compound consists of four main houses, some smaller ones, and the teahouse and several gardens."

They walked slowly through the immaculate landscape that was eye-pleasing despite winter dormancy. "Did you know we Suzukis were active in the Meiji Restoration?" the general asked.

He puffed out his thin chest underneath the warm folds of the cape. "Our honorable ancestors, famous iron producers for centuries, foresaw Japan's need to learn modern techniques for the steel industry. My great-grandfather helped Japan become a modern nation."

Tomi wondered if his mother had planned his nights with Taiko as he translated the boast: A blacksmith Suzuki ancestor somehow had learned western steel-making.

"When Japan modernized, the Suzuki clan, helped by many wise marriages, expanded from steel to chemicals, assorted manufacturing and banking." He let the pride show when he declared in his deep voice, "As Japan grew, so did we."

The general waved his hand. "This is a small part of the result, our own miniature *zaibatsu*, industrial-capital clique."

Tomi wondered, *"Does Mother know how much I love Taiko?"*

General Suzuki's cape inflated again. "In size, we are a flea compared to Mitsubishi, Sumitomo, Yasuda, Mitsui, Nomura and other giants. But we are fierce competitors." He tapped Tomi's new medal and said, "And we have influence."

Tomi ignored Suzuki's boasts and tried to understand why his Mother had used Taiko for his childhood. He hadn't expected to go outdoors and regretted not bringing his tattered greatcoat. General Suzuki glanced at the shivering lad and said with sour envy, "Aiie! The hot blood of youth keeps you warm. You don't know how lucky you are!"

He lowered his voice. "By the time the gardens bloom in two springtimes, Japan will conduct military operations far beyond China. Only a select few know this, but as my only heir, you must understand how the Suzukis are part of the Empire's march into the future."

In his affected palace accent he droned, "The God Emperor and his Imperial Council recently approved an unprecedented buildup of military forces, far greater than next year's modernization of the Army. The Navy is secretly building super battleships that will outgun John Bull's biggest. We're breaking that damned Kellogg Treaty, but the unsuspecting *gaijin* won't know until it's too late. Japan will be the equal of Great Britain, France and the United States."

Tomi gasped at the news and recalled his mother's worry that the 'Strike South' clique was ambitious and impatient. The general grinned at Tomi's reaction. "The West thinks we're satisfied with the occupation of Manchuria, Korea, and part of China. They misjudge us, Tomigawa. The Japanese Empire will control more square miles of this planet than John Bull and Uncle Sam now do! The Pacific Ocean will be the 'Lake of Japan.' We'll capture French Indo-China, British Malaya, Hong Kong, Singapore, the Dutch East Indies and take the Philippines from the Americans, just as they stole it from Spain!"

Tomi asked, "Sir, will it be a sudden-attack quick victory like the Japanese-Russian War?"

Suzuki frowned. "Still seeking combat, are you?" With the self-important scowl of the powerful, he half-whispered in Tomi's cold ear, "The Palace plans for a 30-month conflict at most, and the weak Europeans will eagerly sign a peace treaty after we take their colonies. And the Yankees' isolationist majority will keep America from taking action. Despite appearances, the West's military power and political will are weaker than ours. They will seek peace on our terms."

General Suzuki clapped his gloved hands in cadence with each of his words. "There will be enough battles for honor-hungry young officers serving the *Showa Sama no Dai Nippon Tendo.*" Hearing the sonorous title, 'Emperor of the Empire of Great Japan' in the slow, low-register tones of formal Imperial Court language, Tomi bowed.

Suzuki picked up a solitary leaf from the otherwise immaculate estate grounds. "This leaf is from a white oak tree I had imported. Fallen leaves of most trees quickly rot, but not the white oak leaf. It remains true to its form, through winter and into the next spring. The Suzuki clan is like this leaf. No matter what happens, we don't fall apart. I'm this old leaf of winter and you will be the new leaf. Follow my plans and the Suzuki-Tomigawa tree will flourish. I hadn't expected you to achieve so much so soon. Who knows if it is luck or destiny? You are your father's son."

Tomi wondered if Suzuki's ambition was for Japan or his clan; or were they one and the same? As if reading his mind, the General said, "We Suzukis are in a constant struggle, fighting jealous and greedy enemies, even here in Tokyo. As a Buddhist, you believe we are here because of destiny. I believe it is the result of my planning. Who cares which of us is right? We act according to our natures, just like this white oak leaf."

General Suzuki sat down on a bench and motioned Tomi to join him. The cold stone slab chilled Tomi's buttocks and beyond. His face wounds ached from the chilling wind but he tried not to shiver. Tomi didn't like Suzuki, but his vision was thrilling.

"I've studied the British Empire," Suzuki said. "Its most influential families are those who were active in England's military expansions. They took part in the political process as well as the military. This is the example you and I will follow."

He glanced about but no one was in view except the distant gate guard. Suzuki whispered, "Within the next 24 months, we will get all the resources we now lack: oil, rubber, iron ore, aluminum. Everyone of importance will be rich!"

Tomi's head swivelled with an unasked question. "We Suzukis don't loot like others!" the general said hastily. "Of course there are many warehouses filled with the personal loot of generals and occupation officials, but not the Suzukis. We seek resources and technical information only to improve our industrial base to better serve the God Emperor."

He lifted the side of his gabardine cape and glanced at his German wristwatch. As if he were on a tight schedule, he talked faster, "The Imperial Wish is clear: War will give us what we lack."

Biting cold and pain were forgotten as Tomi imagined a Japan that would not be dependent on the West, which had long denied the Empire its rightful place as an equal colonial power.

Suzuki growled, "Let backward Asian nations undergo the shame and deprivation that modern Japan still suffers at the hands of Europeans and Americans! The Suzukis seek a new, prosperous future for Japan. Tomigawa, can I depend upon you to share these ambitions?

Tomi couldn't imagine Japan ever becoming greater than the British Empire. But Suzuki's vision made sense, even if he was a political general. Suzuki looked at his watch again and snapped, "Well?" Tomi glanced around as if looking for the proper response in the grey light of the fading afternoon. He thought of how his mother had just deflated this general, who lusted for the prestige of the Tomigawa bloodline.

"Sir, you see the foreshadowing of events yet to happen. You make important decisions that I have only read about in books. I am trained to deal with the enemy in front of me in terms of yards, meters, miles and kilometers; while you plan the conquest of the entire Pacific. You ask me to take responsibilities far beyond my limited competence."

Tomi hesitated but the general nodded impatiently. "Sir, I am a simple soldier. But I pledge my life to the Emperor, to the Army and to the Suzuki clan in that ranking order."

Tomi stood and bowed. "I will devote myself to your history-in-the-making in all ways honorable. I hope my service to you includes my destiny on the battlefield. Is this acceptable?"

Suzuki didn't return Tomi's bow. They both knew a Tomigawa warrior had answered a superior of lesser birth. Their noble and blacksmith ancestors stood between them.

General Suzuki replied tartly. "You may travel the hero's path as did your father, but not until the Tomigawa line has joined the Suzukis to produce many sons."

He pointed with a shaky gloved hand and said in a voice husky with unknown emotion, "See that small house over there? Wait in there while I visit with your honorable mother." Suzuki abruptly turned and walked away, crumbling the white oak leaf between his gloves in anger.

Tomi had once seen a fish hawk swoop down and take a salmon from the river. Its talons lifted the fish into an alien world. The hawk, not the salmon, knew what was happening. Tomi felt like that fish as he entered the house.

An elderly woman greeted him. Her dark, brocaded kimono signified high servant status. With arthritic slowness, she got down on her knees and touched her forehead to the floor, chanting, "Welcome, Tomigawa-San, most illustrious guest."

He responded with formality and sat down on the outer platform, glad to be out of the biting cold. She removed his boots and replaced them with a pair of slippers. He was led into a room filled with ancient Korean temple art and furniture, obviously occupation loot. She gave him the prestige position at the low table and served a *koh* of hot sake. It was soon empty.

The outside door banged and Suzuki Taiko entered the room, almost breaking the interior sliding door. Red-faced from the cold, her thick western-style fur coat clashed with the bright yellow and red kimono underneath. She ignored his greeting bow, peeled off the bulky coat, letting it fall on the tatami mat, and sat down with a bottom-heavy thud at the low table. She yelled, "Keiko! Sake. Lots of it! I'm frozen!" Outraged by her bad manners, Tomi almost forgot this unchaperoned meeting was as scandalous as if they had walked naked through the Ginza.

They avoided eye contact as Keiko silently served a tray loaded with five *kohs* of hot sake. The old servant picked up the fur coat, folded it neatly over her arm, bowed and left.

Taiko gulped and refilled her sake cup several times without pouring any for Tomi, an act that would not be tolerated in the lowest whorehouse. Suzuki Taiko was a spoiled bitch with the country manners of her ignorant blacksmith ancestors.

He poured his own sake, raised the cup and said, *"Kanpai."* She ignored his toast.

Tomi stared at the woman who would be his wife. Her outside radiated anger and fear. Why? He thought of several old Japanese proverbs: *Women are demons; There's never a shortage of women;* and the worst, *Never trust a woman even though she has borne you seven children.*

Both heard the old servant make a deliberately noisy departure through the outside door. They were alone. "Well, say something," she demanded.

Unless he obeyed General Suzuki, Tomi's career was doomed. Suppressing outrage, he asked politely, "I know which school you attended, but I don't know your favorite subjects. What are your hobbies? And I'd like to know your social views."

The opening tactic worked. "I shouldn't behave like this, but I'm upset at ... at ..." She left the sentence unfinished with an exaggerated, unladylike wave of tiny hands on thick wrists that protruded from her kimono sleeves.

"Yes, I feel the same way. Tell me, Taiko-San, what's your opinion of the modern world outside of Japan?"

She stared. "How did you know? Oh, Honorable Uncle told you about me."

"No, we only discussed military and family matters. But it is obvious you don't care for traditional ways, so I wonder if you favor Western ways. Is this so?"

Taiko's answering smile exposed tiny white teeth. She might be attractive if she scowled less and smiled more. "I insisted upon going to a school with Western students. Outside the classroom, I learned the *gaijin* thinking. Europeans treat their women much better than we do. It was most enlightening and ah, stimulating," she said with a blush that disturbed him. She was fatally contaminated, not a true human being.

She leaned forward. "Tomigawa, did you know that women are now allowed to vote in the West? "Someday I'm going abroad and learn firsthand how they achieved suffrage. That's the *Eigo* word for the right to vote. We Japanese women should be free of *Seigen*, the Restrictions."

Women voting? End our time-honored Seigen? What next? Women in the Army? Delicately, he probed her lunacy. "Are Japanese women unhappy with the traditional Restrictions?"

"Of course! Can't you see it? No you can't. Oh well, I'll say this for you, you're the first Japanese male to discuss *Seigen* with me. You raised the subject yourself! Most unusual. Do you think the Restrictions are fair? Imagine how you'd feel if you were a woman and required by law to be chattel instead of independent!"

He smiled to mask his disgust for her heretical ideas. "Well, our nation's changing. There is always tension from those who seek change. You're the first woman I know who rejects *Seigen*."

"Oh no I'm not! Your mother, the Lady Tomigawa, cleverly hides her *modan na*, modern thinking behind old fashioned manners." She giggled at his astonished expression.

She was accusing his mother of being modern! Not so. She was the most traditional of women.

"Don't you see that the Restrictions imprison thinking women like your mother and me? Our old fashioned culture is a jail, you men the guards and we women the prisoners!"

He sipped the now lukewarm sake and mulled her words, 'thinking women' and 'prisoners.' This was alien territory. He countered, "The true Japanese spirit remains unchanged, always in balance with nature and our ancient traditions even though our *tamae*, 'outside' appears to be a new Japan to the *gaijin*."

She sneered, "You ask me about my modern views, then you

label them superficial? Is this how you discuss matters important to me? You are a condescending fool."

Tomi realized she was bright as well as spoiled, a terrible combination. He had to disarm her short fuse of anger and retreat from the minefield of gender restrictions. "Taiko-San. We are strangers with no time to get acquainted. We are like two cats thrown into a bag. Frightened and angry, the cats fight, each thinking the other is responsible for being trapped. Let's not quarrel over our plight."

After a half minute of silence, Taiko poured now-cold sake into his cup, a weak gesture of hospitality. With a nervous giggle she said, "We're here because of family duties and we must be friendly." She stood up and pulled a sleeping quilt out of the Korean chest and said with a sarcasm that sounded as if her uncle were speaking, "Now I will do my duty as a Suzuki."

Tomi moved the table as she clumsily spread the quilt on the tatami mat. Suzuki Taiko slowly unwound her obi and disrobed. The winter light filtering through the translucent screen was unkind to her. The more clothing she removed, the less appealing she was, so unlike his Taiko. He knew he was stupid to compare them. Two different women with the same name.

He quickly removed his uniform and wondered if he were capable of coupling with such an unappealing, crazed creature. He grunted when she said coyly, "You have a fine body, Tomi." They crawled into the luxurious floor quilt, without touching. They were naked strangers.

"Well, aren't you supposed to do something?" she demanded in the same tone she used with her servant. "Japanese soldiers are supposed to be lusty. Was I misinformed? Or is it you?"

His military career would be over if he failed to impregnate this lunatic. The threat failed to energize his limp *chimpo*. He viewed this as a military problem. His hands and fingers became patrols probing enemy territory. The nipples of her oversized breasts grew erect. He stroked her thighs, which slowly spread. Tossing off the quilt for freedom of movement, he dry-kissed her toes. Startled, she giggled. "That tickles!" She tried to pull her foot away but he held tightly and continued. She became aroused, but he remained a kite on a windless day. He kissed his way up her thigh to her womanhood. Her groans of surprised delight grew but his *chimpo* didn't. It refused to stand at attention.

Desperate, he fantasized that he was with his Taiko. Finally, he swelled, blocking out the one he was with and remembered the touch, scent, look, and sensations of his own Taiko. His weapon was ready to invade the enemy. Out of habit, he offered his overdue stiffness to the stranger's mouth. To his astonishment, she gritted her teeth, squeezed her ridiculous small eyes shut and turned away. Confused, he wondered if Suzuki's Taiko found his *chimpo* too ugly to kiss? He flopped on his belly to hide his now-soft, diminished member.

He whispered at her silent broad back, "This is new to both of us. Such confusion is natural. I promise that I'll never demand anything of you that doesn't please." She rolled over on her back, but her thin lips remained puckered.

Tomi had been repulsed because he didn't know his enemy. A new tactic was needed. He gently drew the rigid Suzuki Taiko to him. She was stiff but his *chimpo* wasn't. The only tactic left was deceit. "It's a topsy turvy world," he sighed.

"What do you mean?"

"Well, you are the first modern woman I've ever met. I mistakenly thought that modern girls had no inhibitions. Now I understand that you are neither modern nor traditional, just ... different. I humbly apologize for taking too much for granted."

She shifted her heavy body to peer into his face. One of her pendulous breasts touched his shoulder but she didn't move away. "You're wrong about me."

He quelled the urge to quarrel. "Taiko, I am a fool. I apologize if I have offended you."

He was rewarded by a tight hug as she placed her broad face on his shoulder. She whispered, "Yes, you are stupid and will never understand me or your mother or any other woman capable of thinking. I accept your apology because I have no choice."

Tomi thought this spoiled woman should apologize to him for bringing his mother's name into this absurd conversation. Tomi remembered his mission. "Allow me to please you, Taiko-San and we will achieve what your family demands of us. Just close your eyes and trust me."

Taiko took a full minute to ponder the proposal before she closed her eyes. Her lips remained in a thin, unattractive line. He covered the enemy territory with kisses and massages. He gave her every sensual stimulation that he knew. Other than her groans and grunts of pleasure, she was passive, taking the sexual thrills as if she had earned them, giving nothing in return.

When she was ready, he gently inserted his solid *chimpo*, expecting to find a virgin's resistance. He went deeper. Then much deeper. Nothing halted his entry into her inner garden.

Instead of a virgin, he was inside a loose-fitting, much-traveled path. So! She had been afraid of discovery. Tomi wondered how many preceded him. Were any of them *gaijin*? The thought of following a foul-smelling foreigner made him want to retch. But if he said anything about her absent maidenhead, the Suzukis would lose face and destroy him. He had to pretend ignorance. To overcome disgust, he thought of his own Taiko until fantasy replaced this self-centered, well-fleshed person with the same name.

He relived the thousand nights of exploration and discovery with the real Taiko. He thought of how her right lip overlapped the left. And fantasized how his Taiko lifted her narrow hips to meet his thrusts in midair. How her garden clamped him with every stroke and later, the taste of her tears. In his soul was the real Taiko. Beneath him, temporarily connected by reproductive organs, was the insane Suzuki Taiko. Without difficulty, Tomi withheld what the Suzukis wanted from him until she climaxed, expelling a blast of gas. Only then was he able to deposit a small amount of seed in her. He had to do better.

Half-hard and still inside, he probed her moistness and thought of his Taiko nights at home. His *chimpo* hardened and he methodically pumped hard and fast until Suzuki Taiko climaxed again with explosive noise from both ends. He spent himself in throbbing fullness and imagined a battalion of Tomigawa sperm marching up the well-used Suzuki invasion route.

She complained of a cramp and, relieved of duty, he rolled off and thought of General Matsui's army moving up to Nanking. He prayed his seed would have equal success.

"Mmmm. I'm going to like being married to you," she said;

then ruined the moment by adding, "But I won't do anything disgusting. You'd better behave!"

"You have my word as an officer," he replied formally and knew this impure, spoiled person knew nothing about love between a man and a woman. He didn't care how many men had had her. He would be free of the Suzukis after he fathered a son. It was a devil's bargain but at least he would have the Army and his son would be heir to the Suzuki wealth.

He held her in a loose embrace, his hand cupping either the rounded edge of her breast or fat -- he didn't care which. She was no virgin and he was no hero. They were equally false. Taiko sat up and leaned over him, her breasts pressed against his chest as if to emphasize that she was no longer under his maleness. "Tomi, I want to do this often, but let me tell you ..."

He playfully interrupted her by gently brushing his fingertips across her lips. Irritated, Taiko slapped his hand away. In her uncle's voice she snapped, "Hear me! Being your wife will not give you the right to control me or direct my life. I refuse to obey the Restrictions. I'm a modern woman, I think for myself."

She saw that the outburst had startled Tomi and added in a softer tone, "Being a modern woman comes before everything else except family obligations. From early childhood, I knew that my husband would be selected by the family. I accept this. But I will not be a subservient, cringing creature."

Tomi sighed like a tired, old man. "I understand and accept your terms, Taiko." The new hypocrisy came easy to him. He was infected by the Suzukis' political disease. He kissed her pursed lips and playfully asked, "Now, can I enjoy you again before we return to your family?"

"No" she said, looking at her wristwatch that was the exact mate to General Suzuki's. "We've been here too long already. You leave now and I'll follow."

The teahouse was empty. A servant directed him to the main house, where his mother sat with a few Suzuki relatives. The General was absent. Lady Tomigawa and Tomi hastily departed.

They were silent during the trip home in General Suzuki's black Buick sedan. His mother said she had a headache and went to her room. No dinner had been prepared, and worse, Taiko didn't come to his bedroom that night.

The next morning, his mother wordlessly served him breakfast along with a newspaper. The front page photo showed Tomi with the two generals. The caption read: "Medal honoree Second Lieutenant Tomigawa being congratulated by Generals Inukai and Suzuki. Tomigawa-San has been betrothed to General Suzuki's niece for some time. Due to the national emergency, the couple will marry tomorrow in a modest ceremony, after which Second Lieutenant Tomigawa will return to the Nanking battle."

"Mother, where's Taiko?"

"She went to her parents' farm. A family emergency," she said coldly. There hadn't been a phone call or telegram. The crisis was in the House of Tomigawa.

The 'modest' marriage ceremony was held in Tokyo's largest temple; the wedding reception in the Imperial Hotel, designed by the famous Frank Lloyd Wright. Among the throng of luminaries were two royal princes, an uncle and a first cousin of the God Emperor. The generals, admirals, and high government officials were too numerous to count.

Lady Tomigawa was impressed by General Suzuki's power to assemble so many important personages on such short notice. Tomi was praised repeatedly for his bravery and began to think of himself as a worthy hero. Academy cadets from Tomi's class envied his face scars and medal.

None of Taiko's foreign or Japanese classmates had been invited. Tomi suspected that her uncle despised unconventional people and *gaijin* as much as he did. General Suzuki strutted in an aura of self-congratulation with lesser guests and exuded fawning hospitality with superiors.

At regular intervals, General Suzuki's aide escorted Tomi to the general's side for introductions to royalty and celebrities. By the time he had been formally presented to the two princes, Tomi had lost his nervousness.

The late Major Tomigawa's high-ranking comrades stood in a semicircle behind Lady Tomigawa like a royal guard of barons protecting their beloved queen at a hostile foreign court. By contrast, the Suzuki women were ignored. Tomi's new wife often engaged his mother in animated, witty conversations. Tomi didn't understand as they had nothing in common.

When Tomi and Taiko were finally alone in a luxurious suite at the hotel, she announced that the champagne had made her sleepy. Her snoring and his guilt kept him awake and he thought of sad Taiko at home. The next morning, his new wife lazily permitted him to send Tomigawa sperm reinforcements to their target. Repetition didn't improve their lovemaking, but he was used to her grunts of selfish pleasure and climatic wind.

They spent the afternoon at the Suzuki compound with the family inspecting wedding presents. Tomi had never seen so many rare Korean and Chinese works of art outside a museum. Most of it had to be recent loot. Later, when Tomi bid his new wife farewell, she hugged him. It was her first display of affection.

On the way to the airport, Tomi stopped at his mother's house. They stood in the doorway. She looked up at him. "As you grew from child to man, I made sure you had all that you needed, so that you would concentrate on your future. I hope what you now seek is worthy of your ambition."

They gazed at one another. Lady Tomigawa warned, "Your father obeyed General Suzuki as the messenger of the Imperial Wish, but he never trusted him."

"Neither does his son," Tomi responded. "And for the same reasons."

They bowed farewell. She murmured, "I'll use the family's ancient *tanka* code in my letters to you."

In the taxi, Tomi didn't look back but knew his mother wept. Like father, like son, Tomi had no choice and she knew it.

CHAPTER FOUR

The stench of unwashed bodies in wet woolen uniforms filled the crowded tent at the morning briefing. Tomi's eyes stung from cigaret smoke. He didn't command a single soldier, yet was hustled to the meeting the moment he returned from Tokyo. His full bladder reminded him that he hadn't been allowed time to piss after swilling many cups of hot tea.

Tomi's height enabled him to look over the shaven heads and hunched shoulders of the officers in front. Captain Shidehara, a crisp-looking staff officer with a pinned-up sleeve briefed them. He had studied in Nanking as a young man and wryly joked that the loss of his left arm hadn't diminished his fascination for China.

"Below historic Nanking's 20-foot-thick, 50-foot-high walls flows the canal that is the city's defense moat, water highway and open sewer," Captain Shidehara lectured. "Nanking's fortune is written on the water. In good times, the canal is filled with boat traffic. Now it contains the bloated cadavers of unwanted infants, the old and the unlucky, all floating amid the solid waste of Nanking's living. Around them are schools of feeding fish, especially Yangtze 'river pigs' -- big, shiny blackfish. From this foul sewer of life and death comes the adage, 'Nanking's bad luck is good eating for the river pigs.'"

A warrant officer next to Tomi hissed displeasure. "Another one of General Matsui's gook lovers. Too many damn *yasashii,* soft ones, on his staff."

A lieutenant colonel in the front row joked, "How does a fish tell the difference between a gook and his excreta, dead or alive?"

Everyone laughed and Captain Shidehara masked his irritation. The gook haters outnumbered the gook lovers. The captain continued in a stilted tone, "General Matsui plans to soften Nanking's defenses by firing artillery shells over the canal, blasting holes in five of the nine huge gates as well as several weak points on the walls. An unstoppable flood of Imperial troops will pour into the city. The corrupt Nationalists will sue for peace, and Japan will become China's older brother and its protector against *gaijin* powers, who have raped this country for much too long."

Envy chewed at Tomi. He was a rear area flunky hiding from danger with other non-combatants. To look like a warrior, yet not be one, was frustrating.

Another officer replaced Captain Shidehara and droned the order of battle and timetable of attack. Everyone scribbled the vital data in their official diaries except Tomi. He had no unit or battle orders, and didn't even have time to piss, let alone unpack his diary. All he could do was listen to the strategy: Four Japanese infantry divisions, like dragons' jaws of steel, would bite down on the battered walled city while a fleet of Imperial Navy launches sped along the Yangtze to cut off the escape route to the north.

While General Matsui's army made a frontal assault on the city, Tomi's division was to remain in place until long after the attack began, then sweep around the city to link up with naval units at the riverbank. The 16th Division was to continue its reputation for low casualty rates.

An elderly colonel stood and pointed his nicotine-stained finger at the map. "The city is shaped like a delicious pear," he chortled, "ready to be plucked from the tree by hungry warriors!"

The unit commanders laughed loudly, releasing pre-battle tension. From Tomi's position the other close-cropped skulls looked like dark fishing buoys bobbing in a grey sea of acrid cigaret smoke and khaki uniforms. His bladder told him it had reached its capacity.

The colonel bellowed jovially, "Return to your units and tell your men that plenty of food, drink and women, all of them hot, await them inside Nanking's walls. Dismissed!"

Along with other junior officers, Tomi stood aside to let superiors file out of the classroom. He hoped he could get to the nearest latrine in time.

"Second Lieutenant Tomigawa!"

A major grabbed his arm at the tent entrance. "Follow me.

The Division Commander wants you. Hurry."

For ninety minutes, Tomi sat on a low bench in the narrow hallway outside General Nakajima's quarters in a school building. His balloon of hot urine sent urgent void messages to his brain. He tensed his buttocks, sat ramrod-straight with palms on his quivering kneecaps, which reached high above his waist. His wide leather belt pressed directly against his bladder. He felt like a guilty schoolboy and wondered what he had done wrong to be called in by the division commander.

A steady stream of soldiers carrying packages stomped past him into General Nakajima's quarters. They came out empty-handed. No one spoke to Tomi since the major had planted him on the low torture bench an eternity ago. He never had to piss so badly in his life. He feared the unspeakable loss of face if he wet his pants. What did General Nakajima want of him?

His brain had to take control of the bladder. He concentrated on Nakajima, Lieutenant General and commander of the 16th Division, the most feared general officer in the expeditionary force in China. It was said that General Nakajima was powerful because he implemented the Emperor's secret wishes.

Before General Nakajima took over the 16th, he had headed the dreaded *Kempetai*, the military secret police. Everyone in the Army, even Academy cadets, knew that Germany's Gestapo learned their techniques from Nakajima's sadists. Many wondered why the Military Police head had placed himself under the command of Army General Matsui.

Tomi knew the division's combat record. Called the Angels of Terror, the division rarely fought, and then only against the weakest Chinese units. A friend of Tomi's father told him that Nakajima's division mission was to terrorize civilians with a brutality excessive even by Japanese Army standards. The 16th's other speciality was rapacious looting.

Looting was divided into four kinds. First: the organized, recorded transfer of movable valuables and commodities to the Japanese government and the Imperial Army. Second: valuables appropriated by generals and senior officers that are discreetly shipped back to homes and private warehouses in Tokyo for personal gain. Third: small items stuffed in a soldier's knapsack.

Fourth: items stolen from the first two categories. The fourth carried a summary death sentence.

"Hey you! Get in here!" A muscular captain crudely beckoned Tomi with a superior-to-lowly-servant bark. Tomi stood and almost released a flood of urine. He sensed warm dampness where the bulge of his loincloth pressed against his britches. The anteroom looked like a department store. Bookshelves were filled with an array of objects d'art, jewelry, priceless vases, antique scroll paintings, and large jade sculptures.

"Remove your sword and pistol!" Tomi instinctively gripped his sword handle. "Relax, lad. It's the rule here," the captain said with gruff nonchalance. He knocked once on the office door and Tomi heard a high-pitched voice say "enter." Without making eye contact, Tomi saluted and bowed. Without his sword, his left hand felt naked.

"Second Lieutenant Tomigawa reporting, Honorable General."

General Nakajima stared with an intensity that roared accusations. The silence grew to a full minute, then more. Tomi smelled the bulky presence and bad breath of the guard dog captain behind him. Only the sporadic rumble and shudder of artillery intruded.

Tomi suspected it was a military police trick to unnerve him. The pressure-pain of his brimming bladder faded slightly as he thought of General Nakajima's essence and name. *Naka* means inside, and by altering the character, *jima*, island, to *janen*, the general's name would mean 'evil inside thoughts,' Tomi thought with willful irreverence.

General Nakajima stood 5-foot, 3 1/2-inches tall in custom-made British boots that contained lifts. Although he looked and sounded like a little clerk, he was Japan's leading security expert on torture and terror. The Nazi's Himmler was just a small-time German chicken farmer when the God-Emperor appointed Nakajima head of the Japanese Army secret police.

Nakajima had been presented to *Showa Sama* when the God Emperor was Crown Prince, then went on to gain a remarkable degree of royal favor when he alerted the Palace about the army mutiny that resulted in the death of Tomi's father.

Now, 22 months later, he was Tomi's division commander. According to newspaper stories, General Nakajima had many barrels of 'Nanking oil' to destroy Japan's enemies in China. The captain left the room. General Nakajima asked ,"How tall are you, 5-foot-10 or 11?"

"Sir, this unworthy one is much less."

"Are you enjoying your overnight success as a publicized hero, strutting around my camp with those theatrical scars on your face?"

"Honorable General, this unworthy one is most embarrassed by the unearned attention created by accidental events."

"You doubt your superiors' judgement about such important matters and prefer your own opinions instead? Explain yourself!"

If Tomi admitted that he was a false hero, he would be insubordinate, implying his superiors were devious liars. If he said he was a hero, he would be lying to Nakajima, who knew the truth. The only way out of the dilemma was directness.

"Sir, I am the most inexperienced and least worthy officer in the division and probably in the entire Army. Despite such limitations and character defects, I seek only an opportunity to perform the duties for which I have been trained."

"What duties are you capable of handling?"

Instantly hopeful, Tomi enthusiastically responded, "Leading an infantry platoon in the coming attack, Sir."

Surprised, General Nakajima drummed his fingers on the table and realized Tomigawa wanted to get away from the ambitious Suzuki and be in combat. Such a fool had his uses. "No. You'll remain a junior liaison officer between my division and Matsui's headquarters."

Tomi didn't hide his disappointment.

"Your Tokyo patron won't help you here," General Nakajima snapped. "I demand total loyalty. You serve no other master but me. Fail me and nobody can save you. I know all about your secret outdoor conversation with your new uncle-in-law at his fancy compound. The ambitious money-grubbing Suzukis can't hide their secrets from me. My eyes and ears are everywhere."

Surprised, Tomi almost unleashed a hot flood down his breeches. How did Nakajima know about the private talk in the

Suzuki garden? Japanese believe that the stomach is the seat of emotion. This all-seeing general had a black stomach.

Without cause, Nakajima's anger grew. "Your new wife ... I know more about her *gaijins* than you ever will. Now get out of here before you piss your pants and wet my floor. I even know that! No one hides anything from me. If you do any spying, it will be for me. Now get out!" he shouted.

Tomi saluted, made a shaky about-face, and walked out with a fast spreading wet under his belly. He barged through a door marked for senior officers only and fumbled buttons as he stood over the small porcelain toilet hole. His brain and sphincter unclasped together.

General Suzuki and Nakajima were bitter rivals. Nakajima believed Tomi when he asked for combat instead being a staff messenger. Anyone seeking almost certain combat death was idealistic enough to be of use to Nakajima.

Back in his tent, Tomi removed his yellow-stained breech clout for a dry one and pondered over Nakajima's words. The soldier at the Suzuki gate, a Nakajima spy, had been too far away to hear anything. Nakajima was bluffing, hoping Tomi's sense of guilt would trap him.

"Always analyze the motives behind words," his mother had instructed. Why did Nakajima say he knew about Suzuki Taiko's *gaijin* lovers? Tomi was annoyed that his own suspicions were confirmed. But what was Nakajima's motive?

The answer came as he pulled on his brown leather boots. General Nakajima had carefully arranged for Tomi to piss his pants. Had it worked, the humiliation would have destroyed his career as well as the Tomigawa legend that General Suzuki acquired at great cost by the marriage. Suzuki would have lost much face and Nakajima's reputation as the feared ogre would be enhanced. Had it worked, a brilliant political ploy for only a few pots of tea.

Nakajima lost his temper because the elaborately-planned trick had failed. Little Nakajima's weakness was his arrogance and hatred of political rivals. Tomi wondered how many other Japanese leaders wasted time with such nonsense when brave warriors were dying for the Emperor?

***

The siege of Nanking went well for everyone except the outgunned Chinese defenders and Tomi. His only contribution to the distant battle was sore feet as he trekked back and forth on the crowded Zongshan Road. He was the messenger boy between Army General Matsui and Division General Nakajima. His early exhilaration from the dull thuds of artillery and the nearer blasts of mortar rounds faded as his blisters grew.

Tomi knew this was as close to real combat that he'd get. The sporadic firing of light machine guns sounded like flocks of nervous woodpeckers. The deeper clatter of heavy machine guns mixed with the sharp crack of rifles and yells of officers.

When a series of staggered explosions headed toward him on the main supply road, Tomi knew that a hidden Chinese mortar was 'walking shells.' He dove into a muddy ditch and yelled a warning to nearby teamsters leading a pack train. Clumps of dirt, stone and bone clanged against Tomi's steel helmet. He hugged the ground and whimpered as the explosions got closer. A nearby 70-millimeter mortar responded with several rounds that silenced the Chinese mortar.

Shaken and breathing hard, Tomi got up and quickly left the lucky surviving wagoners frantically untangling harnesses from fear-crazed horses. Tomi trotted past scattered pieces of fresh-killed red meat that minutes earlier had been men and animals. He expected another barrage to interdict the important supply artery. Even a glory-seeker like Tomi didn't want an anonymous, instant death without the honor of facing the enemy.

He made record time covering the four miles separating General Nakajima's Division from General Matsui's army headquarters. The generals used Tomi's photographic memory for their running secret debate. Tomi memorized and disgorged sharply-worded disagreements that neither general wanted recorded for posterity or their superiors.

Tomi stood at attention and stared into space as he recited each general's private message to the other. He heard the angry response and walked back to deliver it. General Matsui wanted a 'soft' occupation, just as he had done in Shanghai, where he had donated his own money to a war relief fund to help local civilian refugees. Nakajima, clearly the Emperor's favorite, intended to take his terror campaign into Nanking by declaring it a secret Imperial Wish. Tomi dared not discuss it with anyone. A flunky messenger wasn't supposed to have thoughts, only blisters.

That evening, a message from Tokyo ended the acidic dialogue between the generals. Nanking's occupation would be as Nakajima wished.

Tomi's messenger duties were over and he was demoted to map librarian. In addition to sorting maps, Tomi carried General Nakajima's personal maps when they were in the field.

He hated the big, flat map case, which danced like a black kite in the December wind as it struggled to escape his grip. Tomi followed General Nakajima around like a golf caddy, pulling out maps as needed. Tomi carried the oversized case high in front of him so it didn't bump into his sword, bang against his pistol holster, or get mud-splattered.

Tomi had daydreams of shredding the imitation leather case into black confetti with rapid swings of his sword. The sole advantage of being map boy was that Tomi knew the big picture. While everyone else engaged in the final attack, his division was to stay in place until the city fell, then proceed north to the Ichiang Water Gate, Nanking's door to the Yangtze River, and help the Navy stop the defeated defenders from escaping.

General Nakajima planned to observe the start of the final attack with an important personage and wanted to personally check the Tomb of Sun Yat-sen as a possible vantage point. The huge tomb of the Chinese Republic's founder loomed high on the slope of the Purple and Gold Mountains, a mile from Nanking's thick walls that snaked around the capitol city.

General Nakajima led his inspection party of two colonels, a major and a platoon of security troops commanded by the burly bodyguard captain. Tomi was surprised they lacked the new 6.5-millimeter light machine guns. When he politely suggested extra fire power, the security captain said, "We have two reinforced regiments between us and the nearest gooks. You carry the general's maps. I'll worry about the enemy."

Chastised, Tomi trailed the general's party to the Sun Yat-sen

Mausoleum. They walked through a huge outer gateway inscribed with the Chinese characters, 'Universal Love,' then on a wide tree-lined avenue to a three-arched main gate that proclaimed Sun's message: 'The World Belongs To Everyone.' "Not any more!" General Nakajima shouted. "It belongs to Japan!"

To reach the mausoleum, the group had to climb eight sections of wide stairs. Tomi cursed as each of the 392 steps caused the map case to bounce against his sore kneecaps. The wiry general refused to rest or slow down. At the top, the security platoon took positions outside, facing the steps. The officers went inside the unlit mausoleum, with Tomi in the rear. When his eyes adjusted to the gloom, he saw the general and staff at the large white marble statue of Sun Yat-sen seated on a pedestal.

Four enemy riflemen casually emerged from the darkness behind the statue. General Nakajima, nearest to the surprised Chinese soldiers, spun around with a yelp and ran into the officers behind him. A Chinese fired his German Mauser rifle from the hip. General Nakajima howled and grabbed the seat of his breeches with both hands. The colonels tried to assist him and the trio collapsed in a tangle of boots, binoculars, swords, arms and legs. Several more shots sounded like cannon inside the stone building. The major and captain died before they could draw their pistols.

Tomi panicked. Senselessly holding the big cardboard map case in front of him as a shield, he charged at the Chinese riflemen as he unholstered his 8-millimeter Nambu automatic. A bullet hole appeared next to his head on the map case. He dropped it, pulled the heavy pistol's cocking knob, chambered a round and squeezed the trigger. The bullet turned the face of the nearest rifleman into cherry pulp.

The remaining Chinese took cover behind the statue. Tomi heard the clatter of ejected cartridges bouncing on the marble floor as they reloaded. He sprinted around the massive statue and collided with several rifle muzzles. Stunned and near-blind, Tomi fired aimlessly. Despite the extremely close range, he missed all seven of his remaining rounds. Tomi whimpered, waiting for bullets to rip through his body. The security platoon charged in and riddled the three Chinese. Tomi shouted, "Got to be more of the bastards. Look for a back entrance!"

Someone yelled, "Door's right in front of you, Lieutenant!"

Tomi dropped his empty automatic, pulled out his sword and yelled "Follow me!" He ran toward the dim outline of an entrance. A soldier behind him stepped on Tomi's boot heel and sent him sprawling, face flat against the cold marble floor.

Chinese riflemen waiting inside the circular domed hall fired continuous volleys at the clogged doorway. A hot streak burned his left thigh. He tried to get up but bodies pinned him down, their death scents mingled with the smell of gunpowder.

He felt as much as saw two Chinese attackers use the pile of Japanese dead in the doorway as their firing position. He slashed his blade across their puttee-covered shins. They screamed in pain. Some of the platoon latecomers trampled their own wounded and dead to bayonet the fallen Chinese. The shooting stopped as suddenly as it had started.

Two soldiers freed Tomi from the pile and dragged him back to the outer room. Somebody said, "Lieutenant, you're hit bad. Your eyes are bleeding." Tomi saw only blurred shapes the color of *aoi*, the pale blue-green misty rain of Japan.

Knowing that a dead Nakajima would be better for the Army and Japan, Tomi croaked, "Tell me ... General Nakajima ... is he dead or alive?"

Through loud ringing in his ears, Tomi heard the general's high squeak, "Shot in the ass, but I'm in better shape than you. You've been blinded." Nakajima, flat on his stomach, crowed, "This Tomigawa, his first concern was for his general. Very proper. After you tend me, do him. Except for him, my staff failed me."

Another much calmer voice told Tomi he had cleaned his sword blade and asked permission to return it to the scabbard. Tomi shrugged. A blind man had no use for a sword. He bit his lip to keep from crying. His battle fever was gone and he was a frightened child in the dark.

For the first time, General Nakajima addressed him by his rank. He said in his high voice, "Second Lieutenant Tomigawa, you showed great presence of mind. You and I are the only officers who survived our battle wounds." He nervously puffed a cigaret in his violently shaking hand. "But this idiot who's patching me up insists there are two bullet holes in my right buttock, when I know

I was shot only once!"

Grateful for a distraction, Tomi recalled the adrenalin-filled seconds of the general's cowardly behavior. As his mother would have said, it was a moment that illuminated true character.

"The two wounds can be explained, Sir," Tomi said. "You were spinning around to unholster your pistol and kill the enemy who ambushed you. I believe that the bullet entered one side of your ah, body, and exited the other, a result of your speedy reaction."

"Yes, yes, of course! I remember now! I was spinning around to shoot that fucking gook! Very good of you to remember details in the heat of action, Tomigawa. Only we two remained calm during the ambush. That's why we're wounded instead of dead."

Warming to Tomi's lie, the general added, "If clumsy Colonel Yuzawa hadn't bumped into me, I would have killed that Chinese whore's son. Thank you, Tomigawa, for avenging me."

The medical orderly said, "Lieutenant, the cut over your eye is bleeding badly. Allow me to wipe away the blood." Tomi wept with relief when two swipes of a bandage restored his sight.

The orderly apologized, thinking he had hurt Tomi. "You've also got a bullet graze on the thigh, Sir. Neither wound is serious, but we must prevent infection." Tomi irrationally worried that his best pair of breeches had been ruined.

Tomi's restored sight began with General Nakajima's blood-slick rump, decorated with a large bandage on one cheek. The general was pulled erect and his breeches gently pulled up and over the wad of bandages. When an aide buttoned his fly, the seat of the general's breeches ballooned indecently. Tomi averted his eyes from the comical sight.

Soldiers respectfully laid the dead major and captain in a corner. Colonel Yuzawa, who suffered a severely sprained shoulder from the General's panic and fall, wore a tight restraining sling as he saluted Nakajima. "General, two officers and eight enlisted men were killed, seven badly wounded and ten with light injuries."

General Nakajima ignored him and demanded a complete report from a sergeant named Takahashi, who had led the security platoon rush into the great hall to save Tomi and the general. An intelligent-looking man, Takahashi reported, "Sir, Second

Lieutenant Tomigawa bravely charged the enemy to protect you after you were ambushed."

Given the rare opportunity to speak directly to his general, the sergeant elaborated, "Lieutenant Tomigawa charged directly into the muzzle of the Chinks' guns, firing his pistol until it was empty. Then he drew his sword and killed more enemy after he had been shot and was on the floor, Sir. It was like something one sees only in *Samurai* movies!"

General Nakajima looked at Tomi with open gratitude. A stretcher finally arrived to take General Nakajima down the hill. "Take that damn thing away!" he shouted. "I'm not going to be bounced down all those steps like a rubber ball. Get a strong man. I will ride piggyback. And one for Lieutenant Tomigawa too."

Tomi felt silly, traveling down the six flights of stairs on the back of a struggling soldier whom he outweighed by twenty pounds. In front of him was the stained, ballooned seat of General Nakajima's breeches. The division photographer was waiting at the bottom of the hill to record the triumph. The photo of General Nakajima and Tomi peering over the heads of the two sweating soldiers was taken head-on to hide the ludicrous bulge of the general's bloody ass. Tomi was bareheaded because of the bandage covering his gashed forehead, but General Nakajima insisted on wearing his battle helmet and demanded several poses before he allowed his concerned officers to place him in an ambulance. Nakajima's second in command told the general that his '2-for-1 wound' rated a combat decoration and vowed to start the paperwork immediately.

Weeks later, Tomi learned from Lady Tomigawa's letters and newspaper clippings that the incident was called the 'Sun Yat-sen Tomb Ambush,' in which a large number of enemy defenders were personally killed by General Nakajima. The general was praised for the brilliance of his counter-attack on the strategic heights above Nanking's eastern wall during the siege.

Aware of censorship, his mother effusively described the new wave of patriotism in Tokyo. Everyone was buying 'Nanking noodles' for family feasts to celebrate the imminent surrender of Nanking. "I've never seen such wonderful patriotism and true love for the Emperor!"

In their secret *Tanka* code, which used the first character of every third and fifth line, she wrote: "Things worsen. Nakajima power grows. Be careful."

General Nakajima returned to duty the day after the ambush. Unable to sit, he was irritable and found fault with everyone except Tomi, his new favorite.

At the daily briefing, General Nakajima washed down aspirin with tea and said, "I can't afford to have any more bullet holes in my map case. Therefore Tomigawa will assume command of the security platoon. The war must end soon because Tomigawa has no room left on his face for any more wounds."

Knowing his popularity was temporary, Tomi quickly revamped his new command. Three of the four security platoon sergeants resembled their late captain in appearance and attitude. They were *Kempetai* veterans, who behaved more like lazy thugs than soldiers. Sergeant Takahashi was the exception. His looks hinted of ancestry that probably included a *Samurai* warrior.

Tomi had to quickly gain the sergeants' respect, despite his youth and inexperience. He rumbled in a low voice of near-equals, "Nobody has reason to be proud of what happened at the Sun Yat-sen Tomb. We lost two fine officers, including your commander, an excellent soldier. We all made many mistakes. I am personally responsible and feel deep shame that I did not do more. Because we all failed, General Nakajima was wounded despite his personal bravery. He could just as easily have been killed by the tactical errors you and I made in the Tomb."

The truculent sergeants looked unimpressed. Tomi changed tactics. He bellowed in the military superior-to-inferior voice, "Blind obedience is not enough. Any ox obeys the whip. I demand dedication and constant vigilance by you and your men. As long as I am in command, I will make certain the general's security is ironclad and his orders performed without error. Understand?" Tomi growled in a good imitation of Harada The Bear.

"Fail me and you fail your honorable general. Should that happen, you'll suffer the ugly fate you deserve long before I get my punishment. I will spit on anyone who fails to carry out General Nakajima's orders to the fullest. Woe be to the sergeant who continues lazy, arrogant ways and allows his men to slack off.

Your punishment will be so severe that you will wish you had been killed up at the Tomb. Understand?"

The four sergeants barked *"Hai!"* in unison. Tomi ignored their bows.

"We're going to be the best headquarters security platoon in this army, as well as the finest infantry unit in the division. We will set an example for others. I want every man in each section to be a marksman not only with the Meiji rifle, but also the 6.5-millimeter light machine guns that I've ordered. Several have telescopic sights; ten others have grenade launchers.

"While two sections are guarding the general's headquarters perimeter, I will lead the other two sections into forward positions to get their bellies familiar with actual combat. When the sections are trained and ready, they will shift with each other. Expect neither rest nor sleep until you and every one of your men achieve the proficiency I demand."

Tomi coldly stared down the sergeants' shocked expressions. "Yesterday's blunders must not be repeated, especially the bad shooting. Every man will be trained before the final attack. There is no time to waste. Have sections three and four ready to move out in half an hour!"

For the next 19 hours, Tomi went sleepless. He rotated each platoon section into relatively quiet front-line positions, where other units appreciated the temporary reinforcement. As other divisions crawled into key jump-off points for the attack, Tomi's men provided covering fire without being exposed to heavy gunfire.

During the night, Tomi heard an antique Maxim machine gun on his right flank and knew a Chinese gun crew had infiltrated between his unit and the adjacent one. The enemy would fire in both directions to get the Japanese to shoot blindly at each other.

Tomi ordered his men to fire toward the unmistakable clatter of a hot machine gun barrel inside a water-cooled steel jacket. His unit's sweeping light machine gun fire and a few well-aimed grenades routed the infiltrators.

In the silence that followed, Tomi heard, "Well done, over there! I'm Captain Shimazu of the 13th. I owe you a big bottle of sake for helping us out. What's your name and outfit?"

Thrilled at being praised by a real warrior, Tomi stood up and proudly yelled his name, rank and unit.

Two sniper shots missed him by inches before Sergeant Takahashi pulled him down, "Keep down, Sir! Your white face bandage makes an easy target." Tomi moved fearfully around in a half-crouch for the rest of the night and remembered Suzuki's threat that if he was killed without producing a son, his mother would be punished.

At General Nakajima's staff meeting the next day, he drew Tomi aside. "I understand that you re-equipped my personal security platoon and gave them extra training. I'm pleased, but there was no need for you to take personal blame for the Sun-Yat-sen ambush, which I successfully fought off. The fault lies with the dead officers, Tomigawa."

Tomi was surprised by the general's courteous tone. More important, the general showed trust by letting Tomi know that one of his sergeants was an informer. General Nakajima turned to the assembled officers. "The main attack will be the day after tomorrow. Our orders are to cut off the Water Gate escape route."

He grinned. "I have good news! General Matsui has been ... shall we be kind and say ... promoted? He remains nominally in charge of tactics, but no longer has responsibility for Nanking's occupation. Our patron, The Honorable Prince Asaka, has given this division the honor of occupation security." General Nakajima's smirk vanished when his wounded buttock bumped the table edge behind him.

The Imperial decision overruled General Matsui's original plan to police Nanking with several well-disciplined battalions of soldiers until a new civilian government of Chinese collaborators was formed. General Matsui, Chinese scholar and champion of improved relations between Japan and China, had said when he assumed command in China: "I am going to the front not to fight an enemy, but in the state of mind of one who sets out to pacify his brother."

From the outset, General Nakajima wanted to punish Nanking for resisting Japan. Nanking, a thriving metropolis long before Marco Polo's 13th Century visit, was no stranger to punishment. During the 1912 Revolution, marauding Chinese warlord generals encouraged their troops to terrorize Nanking's cosmopolitan residents.

Led by the brutal 'Pig Tail' Yang and his sadistic subordinate, an ex-bandit called 'Dog Meat' Yang, the so-called liberators set the old royal city afire, destroyed priceless libraries, scrolls and art, as well as many ancient wooden buildings. Yang's men perfected the technique of 'opening melons,' splitting the skulls of prominent Nanking families with swords and executioners' axes. 'Pig Tail' Yang festooned long rows of the severed heads on telegraph wires between poles and called them 'Nanking melons.'

Nakajima was going to add a new chapter to Nanking's tragic history. More than 25,000 Japanese lives might be lost taking Nanking. Japan could not afford to sustain such high casualty rates in future battles against China's vast territory and huge population.

Nakajima told his officers, "A harsh occupation of Nanking will be a cautionary lesson for the rest of China. To avoid Nanking's fate, cities in the interior will surrender without a fight and many Japanese lives will be saved."

General Nakajima ordered that every fourth man in Tomi's security platoon carry one of the new light machine guns. Tomi was informed that ten trucks would be delivered to him; eight loaded with drums of Nakajima's special 'Nanking oil' and two others with rolls of barbed wire. Tomi wondered why so many machine guns were needed after the battle. And what was he supposed to do with the general's highly-publicized kerosene?

**

Early on the morning of the attack, General Nakajima and Prince Asaka began their long climb up Purple Mountain to view the battle from Sun Yat-sen's Tomb.

Prince Asaka laughed, "You, Nakajima, with bullet holes in your ass and I, with a leg brace, limp to victory. A long road from Paris to Nanking, *neh?*"

The prince, a slim, handsome man with a dapper moustache, wore a heavy steel brace due to severe injuries received in an automobile accident that killed Prince Kitashirakawa on a country road outside of Paris five years after The Great War.

General Nakajima, then a captain, served both princes at the Japanese Embassy in Paris. The trio, on secret orders from the Prince Regent, dismissed every pro-Western military attaché' from Japanese embassies throughout postwar Europe. The peace lovers were replaced by the heir-apparent's loyal men, who gathered vital military information.

Thanks to the efficient spy network, Japan knew that their Great War Allies, who continued to thwart Nippon's colonial aims, were weaker in weaponry and political will than re-emerging Germany. The knowledge fed the Palace war clique's dreams of expansion.

Generalissimo Chiang Kai-shek, China's wily military ruler refused to be a puppet of a Japan that demanded much of China, but gave too little in return. Only General Matsui openly respected the Chinese, who had struggled against foreign exploitation as they stumbled from an inept, fragmented empire toward modernity.

The snail's pace of Nakajima's party was set by the handicapped prince. Making several stops to rest, they slowly climbed toward the distinctive blue-tiled roof of the tomb. The strong-willed prince wanted to be able to boast that during the battle he had climbed the famous steps instead of motoring up the back road.

General Nakajima's buttock wounds ached, but he maintained his fawning patter of encouragement as the prince laboriously ascended. Waiting at the summit were news photographers and newsreel cameramen. Prince Asaka posed with one booted foot in front of the other to hide the protuberance of the leg brace on his right leg. He wore a sleek, custom-tailored gabardine uniform adorned with three full rows of campaign ribbons, and insisted upon being photographed from the front-left to display the Imperial Court sword, a personal gift from his nephew, the God Emperor.

The photo of Prince Asaka gazing down at Nanking, half-hidden by the dense fog of gunpowder and smoking ruins, was widely distributed to imply that the Prince, not General Matsui, was responsible for the coming victory.

Despite their expensive German binoculars, smoke obscured

battle's details, so they pretended to track the progress of the attack on maps. General Nakajima was relieved when an intercepted wireless radio message was handed to Prince Asaka. He read it aloud, "9th Division reports advance elements penetrated the south wall and control the Radiant Flower Gate."

The Prince addressed the staff officers, "As we all know, gentlemen, that is our main point of attack. We are victorious!" An elated Asaka dictated a telegram to Tokyo announcing that "Prince Asaka has the honor to inform the *Showa Sama* and the nation that, obeying the Imperial Wish, Nanking has fallen."

The Prince's historic message was quickly broadcast to the nation and triggered spontaneous celebrations. Tens of thousands of citizens poured out of offices and homes to gather along the wide Tokyo boulevard along the Imperial Moat. Throngs fell on their knees and touched their foreheads to the pavement to honor the Living God within the Imperial Palace. That evening, families all over Japan enjoyed special Nanking noodle feasts.

Prince Asaka's message of victory was a few hours old when the Chinese valiantly counterattacked. The badly-mauled 9th Division was forced to retreat, leaving behind its battle flag inside Nanking's Radiant Flower Gate, along with many wounded prisoners who were executed by the defenders. Outraged, the Prince ordered General Matsui to take the city, regardless of casualties. He and Nakajima left in a waiting car that went down the back road. The rest of the dejected party walked down the familiar steps.

A grim-faced General Nakajima addressed the officers at headquarters. "As we drove back, Prince Asaka told me about the famous *gaijin*, Machiavelli, who wrote: 'Taking possession of a state, the conqueror should well reflect as to the harsh measures that may be necessary, and then execute them at a single blow. Cruelties should be committed all at once."

The officers recorded in their diaries, "Cruelties should be committed all at once," in the formal Japanese alphabet composed of classical Chinese characters. The irony went unnoticed. As his division remained in idle reserve, Tomi watched waves of infantry cross the canal on pontoon bridges and overrun perimeter positions.

The Chinese responded with withering gunfire. Despite heavy losses, the Japanese placed long, crudely-made ladders against the walls. Chinese defenders shot down at them with antique rifles, old flintlocks and shotguns. General Suzuki had been correct. Generalissimo Chiang had escaped with his best men and weapons, leaving behind an ill-equipped rear guard to cover his retreat.

He saw two Chinese officers on the wall swinging huge, two-handed Manchurian swords at Japanese platoon leaders, who somehow survived the massacre below them. The Chinese fought with a raw valor. Tomi admired them as much as he did the Japanese officers who led their men into the meat grinder.

Heaps of Japanese dead and wounded grew at the base of the wall until the outnumbered Chinese defenders ran out of ammunition. Fresh waves of Japanese clambered over the walls, and the battle gradually diminished. Tomi returned to the command tent, uncomfortably aware of being relieved that he hadn't been part of the bloodbath.

Someone read the latest report to General Nakajima, who ate standing up. "Our men breached the walls and opened the gates. Organized resistance is over. The Chinese beg for an immediate cease-fire to prevent further loss of life. As instructed, we refuse to negotiate a surrender."

Handing his empty plate and chopsticks to an orderly, General Nakajima intoned, "Now it is my turn. Remember! Cruelties will be committed all at once."

Tomi's heavily-armed security platoon led the division around the city to the Water Gate riverbank without firing a shot.

At the Yangtze River, crowds of terrified civilian refugees had swarmed aboard a motley assortment of junks, sampans and fishing boats to ferry them across the river. Tomi saw no uniformed or armed men on the boats and ordered the platoon to hunker down, alert for any armed deserters who might sneak past.

Although combat ended, the Japanese air regiment continued bombing and machine gunning the retreating masses of refugees and deserters fleeing northward. Attacked from the ground and air, Nanking was a bedlam of fear-crazed survivors.

Poor families marooned on the riverbank wailed in

frustration while those with escape money crammed their children and belongings onto anything that floated. Boatmen viciously beat off refugees who lacked cash. Some desperate men and women swam to boats, hoping some merciful person would pluck them out of the water. Crewmen used hatchets on grasping hands that clung to gunwales. Sickened, Tomi lowered his binoculars.

The ragtag fleet reached midstream before Japanese launches attacked the overloaded junks and sampans. After they used all their heavy ammunition, sailors fired rifles at survivors in the water. There was as little mercy on the Yangtze as there had been on Nanking's walls.

One of Tomi's thug-sergeants ordered his section to shoot survivors who attempted to swim back to shore. Tomi knew he should have given that order. Masses of bodies, mostly women and children, floated silently past in a grisly parade that quivered as the 'river pigs' fed on them.

In late afternoon, General Nakajima held a ceremonial raising of the Japanese army battle flag at the Water Gate. The ever-present newsreel cameramen and photographers filmed his victory appearance as cheering officers and men waved swords and rifles amid *Banzai* cheers.

Because of his height and face wounds, Tomi was told to stand behind General Nakajima and wave the red and white battle flag for the hand-cranked newsreel cameras. Tomi was again a celebrity in an historic battle he had not fought.

The Japanese army unraveled in the confused aftermath. Dusk fell as hundreds of stragglers looted homes for liquor and valuables. To establish order, all troops in the city were ordered to march south, back to their cold, damp tents across the canal. Only two battalions of Nakajima's 16th Division remained in the city to guard against non-existent Chinese marauders.

Neither officers nor the non-coms interfered as the returning soldiers grabbed young Chinese women and dragged them back to camp. During the night, bands of disobedient soldiers crept back into the city and prowled among the ruins, looting, killing and raping. The constant screams of kidnapped women being gang-raped in nearby tents made sleep impossible for Tomi.

The next day, Western newsmen were escorted on a brief tour of Nanking. A heavily-guarded line of staff cars rolled slowly along a few preselected boulevards. The newsmen were told that they could not leave the armed convoy because armed Chinese bandits, deserters and looters were terrorizing civilians and setting fires in the city.

The Western press openly favored the outwardly-polite Japanese over the rebellious, independent Chinese. The press corps was assured that the Japanese army would restore order. American and European reporters filed dispatches about Nanking's occupation from the safety and hospitality of army headquarters. The world was informed that once the outlaws were subdued, Nanking would enjoy the same 'soft' occupation that General Matsui had given Shanghai.

It was not to be. Hours earlier, Nakajima had demanded of Tomi, "Are your men ready to move out with the trucks loaded with my special supplies?"

"Yes, Sir," Tomi replied, "All preparations have been completed as ordered."

"Good. We have new orders from Tokyo," Nakajima told his staff. "All prisoners in Nanking will be summarily executed as outlaws and spies. A tight cordon will be drawn around our sector. Foreign residents and *gaijin* newsmen must not witness our operations."

Tomi hid his surprise, but two other junior officers hissed with sharp intakes of breath. Nakajima said, "We will purge the city of the hundreds of thousands of treacherous Chinese who shed their uniforms and lie in wait to ambush us. Our mission is to inflict a hard, occupation on Nanking, a lesson that will weaken future resistence and shorten the war."

He turned to Tomi. "The security platoon will wear auxiliary military police arm bands and show the other division commanders how to punish criminals. Round up as many Chinese prisoners as possible for an execution demonstration after the foreign newsmen are escorted from the city. Wrap the prisoners in barbed wire and await my arrival with my guests."

Tomi saluted Nakajima and left. He stood alone for a few moments in the cold dawn to gather his wits. The Imperial Wish overruled General Matsui's orders, which clearly stated:*"The entry of the Imperial Army into a foreign capital is a great event in our history ... attracting the attention of the world. Therefore, let no unit enter Nanking in a disorderly fashion. The units entering the walled city will be especially chosen for that purpose. Let the troops be absolutely free from plunder. The starting of fires, even carelessly, will be punished severely. Together with the troops, let the military police and auxiliary military police enter the walls and thereby prevent unlawful conduct."*

Now those orders were to be ignored.

CHAPTER FIVE
NANKING, CHINA

Tomi's convoy rolled through the destroyed Tranquility Gate to begin the first day of Japanese-occupied Nanking on Tuesday, December 14, 1937.

At the demonstration site, they dismounted. In the grey half light of dawn, the men looked like imposters wearing the unfamiliar green and black arm bands of the Military Police. The isolated field that General Nakajima selected was bordered by railroad tracks on the west, the Tranquility Gate on the east and the Water Gate to the north.

What Tomi feared would be the hardest part of the assignment -- collecting Chinese prisoners -- turned out to be the easiest. A black sedan drove up and parked next to the trucks. Four *gaijin* approached and bowed. They must have followed the convoy from the checkpoint.

The *gaijin* leader had a big nose and wore a double-breasted overcoat with a crumpled Nazi swastika armband that kept slipping down. He said in passable Japanese, "On behalf of Nanking's international community, we welcome the Japanese military police here to restore order."

He pointed to a nearby cluster of warehouses. "Last night, our committee persuaded a division of Chinese soldiers to stack their weapons and await your arrival. They are inside those buildings. Their act of trust and goodwill prevents needless bloodshed. We are grateful to your general for sending a police detachment instead of combat troops."

Tomi had to get rid of these foreign witnesses. "Thank you, honored Sirs. We will take charge now. Chinese deserters are robbing and looting in this sector. It is very dangerous. Please return to the International Zone for your own safety."

The German insisted that Tomi sign his prepared receipt for the transfer of the Chinese soldiers to his custody. Tomi quickly inked his official chop and stamped the German's receipt. Relieved by their departure, Tomi's platoon rousted out the battle-weary Chinese soldiers and calmly marched them to the middle of the field. The badly wounded were left under guard in the warehouse with piles of confiscated weapons.

Tomi ignored their pleas for water. He had his men separate the able-bodied from the walking wounded, who were tied with their hands behind their backs in groups of threes, with strips torn from their clothing. Using pantomime because no one in Tomi's platoon knew the Chinese word for 'dig,' they finally got the prisoners to start digging a mass grave with a few trench tools and pieces of wood. Many dug with their bare hands.

Tomi ordered Sergeant Takahashi to position machine-gunners around the field and place checkpoints on the roads to prevent foreign newsmen from entering. The non-com asked, "Sir, shouldn't we make an example to discourage a mass escape before the demonstration?"

Tomi grabbed a Chinese officer from among the diggers and made hand motions to him to leave. Surprised, the officer walked; then, realizing his good fortune, broke into a run toward the railroad tracks. When the officer was 40 yards away, Sergeant Takahashi yelled an order to a machine gunner. A short stutter echoed across the field and the prisoner crumpled. The telescopic sight was perfectly calibrated. "No go! Chinese no go!" Takahashi shouted in pidgin Mandarin to the Cantonese-speaking prisoners. The message was clear.

When his men cut their hands pulling the barbed wire from the large wooden spools, Tomi cursed himself for not bringing leather work gloves. He had the loose end of the wire wrapped around two big prisoners. Like farm animals, the prisoners were prodded to slowly walk away from the bale as a soldier paid out the strand of barbed wire.

The wounded prisoners were shoved into groups of two to three dozen. The two oxen-prisoners pulled the barbed wire around the first group as Tomi's men used bayonets to force the Chinese captives into bunches. When the barbed wire around the

-73-

first bunch fell to the ground, Tomi yelled, "Hold the wire up, you idiots! Hold the wire up!" The prisoners cringed but didn't understand. A prisoner shouted in Japanese, "Please! Honorable Colonel, Sir. Me number one interpreter. I translate and tell fucking gook Chinese your orders."

He was a skinny youth with the pale look of a scholar. Tomi had the man brought to him. "Tell your comrades they must remain tied up until the ration truck comes. They are to hold the wire up at waist level with their hands as it is wrapped around them. When the food truck arrives, we will unwrap the wire, one group at a time, until all are fed. Now repeat my instructions so I know you understand."

His accent was too good for such bad grammar. Tomi suspected the man had once interrogated Japanese prisoners and shoved lighted cigarets into eyeballs to get information. The young prisoner listened intently to Tomi's instructions and relayed them in sing-song Cantonese. A few officers argued and he shouted at them until they sullenly obeyed. Soon, two strands of barbed wire loosely encircled the first bunch of enemy prisoners.

"Think of them as bunches of radishes," Tomi told himself. *"Think how many Japanese they slaughtered. Show no weakness."*

By noon, he had twenty-five loosely tied bunches. Sergeant Takahashi grabbed a wood board, inserted it under the top loop of barbed wire and twisted it like a tourniquet, end over end until the wire loop tightened. Soon all the bunches were tightly-packed. The screams of the outer layer of men made the trench diggers work faster.

Tomi allowed his men to alternate ten minute breaks to eat their combat rations. After all the men were fed, he slowly chewed on a thin slab of tough dried fish and drank from his canteen.

"Please, Sir, water? A little water, please?" Tomi was startled to find the Chinese interpreter squatting next to him. Tomi poured water into the young prisoner's cupped hands. "Thank you. Thank you, Honorable Colonel, Sir," he said.

"I'm neither a colonel nor a fool. Stop pretending," Tomi snarled. He gave him some fish.

"Yes Sir, Lieutenant. Thank you. You are most kind," he said in perfect Japanese.

"You are an interrogator. You tortured captured Japanese."

"No Sir. I never tortured. I was too soft for that duty. I had to find out what kind of man you were before I revealed my fluency. Please, Sir. I want to stay alive. I can guess what you intend to do here. These prisoners are doomed. I want to survive. Perhaps you'd feel better about me if I told you that my father is collaborating with the Japanese in Shanghai."

"Is this true?"

"Yes, if you believe it is so. But if my family were rich and influential collaborators, I wouldn't have been drafted and I wouldn't be here, would I?"

"You are a nuisance," Tomi replied and walked toward the wide ditch the prisoners were hacking out of hard soil. He glanced back at the dejected young man and told him to find a scrap of white cloth for an arm band. A few moments later, the grinning Chinese student handed Tomi a white cloth he had ripped from another prisoner's jacket lining.

"What's your name?"

"Chen Ta, Sir."

"Did you torture Japanese prisoners, Chen Ta?"

Looking straight at Tomi, he said quietly, "I was present, Sir, at the horrible interrogations. But I swear that I did not participate. I was a university student studying Japanese when I got drafted. I just followed orders, as you do now."

Tomi took out a thick fountain pen that once belonged to his father, and inked the characters *tsuuyaku*, 'interpreter,' on the cloth. The ink spread over the loose cotton weave, blurring the characters into broad, bold strokes that looked official.

"Tie this around your right arm and stay close to me at all times," he said. "Do not speak unless I tell you to. High ranking officers will be here soon. Behave as if you belong to me. No matter what happens, stay near and remain silent. Understand?"

"Hai," Chen Ta said, his face aglow with relief.

Tomi's headache eased, but he still had many more prisoners than anticipated. He had Sergeant Takahashi assemble the section leaders and gave them detailed instructions for the demonstration. Then Tomi pointed to Chen Ta. "This man is our translator. He's not to be molested. Now, return to your posts and await General Nakajima's party. The men must behave as though we're on parade. No sloppiness. No hesitation. No weakness. Understood?"

An hour later, General Nakajima's convoy arrived, led by a huge Sumida armored car. The general rode in a 6-wheeled staff car modeled after the Yankee Studebaker convertible. Despite the winter chill, General Nakajima rode with the top down for the photographers.

There were several Nissan staff cars and ten Toyoda trucks filled with men of the division's First Regiment. The soldiers jumped off the trucks, attached bayonets and fanned out around the prisoners digging the ditch. The Chinese saw the menacing bayonets of the newly-arrived troops and knew Tomi had lied. Their moans and wails sounded like the wind of a coming storm.

Tomi ran to the open staff car and saluted General Nakajima, who leaned forward to keep weight off his wounded bottom. His white-gloved hands grasped the sheathed sword between his bandy legs for support. He gaped at the prisoners, surprised that Tomi had rounded up an entire Chinese division. There were far too many of them for an effective demonstration.

Shouting above the prisoners' cries, Tomi reported, "Sir, we await your orders."

"How many damn prisoners do you have?"

"Uh ... uh ... eight-hundred-and ... uh ... thirty-four, Sir!" Tomi stammered. "Several died and one officer was shot attempting to escape." Tomi had erred by not making a head count.

Nakajima asked sarcastically, "And who's this? Your new second-in-command?"

Confused, Tomi looked around. Chen Ta obeyed instructions and stood behind him.

"My translator, Sir. No one in the platoon speaks Cantonese. A temporary expedient."

"You were supposed to demonstrate how we implement the Kill All Prisoners policy," the general scolded. "Other units may not have such good luck in finding translators. Do you think Japanese speakers are found on every Nanking street corner? You have compromised the very purpose of my demonstration."

General Nakajima's anger was justified. Tomi's lack of

foresight was obvious.

"Execute your temporary expedient translator," General Nakajima said.

"Sir?"

"Shoot him now!"

Tomi made a smart turn about and fumbled the Nambu pistol from its holster. He looked at Chen Ta, who stared back in shock. Tomi cocked the automatic, straightened his trembling arm and tried to aim at Chen Ta's head without looking into his eyes. Tomi fired, holstered his pistol, did another about face and bowed to General Nakajima.

"Now, Tomigawa," he ordered, "start the 'special Nanking oil' demonstration with your remaining eight-hundred-and-thirty-three prisoners."

"Yes, Sir!" Nakajima demanded total control. He detested surprises. The general had told his guests there would be a few Chinese, and Tomi made him lose face. It cost Chen Ta his life.

Tomi slowly raised his arm and quickly lowered it. At the signal, Sergeant Takahashi shouted orders. The trucks with 'special Nanking oil' backed up to the barbed wire-wrapped radish bunches. Soldiers tipped barrels over the tailgates and poured the liquid into Chinese army mess kits and old oil cans.

Tomi's men splashed kerosene on the heads of wailing prisoners. It was a slow, clumsy process. One kerosene-drenched radish bunch fell and twenty pairs of feet kicked like a grotesque giant animal lying on its side. The barbed wire kept the screaming bunch intact.

The grave-digger prisoners stampeded. They clambered up the soft earth mounds, and Tomi's men, obeying his standing orders, opened fire. A few escaped. Sounds of shooting, shrill screams and shouted commands added to the confusion. The reinforcement troops fired their weapons. It was a chaotic two-ring circus of death. The high-ranking guests moved their heads from side to side as if watching a tennis match; first at the fleeing diggers, then to the tight bunches of barbed-wire bound captives.

Tomi grabbed an unlit torch and matches from a dumbfounded guard and ran to the first bunch of terrified prisoners. His hands shook. It took two attempts to light the torch and ignite the captives' fuel-sodden clothing.

Compressed into tight helplessness, the prisoners howled as the flames spread. Takahashi and the other sergeants followed his example and soon all the radish bunches were aflame. A stink filled his nostrils. The kerosene was burning too slowly. Tomi guessed what made Nakajima's 'special Nanking oil' special. The kerosene had been deliberately diluted with water to prolong agony. Tomi stared at the pain-wracked men he was slowly burning to death and thought, "I am a monster."

The flames failed to reach prisoners in the center of the bunches. Tomi ordered the troops to continue splashing on more kerosene. Refueled, the flames spread and black smoke curled upward along with the screams of pain. The sweet-sour burnt stench caused Nakajima's party to press handkerchiefs to their noses. Tomi pretended to cough to hide his retching.

Slowly, the bunches cooked down into blackened heaps. The cries and groans of the dying continued. "Shoot the rest!" Tomi yelled and his men used more ammunition than was needed.

After the last screams faded, a staff captain approached Tomi. "The general wants a critique of the demonstration." Tomi looked at the burnt radish bunches, the piles of machine-gunned prisoners in the ditch and scattered bodies strewn about the field. Several of his men vomited, and Tomi wanted to.

General Nakajima snarled. "Fool, you botched everything! What's your pitiful excuse?"

If Tomi mentioned the watered kerosene, he'd end up in a punishment unit. "Sir, the mistakes are my mine alone. The security platoon followed my orders. They are blameless. I am the only one who did not perform his duty. I bear all the shame."

The general was uncharacteristically silent. Nervously, Tomi rattled on, "I should have gathered the prisoners in smaller numbers. My lengthy preparations with too many prisoners complicated matters. Because of my ineptitude, I wasted fuel, manpower and ammunition. I was too eager and thus stupid.

"We're told there could be as many as 200,000 enemy hiding among the civilian population. Because a few Chinese escaped, word may spread, making it impossible to get the remaining outlaws to cooperate as this batch did."

General Nakajima interrupted, "I don't have time to listen to your miserable excuses. The army wants a tally of the mass executions during the months ahead. There must be an exact accounting of executions to determine remaining Chinese troop strength. Your blunders will make the information difficult to get."

Tomi hadn't known that the executions were to continue for months. There wasn't enough watered-down kerosene in Jiang Su Province to burn all its population.

He kept his voice level and bowed low. "With respect, Sir, special units could tally the exact number of executions conducted daily by the roving patrols. Such units, 10 or 20 perhaps, could make spot checks of daily sweeps. However, the disadvantage is ..."

"Silence! You prattle like your uncle. You've brought dishonor to my division. You offend my sense of efficiency as much as the stink of your stupid mistakes."

Tomi stared down and saw a greyish-white splatter of burnt fat glistening on his boot tip. It looked like a badly-formed eye that stared at him in silent accusation.

Nakajima turned and stormed, "Colonel Mori, your inefficient lieutenant no longer commands the security platoon. He will be a clerk and keep score of the summary executions of 200,000 prisoners. No! Make that 250,000 spies, saboteurs, criminals and civilian accomplices who still hide in Nanking. He isn't a leader of men. Perhaps he'll make a better bookkeeper."

Nakajima raised his thin voice and addressed his guests. "With his stiff cock and sharp bayonet, the brave Japanese soldier will give this criminal city the stern punishment it deserves! Now, gentlemen, let's move over to the trench and pose for photographs with the enemy dead."

Tomi returned to camp alone in the back of a truck that rattled with empty kerosene drums. A circle of repugnance surrounded him. No one dared speak to him. Despite hunger, he avoided the officers' mess and remained in his tent cleaning his boots. The servile task fed his self-disgust. He brushed in a steady, trance-like rhythm. One boot tip had a brighter shine from the human fat.

His right hand under the tight cloth strap of the oval Army-issue brush, Tomi stroked the glistening leather with a cadence that matched his new title: *Kaikei gakari, kaikei gakari.* 'Accountant of death, accountant of death.'

The assignment was impossible. General Nakajima insisted he had to personally verify 250,000 executions even though there weren't that many Chinese soldiers still alive. Even if there were half that number, how was Tomi to tally the random, spontaneous executions? He couldn't be everywhere at once.

He had flashes of the burned bodies, the awful stench, the screams and black smoke. The image of Chen Ta looking at him with his destroyed eye. In the background were the railroad siding, the fresh-dug mass grave, the Toyoda trucks and General Nakajima's staff car, dwarfed by the Sumida armored car.

To cancel out the images of writhing men aflame in bands of barbed wire, he concentrated on the Sumida, the first one he'd ever seen. The armored car had a strange wheel and jack arrangement. Its solid rubber tires were for roads and, after a 20-minute conversion, an alternate system of flanged wheel rims that allowed it to roll on railroad tracks.

That gave Tomi an idea. He pulled a Nanking street map out of his case. Railroad tracks ran from the terminal in the government district, north to the main line that hugged the south bank of the Yangtze. If the tracks hadn't been hit by bombs, the Sumida armored car could be used as a quicker way to tally the body count at executions. He would travel on Nanking's north-south railroad tracks, then switch to road tires to patrol the east and west sectors.

The next morning, he approached Major Okada, a supply officer, with a requisition. "An interesting list, Lieutenant Tomigawa." He glanced around, then lowered his head as if scrutinizing the list. He whispered between unmoving lips. "Don't feel bad, lad. Many of us know the kerosene was deliberately diluted. Not your fault. You did well despite all."

Major Okada flicked his finger at the requisition sheet and said in a loud voice, "Honorable General Nakajima wants you to form a clerical unit for an important duty. You'll need personnel, transport and a work place. Very unusual request, this Sumida armored car. Not easy to get. But since the criminal execution tally has the high command's attention, it might be possible. General Nakajima ordered me to remind you that the execution total must be 250,000, not one gook less! Understand?"

"Yes, Sir."

"Now, Tomigawa, what about your personnel? Anyone in mind?"

Startled, he hadn't expected to be given a choice. Nakajima was sure to have several informers, so Tomi needed to ask for someone trustworthy.

"Sir, may I request Sergeant Takahashi of the security platoon?"

Major Okada looked up in surprise, then smiled as he saw the logic. He leaned back, lit a cigaret and blew smoke down at the requisition form.

"Yes, an excellent non-com, Tomigawa. And your men?"

"Sir, I'll let Sergeant Takahashi select them."

Major Okada grinned. By leaving the choice of personnel to Takahashi, Tomi might get good men instead of misfits who were shuffled around on temporary duties.

"A final important point, Tomigawa. General Nakajima wants your records and correspondence to show that you are operating under the personal command of General Matsui."

"General Matsui? But ..."

"Even though General Matsui is no longer in operational control, he remains titular head of the campaign. General Nakajima's instructions are clear. Your accounting reports will show that the "Kill All Prisoners Program is under General Matsui's command. Comprehend?" Major Okada's voice rose with meaningful inflection and Tomi nodded. General Nakajima wanted responsibility for Nanking's punishment to fall upon General Matsui, the man who tried to prevent it.

Tomi was assigned a small office in the shell-pocked railroad station, near Prince Asaka's headquarters. Sergeant Takahashi dragooned eleven capable men, plus a clerk with accounting experience. Tomi was given temporary use of a Sumida armored car and its 6-man crew.

As he inspected the Sumida, he heard Sergeant Takahashi curse when he failed to start the dilapidated Toyoda army truck they'd been issued. The motor wouldn't kick over even after installing a battery that he stole from another regiment's vehicle. Tomi lifted the truck hood and smelled raw gasoline. "It's flooded, Sergeant. Turn it off." Tomi reached under the carburetor, twisting the air and fuel mix screws in opposite directions.

"Try it now, Sergeant."

Takahashi pressed the floor starter several times. The engine backfired and chugged into a rough idle until Tomi adjusted the fuel mix to smooth it. Takahashi was surprised. It was the first time he'd seen an officer dirty his hands on an engine. He prudently placed a guard on the repaired truck to keep it from being stolen.

Tomi told his new clerk-accountant to paint a large chart on the wall titled 'The Nanking Account by order of General Matsui.' Above the chart he had '250,000' written in large Arabic numerals -- Tomi's goal as Nanking's Accountant of Death.

Sergeant Takahashi returned with an abacus, a ream of paper and an Army calendar that he had liberated from a careless unit. With Takahashi's help, Tomi looked organized even though he lacked a plan. Before they started their count, Tomi inspected the hybrid Sumida with bewilderment. Why put a weak, 40-horsepower engine in a 10-foot high, 21-foot long steel monster?

Why did the 6-man crew have only one heavy machine gun in the turret, plus a few rifle slits? Tomi assumed the Sumida design wasn't a good example of Army planning. Chatting with the crew, Tomi learned that the turret gun frequently jammed. Tomi had light machine guns shoved into the side rifle slits. It was uncomfortable but Tomi wanted firepower.

Clinging to the outside of the Sumida's turret, Tomi and Takahashi slowly began their death accounting. Dense smoke filtered the fragile winter sunlight. A third of the city was ablaze from Japanese arson squads busy in the poor districts. Entire blocks of wealthy homes were untouched because the Army planned to requisition them after the official looting.

The railroad line was damaged in many places, but Tomi stubbornly ordered the Sumida crew to drive onto the rails. Four built-in jacks lifted the 7 1/2-ton monster and its six solid rubber tires were replaced with flanged steel railroad wheels. The armored car could not exceed 20 miles an hour on the rails, and worse, the track was littered with debris. After many starts and stops, Tomi realized the Sumida was useless and cursed its designer. Embarrassed, he told the crew, "I've caused us needless labor and time. Please put the solid tires back on."

They rumbled down a main avenue two blocks from the protected international zone, making sharp turns to avoid the scattered corpses surrounded by packs of dogs and bold rats.

Over the engine roar, Tomi heard muffled shots coming from an apartment building. He yelled, "Halt!" down the turret hatch.

Sergeant Takahashi carried a light machine gun by its steam-kettle handle and followed Tomi into the building. Seven Japanese soldiers were taking sexual comfort from four women. Men and children, some dead, some dying, were heaped against one wall. The soldiers got to their feet and hastily stuffed themselves back into unbuttoned breeches.

"Are those enemy soldiers?" Tomi demanded. The men shrugged.

"What is your unit?"

"General Yanagawa's 4th Division, 2nd Battalion, Sir." This was the unit that had suffered the heaviest losses at the city walls. Tomi shook his head and walked out. Off-duty soldiers were encouraged to enter Nanking and take personal revenge on civilians. It was bad luck to be Chinese in Nanking.

Around the corner, was a special operations squad. The corporal in charge crisply reported in his distinctive Okinawa accent, "We executed 35 to 40 Chinese this morning." None had been armed or in uniform, and women were included in the count.

Tomi and Takahashi returned to the armored car and drove to the ancient Ming Palace, where civilian prisoners were being used as bayonet practice targets. The screaming and blood was more slaughterhouse than military. War was nothing like what Tomi had expected.

He saluted a captain wearing transport insignia of the 13th Division. When Tomi requested a count of the executed, he was told, "Ah, 80, 90-odd, I should think. We lost track in the confusion, Lieutenant. It's my unit's first time at this sort of shitty work. But the colonel wanted us to get killing experience because we're all reservists."

"Sir, how many are enemy soldiers?"

The captain glanced at Tomi's open notebook and studied him before judging him a 'safe ear.' He asked, "What answer do you need for your report? My numbers will show that all the executed were soldiers, because I have a quota. But 8 out of 10 are civilians, including females and kids. The bayonet doesn't distinguish. One gook's soft belly is as good as another."

Over the next several hours, Tomi gathered reports from special operations units, ranging from squads to entire companies. The responses were similar. The liars swore all the executed were Chinese soldiers, and the honest ones admitted most were civilians, unless the Chinese army drafted women and children. There was no resistance or armed bands in the city.

At a major intersection close to the International Safety Zone, Tomi was startled by a tall foreigner in a strange uniform who used the Japanese army hand command, 'Proceed to me.' He dismounted and saluted an angry German general who said, "*Watashi wa Taisho von Falkenhausen.*"

"Ich bist Unteruitnant Tomigawa, Herr Generar," Tomi responded in an even worse German that omitted the 'L.' They stared at each other, eyes smarting and tearing from the smoky haze carried by the cold breeze. Both had exhausted their vocabulary in the other's language until a comical-looking little man in a lumpy overcoat with the round Nazi Party pin on the lapel joined them. His arm band had slipped down to his elbow, crumpling the swastika symbol. Tomi recognized him as the German who had insisted on getting a receipt for the Chinese soldiers at yesterday's disastrous demonstration. Fortunately, the German didn't recognize him.

"My name is John Rabe," the little German said in his fluent, accented Japanese. "I'm with the Siemens Company and a member of the Nazi Party. I reside in Nanking permanently. This is Herr General Ernst von Faulkenhausen of the German Wehrmacht. He was a military observer with the Chinese Nationalist forces. Because of the new relationship between our nations, he will remain in Nanking to liaise with the Japanese army. Who is your supreme commander?"

Tomi followed Nakajima's instructions and lied, "Nanking is under the direct command of General Matsui, Sir."

The little German grabbed his arm and said, *"Der kinder … todt."* He switched to Japanese. "The children. Dead! General Matsui's troops are raping, torturing and murdering children."

The tall general spoke rapid German. Rabe nodded and said, "Come this way, please."

Tomi yelled to Sergeant Takahashi to join them. Takahashi carried his light machine gun because foreigners were not to be trusted. The *gaijin* led them inside a large building.

Rabe's voice trembled, "This was a girls' school." He opened a door. "Look inside."

It was a sickening, nightmarish jumble of human debris. The classroom floor was littered with a tangle of naked bodies and broken furniture. The mutilated corpses had once been immature girls. The walls and floors were smeared with long trails of blood, indicating that they had been alive when they suffered atrocities beyond rape. Sergeant Takahashi muttered, "Animals!"

The Germans stared at Tomi in angry accusation. "Why?" roared the German civilian. "For God's sake, why?"

Tomi shook his head. Rabe blurred his Japanese in a nervous, stream, "We urged the girls to seek safety from marauding soldiers by staying together in the school with their teachers and await the arrival of Japanese military police, who would restore order. The teachers and children obeyed us. Your troops came and shot the teachers. Herr General and I returned, along with an American YMCA official, but your soldiers chased us away. They fired warning shots in the air." Rabe sobbed, "We heard the girls' screams all night long." He wiped his tears with a clenched fist and pointed at the disfigured, waxy corpses. "How could you do such things? You deliberately tortured and killed innocent children! Why?"

The grim-faced general spoke. Rabe composed himself. "Herr General says he was on the Western Front during the Great War, but this is far worse. Herr General saw officers here last night. This was done by depraved criminals who acted under orders."

General von Falkenhausen glared at Tomi as Rabe continued to translate. "We are only a handful of Europeans. We cannot protect all the Chinese. These crimes are against the laws of civilized nations. The highest ranking Japanese officers in Tokyo must be notified immediately that General Matsui's troops are committing atrocities."

The short German stood as tall as possible and said with formality, "I add my own feelings to Herr General's. As a member of the Nazi Party, I will inform Chancellor Hitler himself of these crimes. I will tell him that General Matsui is the Beast of Nanking!"

The *gaijin* blamed General Matsui, unaware that he had tried to prevent such crimes. Tomi bowed. "I understand, Sirs, and will inform my superiors. Good day."

The German general didn't return the salute. Tomi went outside to stand beside the armored car. The throat-catching fumes were a relief compared to what he had seen. Who in the Imperial Palace overruled General Matsui? Who wanted the hard occupation? Who gave the 'kill all prisoners' order? And why make war on children? He was ashamed for Japan.

Tomi told Sergeant Takahashi that they must file a formal report. Takahashi bluntly replied, "No, Sir! We can't report this! Let the *gaijin* go to higher command. If we report this horror, the only ones punished will be us. We didn't see a fucking thing, Sir!"

Tomi knew Takahashi was right. They avoided looking at each other because neither wanted to see the other's shame. Disloyal thoughts were the least of Tomi's problems. He had to write a credible report showing 250,000 soldiers, identified as bandits and spies, were or would soon be executed. In the conversational style of equals, Tomi said, "Takahashi, I want your opinion. How can I document the fictitious 250,000 goal?"

Takahashi's personal opinion had never been requested by an officer, and he replied truthfully, "Sir, ten years' service taught me that, if a general believes that many enemy still lurk in the city, then your arithmetic must match that number."

Tomi nodded. "Today's total came to 976 confirmed bodies of enemy soldiers ... or was that 12,367? Yes, it's the larger number. And your count matches mine, Sergeant Takahashi."

When the armored car reached the Water Gate sector, the road was filled with a long column of prisoners wearing Chinese Army uniforms and bound with telephone wire. Tomi saw Major

Tanaka, a close advisor to Nakajima. "Congratulations, Sir, It appears you've captured an entire Chinese army," Tomi shouted down from his turret perch.

Another great victory for General Nakajima!" Tanaka crowed. "The general personally accepted the surrender of two Chinese divisions without firing a single shot. We are herding the gooks to temporary pens the general had erected. Move your armored car into the column and help us guard these sub-humans."

The prisoner pens were rows of crude squares made of barbed wire strands on poles. Nearby were stacks of drums that contained gasoline instead of diluted 'Nanking oil.' By dusk, all the prisoners were behind wire. As soon as the Japanese troops finished their cold field rations, Major Tanaka, a strict teetotaler, distributed generous portions of Chinese wine and Army sake to his troops. Tomi kept a running total of the executions as half-drunk guards splashed gasoline over the huddled prisoners.

Major Tanaka bellowed, "Guards! Light the *choochin,* paper lanterns." Flaming torches were tossed at the fuel-drenched prisoners. Men howled, twisted and spun in pain against the barbed wire. A few guards laughed at the frenetic, grotesque movements of men dying in excruciating agony, but the majority turned away in horror at the sights, sounds and stench.

"General Nakajima calls these gooks his *choochin.* He and his guests want to see the lanterns' glow from where they are dining, almost a mile away," the major explained.

The screaming lanterns were bright enough for Tomi to record numbers in his accounting ledger. When he completed the sickening tally, he was denied permission to leave. "Now count the beheadings!"

Major Tanaka ordered Tomi to stand next to him with a notebook, recording the number of Chinese officers executed. The sword-wielding junior officers made wagers about who could sever ten heads the fastest. The single beheading strokes soon increased to fumbling non-lethal wounds as the swordsmen got drunker. The mound of heads was decorated by officers, who placed lit cigarets and severed genitalia in the death-widened grimaces. The sake and gasoline ran out before the supply of prisoners. Several hundred wailing, terrified prisoners remained.

Major Tanaka yelled, "Tomigawa! Move the Sumida into position! Use your heavy weapon on the remaining prisoners!"

After a half hour of constant firing, the overheated turret gun jammed. Takahashi and the crew continued to use the light machine guns until no prisoners were left standing. The guards used bayonets to finish off the wounded. Tomi's pistol never left its holster. Instead, he flicked a hand-held abacus and noted that 3,000 prisoners had been executed by fire, sword or bullet.

Takahashi scowled. "Sir, perhaps that should be 35,000. General Nakajima will say he captured five full divisions with many Chinese killed. Headquarters will never know that his prisoners were two under-strength divisions of draftees who surrendered voluntarily. An accurate accounting makes him a liar. You and I could end up in a punishment unit."

Tomi revised the death tally, and they slept next to the armored car that night. Chen Ta, the interpreter Tomi had shot, appeared in his dream. Tomi vowed he'd never forget him after Chen Ta said, "I hate being dead and forgotten." Chen Ta cried red tears from his destroyed eye when Tomi said Nakajima's executions would go on for many months. Tomi begged forgiveness but Chen Ta said *"Katoo. Katoo.* Vile. Vile."

CHAPTER SIX

"Hiroshi put a bullet in his brain," Sergeant Takahashi announced sadly when Tomi entered their office. Hiroshi was Takahashi's closest friend.

"Hiroshi had two sons. He was assigned to an interrogation team. Yesterday they questioned a family, including small children, about some suspected buried wealth. The team forced the parents to ... to eat body parts sliced off their children. They tried to make the Chinese reveal hidden wealth that they didn't have. Fucking sadistic bastards."

General Nakajima's rule was that anyone who exhibited pity was *yasashii*, soft, and was swiftly transferred to duties in a punishment unit and almost certain death.

"Hiroshi loved the Army. He chose *jisatsu*, suicide, rather than dishonorable duty. Many suicides and nervous breakdowns go unreported. Nanking is a curse for all of us."

Tomi didn't tell Takahashi that many in Tokyo shared his opinion. The coded message in Mother's last letter reported that several generals, outraged by the horrors, called Occupied Nanking's three months of terror 'The Army's Days of Shame.' But the hard men who ordered Nanking's stern punishment had Palace support. In another coded letter, she wrote that those in power referred to the mass brutality as 'Matters Best Left Unsaid.'

Tomi's death accounting report had been sent to Tokyo with charts and statistics that proved more than 149,000 military prisoners had been executed. Although much less than General Nakajima's initial goal, the number was impressive. And everyone knew it ignored hundreds of thousands of civilians casually killed in unreported incidents.

Also missing from the tally were the many thousands of

young girls sent to comfort woman brothels, and the tens of thousands doomed to be worked to death as slave laborers. 'Days of Shame' seemed a more fitting description than the poetic 'Matters Best Left Unsaid.'

High command lauded General Nakajima for the death accounting. Instead of being praised, Tomi and Takahashi were ordered to destroy all their statistics and paperwork. Nakajima said, "Our enemies tell monstrous lies to belittle our glorious victory here. No records must remain that might be twisted into falsehoods about the honorable conduct of the Japanese Army."

When the mass rapes and executions finally ended, Tomi foolishly expected normal life would resume in Nanking. Instead, a frenzied hunt for hidden riches began. Wealthy Chinese families and their servants were jailed and tortured.

By the time General Nakajima's interrogation teams pried off the second or third fingernail with a bayonet, the master, mistress, child or loyal servant readily told the location of a family's buried wealth. Those who had no wealth to reveal suffered the most.

Interrogators called cooperative captives 'one- and two-fingernail talkers.' Then more fingernails were removed to get the names of others who might have hidden wealth. Crazed with pain, prisoners screamed the names of innocent relatives, friends and acquaintances. But torture failed to produce more riches. Despite the diminishing amount of treasure revealed, General Nakajima stubbornly believed the gardens and parks held gold and jewelry hidden from Chinese tax collectors, marauding war lords and invaders. He assigned Tomi and Takahashi to study interrogation team reports for new clues.

Tomi realized that hardly anyone of consequence was left to torture. But Nakajima expected him to provide new victims for the teams of sadists. Tomi and Takahashi studied the interrogation confessions but uncovered only more proof of brutal Nakajima's greed. The gruesome details sickened them. No wonder Sergeant Hiroshi shot himself.

When a hidden crate filled with gold and jewels was accidentally discovered in a warehouse in Nakajima's sector, the general's superiors taunted him about it. "You lazy scoundrels embarrass me!" Nakajima stormed at the assembled interrogation teams. Takahashi, a veteran of the tirades, advised Tomi to sit in the rear with him. "He singles out one unlucky person to punish as an example to the rest. The more he talks, the angrier he gets."

Nakajima shouted, "You are all guilty of stupidity, laziness and worse! The gooks make fools of you because I've been too easy on you! Unless the hidden wealth is soon uncovered, I'll assign others to the job and you will all be sent to a lice-ridden outpost along the Russian border, where you'll shit icicles and fuck diseased camels."

He looked around. Tomi's height made him the target. "Tomigawa! You can't hide from me," he squeaked. "Your fancy charts and bullshit statistics don't fool me! You sit on your ass like a clerk instead of hunting for the money! You daydream about returning to Tokyo to lick the boots of your uppity relatives. I hold you personally responsible for locating the treasure in our sector. If you fail, you'll be broken in rank and sent to a punishment unit, along with your lackey sergeant!" Takahashi was included because his spy reports failed to reveal Tomi's weaknesses.

Back in their office, Tomi stared at the schematic he had drawn of the Chinese families tortured for information. He tasted stomach acid and forced himself to concentrate on the chart, which looked like an upside down genealogy tree of doomed souls.

"Takahashi, our chart winnows the 200 wealthiest families down to a mere 32. All of them confessed and still Nakajima got nothing. So much for the value of torture."

Tomi looked up at the wall where the original execution goal was painted in red numerals. The actual number of executions during 'Matters Best Left Unsaid' was unknown.

Given the ultimatum, they had no choice but to act as if there was buried treasure, even if it only existed in greedy dreams. They had to convince Nakajima that they believed gold and jewels were hidden in Nanking's blood-soaked soil.

Tomi demanded of Takahashi, "Who's still alive? Who hasn't been snared by Nakajima's net of pain? Whose fingernails are still attached? Who are we overlooking?"

Takahashi, depressed at the thought of losing his hard-won sergeant's stars and ending up with Tomi in a punishment unit, said mournfully, "Only the Lord Buddha knows, Sir." He blinked and repeated his words as a question: "Only Lord Buddha knows? Sir, do you have the locations of the 32 families' residences?"

Tomi handed his file to the sergeant, who marked the family homes on an overlay of the Nanking street map. "Look! 24 of those families reside in the quadrant between the North Star Gate Road and the river."

"Could just be a coincidence, Takahashi. Search parties dug up nearly every one of the families' courtyards and gardens, and all they found were a few small bags of jewelry, some money and sentimental items. There's nothing hidden that's valuable enough to satisfy the general's hunger."

"Please, Lieutenant, look at the street map. Do you see what I see? Only Buddha knows!"

"Nothing except a park we dug up and the temple. The temple! Of course! Buddha knows!"

"Yes Sir. The Buddhist temple is within walking or carrying distance of the family homes. The temple probably was looted, but the priests may have secret places."

"Be logical, Sergeant. If there's treasure hidden in the temple, why didn't those Chinese families confess during torture?"

"What if they didn't know, Sir? Imagine yourself a rich elder in a city that's been invaded many times. You won't tote your wealth amidst a fleeing horde of refugees, where everyone steals to survive. And if you bury your wealth, the invaders may unearth it. So you give your gold and jewels to the Buddhist priests to hide without telling anyone who remained behind because they'd either steal it for themselves or confess under torture. Priests can be trusted because wealth is meaningless to them. You flee and after the fighting and looting end, you return and reclaim it. None of the priests was interrogated by Nakajima's teams."

"If you're right, Sergeant, the senior priests are hiding the wealth of 32 rich families stashed somewhere in the temple ... surely enough to satisfy Nakajima." Tomi thought of the priests under torture, and said, "I'll go to the temple alone and plead with them to tell us."

"No, Lieutenant!" Takahashi snapped. "If you went to the priests, they'd move the treasure. If the priests could be coaxed into giving up the treasure, they'd have done so to save all those families from torture. Some Buddhist priests would die rather than talk.

"Your action would do nothing but cause your own execution. Besides, the general has spies everywhere. We're a two-man team and I am ordered to inform on you! The general will eventually learn that you acted on your own and alerted the priests. We would both suffer."

"You're right, Takahashi. I'm using poor judgement. Thank you for your advice, my friend." Tomi bowed low to show that Takahashi was his intellectual and social equal.

"You remind me that many priests would die rather than violate a trust," Tomi said. "That will be my argument to the general." We need another path to the priests' secret."

Takahashi smiled. "I've got a daring one," he said, and he told Tomi his ingenious plan.

***

On this, his second wait in the general's anteroom, Tomi arrived with his bladder empty. When he was finally summoned, General Nakajima and Colonel Mori were drinking sake. The general munched lychee nuts and glared as Tomi saluted.

"Have you any results to report, Accountant Tomigawa, or are you here to waste my time?"

Tomi unrolled the map overlay showing converging lines to the temple. In a deferential tone, he repeated Sergeant Takahashi's theory as to why no treasure had been uncovered by torture.

Nakajima slammed his open palm on the table and said through a mouthful of nuts, "See, Colonel Mori, unlike you, I used fear to prod this lazy fellow into solving the problem. Very well, Tomigawa, have the priests brought here for interrogation immediately."

"Sir, if it pleases the General," Tomi said, "it is your Sergeant Takahashi who deserves full credit for suggesting the Buddhist temple. He and I have discussed the matter most thoroughly. Despite skillful interrogation, the priests will allow themselves to die before divulging their secrets. Proof of this is their persistent silence despite the fate of so many neighborhood families. As a

Zen Buddhist, I know priests can will themselves into a coma or death. They will take their secrets into the next life."

The general's frustration showed, and Tomi quickly added, "Request permission, Sir, to examine the temple for possible hiding places before the priests are interrogated."

"How will a youth like you uncover what those clever Buddhist priests hide? Their artful deception exceeds your puny experience."

"Yes Sir. It is because I lack the required abilities that I request the loan of experts from the following units: *Kohei, Kahei, Bokurentai. Shinajin no yakusha; shoshite san ooki na hachi.*"

Nakajima stopped chewing. Why did this peculiar officer want an engineer, a chemical warfare specialist, an anti-aircraft defense officer, an interpreter and three large cooking pots? "Accountant Tomigawa, explain this odd request of yours to Colonel Mori."

Tomi outlined Sergeant Takahashi's devious plan, and Nakajima burst out laughing, spewing wet lychee nuts on the table. He slapped the giggling Colonel on the back and bragged, "See how much brighter my security sergeants are than little Matsui and his entire staff! Request approved, but you'd better produce results!"

The next morning, a cordon of infantry surrounded the temple with orders not to mistreat the four priests and two novices detained inside. Tomi explained Takahashi's plan to the specialists, who waited outside with the troops.

Tomigawa and his sergeant entered the silent temple. Takahashi stood next to the translator-sergeant and chief priest. Tomi walked to the large gilded statue of the Lord Buddha and bowed. He lit an incense stick and prayed Takahashi's trick would work. He placed his red prayer paper on the altar, clapped his hands softly and turned. Tomi clasped his hands in front and bowed rapidly to the chief priest in the ancient Chinese fashion.

"*Sooryo-Sama*, Most Honorable Buddhist Priest," he began. The Chinese gasped. He was the first Japanese officer ever to show traditional courtesy. Tomi waited for the sergeant-translator to repeat his salutation before he said, "Most humbly I beg your forgiveness for this intrusion. It is my unfortunate duty to locate certain items of high value that my superiors know are hidden here. I will lose merit and suffer in the next life for my evil deed, but it must be done. I have no choice but to follow the path laid out for me. My profound apologies, *Sooryo-Sama*."

He bowed again. Sergeant Takahashi signaled a waiting procession of soldiers to carry in three large cooking pots, three car batteries and the anti-aircraft listening equipment, which resembled three oversized loudspeakers. As the gear was set up, Tomi said in slow, hesitant phrases for the translator to properly communicate the complex information: "Honorable Priest, the scientific equipment before you is a new invention that generates powerful radio waves able to liquify metals and burn wood.

"The radiating waves, much like the invisible X-rays used in Western medicine, goes through thick stone and destroys everything within its range. Soft metal, like gold, melts instantly. Then the liquid gold seeps out to reveal its hiding place. Ceramic, paper, wood, cloth ... all are set afire or damaged by the destructive rays. My superiors have given me permission to demonstrate the rays' power so you are forewarned that the temple's treasure will be destroyed if you do not reveal the secret hoard. Please observe."

Tomi berated Takahashi. "Sergeant! Don't place the demonstration pots so close to Lord Buddha's statue. It will surely be damaged or destroyed!" Takahasi bowed his apology and shoved the pots away from Buddha.

The translator repeated Tomi's words to the priests as soldiers rolled in the firefighting equipment and a tank of hot water. Takahashi carefully aimed the sound detector 'ears' at the pots, now filled with water. When the wires were connected to the batteries, loud, irritating acoustical feedback filled the temple. Everyone covered their ears. Unseen, Sergeant Takahashi deftly dropped a small block of solid sodium into each pot as he put on the lids. The aircraft defense officer twisted dials on an impressive control box and nodded his readiness.

Tomi yelled, "Launch radio beams at weakest intensity!" The screeches rose in volume but nothing happened for a half minute. Tomi and Takahashi worried that the water wasn't hot enough to melt the thin wax coating they had smeared on the sodium blocks, but then the pots exploded and overturned in staggered order.

Water gushed across the floor. The priests, interpreter and guards were startled. The exposed sodium reacted violently to the water, just as Takahashi had remembered from an Army demonstration.

As if the pots were dangerously hot, Takahashi ordered the firefighters to hose them down. The spreading water reached the sandals and robes of the priests, who now believed that the Dwarf Bandits' secret weapon could penetrate thick walls.

"You have witnessed the destructive power of the rays," Tomi said. "Warrant Officer Takaji, aim one of the ray weapons at Lord Buddha's statue and the other two at the nearest walls. Await my command to fire."

When the equipment was repositioned, Tomi went to the head priest and, oblivious to the puddled water, removed his helmet and sank to his knees. He thought of the pig farm bayonet lesson; beheading Captain Yu; shooting Chen Ta; setting men afire; Yangtze's floating dead; and Nakajima's 'lanterns' of screaming prisoners. Tomi, Nanking's official accountant of death, knew he was a despicable wretch without honor.

He pressed his forehead to the floor and mumbled, "I will suffer in the next life for my terrible deeds in this one. I beg you, Honorable Priest, keep me from adding to the mountain of evil I have heaped upon myself. Please help me."

Shocked, the sergeant-translator hesitated until Sergeant Takahashi prodded him. Then Tomi's words were repeated in hushed Mandarin. Tomi knew his next life would be far worse than this one. Suicide was not a solution. He had lost his way.

The priest's withered hand reached out and touched Tomi, who looked up. The priest searched for the truth behind Tomi's tears of self-pity. Without taking his eyes from Tomi's, the priest spoke. The translator repeated, "Young man, you shall have what you came for. But from this moment on, everyone in this temple, especially you and me, is cursed. The Wheel of Life turns, and all here will die amidst much unhappiness. We will all regret our next existence."

Tomi bowed, not caring about loss of face. He knew that he had accepted a defeat, not a victory. He rose from his knees; his scabbard slid roughly on the stone floor, making a strange, rude sound. The priest moved close to Tomi as if sniffing for truth or the foul source of evil.

The priest sighed, went to a side wall and pressed unmarked places in a blur of fingers. A spring clicked and a panel slide open. Inside was a large, shallow shelf with a number of wrapped objects. Everyone gasped. The Japanese officers and non-coms ran toward the trove. Tomi thundered, "Halt! And remain silent!" Even the captain obeyed the harsh command.

"Translator, tell the honorable priest that I alone, not he, bear the guilt for removing that which has been hidden. Let the curse fall only upon me and not on anyone else here," Tomi said.

The priest smiled wanly as if he had expected those words. He spoke through the translator, "At last, you begin to understand. Only you and I bear the weight of this sacrilege."

Time slowed as the priest guided Tomi through a ritual of solemn transfer. The priest unwrapped thick coverings of raw silk cloth, yellowed by time uncounted. He recited each object's history before he presented it to Tomi, who carefully placed it on the floor. Each time the priest bowed to an uncovered artifact, Tomi followed suit as if he were the priest's novice.

The ritual continued until the ancient vases, urns, jewelry, sculpture, pottery and large jade pieces were displayed in a long row. The surprised Chinese priests murmured sad appreciation and the Japanese craned their necks for a glimpse of the treasure. Tomi and Takahashi had uncovered ancient treasure hidden for centuries, not years.

Three bundles remained unwrapped. In a quavering voice, the old priest announced to Tomi, "The Sung Dragons, most venerable of the Middle Kingdom, made by strangers from beyond." He unwrapped the smallest bundle with shaking hands, then the two larger ones.

Sung art, created ten centuries ago when Europeans lived in squalor and ignorance, achieved an aesthetic creativity unrivaled by any civilization until then. It was as if superior beings had visited Earth and gifted the human race with new beauty.

The three dragons were poems of ceramic, jewels and gold. Five claws on each dragon's foot signified they had been created for a mighty Emperor. The priest handed Tomi the smallest dragon and waited expectantly. Despite the chilly dampness of the unheated temple, the dragon warmed his palms. Tomi sensed he was holding onto calm serenity. He looked up in wonder and the old priest's eyes sparkled. They shared their secret in silence as everyone watched. Reluctantly, Tomi placed the dragon on the floor but the strange warmth stayed with him.

The priest handed Tomi each of the two remaining dragons according to size. Tomi was silent as he twice again experienced that same sense of calm warmth. This time the priest closed his eyes and faintly smiled. "Young man, you have what you sought. Describe what is in your heart."

"There is much that I do not understand, Most Honorable Priest. I will not survive this war, but until I die, this moment of awe will be remembered with the deepest of humility."

After the sergeant-translator repeated his words, Tomi took a big risk and snarled at the priest. "Translator! Tell this priest that now is neither the time nor place for such conversation. Time is far more precious than one realizes and should not be wasted with words."

The abrupt change in attitude surprised the translator as well as the priest when he heard it in Mandarin. Tomi used the harsh tone of an overbearing Japanese officer and said, "Now, translator, make certain you tell the old priest the following exact words: 'Stop bothering me, old man. Get out of my sight! There is little time left and I will have many severe military duties to perform when I follow the orders of my general and not Lord Buddha. Understand?"

The Army translator repeated Tomi's words in the same arrogant tone.

The priest hesitated, then nodded. The message Tomi hid from the sergeant-translator had been received. The priest replied to the translator, "Of course I understand. Those of us now living are thieves who take from the past as well as the present. We breathe each other's air. We eat each other's food. We take from one another in war; one generation takes from another."

The priest placed his hand on Tomi's arm, thumb pressed through his uniform with surprising strength. The translator listened to the priest, shrugged, and repeated his words.

"The Sung dragons have passed through countless hands. No

one truly owns the dragons, now or in the future. It is your sad destiny, young officer, to be forever haunted by the evils of what you have witnessed, what you have done and what you will do. You will not die in battle, although you'll wish you had. You are cursed to live many more years than you desire, unable to forget."

The priest looked at the dragons and in a voice of prayer, intoned, "There is but one way for you to gain merit in this life. When it is within your power, you must honor the three Sung dragons by placing them among deserving people."

Tomi demanded, "Are you sure that's what he said?"

The translator replied, "Yes Sir. The old dog doesn't make much sense, does he?"

Tomi wondered how he was supposed to protect the Sung dragons. The translator waited for a response, but Tomi waved a negative hand.

"Now that your superiors have what they want, this temple is without value to anyone here," the old priest said in a flat tone.

"Yes," Tomi said, "when I return tomorrow, I will not pray as I have today."

The priest gazed at the ancient treasures that he had guarded for most of his life. Puddles of water on the floor looked like blood in the shadows. The old priest motioned for his tiny band of priests and novices to follow him into the courtyard. Tomi yelled to the guards, "Let them pass!" They walked slowly away and never looked back.

At headquarters, General Nakajima chortled, "I knew you'd come up with something, Tomigawa, but I didn't expect anything this grand."

Colonel Mori whispered something to the general, who nodded. Colonel Mori demanded, "Give me your inventory list, Tomigawa."

"I'm sorry, Sir. There wasn't time to make one. Once the artifacts were secure in the truck, we came directly here."

Nakajima said, "They belong to Japan now. Colonel Mori, catalogue the shipment. Tomigawa, you and your men are dismissed. Well done. I knew you and my Sergeant Takahashi would produce, once I planted my boot in your lazy bellies."

Alone in their little office, Sergeant Takahashi said, "Everyone praises you for tricking the priest by acting strangely," he said. "But it wasn't an act, was it?" Instead of waiting for an answer, he handed Tomi a paper, "I listed every item and the translated words of the priest."

"Did anyone see you make this list?"

"No, Sir, I know better than that."

"Good. Destroy it before the general learns I lied to him."

"Please listen. Before you joined the division, an innocent officer was accused of stealing one gem in a large batch claimed by General Nakajima. The officer couldn't prove his innocence. He was executed. I knew someone else stole it.

"This list is the only proof of what you gave the general. That's why Colonel Mori asked you for a written inventory. What's to prevent the general from swiping one of the pieces and claiming we took it? By now the general's informers have told him about your strange conversation with the elder priest. And freeing the priests before an interrogation team gets a crack at them wasn't smart, Sir. You'd be in a lot of trouble right now if the general wasn't so dazzled by the temple loot. This list will prove our innocence if there's a high-level theft."

"Takahashi, I'll copy the original and destroy your list. Should there be trouble, you were unaware of my strange actions. Understand, my friend?"

Takahashi handed his list to Tomi, who made a coded copy in an undated letter to his mother and put it in his pay book. The next day the temple walls were torn down in a vain hunt for treasure. For some reason, General Nakajima and Colonel Mori never mentioned the temple treasure again and Tomi went unpunished for freeing the priests. Perhaps they wanted to forget the incident. Later, Tomi learned the Sung dragons had surfaced in the Imperial Palace.

CHAPTER SEVEN
TOKYO, JAPAN   MARCH 1939

Crouched on Suzuki's desk was the smallest Sung dragon. Despite the morning sun, it looked dull and lifeless. General Suzuki waved Tomi to the least-prestigious chair; a reminder that he had failed to impregnate the general's niece. The gesture showered grey ash from his cigaret holder onto the rug, decorated with the round Chinese good luck symbol. Suzuki stared through his monocle; the other eye squinted from smoke.

Suzuki's office, in the building adjacent to headquarters, had a prestigious east view of the Imperial Palace, but Tomi's attention was drawn to the Sung dragon. Such a gift from the Royal Court was worth more to 'The Number One Suzuki of Them All' than all his wealth.

The general smirked. "You look like you've seen a ghost. Is something amiss, *Chu-I?*" Another reminder to Tomi that his promotion to First Lieutenant and return to Tokyo were reasons to be grateful he had married a Suzuki. After 17 months in China, Tomi was relieved to be away from Nakajima and the brutalities of the occupation.

"No, Sir, not at all, General." Tomi wondered if the old priest was still alive.

"Must I remind you again? When we're alone, call me Uncle. In public, I prefer 'general,' even though I won't be on active duty much longer," he smiled. "Much of my time is spent with the new China Affairs Board. Soon I will work full time on industrial policies necessary for the 'Strike South' campaign. Two weeks ago, I overheard a chance remark about my Sung dragon and thought about the rest of the Nanking treasures you uncovered," he said in a conspiratorial whisper. Tomi had naively assumed that his return to Tokyo was to plant more seed in Suzuki's niece. Now he waited for the next layer of many to be revealed.

"Tell me in detail, Nephew, about the discovery of the temple treasure, as well as the aftermath." The general removed his monocle, closed his eyes and stroked the Sung dragon as Tomi recounted Sergeant Takahashi's brilliant initial deduction and successful sodium-in-the-water trick. Tomi concluded with Colonel Mori's demand for his written inventory.

Tomi omitted the Sung dragons' strange inner warmth; the promise to find a future place of honor for them; and how he had saved the priests from Nakajima's interrogation torturers.

"How many objects did you remove from the temple?"

"Eighteen, Sir."

"Certain it was 18 pieces, not 13?" Suzuki demanded as he unlocked a desk drawer and withdrew a thick file.

"Yes, Uncle. I made an inventory later that day with descriptions of all 18 objects. I put it in code because personal papers are always searched. The list is hidden in my mother's house." Suzuki read as Tomi recited the inventory from memory.

"What greed! Sadistic little man kept the 3,000-year-old ceremonial jade scepter, 3 priceless bronze ritual food chalices from the Eastern Zhou Period, and the bronze ceremonial decapitation axe of the Sung Dynasty. Unbelievable! This time Nakajima has gone too far. Stealing from his patron, Prince Asaka! Bring the original list to me first thing in the morning."

Suzuki stared out the eastern window. "This is a matter of great sensitivity, Nephew. After you deliver the list to me, forget everything about it. Don't mention anything to ... what's your clever sergeant's name? The one you asked to be included in your transfer?"

"Takahashi, Sir."

"Yes. He's not to know anything." Suzuki inserted a fresh cigaret in the holder and lit it. "You've made a major contribution to the army and to Suzuki Enterprises."

Tomi tested the gratitude without much hope, "Sir, is an infantry assignment now possible?"

"Of course not! Taiko isn't pregnant yet. Your chemistry trick prompts an idea. There's a secret research unit in Harbin,

Manchuria. It is commanded by a Colonel Otomo. He gave Suzuki Construction the initial contract and promised more but nothing's happened. I want to know why. Otomo is a strange ladder-climber."

"Strange in what manner, Uncle?" Tomi asked, masking disappointment.

"Talented scientist. Otomo and his powerful connections convinced the Palace and General Staff to commit huge sums of money to biological warfare research. He is as brash as an American, but a brilliant, dedicated officer. Much too unorthodox for my taste. An ambitious man like that is likely to award the biggest contracts to my competitors and toss me a few crumbs.

"Nephew, I want you to visit Otomo's unit as a lowly budget specialist. Bring back as much contract-specific information as you can. Otomo is reluctant to discuss future manufacturing facilities until he's quite ready. Just like a scientist! I want Suzuki Enterprises to be one of the main contractors of what some call the Bacterium Bomb, or B-Bomb."

"Forgive me Sir, but lacking a scientific background, how will I know what to ask?"

"Read everything in our library about military plague weapons. Your Inspectorate job will be budget planning of new projects. Scientists are a greedy lot when it comes to research funds. Enough is never enough. Otomo's staff will use layman language to explain future needs and we'll have inside information about B-Bomb production line specifications."

"But I know nothing of budgets. I am an infantry officer."

"Stop this dithering and false modesty! The General Staff was impressed with your Nanking Accounting Report. It gave us a clear statistical picture. I wish all the paperwork that crosses my desk were as concise and comprehensive. While you study plague warfare in the library, that Takahashi fellow of yours will take an Army Accounting course, if he has the brains for it."

"Sergeant Takahashi prepared the Nanking numbers. He will do well."

"Should Otomo give technical data to our competitors before us, we lose much. Future wars will be won with such weapons and Suzuki Enterprises must share in the victory."

When the general said *shoori*, 'victory,' Tomi knew he meant *reiki*, 'profit.'

"Now let me show you where you're going, Nephew." Suzuki spread a map on his desk next to the Sung dragon. "Here!" Pointing his cigaret holder at Harbin. Tomi hadn't known the Manchurian city was so close to Soviet's Vladivostok. "With the data you bring me, I'll have an idea of what kind of factory we'll need to build Otomo's B-Bombs."

Tomi leaned over the map and gently touched the Sung dragon, expecting magical warmth. It felt like a lump of cold clay.

***

The flatulent noise of his wife's orgasm abruptly ended Tomi's wandering thoughts about the secret chemical unit. Making every thrust a prayer for conception, he finished.

Taiko panted, "So, you missed me." Not "How bad was it for you in China?" She was so unlike his beloved Taiko. All they had in common were first names and his sperm.

"Of course," he grunted. She patted his wet genitals as if he were a pet dog who had performed a trick. Tomi awaited her pillow talk debate.

"Tomi, why do we Japanese claim superiority over other races?

"Because we are."

"Ah so, the super-patriot."

Tomi suspected that their post-coital quarrels prevented her from getting pregnant. Her crazy modern thinking and sourness repelled his seed. "Taiko, must we always quarrel after sex? What pleasure do you get from mocking our society and baiting me?"

"I'm trying to remove your blindfold of self-delusion. Education opened my eyes, while yours are shut. Japan's superiority is nothing more than lies you learned at the Military Academy. You know so little, yet revel in so much arrogance!"

"Western education has put strange ideas in your head. What do you know that I don't?"

"You never heard the Chinese word, *nu*," she snapped, knowing Chinese was his weakest language. "*Nu* means primitive slave. That's what our ancestors were called by Chinese explorers who landed here a millennia ago. We were unwashed, ignorant barbarians lacking a written language. We couldn't grow rice or work metals. We were just Stone Age animals."

Tomi sat up and glared at her. " *Gaijin* lies! How dare you insult Japan's glorious past?"

"It's true! Educated Europeans aren't ashamed of their crude past. Why do we deny the obvious? The Chinese gave us their alphabet and taught us, the primitive *Nu*, everything: literature; art, religion, philosophy, government, science, agriculture and even your precious military tactics. Thank the gods those early Chinese and Koreans interbred with us dirty savages."

"There was no foreign contamination! We are the superior civilized ones! Whatever we learned from gook dog-eaters, we improved upon centuries ago. *Shogun* Hideyoshi even invaded the Asian mainland, as we do now."

"Simpleton! Hideyoshi was a cruel warlord who attacked peaceful, defenseless coastal cities. He brought back tens of thousands of noses chopped off captive Koreans and Chinese. He displayed them as gruesome souvenirs in a stinking war monument only three hundred years ago! Asia gave us civilization and a royal line, and we gave them senseless brutality!"

Tomi shifted from her uncomfortable accusation. "We never interbred with mainlanders."

"Why does the Imperial Palace refuse to let archeologists dig up any more ancient burial mounds in Kyoto? They contain records showing our own nobility flows with Chinese and Korean bloodlines. Japan's racial superiority is a myth."

"Enough of this traitorous shit!" He scrambled out of bed.

"We Japanese conceal the truth from ourselves ... *Kakureru!* Hiding from reality, past and present. *Kakureru* is our fatal flaw!"

Tomi refused to argue with a demented person. He hurriedly put on his uniform without taking time to wash off the sex slick. Taiko smirked like her uncle. She stretched her thin arms over her thick body as she watched him fumble into his uniform. No wonder she was barren despite his earnest, repeated efforts. Modern women only bred headaches.

"Where do you think you're going on your first night home?"

"I'm going to visit my mother."

"At this hour? Good night, dutiful son," she drawled and rolled over to deliberately expose her naked backside.

***

Tomi's taxi stopped behind a parked civilian car guarded by a chauffeur in Army uniform. When Honorable Father was alive, the Tomigawas never entertained visitors at this late hour.

Taiko greeted Tomi at the entrance, and they embraced for a hurried kiss before she broke away to remove his boots, much more slowly than usual. She whispered, "Oh how I missed you, Tomichan! Are you well? The Lady Tomigawa has a guest, Major General Hashimoto. Forgive me, but I must announce you."

Why did he have to be formally announced in his own home? Taiko led him through the small house as if he didn't know the way. His mother embraced him and searched his face. What was she seeking: his old scars, or fresh suspicion about her guest?

Major General Hashimoto, handsome in a well-cut tweed civilian suit, sat at the place of honor, Honorable Father's position. After an exchange of bows, the general said cordially, "Delighted to see you. Congratulations on your promotion."

Lady Tomigawa smoothed her kimono, the same one she wore at Tomi's wedding. "The telegram said you'd visit tomorrow. This is a surprise." She signaled Taiko to bring more hot sake.

General Hashimoto's looks, physique and even his mannerisms reminded Tomi of his father. He was not as well-born as the Tomigawas. A bright, forthright man, he had been Major Tomigawa's closest friend. Neither he nor Lady Tomigawa seemed embarrassed by Tomi's presence.

General Hashimoto smiled. "Your arrival is opportune, Tomigawa. We were discussing your immediate future. Please tell me, how did your meeting with General Suzuki go, now that he's finally freed you from Nakajima's 16th?"

Hashimoto's question was a deliberate message that he had a spy in Suzuki's office. Despite Hashimoto's candor, Tomi could not reveal Nakajima's theft of temple artifacts, or Tomi's temporary assignment to the secret chemical warfare unit.

"I was hoping for front line duty, but apparently not yet."

"A staff inspector can learn much in *Manchukuo*."

Everyone spied, everyone lied and Tomi was the last to know. Taiko brought sake and left.

Lady Tomigawa said, "The general was explaining some new military developments about which I'm woefully ignorant." Her false, innocent tone normally directed at unwary enemies was now used on Tomi. It was insulting. She knew more about Army matters than most staff officers. He dared not relax in the house where he had been born.

General Hashimoto casually asked, "How familiar are you with *kansen sensoo?*"

"Infection warfare, Sir? Ancient archers dipped their arrow heads in corpses, and Europeans catapulted the dead over the walls of besieged cities to spread disease."

Lady Tomigawa chided, "We're discussing modern times. Hashimoto-San said that during the Great War a German naval captain sneaked into America and injected plague bacteria, anthrax and Glanders Disease into horses and mules awaiting shipment to the English Army. He planned to wipe out all the Allied draft animals in France. The human casualties would have been awful."

"Yes, but the inoculations didn't take," Hashimoto said. "Had the scientists done their work correctly, the Kaiser might have won the war. Anthrax is deadly. The bacterium is found in soil and sometimes wipes out herds of grazing beasts." He leaned forward. "Humans suffer painful death; their bodies become covered with black lesions and boils. That's why its other name is the Black Bane. Anthrax is as gruesome as leprosy, but faster."

Aware that Taiko was in the traditional servant position outside the sliding panel, General Hashimoto whispered, "China's strategic depth has bogged us down and conventional arms won't bring victory. The General Staff is secretly spending a fortune researching anthrax, smallpox and other plague weapons.

"Infection bombs are cheap to produce and fit our surprise attack doctrine. Much experimentation is needed before we get reliable weapons. But if we use plague weapons and fail as the Germans did, it would be disastrous for us."

"My apology, Honorable General. I have no knowledge of such things." Tomi said, thinking of *Kakureru*, the concealment of oneself from others. His mother said in her softest voice, "Please explain to my son your reluctance about plague weapons."

General Hashimoto said, "Your honorable father and I never favored biological warfare. History tells us that the introduction of a new weapon or tactic prompts the enemy to improve upon it. Examples include cannon, shrapnel, repeating rifles, machine guns, airplanes, tanks and poison gas. But a germ bomb is not like other mass destruction weapons. An artillery shell or bomb kills upon impact, but a germ bomb keeps on killing, because its victims transmit living anthrax to others. Imagine a surprise attack on a capital city."

His mother completed his thought in a very unJapanese manner, " ... but no one owns science. An enemy can counterattack with his own pestilence, just like poison gas in The Great War."

General Hashimoto stared fixedly at the opposite wall, as if it were a talking picture screen. "We are the most densely populated nation. Our vulnerability exceeds our defenses in an exchange of anthrax. The Russians, Europeans and Americans would all retaliate with bacterium bombs on our crowded cities. Our casualties would be greater than theirs."

Lady Tomigawa's eyes flicked between General Hashimoto and her son. She whispered, "A few outsiders know the Kwantung Army conducts germ research in *Manchukuo*. But how can an arrogant war gambler on a winning streak be convinced that his next bet will lose? The new weapon might contain unforeseen results, as well as germs.

Tomi's mother called The God Emperor a war gambler! *Muhon*, treason! The general and lieutenant avoided eye contact. Officers loathed such talk, even when true. Tomi wondered if this friend of father's took comfort from his mother's aristocratic body, which had produced him.

General Hashimoto interrupted his dark thoughts. "Tomigawa, the Kwantung Army is noted for its, ah, initiative." Everyone knew the Emperor favored the victorious Kwantung Army, which openly financed its independent actions through mainland opium trade. The Kwantung Army deliberately started the successful Manchurian War and now the one in China.

"Japan's elite is addicted to conspiracy," his mother said. "Plotters, counter-plotters, secret societies, fanatics and informers abound. Some generals, like Hashimoto, favor a strong army immune from politics, while the radical *Kodo*, Imperial Way Party, wants the Emperor and Army to be free of political or moral restraints."

"And what of General Suzuki?"

"Such men are different, my son," Mother replied. "They cynically play all sides to gain profit and power for themselves." She frowned. "Selfish schemers like Suzuki are weeds found in every country. Their reckless greed, disguised as patriotism, creates chaos. Then they stand aloof, encouraging honorable warriors to shed blood to undo the disasters they have created."

General Hashimoto added, "Japan is at a crossroads. One path is the slow and steady growth of the Empire through trade, diplomacy and occasional low-risk war. This destiny is favored by the pro-Western minority to which Lady Tomigawa and I belong. The ultra-patriots and the profit-seekers want a germ bomb for surprise attacks that will stun the *gaijin* and give us cheap, quick conquests. We desperately need more arable land, but these war gamblers ignore all the risks. It's as insane as doing mathematics without the minus sign.

"Our people will pay an awful price if the germ war strategy backfires. The risk is not worth the reward."

Tomi was struck by how his mother and General Hashimoto thought alike, as if they were equal partners. He remembered how Suzuki's Taiko called his mother a modern woman in disguise.

In a command voice that carried a studied subtlety, General Hashimoto said, "Lieutenant Tomigawa, without violating your code of honor or the orders of your superiors, any unrestricted information that you can provide me about Unit 731's completion schedule will be appreciated. It might help me tilt the current debate at Headquarters. We will meet here upon your return."

Tomi saw his mother give Hashimoto a surprised look. Her co-conspirator and lover wanted him to be a spy, yet his mother remained silent.

Tomi imagined they did the same things Taiko and he did

under this roof. How could she evoke his father's spirit, yet couple with this man? She was not the dutiful widow.

To quench evil thoughts, Tomi tried to see the world from her viewpoint. She had warrior spirit but the Female Restrictions hobbled her. Having General Hashimoto as her front allowed her to use her intellect and political skills. But taking him as her lover was obscene.

Anger and self-pity churned in Tomi's belly. The Suzuki marriage made him a dupe and his mother made him a traitor. Had she been General Hashimoto's lover before his father's death? Was it lust, politics or both? Suzuki's Taiko openly rebelled at the Restrictions, while his mother slyly hatched treason behind them.

Everything had been said and they were silent. The sake was cold but no more was offered. His mother wanted him to leave, but he wanted to be with Taiko tonight, the first time in 17 months. Tomi rose, hoping his mother would urge him to stay. Instead she said flatly, "Please extend my regards to your honorable wife and General Suzuki."

Taiko wept silently as Tomi angrily wrestled on his boots at the front door platform. They were about to kiss goodbye, when Lady Tomigawa called from within, "Taiko! More hot sake, please."

Outside, the waiting army chauffeur saluted him. Tomi wondered how many more hours the soldier would wait. Tomi decided to walk off his anger to the Suzuki compound, tasting bitter treason instead of sweet Taiko. It was near midnight and the empty streets echoed his boot steps. He heard the familiar, comforting clacks of a neighborhood fire guard hitting his wooden sticks, assuring all that he was on the alert for fire. His mother and lover were using him like a lowly fire guard. When he sounded the alarm, he'd be a traitor like her.

***

For the next several weeks, Tomi endured strained eyes and headaches learning about military diseases and plagues, while Sergeant Takahashi incessantly clicked his abacus, mastering arcane military accounting. Sitting at a library table for eleven hours each day, Tomi skimmed the centuries, learning the diseases of invading armies.

Unpredictability was the biggest problem with modern germ weapons in tactical situations. A commander had to launch a B-Bomb attack too far away from his own troops. The ideal target was an enemy civilian population, but delivery methods were crude and uncertain.

It was simpler during the French and Indian War, when the British distributed blankets of dead smallpox victims to pro-French Indian tribes around Fort Pitt. The English and their colonial allies, including young George Washington, were safe. Having unsightly smallpox face scars was proof of immunity.

Tomi was fascinated by the many spy reports he saw on *gaijin* plague research. Except for the lax Yankees, the other major powers were in a race to solve the vexing complexities of infection warfare. Even germs found in nature were nasty. Excluding the Great War, for every soldier killed by a bullet, bayonet or shrapnel, at least one or two others died of disease. The Yankees, out of ignorance and poor leadership, lost 15 to 20 soldiers to tropical diseases for every one killed in the Spanish-American War and Philippine Insurrection. Yankees were blind to the lessons of military history.

Not so Imperial Japan, which led the world in preventative military medicine and sanitation. When the Russians were defeated at the century's start, only Japan had sanitation, water testing and purification units. This saved Japan's soldiers from cholera, typhoid and dysentery.

Getting soldiers to voluntarily swallow vile-tasting creosote pills for the prevention of intestinal diseases was solved with typical Japanese ingenuity. The pills were distributed in small tins that bore the message: "It is the Emperor's Will that each soldier take this medicine after each meal." A soldier would rather starve than skip his pill.

And now the brilliant Colonel Otomo was transforming mankind's ancient diseases into modern biological weapons at his secret unit. Tomi hoped he'd get a chance to meet the famed scientist during his short visit to Harbin.

When Tomi wasn't studying, he fretted over General Hashimoto's and his mother's patriotic but weak worries about the new weapon's unintended consequences. It was impossible to obey the conflicting dictates of his mother's lover and General Suzuki without dishonor. Tomi regretted his existence, just as the old Buddhist priest had predicted.

CHAPTER EIGHT
MANCHURIA, 1939

Sergeant Takahashi's clipped *Miyagino* accent brought them luck as the old train rattled across the Manchurian Plain to Harbin. They were in a second class railway coach with a noisy group of newly-recruited technicians assigned to the Bacteriological Experimental Center. A fat, middle-aged civilian walking down the aisle overheard Takahasahi's accent. He introduced himself as a Tohoku Imperial University professor returning to duty after home leave. When he heard Tomi's name and assignment, Professor Toda Hideo invited them to his private railway compartment for excellent green tea.

"You two are fortunate we're arriving on a Tuesday," he said jovially. "On Mondays and Fridays it is less than pleasant. When I first arrived, I gagged for days." He answered Tomi's quizzical look. "The stink from the crematory smokestacks. When there is no wind, the entire complex reeks of burning *murata*. But one gets used to the smell."

"*Murata*? Tree logs?"

Professor Toda giggled, his double chin quivering. He was a rarity -- an obese Japanese. He looked like a dwarf *sumo* wrestler in a travel-rumpled business suit. "Forgive me, First Lieutenant Tomigawa. It's a joke. When the new facility was built south of Harbin, the local laborers who cleared the land were told that it was for a lumber mill. Some witty person called our laboratory subjects *murata*, logs, and the name stuck."

"Logs? Subjects? My apologies for not understanding."

"Gooks. Non-humans. Criminals and spies used in our experiments. Someday the world will honor us for our scientific discoveries. We are learning much about treatment of combat wounds and surgical techniques, as well as new cures for frostbite, childbirth aberrations, malnutrition and many communicable diseases, including venereal. Colonel Otomo's team is expanding scientific knowledge. Japan's foremost universities send their top medical students and researchers here for training. That's why we use up so many 'logs.' The stink is nothing compared to the knowledge we will give the civilized world."

Professor Toda looked out the window. "Right on schedule. We transfer to the Pingfang local. Not enough time for you two heroes to sightsee Saint Sophia's Church or enjoy a White Russian whore, but try a beer. The Kwantung Army owns the old Russian brewery. It's a patriotic drink."

Despite the professor's cheer, Pingfang was grim. Only the minefield warning posters were familiar. The surrounding land was desolate, lacking hamlets, grazing herds, cultivated fields and people. The outer ring of the sprawling complex was ringed with earthen breastwork, guard towers and a high wall topped with barbed wire and high-voltage electrical fencing.

All the guards wore the black and green insignia patch of the *Kempetai*, Military Police. It took 3 men to push open the 2 huge iron doors, revealing a medieval-looking drawbridge over a deep moat. Even on the endless Manchurian Plain, the Japanese island people set themselves apart with moats, bridges and enclosures. The strange place hid behind many names, including *Kamo* unit and *Togo* unit, but it was better known as Unit 731-T.

Inside the heavily-guarded perimeter where Tomi expected white-coated scientists in pristine laboratories, there were rows of windowless barracks constructed with the dark brown wood the Army favored. The crematory's two widely-spaced smokestacks dominated the complex

Colonel Otomo greeted the new arrivals personally; no introduction by a fawning aide or the usual patriotic preamble. He said, "I'm Doctor Otomo, head of the Epidemic Prevention and Water Purification Department of the Kwantung Army." Everyone in the room, including Tomi, was impressed by the handsome man in his late forties, with full lips, high forehead and penetrating eyes that moved expressively when he spoke.

"It is the Emperor's wish that we save lives. For every hundred laboratory subjects we harvest, the lives of 3, perhaps 4

Japanese soldiers are saved. A worthwhile ratio. As you witness unfamiliar events, remember the rule: The logs are used to save human beings like your brothers and sisters. We advance science in many disciplines as well as medical research and training, disease prevention, weapon development and field applications."

He spoke in a matter-of-fact voice that carried confidence. Tomi had read that Dr. Otomo toured the United States and Europe years ago on his own scant funds to study.

Colonel Otomo scanned his audience. "You are here because you are Japan's finest scientific talent. Be diligent, work hard and remember our objectives. Someday you will be proud to say that you served here. Report to the billeting officer for your quarter assignments and duty rosters for tomorrow's assignments. Dismissed."

The newcomers stood and glanced around. No *Banzai* cheer. No bowing. Dr. Otomo raised his voice, " *Chu-I* Tomigawa and *Gunso* Takahashi! Come with me."

They entered a functional office lined with shelves of textbooks. The only wall decorations were photographs of The Emperor and Otomo's mentor, General Tojo, former *Kempetai* chief of the Kwantung Army. Otomo sat at his desk and demanded, "Sergeant! State your mission here."

Ignoring Tomi was a breach of military courtesy. Takahashi recovered and bowed, "*Taisa-San,* Honorable Colonel, my humble duty is to assist First Lieutenant Tomigawa in working with your staff on budget estimates."

"What experience have you?"

Takahashi said, "None, *Taisa-San.* I only recently completed my army accounting course."

"And you?" he asked Tomi.

"Even less, Honorable Colonel. I am without accounting experience. I was told that *Gunso* Takahashi and I were selected because of the accounting reports we wrote at Nanking."

"A waste of laboratory subjects. What is your real purpose?"

"Sir?"

"Otomo Rule Number One: Never lie to me. Rule Number Two: Liars get punished. Now, strike your sergeant's face. If you soften the blow, my guards will do it for you, much harder."

Tomi said, "So sorry," and knocked Takahashi sideways with an open slap. Takahashi's cheek bore a red imprint and his eyes watered. He recovered, stiffened to attention and returned Tomi's low bow of apology with a deeper one that forgave Tomi.

"Sergeant, do the same to your lieutenant." Takahashi hesitated but Tomi nodded. The blow was hard and Tomi's knees buckled under the more experienced hand.

Colonel Otomo said, "Tomigawa! Inform General Suzuki that when my project is ready, construction will be done by five groups, of which Suzuki gets one-fifth -- no more, no less.

"Your mother's situation, however, is unique. Lady Tomigawa's close friend, General Hashimoto stepped in front of a speeding taxi outside Headquarters and died two days later. Your mother was so distraught that she was placed under proper Army care at home."

Tomi shuddered. His mother and Taiko were under *Kempetai* house arrest or worse. Surely, Hashimoto had been tortured until he revealed the names of fellow plotters; then executed. Tomi would not have a quick death, and Takahashi would be executed for having a fool for his superior.

Tomi would have to shoot Takahashi, then himself. But his hand froze at his holster when Otomo said without emotion, "Lady Tomigawa's life depends upon your next move."

"Shit!" groaned Takahashi, the unwitting pawn. Otomo droned the three words that define Japanese character: "Duty. Hierarchy. Harmony. All that prevents your mother from joining her friend Hashimoto is my evaluation of your sense of duty."

Tomi felt the portrait of General Tojo looking down at him. The *Kempetai* knew everything. His mother and Taiko would suffer horribly if he committed suicide. He choked out, "I obey."

Colonel Otomo shoved a sheet of orders across the desk. Tomi was assigned to Unit 731's *Kempetai* as head of security with Takahashi as his senior non-com.

***

Harbin and Hell were joined by 60 miles of shiny railroad tracks that sliced the Manchurian plain. Tomi accepted delivery of new 'logs' in civilized Harbin and took them by train to their final destination. During the first awful weeks, the prisoners' faces made a nightly appearance in his nightmares. He understood why the captain he replaced had suffered a nervous breakdown and was hastily transferred a few days before Tomi's arrival.

Harvested logs were burned on Mondays and Fridays. Tomi retched from the plumes that poured from the twin smokestacks and didn't think he would ever get used to the stench. The mountain of grey ash and bone behind the crematory grew, despite the demand for fertilizer.

Tomi and Takahashi constantly checked on their *Kempetai* who guarded the barracks, laboratories, dormitories, jail, classrooms, and surgeries, as well as perimeter security and the bombing range. With the exception of the starvation studies, logs got the same rations as his *Kempetai* soldiers because Colonel Otomo wanted healthy test subjects. Even the women and girls in the pregnancy and venereal disease studies weren't badly mistreated until harvesting.

Colonel Otomo ordered Takahashi and Tomi to attend several harvests. "There's an elegant contradiction to Unit 731's mission that you must appreciate beyond what laymen regard as unpleasantries," he explained. "We work for 10,000 tomorrows. Through medical research we will save lives, and through biological warfare testing we will destroy the Emperor's enemies. You two are ignorant of research methods. The scientific reason we vivisect is to examine living organs uncontaminated by anesthetics. The scalpel is the sword of Japan's future."

Otomo's words lost their grandness the first time Tomi watched a pregnant woman dragged into surgery and strapped down. Before a nurse stuffed a rag into her mouth, she begged for her unborn child's life. Without anesthetic, she was opened with the graceful sweep of a scalpel. Deft, busy hands of white-clad doctors and nurses took her apart and ignored her muffled screams. Bright blood rivulets raced down the operating table depressions into waiting cans beneath. The woman's contents were placed into numbered white enamel pans and taken to an adjacent laboratory for study. The recorded data grew as fast as the crematory's mountain of ash.

The prisoners were not haphazardly brutalized and

slaughtered like Nanking's victims. Here, dispassionate men and women of science followed rigid academic and medical protocol to discover new facts amid the disciplined gore.

Unlike Unit 731's scientists, who learned but didn't feel, Tomi felt but didn't learn. He lacked the detachment that disconnected scientists from the horrors. Tomi's perfect memory made him imperfect for Unit 731 duty. He and his *Kempetai* routinely brought children of criminals to the complex. They were injected with typhus, cholera, smallpox, plague, anthrax or syphilis germs.

When the awful symptoms ravaged their small bodies, the doctors frantically worked to cure them, without much success. Death was a child's only friend in Pingfang.

Yet Tomi grudgingly approved as medical students learned the latest surgical techniques under combat-type conditions. Healthy prisoners of military age were carefully shot, then treated without anesthetic. The screams, curses and moans made these programs the noisiest and most unruly. They required the biggest, meanest guards.

In the starvation wards, subjects often lived weeks without food or water. The skeletal logs moaned their way to harvest.

"Death by starvation is the constant of inferior races," Major Mutsu said as he made rounds with an orientation group that Tomi and Takahashi joined. "The study of malnutrition isn't necessary when there are unlimited supplies of slaves. Think what will happen when we occupy a country after its population has been decimated by our mass plague and poison gas weapons. If we've done a good job here, the enemy's civilian casualties will result in a labor shortage.

"We will put survivors to work rebuilding the cities we occupy. Food will be scarce, yet the labor force must be able to do hard work. During a war, every gook's death is our advantage. After surrender, every gook's death is our loss," Major Mutsu explained.

"How many precious grains of rice does it take to keep a slave laborer digging a ditch? Until the advent of modern germ warfare, this question wasn't relevant, and there's scant data in scientific literature. We must know the amount of calories needed for a non-human's survival. Consider a gook's ration. Too little results in illness or death. Too much food is wasted shit."

Major Mutsu was an Army doctor who used a logic that Tomi understood. Soldiers go into combat with only enough rations to keep them going. To carry excess food instead of ammo was an error. But in combat, the rules were simple: Be brave and kill the enemy. At Unit 731, nothing was simple except suffering and the stink of science.

Takahashi added harsh words to Tomi's inner feelings as they unloaded a roped line of small children marked for vivisection. Takahashi spat and murmured insubordination for Tomi's ears only. "This fucking place is just as crazy as Nanking, but with white coats and polite talk.

"Even a lowborn like me knows that three Japanese aren't saved for every 100 logs murdered. Half these fucking doctors are crazy and the other half don't know what they're doing. If these misguided eunuchs want to know about combat wounds, let them go into battle with us. If they want to learn about malnutrition, let them visit my poor farm village. Bah! Education flushes common sense out of the brain!"

Tomi didn't reply, but knew that Takahashi's class hatred blinded him to the partial higher good. The death factory's revolving door was horrible, but valuable knowledge was gained with each spin. Takahashi didn't understand the rigorous scientific discipline. He was like the ox plowing a rice paddy, part of a complex process that it didn't comprehend.

Unlike Takahashi, Tomi didn't blame everything on the cold logic and busy scalpels of unemotional scientists. The logs were eager to please, like a dog that licked the hand of the master who beat it. Except for the pregnant ones aware of the life within, they cooperated even when they were about to be harvested. Their lack of honor and dignity angered Tomi. Perhaps that's why the gods made them gooks. A human being with *Nihonjin* pride would never be so docile. If Tomi were a log, he would try to escape or die fighting his zoo keepers. He would never allow himself to be humiliated or let a scientist slice him open without anesthetic.

The passivity of the Russians, Chinese, Manchurians, Koreans, Jews, Armenians and Asian tribesmen made Tomi's job easier. His strict discipline, enforced by Sergeant Takahashi's vigilance, kept his *Kempetai* thugs alert and efficient.

Self-absorbed doctors and scientists cared only about their own projects, not the total number of subjects. But Academy-trained Tomi felt blind without an eagle's view of combat's chaos to make sense of the whole. At Nanking, they had made a rational total from thousands of irrational incidents. Unit 731's rational details were so well controlled and measured that the grand total of processed humans had no scientific value. But security demands were different.

"Logs, lab rats or rabbits, the gross total used has no scientific value," Otomo said when Tomi proposed a status chart. "Each applied research project is its own discrete universe. How many logs or rats the unit uses in a month or year is meaningless, as long as we have sufficient test subjects to generate the end product: the scientific data.

"However, if for security reasons you want to count grains of sand in the hour glass before they drop to the bottom, do so. Just keep the flow of new logs maintained."

Tomi made a status board to track every prisoner's progress from railroad boxcar arrival to the inevitable crematory. From pregnancies to plagues, only the times differed. Takahashi and Tomi usually worked 14-hour days to make certain the hell in which they were trapped was escape-proof. They conducted surprise inspections and roll calls to prevent sloppiness. Tomi knew that as long as he was efficient at his grisly duties, his mother and Taiko stayed alive. Takahashi, trapped by Tomi's actions, vowed not to make that mistake again.

The men in the *Kempetai* unit were frightened of the test range, where germs and poison gas infections lurked. The easy part was taking healthy people out beyond the fortress perimeter to the bombing range. Men, women and children were chained to wooden posts arranged in concentric circles of a huge target.

After Tomi and his men were safely away, and if the wind sock pointed in the right direction, a low-flying Army bomber dropped a test weapon. It might be a dense cloud of plague-infected fleas, a ceramic bomb filled with anthrax germs or a dull steel canister painted with the grey, yellow and white bands indicating mustard gas, blister gas or some other poisonous brew.

A range safety technician in a protective suit checked the air with a detector after 24 hours. Then the all-clear sounded and the duty got dangerous.

Tomi and his men awkwardly wiggled into reddish brown rubberized fabric suits that resembled deep sea diver outfits complete with attached boots. With their hoods, special gas masks and elbow-high gauntlets, they lumbered around like red-skinned creatures from Mars. Inside their protective cocoons, sweaty, frightened men moved around half-blind because their goggles fogged up with condensation inside their gasmasks. They panted nervously, inhaling a noxious stench that was a blend of their own waste, mildew and cheap rubber.

No one had confidence in the suits. Each time Tomi carefully mounted his horse, he prayed the rubberized suit wouldn't come apart at the seams. The horse was completely clad down to its fetlocks in the same rubberized cotton fabric, with oversized goggles over his eyes. His hoof leggings widened to the straps across his withers. But the manufacturer of the bizarre equipment had forgotten to add a diaper, and the skittish nag voided the moment it was enveloped in its rubber suit. Hobbled in its own urine-soaked manure, the horse was difficult to control, forcing Tomi to grip the saddle's small brass square pommel like a recruit.

The horse was part of the test. After several border skirmishes with the Soviet Army, the Kwantung Army ordered Unit 731 to develop anti-poison gas gear for its horse cavalry in the event of a Soviet attack on Manchuria. Nothing was learned except that they became wildly incontinent.

Unlike a poison gas or high explosive test, where death was immediate, most prisoners survived a germ bomb, except for a lucky few at ground zero. Chained overnight to T-frames with arms outstretched, they screamed when Tomi approached. To them, he was a monster riding a goggle-eyed dragon, leading other slow-moving monsters, whose terra cotta-colored skins glistened in the sunshine.

They unchained the survivors and forced them back to distant lab cages for medical probing, study and eventual harvest. Guards who normally walked with a swagger took small, mincing steps like delicate *geishas,* terrified of tearing their fragile suits.

They were an assortment of sadistic thugs, ambitious careerists, former civilian policemen and super-patriotic idealists, plus a sprinkling of crazies. They were what General Tojo wanted when he created the Kwantung Army's military police. The brutes would have been ideal for General Nakajima's 16th Division at Nanking.

These tough *Kempetai* blubbered over a skin rash, pimple, mosquito bite or razor burn. Tomi's inner fear also overflowed like an old latrine, but he hid it well. All had seen Colonel Otomo's devil-germs at work. Most flea-borne and rat-sick bubonic plague experiments were failures. Worse, Otomo's cure rate for other diseases was near zero.

After infected subjects were locked up, Tomi and his men decontaminated themselves while still entombed in the rubber suits. They showered outdoors several times and dusted with a variety of chemical douches, depending upon the test weapon of the day. Often it was 'slurry,' the crude Great War decontamination solution of baking soda and water. Other times they used chloramine-T, chloride of lime and other smelly chemical combinations. Only then did they remove their claustrophobic, waste-filled suits and breathe fresh air.

Naked, they splashed themselves with alcohol until their most sensitive parts stung. Then the men blissfully soaked in communal hot tubs, the epicenter of Japanese culture. Tomi made sure the men had generous sake rations to numb their constant fear of invisible death, which came in bewildering forms.

Prisoners infected with bubonic plague or anthrax usually suffered a sequence of incessant coughing, fever, nausea, ugly flesh-eating sores and suppurating black tumors that spread rapidly. Convulsions were followed by coma, then death. The *Kempetai* guards knew that all that protected them from the anthrax germs in soil was a thin, rubberized fabric. Having seen gruesome death, many were hypochondriacs and all knew panic.

Tomi and Takahashi promised each other a bullet in the brain if either got infected but was too weak to pull the trigger. Fear prompted Takahashi to secretly test all the protective suits. He inflated each one with tire pumps, then immersed them in vats of water. Air bubbles leaked from one out of every 15 suits.

"What rotten bastard sold these cheap death suits to the Army without testing them? Fucking traitors!" Takahashi stormed. Not wanting the men to know how perilously close they were to death, he and Tomi carefully patched the leaking seams themselves. Tomi immediately requisitioned new suits and discovered the manufacturer was Suzuki Chemicals.

At the officers' club, Tomi heard a relaxed Colonel Otomo candidly discuss his problems. "Our planet and our bodies are home to many thousands of bacteria, some good, some bad. The toxic ones are living weapons that reproduce rapidly. But only a few microorganisms can be tamed for military use. We search for microbes that are cheaply and quickly produced; colonies that remain alive after a bomb shell explodes, then spreads like wildfire on a city's population.

A young Army doctor, aglow with admiration, asked, "Sir, of all the weapons we test here, which one do you think will have the highest success against our enemies?"

Colonel Otomo laughed ruefully. "Exactly what my superiors ask me every time I'm in Tokyo. It's no secret that my personal preference is *Bacillus Anthracis-San*. But we need much time to polish his social skills before we introduce him to our enemies."

Everyone laughed at the honorific he gave his favorite bacterium. *Anthrakis* was Greek for coal because of the black color of anthrax boils, tumors and lesions on a victim's body.

"Anthrax is a good offensive weapon, but he's unruly and has yet to reveal how we can make ourselves immune from his embrace. But I'm as stubborn as he is," Otomo said. "If Mr. Anthrax doesn't live up to his promises, there are several other germ weapons waiting in the wings.

"It's only a matter of time before we have an arsenal of germ and gas weapons. We know the Soviets have a germ war research center north of the Caspian Sea, so we must not waste time. Japan needs a super bacterium bomb for surprise attacks against our stronger enemies, north and south. Tokyo wants a quick, one-strike war, but we cannot allow Japan to be the target of an enemy's germ counter-attack."

These were almost the same cautionary words that Tomi had heard from his mother's late lover. When General Hashimoto said it, it was treason. Now it is Army doctrine. Tomi prayed his mother and Taiko were not being ill-treated by the *Kempetai.*

Pragmatic Colonel Otomo didn't punish Tomi for attempting to spy. Such behavior was normal in the Japanese military. With Lady Tomigawa held hostage, Tomi performed brilliantly as security chief and Otomo honored him by personally attending an inspection of the all-important records buildings, where Otomo's precious research data were stored.

Takahashi and Tomi held several rehearsals to correct any flaws before their master's inspection. The sheer tonnage of Unit 731's research data storage was astonishing. Five barracks-type buildings were filled to the ceilings with rows of wooden cabinets, crates and bins. Each file contained detailed statistics of the many thousands of harvested subjects.

Colonel Otomo cheerfully asked Tomi, "*Chu-I*Tomigawa! Do you realize that you are protecting the most far-reaching documented research in the history of science? The *gaijin* don't have a fraction of what I have stored here. It's priceless! When I toured the Yankee capital, their Army Institute of Pathology contained only cadaver parts and organs from their Civil War, as well as a collection of defective embryos. When I asked to see their medical statistics, they sent me next door to the Smithsonian to read worthless records! They saved old pathological specimens, but ignored modern science and statistics! Americans are the most stupid of all *gaijin*! "Germany invented modern chemical warfare, but now we're the leader. This is the most important research repository on earth. Tell me, do you appreciate what you are safeguarding?"

Tomi ignored the question with an insubordinate silence that was as dangerous as walking barefoot on the anthrax-contaminated soil at the range.

"What the hell's the matter with you?" Otomo snapped.

Tomi touched the thick wooden frame of the nearest record bin marked "Advanced Syphilis Experiment Females." Unit 731 had several research studies on venereal diseases that were a major problem, despite official Army sex slave brothels. Japanese soldiers considered condoms unmanly.

"Your important repository is endangered by fire hazard,

Colonel Otomo," Tomi said bluntly.

"Is this so?" Otomo asked his chief of facilities.

Major Iyoshe pointed to the ends of the long building, where fire extinguishers, buckets of water and sand were clustered under the fire alarm, the traditional hanging iron bar and hammer. "We're well prepared. What the hell do you know about fire hazards, Lieutenant?"

"Major Iyoshe, may I be permitted to inquire about the time elapsed during the last fire drill?

"Fire drill? Timing? You don't understand. No evacuation is needed. There are guards at both ends. No smoking, and it's off-limits except for daily visitations by a few clerks," he said testily.

Tomi bowed to both superiors. "Honorable Sirs, I humbly request permission to experiment. I would like to determine the time required to quench multiple paper fires after the alarm is given. And I have not alerted the guards in advance." Tomi had deliberately used Otomo's favorite term, *shiken suru*, to experiment.

"Proceed. I'll observe," Colonel Otomo said. Takahashi and Tomi each hauled two fire buckets filled with sand to different aisles and piled crumpled waste paper on top of each. When the second hand on Tomi's wristwatch touched 12, they set the paper mounds aflame in rapid sequence.

Colonel Otomo glanced at his watch as Takahashi raced to the fire alarm and repeatedly beat the hanging iron bar with the hammer. He bellowed *"Kaji, Kaji, Kaji!* Fire! Fire! Fire!"

A startled guard grabbed a water bucket and spilled half the contents on the floor before he quenched the first fire. Two of the three remaining test fires burned themselves out before other guards arrived to form a futile bucket brigade.

"Seventy-three seconds, Sirs," Tomi said.

Otomo corrected him, "No, seventy-three-and-one-half. Even with a faster response, my records could be destroyed."

"Unless we installed an overhead system, Sir," Tomi suggested.

"Already looked into that," grumped the major. "The *gaijin's* fire sprinkler systems require higher water pressure than we have. Our damn plumbing can't take the increased pressure. One burst pipe or defective sprinkler head would turn our records into soaked garbage."

"There may be another way, Sirs."

Colonel Otomo's raised eyebrows gave permission to Tomi to continue. "We might use a fire retardant made of crematory ash mixed with baking soda. We have an unlimited supply. A thick layer of bone ash and baking soda in thin balsa wood trays could be placed on top of file cabinets. The fire burns the tray and dumps retardant on the files before too much damage is done."

Major Iyoshe objected, "We'd end up with filthy records."

Otomo said, "Put the fire retardant in tightly sealed waterproof paper packets and place them over every file, not just on cabinet tops. Add metal braces to reinforce shelves.

"I want engineering blueprints within the week, Major. Meanwhile, start testing four different mixtures of dry retardant. And from now on, we will ship duplicate records to Tokyo every month instead of semi-annually. That's our temporary solution.

"The best sprinkler systems are made by Germans and Americans. We will install a separate water pipe system, including pumps! My patriotism doesn't include using inferior Japanese products that endanger my records."

He turned to go but an afterthought halted him. "One more thing. Requisition typewriters and get clerks that type. No more using water soluble ink on permanent records. This is modern science's Library of Alexandria. It must be protected at all costs." As he and the embarrassed major left, Otomo murmured, "The fresh eye sees more."

After they were gone, Tomi bowed to Takahashi. "Your fire drill idea won the day, my friend. I am indebted to you. As always, you make me appear far smarter than I am. You are the one who deserves praise."

"Praise is useless, Tomi. I just want to leave this crazy fucking place before next winter."

***

Everyone at Unit 731 talked about the Manchurian winter and Colonel Otomo's frostbite treatment study in -15 degree

-126-

temperatures. Dozens of naked prisoners were tethered to outdoor leashes like sled dogs as new frostbite cure theories were tested on all body parts.

The Kwantung Army suffered a high incidence of frostbite amputation cases, while their spies reported the Siberian border troops were unaffected by frigid weather. Because of increased tensions, Colonel Otomo planned to resume experiments in December. Tomi hoped General Suzuki could arrange to have his mother freed before then and get him reassigned.

The large civilian staff at Pingfang were given comfortable living conditions, extra pay, special privileges and career-enhancing experiments. They revered Colonel Otomo. One earnest project chief bragged, "When the world finds out what he's done here, he'll be as famous as Pasteur and the Curies!"

Otomo's chief patron was General Tojo, a rising star much favored by the Imperial Palace. Unit 731 was the result. Colonel Otomo was idolized for his work and Tomi scorned for his. On his single day off every second week, he fled to Harbin to escape Pingfang's organized hell. Even there, his *Kempetai* insignia, the black horizontal jagged stripe outlined in green over his right breast pocket, marked him. Fearful civilians hastily left half-finished meals in restaurants when he walked in, and off-duty Japanese soldiers were uncomfortable.

None of this bothered Tomi, who usually strolled along the river bank in solitude. Harbin wasn't cosmopolitan Shanghai, but the Manchurian city got its unique nature from its polyglot people and architecture. In the park-like grounds of Wen Miao, a Confucian temple with golden dragons on its many roofs, Tomi reverently touched the ancient stones in the garden. But he refused to accept the ugly truth that Japanese were ignorant savages when the Chinese holy steles were inscribed.

Unlike Japan's homogeneous race, Harbin contained 40 different ethnic groups, including the Han, Korean, Manchurian, Tibetan, Ewen, Oroken, Miao, Zhuang, Daur, Xibe, Hez, Tujia and Uygur, plus Russians of every color and religion.

Twenty years earlier, 500,000 Czarist Russians fled the Revolution and settled in Harbin. It was called 'Little Moscow' because it had the largest Russian population of any city in the world outside the Soviet Union.

To its credit, the Kwantung Army didn't destroy the architectural symbols of Russian Imperialism, particularly Saint Sophia's Orthodox Church. With its elaborately-carved red stone walls, arches and the cross-bearing green cupola, it belonged in a child's book of fairy tales.

The city's harmony remained intact after the Japanese took the city from the Russians. There were more than a hundred places of worship: Buddhist, Taoist, Confucian temples; Muslim mosques; Christian churches and a Jewish synagogue. Perhaps the isolation of long, bitter winters created harmony.

Tomi was depressed and lonely, but declined the readily-available sex in Harbin or the clinical variety at Unit 731. His spirit was infected and his destiny spiraled downward, just as the old monk in Nanking had predicted.

Unexpectedly, Takahashi requested an off-duty meeting on an urgent matter. Because of ever-present spies, they met in Harbin's Daoli district and, over Russian beer, openly took notes detailing the pedestrian flow as if they were planning a log collection in Harbin. With alibis established, Tomi led Takahashi to the isolated river walk.

At a desolate spot, Takahashi pulled a familiar object from his pocket. It was a tag from Tomi's log chart. The color code indicated a pregnancy study subject. It was forbidden to remove a tag until the log went to the Crematory. Takahashi had defied Tomi's orders.

Japanese males dammed their emotions within their *honne* until pressure, like earthquakes or tsunamis, vented in violence or breakdown. Takahashi sat on a fallen tree trunk, head lowered, and wept, "I love this woman and she's having my child."

The pregnancy study was the most popular among Unit 731's staff because its purpose was to statistically prove the obvious: Japanese penises were superior and their sperm was more potent than all other races. Officers, non-coms and civilians volunteered for the pregnancy study because the subjects were the prettiest, healthiest females. Tomi had declined to participate because he didn't want his offspring, half-breed or not, harvested for science.

Takahashi explained, "She's special. Very bright. She was a

language student and speaks Japanese. Her name is Ruth."

"Ruth?"

"She's *Wei Wei.*"

"What's that? A local nomad tribe?"

"No. *Wei Wei* in Chinese means 'from the West.' She's Chinese Jewish."

"But Jews are *gaijin.*"

"That's what I thought. Ruth said that Jews had been traders along the Great Silk Road for centuries. They so impressed the Sung Emperor that he asked them to settle in his capital, Kaifeng. The Emperor couldn't pronounce their Hebrew names, so he gave them seven Chinese family surnames that are still used to this day.

"The single men married local women because there weren't enough Jewish women in the colony. Chinese wives always take their husbands' religion and China's Jews, who are Chinese in appearance, have been called *Wei Wei* ever since."

The second-hand history lesson annoyed Tomi. This woman had sexually bewitched Takahashi to save herself. His non-com's softness was a huge, unnecessary risk to Tomi's mother and Taiko. But Takahashi was trapped because of Tomi. He sucked air between his teeth. He had to honor Takahashi's plea for help.

"Ruth will be split open like a ripe melon. I must free her."

He flinched when Tomi snorted, "Impossible! The only escape is up the smokestack."

Please, Tomi, we must think of a way!"

"She can't get past the electric wire and the kill zone."

"Can we bribe someone to hide her in a crematory cart?"

"No. Everyone spies at Pingfang Fortress. We can only trust ourselves."

"I've got to save her and my unborn child!"

Tomi knew his comrade was temporarily crazy when he said 'my unborn child,' yet could not come up with one of his inventive schemes. Tomi was angry at Ruth the *Wei Wei,* who would get them all killed.

He slapped a mosquito on his neck and rubbed the swelling. He hoped the bite closed before they went to the bombing range the next day for a routine germ-shrapnel test. Tomi's men preferred to collect bloody pieces of bomb-blasted subjects than handle those infected with anthrax. The gruesome corpses were safer than invisible germs. Tomi wondered how they could create an illusion that would made Ruth invisible.

Foolishly, he blurted a half-formed idea. "What if we put her with the test subjects on the range? The night before a bomb drop, we sneak back, unchain her and send her off with food and money. We replace her with other body parts, making the mess look like two people instead of one. With luck, she'd make the 60-mile hike to Harbin. Her family can arrange her escape."

"Wonderful solution!"

"Wait," Tomi warned. "How do we get her out of the study and sent to the range? If Ruth just disappeared, they'd know she had inside help. We'd be tortured and end up as logs ourselves. I'm afraid your Ruth is doomed."

"There is a way," Takahashi said mournfully. "You know Haruo, the commissary sergeant?"

Tomi nodded. Takahashi used Haruo's commissary as a cover for his own black market dealings. Takahashi had more money than a sergeant should. Fortunately, he sent all of it to his Sendai family instead of drawing attention as a spender.

"We both volunteered to impregnate women in the study. Haruo's woman was taken out of the program after she was caught in bed with a young intern. The doctors said she ruined the study because there was no way to record her intercourse frequency."

"What happened to them?"

"The intern was transferred and the woman was put in the gonorrhea infection program for quick harvest. Haruo was upset because the intern had forced her to submit."

"Takahashi, how can we get someone to, ah, disqualify Ruth? And how can we keep her from being transferred to the venereal disease ward and harvested?"

Takahashi mumbled, "You've got to visit her during your nightly inspection rounds. I'll discover you in the act. You claim Ruth seduced you. Everyone knows you're as celibate as a monk. You insist that she join the morning's march to the bombing range because only her immediate death will allow you to save face."

Tomi hissed, "*Jodan ja nai!* You must be kidding!"

"It's the only way."

"If anything goes wrong, she'll be harvested. Of course, we'll just pretend it happens."

"No. They examine them. If there's no semen, they may keep her in the program. We need evidence of intercourse."

Tomi would not ask another man to have sex with his Taiko, even to save her life. He lacked Takahashi's selfless love. "I can't do it. It would end our friendship. Honor prevents it."

As if Tomi were a lowly recruit, Takahashi snarled, "Honor? Where is your fucking *Samurai* honor in our rotten world? I beg you to save my woman and unborn child from this death factory that you put me in, and you babble of honor? Are you my friend or just a highborn prick using a peasant's neck as your footstool?'

Tomi said evenly, "I'm your friend. If I had a brother, he'd be like you. This crazy scheme will get us all killed, including my mother and Taiko. So we must plan every detail carefully, and pray our ancestors will rain luck down upon us."

Tomi bowed low to Takahashi. As suddenly as a summer rainstorm, the two men wept. Both were risking their loved ones in an escape that might well end in disaster.

***

The scent of a sleeping woman was exciting, and an entire dormitory of them was like inhaling a blossom-filled night garden. Despite tension and stealth, Tomi had an unwanted erection. He told himself it was not the prospect of sex comfort for the first time in months. Tomi had ordered the outside guard to remain at his post while he checked the other guard at the opposite door.

Tomi walked down the double row of sleeping women, stopping at the eleventh bunk on the right. Empty. He briefly flicked on his flashlight to read the name on the hanging medical chart. It was Ruth's bunk. Tomi heard a noise and went to the unlit *benjo*, toilet. On the wooden slat floor a woman struggled, her head moving violently from side to side. The thrusting man on top had her arms pinned.

The flashlight beam revealed the face of a startled guard. Tomi roared, "Cockroach! Desert your post, will you?" The man scrambled off Ruth and Tomi knocked him down, kicking his exposed genitals repeatedly.

When he was certain the guard was unconscious, he turned to Ruth, who cried in Japanese, "He force me. Sorry, so sorry, Sir!"

"Silence, Ruth," Tomi whispered. "I'm Takahashi's friend. No matter what I say or do, just tell the truth about being raped. All will be well." Terror failed to hide her remarkable beauty.

Tomi bellowed, "Guard! Guard! In here at once!" The row of hanging light bulbs flickered on and awakened women stirred, then rose to stand dutifully next to their bunks as the other guard raced through the barracks.

"So! You were his lookout while he fucked a log. Had your turn already, did you?"

"No, Sir! I didn't do anything, First Lieutenant Tomigawa, Sir. I swear it. I never touched a log. Never! I knew nothing about this. I was at my post the whole time!"

Takahashi ran in and saw Ruth wailing, her blouse ripped, face bruised, and lips swollen; as well as an unconscious guard naked from the waist down, bleeding from his battered crotch.

Tomi pointed to the fallen guard. "Sergeant Takahashi, I caught this scum of yours fucking a log. She claims that he forced her. I doubt it. Obviously, your cursed guard has been taking comfort from logs every time he is posted here. Is this how you command a guard detail? I hold you personally responsible for contamination of the program!"

"But Sir. I inspect this dormitory twice a night. This is the first time such a violation has ever happened." Ignoring the sobbing Ruth, he asked, "What are your orders, Sir?"

"Call out the entire detachment. I want the men to punish this lowlife slowly and without mercy. He contaminated Colonel Otomo's project. He disgraced us. Let his death be a warning to anyone who violates the trust the Colonel placed in us."

"Yes, Sir."

"Sergeant, this damn log is disqualified from the program. Take personal charge of her. See that she goes to the bombing range with the morning batch. I don't want her around here. This sorry mess is your fault. I warned you not to be soft on your men!"

"Yes, Sir, I apologize." He bowed. "I am responsible for my

men's conduct. It is my fault."

Tomi slapped Takahashi's face. "You failed your duty and embarrassed me. By morning, I'll be the joke of Unit 731." Tomi gave the innocent guard a double slap.

"Sergeant Takahashi! Interrogate all the guards and question every idiot log in this whorehouse too. Find out if this contamination has spread. You will personally add this log to tomorrow's range fodder. Then awaken the project scientist and report what happened. Tell him I will personally apologize to him."

Takahashi understood the hastily changed plan. By breakfast, everyone would gossip about the rapist's bad death and a guilty log sent to the bombing range. Tomi had lost so much face that no one questioned why he hadn't sent the errant log into another lethal experiment. The spectacle of a *Kempetai* officer losing face was an event everyone enjoyed. Even Major Iyoshe, whom Tomi had shamed with the fire threat to Otomo's precious records, would savor Tomi's public ridicule and did not question a worthless log's fate.

By afternoon, the subjects were chained at the range. The fearful guards averted their eyes when Takahashi and Tomi dragged Ruth to the T-frame farthest from target center. The *Kempetai* guards knew their tough, demanding superiors wanted her to suffer much before she died.

Takahashi had coaxed her to overeat and drink copious amounts of water before her ordeal. As Ruth was being chained, Tomi glanced north toward Harbin where she would flee. Several hundred yards away, a work party was digging holes, while others unloaded objects from trucks. Tomi didn't have his binoculars and fretted over the unexpected development.

He went to the office of Captain Kisho, the range safety officer whose addiction to Virginia tobacco made him a steady customer of Takahashi's black market. Kisho eyed Tomi's knapsack and pumped for juicy details of last night's scandal. Tomi pulled out two cartons of American cigarets and said, "I need an overnight delay. My troops are exhausted. I spent the night questioning all of them. Fortunately, it was an isolated instance."

Kisho readily agreed to reschedule the test until the next

morning. After he locked the cartons in his desk drawer, he leaned back and laughed, "Tomigawa, you gave me *Amerikanjin no tabaco* for nothing. I already postponed today's test. My men found active traces in the soil after the bacterium bombing the other day. Damn new stuff acts different from anything we used before. Surprised no one informed you before you took today's batch of logs out to the target area. I guess you were too busy."

Tomi felt itchy. He and Takahashi had touched the soil when they chained Ruth to the cross. He stormed, "My men were exposed to some new germ because you didn't inform me?"

"Don't brown your breech-clout, First Lieutenant Tomigawa," the captain snarled. "You're the one who didn't want your men suited up in protective gear when the logs were taken out. In the future, maybe you people should wear your rubber suits going and returning!"

Tomi bowed a silent apology. "Kisho-San, speaking of things I don't know but should, why is a big work party out there today? Are they putting up more perimeter fencing?"

"No, the engineers are laying another minefield. Major Iyoshe is afraid the project won't be finished before the ground freezes."

"Another mine field? I didn't see any warning signs!"

"Work was held up for a while due to a lack of mines. The Kwantung Army has planted every available one along the Soviet border. When old Iyoshe lost face over your fire drill experiment, he pulled strings and got a partial shipment of assorted mines from the Navy. Iyoshe was worried that you'd find some perimeter weakness and wasn't going to let you embarrass him again."

"Let's see the mine field map," Tomi asked. Kisho lit a Lucky Strike and inhaled before putting a tissue overlay on the map.

"Don't worry about your men. Major Iyoshe is planting the mines at the north end. He posted plenty of warning signs there. Not even close to the target area."

Tomi aligned the rectangular overlay on their marks and memorized the schematic. The incomplete pattern was simple; an oval within an oval. Kisho had used red ink to mark the planted mines, which formed a double arc.

"When was this updated?"

"Couple of days ago. Iyoshe said his men added a couple

more rows since then and would update my map when he got a chance."

The memorization was useless. They were going to walk through an unmarked minefield.

"Kisho, why two different symbols marking the mines?"

"They shipped us both Model 93 and the new Model 96. We need to know which is which." The 93 was a standard pancake mine that exploded when its top plate was depressed. It was issued with a choice of triggering weights from 20 to 200 pounds.

"What fuse are they using?"

"Less than usual. No Russian tanks will be rolling around here," he laughed. "Damn thing will go off if a butterfly lands on it."

"What's a Model 96? Don't think I ever heard of it."

Kisho said, "Army Ordnance adapted a 100-pound naval mine for land use with a trip wire system. Snag the wire and 46 pounds of TNT goes boom."

"This map doesn't show the layout."

He gave Tomi a sharp, suspicious look. "You're not planning to take a stroll there, are you? Frankly I don't know or care how the damn trip wires are arranged."

"You're right, Kisho. Only a fool, would wander out there." Tomi grinned. "I guess you'll also cancel tomorrow's bombing run because of plague traces."

"Won't know 'til my troops do a final check. We'll probably send out the bomber after breakfast tomorrow. The new plague germ is different from anything they've cooked up before."

***

When he heard about the mines, Takahashi refused to let Tomi accompany him.

"No. It will take both of us to get Ruth through the minefield. I'll lead. You're lookout."

"I'm sorry I got you into this, Tomi."

"If positions were reversed, you wouldn't desert me. Anyway, if I stayed here and you got blown up, they'd suspect me anyway."

Takahashi groaned when told about the Model 96 mine. He squinted at Tomi's minefield sketch. "Hey, this doesn't make sense. The gap between the 96ers is too long. The trip wires would sag." He closed his eyes and rubbed his nose as he worked through the problem. His features were as noble as Tomi's. Only his accent revealed a peasant birth. But Takahashi didn't think like a farmer. His eyes opened wide, as if he'd been punched. "Oh no! They probably strung hand grenade booby-traps between the big mines to keep the trip wires high enough off the ground!"

Every Japanese infantryman made the simple device: A sharpened stake was shoved into the ground; tied to it was a wax paper tube with a hand grenade stuffed inside. The grenade's safety pin was tied to a taut trip wire. When the wire was moved even an inch, the grenade would explode in seconds and set off nearby mines in a chain reaction. The two men looked at each other, neither hiding his fear. Ruth was chained at the range and could not be retrieved. They had no choice but to proceed despite worsened odds.

After dark, they sneaked past the range guard shacks. They had rubberized boots over their own. An extra pair for Ruth was tied around Tomi's neck. Takahashi carried a loaded knapsack.

They unchained Ruth, who couldn't walk in the oversized boots they had brought her. Takahashi half-carried her and Tomi led the way. He visualized the incomplete map overlay with each tentative step. Four times he felt unexpected trip wires and moved around them.

When they had reached the far side of the mine field, Tomi knew he could not safely retrace his steps. He and Takahashi would die instantly, but his mother and Taiko would die slowly.

Takahashi retrieved a Buddhist priest's tattered saffron robe, male undergarment, sandals, food, money and a begging bowl from the bulging pack. He handed Tomi shears to cut off Ruth's hair and dry-shave her scalp. Despite being cut several times, she remained quiet.

Tomi scooped up her black tresses from the ground and handed them to her. "Ruth, when you are several *li's* away, scatter the hair off the road, a little bit at a time."

She nodded as Takahashi dirtied her bare head and face with caressing hands. In the dark, she looked like a lowly beggar monk. If she could fool curious peasants and soldiers, she might be able to walk to Harbin in three nights and two days.

Tomi looked away as Takahashi helped her out of her waste-stained clothes and tenderly cleaned her before she put on the monk's robe. Takahashi handed her a small knife and said, "Defend yourself and our child. If I'm still alive, I promise to find you both."

"Yes, beloved. I will wait for you, no matter how long or what happens."

She left. Both knew they would not see each other again in this life. The sweat Tomi wiped from his face was from fear. "The booby traps are staggered without a pattern. We can't retrace our steps without getting blown up."

Takahashi thought about the work party that had rigged the grenades and mines. "The officers were probably too scared to be near the men who planted the mines. Unsupervised, they would have done the job the safest way. My guess is that the trip wires are set in straight lines."

Takahashi was right. Fearfully, they crawled past monster mines to safety.

***

At morning formation, Tomi told his troops, "After today's bombing run, Sergeant Takahashi and I will go out to test the soil and air for plague germs. You men stand by. We will return to lead you out to the range if my detector shows no contamination."

When the thumps of bomb explosions faded, Takahashi and Tomi wiggled into their protective suits and slowly lumbered to the range. They dragged a torso and other unidentified body parts to Ruth's empty post and spread the gory mess until her post looked like the rest. Four posts away, a young female stubbornly clung to life. Eyes alert, she pleaded to them in an unknown language. Survivors were routinely questioned by the medical staff before they were vivisected. Tomi gave her a more merciful death. He cut her throat.

CHAPTER NINE

He was a coward and voided as loosely as a log at harvest. The sun competed with the heat of furiously burning wrecks of the one-sided tank battle. Tomi and Takahashi cowered behind Captain Hara's burning tank as enemy tanks punched holes into the fleeing Japanese armor like fists through *shooji*, paper screens. The odor of Tomi's waste mixed with the overpowering sweet-sour of roasting bodies and gunpowder.

"Stink's no different than Nanking or Pingfang," Takahashi said without emotion. "Only this time it's the Japanese who are roasting. We all smell the same."

This was not how Tomi wanted to find glory in combat. He wasn't able shout brave words over deafening explosions or swing his sword into enemy flesh. Their 'weapons' were backpacks of plague germs that sloshed in fragile glass jars cushioned by straw.

A fresh barrage of tank artillery bursts rained dirt, metal and body pieces on the two men. They hugged the ground and scrambled side to side like two frightened crabs desperate to avoid the cooking pot.

Deafened, Tomi expected the next explosion to get them. Instead, there was a sudden lull. Tomi timidly raised his head and saw his cowardice reflected in the wide-open eyes of Hara, hanging head down, his remaining foot caught in the burning turret of his command tank. His bottom half smoldered. Two classes ahead of Tomi at the Academy, he had been the superior athlete. Tomi whimpered. He didn't want to die like Hara.

Yesterday, Tomi had visited Hara and they drank tea next to the tank in stifling heat. Hara told him, "When our tanks attack in the morning, it will be very Japanese."

"What do you mean?"

"Imagine being inside my tank, Tomi. We're packed in a noisy, cramped hunk of metal trying to see the world through a tiny slit, but we only see what's directly in front of us. Yet we speed ahead, part of a 91-tank formation moving as a single unit. That makes it so Japanese."

"But Hara, the same can be said for any military formation. I envy you going into battle tomorrow with this brand new tank."

"Ah yes, tomorrow's battle in our new tanks." He looked into the distance. "Many young men will die tomorrow because of the bad judgement of old men. The myopic ones in Tokyo overruled our request to improve this." Hara affectionately patted the narrow track of his Type 89 medium tank. "They refused to replace our short-barreled 57-millimeter cannon with the higher-velocity gun we requested."

"Why would they deny an armament upgrade?"

He looked at Tomi as if he were still an underclassman. "The General Staff said what worked in China will also succeed against the inferior, stupid Soviets. The old generals forgot that the Chinese had only antique tanks. The Russians are different. In the morning we will be in the world's first major tank battle with the wrong weapons."

He waved at the vastness of the steppes. "Look around you. We're going to fight on a vast plain as flat and wide as the ocean. No trees, no mountains, no cities. It is perfect tank country for the superior tank, which travels faster and shoots farther with more punch than its thin-skinned opponent. Our tank regiments face the Soviets T-34s." He lowered his voice to a mournful whisper. "It will be another Yamagata slaughter."

Tomi almost dropped his canteen cup. Three months earlier, fighting had broken out on the disputed border between Japan's Manchukuo and the Soviet's Mongolia. Tokyo didn't want to get into a full scale war with the Soviet Union. The High Command issued orders not to counter-attack.

But the arrogant Kwantung Army, knowing the Imperial Wish, disobeyed as usual. The Kwantung Army sent its Yamagata Strike Force to drive out the Mongolians and their Soviet masters from the disputed territory. But the force was quickly encircled by a brilliant Soviet maneuver and annihilated. The Kwantung Army mistakenly believed the Soviet Army was leaderless after Stalin had exterminated most of the officer corps in a political purge.

Humiliated, the Kwantung Army counterattacked with the 23rd Infantry Division, plus two tank regiments, including Hara's. They pushed the Russians back east to the banks of the Halha River and both sides dug in.

The glass jars of plague germs Takahashi and Tomi carried were Colonel Otomo's gift to the Kwantung Army to avenge the Yamagata defeat. Otomo sent them instead of scientists because of their Nanking battle experience. Tomi was instructed to scatter his germs upstream, infecting the Soviet troops during the stalemate.

But when Tomi and Takahashi reported to General Komatsubara of the 23rd Division, he roared, "Fools! My troops drink out of the same river. You dump your germs behind their lines -- not in the river or near my men."

Takahashi and Tomi had lugged their heavy backpacks as far as the leading element of the 3rd Tank Regiment, hoping to slip through a gap in the Soviet lines, when Captain Hara stopped them from certain death.

"You'll never get through now. The Soviets are massed for an immediate attack," Hara had warned. "Our listening posts reported they've been bringing up armor all day. What used to be a porous infantry line yesterday is now a solid line of Russia's new wonder weapon."

"Wonder weapon?" Tomi asked, thinking his jars of germs were the newest weapon.

"Production prototypes of their new T-34 tank. Best in the world. Thick, sloped armor and with a long-range cannon, plus machine guns. My tank's 150-horsepower gets a top speed of 25 miles an hour. The *Roshiya* T-34 has over twice my horsepower, is much faster and gets better mileage! Both tanks were designed two years ago. The Russian diesel engines are reliable and easy to fix, while a third of our tanks are always down for repairs. Wish we had their tank and they had ours!"

"Why are our tanks so lacking?"

"Obsolete design, inferior workmanship and arrogant generals who disregard the advice of younger officers with experience. So we fight with poor equipment. It's our fucking archaic system, Tomi! Custom demands that we keep our critical opinions hidden because our superiors demand blind obedience. Self-delusion is an insane way to run a modern army!"

Tomi thought of his Sumida armored car in Nanking. It had been designed six years before Hara's tank, yet the Army continued to build overweight, under-gunned combat vehicles. How can crude Slav communists design better tanks than the Japanese? And how did they outmaneuver the Kwantung?

Dead Hara's prophetic words echoed as he inhaled his classmate's burning flesh. Takahashi yelled into Tomi's deafened ear, "Battle seems to be moving away." Defeat was confusing and tiring. They slipped off their backpacks and rested.

Colonel Otomo had sent Tomi and Takahashi because they would die rather than allow the enemy to discover Unit 731's germ warfare secret. Colonel Otomo refused to tell Tomi which plague germs they carried. "It might distract you from your mission. Just think about your mother," he warned. Takahashi suspected the jars contained anthrax, Otomo's favorite germ.

Takahashi and Tomi searched for an infantryman's trench tool to bury Otomo's devil's brew. They wandered among the dead and debris of the battlefield. Hidden behind a blasted tank hulk was an abandoned but undamaged *Sanrinsha*, the Army's 3-wheeled motorcycle cargo carrier.

Tomi saw black dots on the horizon moving toward them. Enemy troops. That's why the shelling had stopped. Tomi mounted the motorcycle and frantically tried to kick-start the cold engine until his right leg ached. It wouldn't start. Fear and frustration twisted Tomi's gut. He gasped for breath and felt the coward's slippery excreta he sat in.

Takahashi unscrewed the gas cap and grunted, "Empty."

Tomi was ashamed that he had revealed his fear. He had to do something honorable before the Russians killed them. Enemy equipment always fascinated soldiers. In Nanking, Japanese troops clambered like children on Chinese trucks, military equipment and *gaijin* autos. The Russian and Mongolian troops might consider the cargo motorcycle a toy, perhaps even tow it back to their camp.

Tomi put the knapsacks of liquid disease in the empty cargo bed, and with shaking hands he donned a surgeon's mask and rubberized gauntlets. He told Takahashi to move away upwind. Holding his breath, Tomi opened the sealed bottles and clumsily splashed the living contents on the handlebars, saddle seat and cargo space.

He felt something cold and saw that several drops had landed on his sleeve and soaked through to his skin. If the secret liquid was anthrax, Tomi was a dead man. Breathing anthrax spores was lethal and his flimsy nose mask was useless. He imagined the anthrax germs were invisible screws burrowing into his lungs and organs. Barehanded, he tossed the wet gauntlets away from the disease-dripping vehicle. He had one to six days of agony, then death.

Takahashi rushed over. "Tomi! What happened?"

Tomi screamed, "Don't touch me! I spilled some! I'm infected!" Takashi quickly obeyed. Wet from sweat, Tomi stooped to wipe his hands on the long grass of the steppes in a foolish attempt to soothe the imagined itching and burning. Irrationally, he dropped his breeches and carefully cleaned himself with handfuls of grass. He threw away the stinking breech clout, wondering how long he would be able to wipe his ass before the filthy black pain took command.

"I have four morphine shots," Tomi said. "I'll use them."

"We don't know for sure that Otomo's crap is anthrax. What if it isn't? Don't do anything stupid. If it isn't, you'll survive. If it is, I promise not to let you suffer."

Exhausted, Tomi nodded. He looked at a charred corpse next to a miniature tank. He thought of Hara's scorn for flawed military thinking. The tankette, copied from an old English Army model, weighed 3 tons but carried only two men and a machine gun.

The corpse suddenly waved to Tomi with a blackened arm. The mouth on the burned face moved but Tomi was still deaf from the shelling. He looked nervously around the grassy plain littered with hundreds of Japanese corpses. Nothing moved, but he felt ground vibrations from explosions through his boot soles. He did a 360-degree sweep with binoculars. Despite the heat distortion and sweat stinging his eyes, he saw many Russian tanks chasing one Japanese tank. The battle was almost over.

Takahashi emptied his water canteen into the ruin of the man's mouth. He wore the insignia of a colonel. Tomi took two ampules from his kit and injected morphine into a charred arm. There were so many dead that it was difficult to walk without occasionally stepping on flesh. Takahashi found a dead infantryman without much gore, and the two men removed the rolled canvas from his pack. Returning to the burned man, they rolled him onto the spread canvas. Pieces of skin sloughed off and left a black and red trail from green grass to the brown canvas. Screams contorted his blackened face.

"We've got to get away from here. Tanks and infantry are coming in to mop-up," Takahashi said urgently. They wrapped the shelter half cords around their fists and with heads down, slowly dragged the screaming man toward the rear. Five soldiers stood in front of them. A corporal saluted.

"Where are your weapons?" Takahashi demanded. Retreating soldiers who abandoned their weapons were supposed to be shot. The man shrugged. "Have any water?

The corporal handed over his full canteen and Takahashi offered it to Tomi, who refused to drink despite his thirst. He was afraid of contaminating the others.

The corporal's tunic badge was bright white outlined in green. "You are a musician?" Tomi asked incredulously.

The man nodded. Takahashi said, "I'll bet an overconfident battalion commander planned to entertain his victorious troops. Could be this colonel we're dragging. Let's move."

Other dazed and wounded stragglers joined them. The further they traveled to the rear, the more men they collected. They reached a field hospital tent, where a thin, harried doctor peered through thick eyeglasses at the burned colonel; then sadly motioned to his assistant to drag him to triage with the rest of the dead and dying.

The doctor demanded, "Morphine! Have any morphine?" Tomi hesitated, then handed over his last two ampules. Takahashi gave the doctor his four vials. The doctor injected partial amounts of each ampule into a few patients writhing in pain. He returned and said, "We're completely out of supplies." He bummed a cigaret from a straggler and moved from stretcher to stretcher, puffing nervously as he soothed those he could not help.

Suddenly, many of the wounded scrambled off their stretchers and tried to crawl out the open-sided tent. One patient, both legs in splints and on his belly, clawed the ground like a turtle. Takahashi and Tomi were confused until they saw tanks and a skirmish line of infantry headed towards them.

With his longer legs, Tomi sprinted ahead of Takahashi and the others. He led the running men when a fist of heat hit his back. Takahashi helped him to his feet. A Soviet tank had opened fire. The first sighting round had gone long and hit those running away. The musician-corporal who had given them his water canteen was among the newly dead.

Survivors ran, hobbled and limped away until the Soviet tanks halted at the field hospital. They were still within cannon range, but Tomi was exhausted and had to stop. He waited for Takahashi and the others to catch up, and he wondered why he had bothered to run so hard. He might escape the Russians but not the anthrax inside him.

The men looked at him, awaiting orders. Tomi faked calmness and scanned the hospital with his binoculars. The Russian and Mongol soldiers were bayoneting the severely wounded. Tomi handed the glasses to Takahashi, who cursed, then passed them to the doctor who had been last to join the group because he was assisting a man with a bad leg wound.

The doctor twisted the lens rings to focus the binoculars against his thick eye glasses and instantly regretted it. He cried as he watched the massacre. Unlike the uncaring doctors and icy scientists of Unit 731, he mourned the slaughtered as if they had been his children.

"Who has weapons, food or water?" Takahashi gruffly demanded.

A trembling soldier with a shredded arm said, "Here, Sir," and gave Tomi a German-style potato masher grenade. Tomi shoved the smooth-cylindrical grenade into his sword belt. The 20-ounce heft felt good. Another patient gave Takahashi -- of all useless things -- a vomiting gas candle. He shrugged and stuffed the thin, 7-inch tube into his belt. No one had water or food. The only weapons were Tomi's pistol and sword, Takahashi's pistol and a few sharp instruments in the doctor's bag.

There were 35 in the group but Tomi, Takahashi, the doctor and his medic were the only ones who were not wounded. Takahashi drew Tomi aside and whispered, "The *Rushiyajin* are between us and our lines. Our only choice is to hide until nightfall; then try to sneak back."

Tomi checked his compass and Takahashi formed the men in a vertical line aimed toward the Japanese lines. He placed the less injured soldiers between severely wounded men and ordered them to be responsible for the weaker comrades' safety. No one was to move or talk.

The doctor tugged Tomi's sleeve. "I must move up and down the line."

"You'll give away our position to the enemy!"

"Some patients may bleed to death if I don't tend them."

Tomi cursed, then relented. "All right. But stay low. Order your patients not to cry out in pain or moan. If they make noise, the Russians will kill us all."

The doctor sighed. "I will try to do as you ask." He started to crawl away.

"Wait! I'm not finished. If a patient gets delirious or cries out when Russian infantry is nearby, I order you to silence him with your scalpel. Sacrifice one man to save 34 others. Remember what the *Rushiyajin* did at your hospital. Understand?" The doctor's meaningful stare held the promise to follow orders.

The men were frightened and Tomi didn't insult their intelligence by making the usual patriotic speech that Japanese officers usually did in hopeless situations. "Everyone lie down. Burrow yourself into the tall grass and remain still. If you shift your body, a sharp-eyed Russian will wonder how the grass moves without wind," Tomi said in a low voice. "We remain in place until dark. Then we'll move in a tight column to our lines. I'll lead. I have a compass so we won't get lost, as long as each of you follows the man in front. When we're moving, whisper my orders down the line from man to man. We will go at the slowest man's pace. No one will be left behind. If you hear the enemy approaching, don't panic and run. Our only hope is to remain hidden, no matter what happens. If you have to piss, do it in place."

Takahashi added, "That's better than having your big cocks shot off by a jealous Russian." The men giggled. Tomi was grateful his sergeant could relieve the fear and tension. He looked up at the sun. Four long hours until the cool darkness would fall on the baked Manchurian Plain.

Tomi had to give the hope needed for survival. "I want each of you to be a *tora,* a tiger, hiding in tall grass. You are sly and secretive. The near-sighted Russian bear cannot see the invisible Japanese *tora.* Those of you who had the foresight to bring along a bottle of sake and your number one geisha have my permission to enjoy yourselves as long as you remain horizontal and keep your pleasure groans to yourselves. Alas, I neglected to bring my favorite geisha. I'll never be promoted to captain with such lack of preparation." The men laughed.

"Now hide well, my *toras.*" As for the rest of you, those without caps, use a piece of khaki cloth or weave grass stalks to protect your heads from the sun. Doctor, move down the line and cut a button off each man's tunic. Soldiers, put your button in your mouth and suck it. The saliva will ease your thirst. Sleep if you can, or rest. We've got a long march tonight before we rejoin our comrades for breakfast."

After the men settled down, the only sound was the chatter of distant machine guns. Tomi wondered why Japanese long-range artillery hadn't opened up on the advancing enemy. They all heard the heavy rumble and Takahashi yelled above the noise, "A single tank is headed this way. No infantry. Everyone stay in place and hug earth!"

Tomi removed his steel helmet and raised his head for a peek. The T-34 was closing in at an angle. The tank's bow machine gun barrel moved back and forth like an insect's antenna, hunting for prey. The T-34 was so close Tomi could see the steel flanges of the bogey wheels turning the track. He gave the 'Stay in place' hand signal to Takahashi and crept through tall grass to the left side of the slowly moving tank.

When its turret was past him, Tomi got close and inhaled belching exhaust. Too bad the fumes can't kill anthrax, he thought, but the tank was his opportunity to die honorably. In a low crouch, he kept pace with the tank. The metallic clanks, clatters and rumbles of the 10-ton monster were the sounds of his approaching death.

Tomi pulled the potato masher grenade from his belt, unscrewed the safety cap and hooked his finger inside the ring attached to the fuse wire. The grenade was activated when the thrower, who held the fuse wire ring, flung it at a target. But Tomi would have to shove the grenade deep inside the gap between the links in the track and one of five bogey wheels. If he acted too soon, the chemical fuse would be destroyed before it ignited the explosive. Tomi knew there was a five-second safety delay, but accurate fuses were rare.

The tank increased speed and ruined his timing. Gripping the grenade, he yanked the fuse wire ring with his right hand and counted, *Ichi. Ni. San.* When he reached, *Shi,* four, he shoved the grenade, handle first, deep between the steel track and flanged wheel. His fear-heavy feet dragged, and to keep from falling underneath, he grabbed the tank's sloping armor.

The dangling fuse wire wrapped around the revolving bogey wheel and tightened, trapping Tomi's finger in the grenade ring. He was hooked, and was being reeled in like a fish. His blubbering escalated into a long scream. Helpless, he shut his eyes as he was pulled to a certain gory death. The bogey wheel completed a rotation and released the wire and Tomi with it. Instead of losing his life or arm, Tomi only left behind half his trigger finger.

He rolled away from the tank as it rumbled toward Takahashi and the men. The fuse was probably crushed before igniting. Tomi's clumsiness would kill his men. His thoughts of defeat were shattered by an explosion, and he thanked the gods for sloppy fuse makers.

The left steel track traveled through the bogey wheels and flopped off. But the right track continued and spun the tank around toward Tomi. A pair of round green eyes stared at him through the horizontal slit visor. He dove under the tank. There was just enough space to crawl to its midpoint as the crippled tank revolved in a tight circle. The machine gun chattered and the cannon fired a round harmlessly into the distance. The tank engine stopped, and all was quiet.

He frantically thought about how to exploit the tank crew's momentary confusion. If he fired his pistol into the slit, other *Roshiyajin* would close the visor and spray the area with gunfire, killing his men.

Takahashi approached the tank from the rear, holding the vomiting gas candle. The Russians' bow machine gun fired aimlessly, high in the air. Tomi crawled out and saw Takahashi yank the bottom metal ring and drop the candle into the open slit.

The cannon turret was located far forward, enabling Tomi to climb up the rear deck and perch behind the turret hatch cover. Takahashi joined him, pistol in hand. They didn't know how many men were inside or if there was an escape hatch underneath. Takahashi cocked his pistol and Tomi held his sword in his bloody right hand.

The turret hatch cover banged open and a brown leather aviator's helmet popped up. Tomi swung his sword and the man fell back inside the tank. The hatch clanged shut.

Tomi had been overanxious. Takahashi swore and yelled, "Let me get the next one with my pistol!" The vomiting tank crew could remain safely buttoned up until help arrived. Or they could discover that the Japanese on their tank were toothless.

Tomi and Takahashi heard the men cheering. They stood in full view if they were at a schoolyard game. Afraid that the machine gunner would mow them down, Tomi stamped his boots on the turret and angrily yelled, "You fucking fools! Get down! The *Roshiyajin* will shoot you."

The hatch opened and a raised pair of arms emerged. The tankers thought Tomi's irate boot stomping was the sound of a satchel charge being attached. Takahashi barked, " If they find out how fucking weak we are, we'll be the prisoners."

He grabbed one raised arm and twisted it up. The screaming Russian quickly emerged. Takahashi clubbed him with his pistol butt, kicked him off the tank and yelled to the men, "Grab him!" The second and third crewmen followed and were shoved off the tank, half-blind and still vomiting. Tomi looked inside the tank and saw the skull he had sliced with his sword.

A Russian on the ground realized the Japanese were unarmed, wounded wretches and babbled in his ugly language to his comrades. "Doctor," Tomi ordered, "silence that Russian!"

The doctor calmly adjusted his glasses, inserted his scalpel in the man's neck and deftly released blood from the carotid artery he had opened. Now there were only two prisoners.

Takahashi yelled, "Unwind your puttees and bind and gag the prisoners as tightly as you can!" Squatting on the turret, Tomi scanned the horizon with his binoculars. No enemy. The men stared at the blood that flowed from his severed finger.

After the vomit gas cleared, Tomi ordered the men to search the tank for hand weapons, ammo, food and water. Three water canteens were found and two were given to the badly wounded. He wondered why the tank carried no rations.

The doctor stopped Tomi's bleeding and bandaged the half finger. "Attention!" the doctor shouted to the motley bunch of wounded stragglers. "Soldiers of Japan," he declared, "you will remember this day for the rest of your lives. Armed only with a sword in his bloody hand, this valiant officer and his sergeant captured a modern enemy tank. The *Samurai* spirit of these two heroes is more powerful than enemy armor."

Tomi and Takahashi flushed with pleasure as the bedraggled men roared *"Banzai!"*

With false sternness that earned more grins, Tomi said, "Before you celebrate with all the hot sake that we don't have, the plan is unchanged. Hide until dark and sneak back to our lines. We're taking the prisoners with us."

Even though he was a major, the doctor bowed and saluted. "Speaking for my patients, we are confident that your inspired leadership will see us to safety." Tomi returned his salute.

The doctor introduced himself as Major Okita. For a few exhilarating moments, Tomi forgot he was a walking dead man. He didn't tell the doctor that he was a probable plague carrier. Both he and Takahashi were needed to get the group to safety. And they did, reaching the Kwantung Army lines shortly after dawn, exhausted and dehydrated but safe.

The defeated army was a sad sight. Confused men wandered around aimlessly and few orders were given. Takahashi stayed with the men while Major Okita and Tomi went to the commanding general's tent. Two officers were holding General

Komatsubara's arms. "I must kill myself! Release me," he begged. "I've disgraced the Emperor and the Army."

"Sir, we need your valuable guidance now more than ever," a colonel pleaded. "Please, Sir, save what's left of the division. You haven't slept or rested. You're exhausted. This defeat isn't your fault and you know it."

The general slumped into a chair. He looked older than when Tomi had seen him two days ago. Embarrassed by the scene, the staff officers turned to Major Okita. "*Okita-San*, so glad you made it back. We had a report that your field hospital was overrun. How did you escape?"

Major Okita told how Tomi and Takahashi had disabled an enemy tank. "I will never forget how he stood on the tank, sword in his bloody hand and stomping on the turret hatch. If not for his outstanding leadership and that of his sergeant, 35 of us would not have made it back through the Russian lines."

A colonel exclaimed, "One officer destroys a T-34 tank! What a wonderful thing! What is your name?"

Tomi saluted, bowed and gave his name. The officer stared at his tunic badge. "Tomigawa? Are you ... yes, of course you are the Tomigawa. But I thought you were Infantry, serving in Nanking. Since when are you *Kempetai*?"

"I'm temporarily assigned to Water Purification Unit 731 in Harbin, Sir."

Every field grade officer in the Kwantung Army knew the unit. Tomi and Sergeant Takahashi now had special status because they reported to Colonel Otomo, who reported to General Tojo, who was favored by *Showa Sama*, the God-Emperor. Japanese are not comfortable until they know each other's status, family background and connections.

"Ah! Now I remember you," General Komatsubara interrupted. "Did you distribute Colonel Otomo's gift? Not that it matters now."

"Sir, I failed to reach the enemy's water supply. I planted the material in a vehicle behind their lines."

"How soon will we know if it works?"

Tomi knew he had five days left if he had carried anthrax. He replied, "Within six days, Sir, if it's one bacterium, and ten days if it's another. I wasn't told which one we brought."

Doctor Okita took him to the crowded hospital, where they found Takahashi with the wounded. Okita disinfected Tomi's throbbing finger stump. "I must operate. Need to trim the bone and tissue for a proper skin flap," he said. "If I don't you'll have ugly scar tissue."

Tomi looked around the ward. Badly wounded men cried in pain but there weren't enough doctors or medics to care for them. Defeat overwhelmed everything. Nodding toward the confusion, Tomi said, "If not for me, you'd be helping them. Doctor, you're needed out there."

Okita hesitated, then nodded. "Take a bath and soak. Keep the wound absolutely dry. Get some sleep and meet me back here at nine." The doctor hurried away.

Takahashi scolded, "Tomi! Why didn't you tell the doctor about your germ infection?"

"I don't know what Otomo gave us. If it's anthrax, there's no cure. If I'm a plague carrier, you are one too. So it's too late. If we are not, why add panic to this sorry mess? Both of us were needed to get through the lines." Takahashi gave Tomi a sour look and went to the non-com's area. Tomi went to the officers' section.

So many officers had been killed or missing that Tomi had his choice of bunks. The division had been pushed back 20 miles, turning the elite division into a useless mob.

That night, Dr. Major Okita led Tomi to a tank repair shed, where they joined a somber group of officers. The mechanics had fled with other rear echelon troops. The disabled tanks around them were as useless as the ones destroyed in battle.

Tomi wondered why he was included in this private meeting. Amid metallic grime and the stink of grease, the officers squatted on ammo boxes arranged in a circle on the dirt floor. They chewed common soldiers' combat rations of canned fish, rice, salt and stale biscuits. Typical of the army's uneven supply system, food was scare but rice wine wasn't. They gulped large amounts of cold sake directly from big green bottles. When everyone was through, there were polite belches and all but Tomi lit cigarets.

The senior staff officer announced, "General Komatsubara is resting comfortably. His replacement arrives tomorrow. When we informed Kwantung HQ that the Russians unilaterally halted their advance, we were ordered to stand down. No counter-attack, no patrols or artillery barrages. In effect, it's a cease fire."

They silently absorbed the meaning. Defeat was final. The army would not send fresh troops to restore this battered division's honor. The senior officer continued, "Major Okita, I asked you here because we need some good news for a change. Would you please repeat the account of our guest's bravery?"

Okita's spirited retelling was accurate, but sounded like a knight's tale of old. Tomi noticed that ranking officers deferred to the doctor. For some reason, he enjoyed high status.

An infantry major asked Tomi, "What gave you the idea about stopping the tank?

"Desperation, Sir. I'd have shoved a rock in the tank track if that was all I had."

The officer scowled. "Tomigawa, your tank-destroying method can be copied by our infantry using satchel charges. What do you think of that?"

Tomi remembered how Hara's tank regiment was destroyed by the superior T-34's. To honor Hara's memory, Tomi said, "My encounter is a poor one to use as an example. My sergeant and I had extraordinary good luck, not skill. It was a solitary tank moving slowly. Trying to plant a heavy explosive on a fast T-34 tank with infantry support is suicidal."

"Nonsense!" the major blustered, "all we need are valiant men willing to die for the Emperor. After the enemy tanks pass our men hidden in camouflaged holes, they will sneak out and attach their charges." He sneered. "I was going to call it the Tomigawa Technique, but your lack of enthusiasm precludes that honor!"

"Thank you, Honorable Major, for not connecting my name to certain failure!" Tomi retorted. The officer's eyes flicked to Tomi's *Kempetai* badge, tightened his lips and left.

"It's because of that fucking Zhukov!" someone said to change the subject.

"Forgive me, but what's a Zhukov?" Tomi asked. Everyone laughed.

The senior staff officer smiled ruefully. "Not what. Who. Zhukov is the Soviet lieutenant general who defeated us with his speed, shock and surprise tactics." He arranged empty food cans and trash to represent the order of battle. Given war's confusion, military men needed to make sense of what happened. Learning defeat's lessons might result in future victories.

The colonel said, "Zhukov has reinvented warfare. Somehow, he and his brilliant chief of staff, Shtern, escaped Stalin's officer purge and took command at the border in June. The paranoid Soviets feared that the Kwantung Army was going to cut their Trans-Siberian railway, which was not true. Stalin gave General Zhukov 500 new T-34's, 500 aircraft, 20 cavalry squadrons and 35 infantry battalions."

The colonel sighed in rueful admiration. "Zhukov had the perfect corps for his new tactics. We were outnumbered 3 to 2 in infantry, and 3 to 1 in cavalry squadrons, plus all those T-34 tanks. The Russians also were superior in intelligence, command and control. Zhukov radioed misleading orders in an old code that he knew we had.

Because of this misdirection, we expected the Russians to form a defensive line for a prolonged stalemate. Captured Soviet officers we interrogated hours before the attack were unaware of Zhukov's true intentions. Then he attacked on August 20th. We were completely fooled.

"In the sky, Soviet bombers and fighters ripped through our air regiments in new 'zoom and boom' attacks. We were stunned by Zhukov's concentrated air, artillery and infantry assaults. It was unlike anything we had ever seen before. His Russian and Mongolian infantry were well-trained and well equipped, not like the disorganized peasant-draftees we beat in China. When we moved up our reserves to reinforce the entire front, Zhukov's main tank force speared through our flank like sword through paper, and surrounded us. When we reacted to the threat, Zhukov used armor units as pincers, making inner encirclements. At that point, Zhukov's corps was the meat grinder and we the pork."

Tomi remembered all the burned bodies and knew he was a coward, but the incompetent generals in Tokyo created the defeat. The colonel said, "Do not repeat this, but we lost 20,000 to 25,000 of our troops. Another 20,000 are wounded or missing. About 40% of our tanks were destroyed or badly damaged."

"What happens now, Sir?" Tomi boldly asked him.

"Only a commanding general can give an informed answer, and my personal opinion might be unpopular," he nodded to Tomi. "You have an honorable reputation. I trust you not to repeat what I say here." Tomi bowed low in agreement.

The officer said slowly, "The empire can only be expanded to the south, against weaker, less alert *gaijin*."

After a meaningful pause, someone said, "The Soviets call their victory 'Khalkin-Gol,' or the 'River Halka Battle.' Tokyo calls it 'The *Nomonhan* Incident,' after the village where the battle started. In Mongolian, *Nomonhan* means Peace."

The colonel added, "The Soviets don't want to start a war. Stalin ordered Zhukov to halt after giving us a bloody nose. Gentlemen, forgive my sake-oiled tongue. I've mislead you into a speculative discussion beyond my knowledge and authority. Analysis will be done by our knowledgeable leaders. Let's get some sleep. Our new division commander arrives tomorrow."

Tomi's thoughts burned with treason. Tens of thousands soldiers died because the Kwantung Army had lost face in an earlier border skirmish. Did anyone but map makers care what side of the Halka River the Mongolians pissed into? Tomi no longer lusted for a hero's death. He knew that soldiers in all armies were tiny ants who all smelled the same when roasted.

CHAPTER TEN
TOKYO, SEPTEMBER 1939

Doctor-Major Okita was the eldest son of an influential newspaper publishing family. His hero-worship and the government's wish to mask the defeat made Tomi and Takahashi valiant heroes of the *Nomonhan* Incident. The *Kempetai* produced a recruiting poster showing an idealized Tomi and Takahashi on a destroyed Russian tank with piles of bodies around them.

Tomi was grateful for the accolades that had freed his mother and Taiko. But they both behaved strangely at their brief reunion. "Were you harmed or mistreated?" he asked his mother.

"Of course not! We were threatened, but unmolested. Still, it was a frightening experience. Wasn't it, Taiko?"

Taiko nodded silently. Lady Tomigawa sighed. "Living with fear is the same as living in a prison. But thanks to you, my brave son, we are free again. All is well now, isn't it, Taiko?" Without waiting for a reply, she told Taiko to prepare green tea.

"Tell me everything that happened from the moment you reported to Colonel Otomo."

Tomi omitted the horrors of the logs and helping Ruth the *Wei Wei* escape. His mother, in turn, gave scant details of her house arrest. Neither mentioned General Hashimoto's torture-murder. The reunion was crowded with unspoken thoughts.

Perhaps that made Tomi untypically blunt when he later reported to General Suzuki. "Since Colonel Otomo promised Suzuki Enterprises a fifth of all contracts, my attempt to get information was unnecessary, Sir."

"Yes. But it was your mother who attracted suspicions and placed you in jeopardy. It is lucky things turned out well," Suzuki retorted. "Are you following European events?"

"I'm sorry. I haven't had time, Uncle."

"The outbreak of war gives us a golden opportunity, but we must hurry before our friend, Hitler, grabs all the spoils. I am supervising a number of civilian programs to put us on a war footing. It is where I can do the most good."

Most good for Japan, or Suzuki Enterprises? Tomi wondered. He tried to discuss quality control of Suzuki bacterial protective gear and fuses, but the general interrupted, "Save those boring subjects for another time, Nephew."

Hara's ghost made Tomi persist. "Sir, will the War Preparation Board create a quality control inspectorate? It would improve Army procurement. And, considering our recent failures against the Soviets, will there be a armament improvement center as well?

Suzuki aimed his monocled eye at Tomi, "For some reason, your Mongolian skirmish has altered your interests. And not for the better."

"My apologies, Sir, for being so forward, but the views of experienced combat officers might be valuable when new designs are made. If our medium tank carried the high velocity cannon that many tank officers had requested, we would have acquitted ourselves better."

"Experts more knowledgeable than you are in charge of quality control. The designers and engineers know the limits of our resources better than junior officers! It is not your concern. Concentrate on matters closer to home, Nephew, especially with Taiko. Your days of risky escapades are over until you give us sons! You are capable, aren't you?"

Tomi knew Hara had been right: Many would die because of leaders like his stubborn uncle.

***

Tokyo was gloomier than Tomi remembered. With Imperial Palace approval, Suzuki and his clique of industrialists instituted price controls and import restrictions, which created instant shortages. Fleets of charcoal-burning buses replaced the gasoline burners. Consumer goods became scarce as factories shifted to war production. Patriotism became superheated and dissent was squelched as government ministries put a Japanese face on propaganda copied from ruthless Axis partners in Berlin and Rome. All things Western were frowned upon, from women's hair permanents to once-popular European-style clothing. Patriotic men began to wear khaki-colored 'people's uniforms,' and women, *mampos*, work pantaloons.

Tomi's western-educated wife no longer baited him during pillow talk. "It's difficult for us, Tomi," she complained moments after they had finished routine sex.

"Western goods are scarce even at the best *departmento* stores. I've heard that many imported items can only be gotten through the black market, run by horrible *Yakuza* gangsters. If it weren't for Uncle's influence, we'd be wearing rags."

Several days passed before Tomi found an excuse to visit his mother overnight. When he tried to make love with Taiko, she refused. "What's wrong, beloved?" Tomi held her. In a dead voice she whispered, "They came to my room every night."

"Who?"

"The *Kempetai* guards. One of them hurt me. He said I deserved sexual punishment for serving in a bad household. I pleaded. I begged. He showed no mercy. I am so sorry, my love."

Tomi was filled with anger, guilt, pity and hatred. Taiko suffered because of his actions and his mother's feeble conspiracy. Yet Taiko comforted him as he wept in helpless rage.

"What about the female chaperone?"

"No chaperone. The filthy ones said that if I failed to cooperate with proper enthusiasm, they would take sexual comfort from Lady Tomigawa, turn me into a comfort woman and send my family to a labor camp. I had no choice. They injured me badly, *Tomichan*. I go to the medical clinic every week. I can only give you my spiritual love. All else is gone. Dishonor and disease fill my body. I am so sorry. I wanted to see you tonight, one last time before I kill myself."

Tomi tried to kiss her, but she turned away. "No! I'm a diseased shell. Nothing is left of me."

Silently, they held each other through the night. No words existed for such loss. It was as if they were dead, but still able to suffer. Tomi regretted that he hadn't stepped on a mine in

Pingfang.

"Bad things happened to you because of me. Mother and you were confined here because of my actions. What the guards did is my fault. I am the guilty one. If you kill yourself, then tomorrow I too, will die so that our spirits will join."

"No, *Tomichan!*" She leaned down and kissed the ugly scar of his finger stump.

Erotic memories flooded him. Tomi gasped, "As long as you remain in this life, I will also remain. Take your own life, and I will follow you. Please stay alive for both of us."

Taiko was quiet for a long time, then whispered, "I'll remain alive for you."

Their tears mingled and she let him kiss her chastely before she left. The sad night mocked old memories. They were now different people.

If Taiko took her life, he doubted that he would follow her. But he had to avenge her dishonor. He left before dawn without farewells. If he saw his mother's aristocratic face, he would lose control. Taiko suffered to save Lady Tomigawa from humiliation.

The next night, he vented his impotent rage on his wife with repetitious intercourse. The selfish one wallowed in comfort and the selfless one suffered.

***

Lady Tomigawa pretended all was well when she joined a beaming General Suzuki and his niece in General Tojo's office for a private ceremony honoring Tomi's heroism. Tomi cared only that Tojo once headed the Kwantung Army's *Kempetai,* among other influential posts. The Palace's ascending star, Tojo was nicknamed *Kamison,* 'The Razor' for his keen intelligence. He was now Vice Minister of War and head of the Secret Service.

His dark eyes and thin lips were exaggerated by his shaven head, grey-black moustache and dark-framed glasses. He was cordial as he awarded Tomi the highest level of the Order of the Golden Kite; another Wound Badge; and the Order of The Sacred Treasure for *Koro Sho,* exceptional service.

General Suzuki pompously thanked Tojo for the high honor

bestowed upon the Suzuki-Tomigawa family, who would strive to excel in its loyal service to the *Showa Sama.*" Tomi would have been happier if Suzuki had pledged quality control of his military production lines. After posing for the official photograph, General Suzuki lost face when General Tojo pointedly asked Tomi to join him in an adjoining office.

"You will immediately return to Harbin," Tojo ordered.

Tomi hid his panic with a calm bow. "Yes, Sir."

General Tojo softly waved a negative hand gesture. "Hah, forgive my little jest. You will be there for two months to train your replacement. It is Colonel Otomo's express wish. I have new duties for you here that will prove interesting."

Relieved that his days at the death factory would end, he took a risk as great as inserting the grenade in the tank track.

"General Tojo, Sir. I apologize for what I'm about to ask. Please forgive me."

"Asking forgiveness at a medal ceremony? I was told you are an odd one."

"Sir, I would gladly exchange the great honor you have given me for two requests that only you have the power to grant." Tojo's wary nod permitted Tomi to continue. He bowed and held the low position. Staring at the floor and quivering with fear, he used the formal classic style. "This humble person, with temerity beyond his station, begs for the names of two who guarded the Lady Tomigawa during her recent house detention."

"And your second request?"

Tomi straightened. "Sir, Doctor-Major Okita, 35 wounded soldiers and I are alive because of the bravery of this humble one's sergeant. When I depart from Unit 731, security will be more efficient, thanks in part to this Sergeant Takahashi. But his value to Unit 731 will diminish should he remain there after my transfer."

Tomi returned General Tojo's stare, fearing Takahashi would be left in the medical madhouse.

"Have you been informed about what is happening in Mongolia?

"No, Sir."

"An epidemic is sweeping through the Russian border

divisions. Our spies tell us that Soviet first aid stations and hospitals are crowded with patients having fever, dysentery, coughing and debilitating headaches. Do you know what disease they suffer?"

"No, Sir."

"Typhoid. Colonel Otomo insists it is no coincidence. He was most pleased with your delivery of his bacteria during the tank battle. This may bode well when you request your sergeant's transfer from Colonel Otomo. Your first request is out of the question. Your motive may be understandable, but the outcome is not in the national interest. Forget petty, personal things. *Dai Nippon Teikoku*, The Empire of Greater Japan, requires the zeal of the *Kempetai*. Every military police officer knows he will be punished for under-performance of duties, but never for exceeding them. Think of what is best for *Nippon*, not your own interests.

"Upon completion of the Pingfang training, report back here. We will see if your strange way of solving difficult problems has more value than your lost trigger finger." General Tojo showed his mild irritation over Tomi's impertinence by ignoring his salute.

Takahashi's fate hung in the balance, and Tomi could not inflict revenge on Taiko's torturers. He had medals but no power. The Nanking priest's words haunted him.

Tomi escorted his mother home in silence. Inside the house, she shed all pretense and sighed. "Poor little Taiko is at the clinic for her weekly treatment. Nasty complications."

"Where's your decency? You know what she means to me, yet you didn't help her. You slept as she was being savaged. Why didn't you beg your influential friends to do something? When your safety and comfort are at risk, you are selfish and callous!"

"Are you quite done?" Her flushed face showed hurt. "You, who lack political comprehension, are a blind man who stumbles about in a world of all-seeing eyes. I'll teach you a few obvious truths, but after I'm gone, don't expect your bright but spoiled wife to be as patient.

"Had I been sexually abused by those barbarians, I would have committed suicide and the *Kempetai* would claim it was an admission of guilt. And you, my son and fellow conspirator, would have been arrested, tortured and executed, just like my dearest friend, General Hashimoto. I could not let you, the last Tomigawa, die in disgrace.

"By brutalizing little Taiko right under my own roof, I lost face, but the *Kempetai* were content with that punishment. We were viewed as political opponents, not spies or traitors. It's the difference between a horrible death and a shamed life. Had I allowed my maidservant to die by her own hand, the Tomigawas would lose face and signal the end of the family legend. And you would have rotted in Harbin while General Suzuki would get someone else's sperm. Or, if servant rumors are to be believed, added his own to continue the dynasty."

Ugly reality jolted Tomi out of his blindness.

"My only counter-move was silence. Yes, I heard poor Taiko being sexually tortured at night. It was horrible. But to save you and the Tomigawa line, I said nothing. Had Taiko been my daughter, I would have done the same. The family must not end this way."

Her voice was strong, her gaze direct. "You were as much a hostage as we were. As long as you were alive and at risk, I restrained myself from stabbing or poisoning those *Kempetai* beasts. Saying and doing nothing was the hardest thing I ever did. I love Taiko as much as you. When trapped by Destiny, one endures what cannot be endured. May you never have to face this choice."

"Their names?"

"They never formally introduced themselves," she snapped. But he knew that look. She was the cat about to pounce on the unaware mouse. She wanted something from him.

"You found out from other sources?" Tomi demanded. Her silence revealed that she knew and was still involved with her amateur conspirators.

"Their names?" Tomi repeated through gritted teeth.

"A trade: Their names for your vow to seek revenge my way ... not yours."

"Why should I agree?"

"Your foolish kind of revenge will end in your death. If you want *fukushuu*, vengeance, first swear upon your honor that you

-161-

will follow my strategy. The details I leave to you."

Lady Tomigawa revealed her scheme after he uttered his vow. His hot anger blended with reluctant admiration for her logical, cold thinking. She was a witch.

"Now, tell me their names."

She said each syllable as a profanity soiling her lips.

***

Neither Colonel Otomo nor Unit 731 had changed. The colonel looked at Tomi's ugly finger stump with clinical interest. "Untidy amputation. A butcher could have done it better."

"There wasn't time to do it properly, Sir."

"It will bother you later. Does it hamper your brush work?"

"I try to write with my other hand now."

"I am told you compose poems."

"A long time ago, Sir. No longer."

If Tomi's poetry was news to Otomo, it meant he had just received an updated *Kempetai* report. Yet Otomo's attitude was casual, not angry. The scientist wore his newest medal for infecting Soviet border troops with disease.

Tomi's initial meeting with Otomo was a political game of *Go*, a game with simpler rules than chess, but more complex in strategy. "I never cared for poetry, except for a line by the American, Emerson," Otomo said, turning a framed calligraphy toward Tomi. The exquisite Chinese characters read, "All life is an experiment. The more experiments you make, the better."

"Certain personages in Tokyo said you requested that Sergeant Takahashi return to Tokyo with you. The decision is mine. Why should I release a good non-com?"

"Sir, to answer that question, I first must point out two areas of weakness at Unit 731."

"Weaknesses? You, the security officer, indict yourself?"

"Hardly, Sir," Tomi said with a pleasant smile that didn't offend. "While I was completing the Mongolian mission, I thought about our security arrangements. With your permission, Sir? Here are the two weak points," Tomi said, pointing to the pregnancy dormitory and minefield on the wall map. "Sir, you may recall my

-162-

embarrassment when I found a guard inside a pregnancy log."

"Of course. You did well to quickly execute him and get rid of the subject."

"Thank you, Sir. But the possibility still exists that a guard might be secretly taking sexual comfort from a log, or even helping her escape through the minefield to waiting accomplices."

Otomo chuckled. "What a bizarre thought! Who would want a log that badly?"

Knowing Otomo's craving for precision, Tomi said, "Given the current security status, I estimate the likelihood of such an event to be 3 to 5 percent. Unit 731 is vital and requires nothing less than 100 percent security."

"And you propose ... ?"

"Expand the punishment, Sir. *Kempetai* suspected of taking unauthorized comfort from subjects and all other guards at or around the same location should be put in the harshest experiment projects instead of the quick death that I, in my anger, imposed on the guilty one. To save their own skins, the guards will constantly monitor each other. No one will contaminate your pregnancy research study again."

Colonel Otomo laughed, as if he knew something that Tomi didn't. "Now what's this nonsense about escaping through the minefield?"

"Why does Unit 731 have to use big, clumsy Navy mines festooned with trip wires that are visible to trespassers? Only modern anti-personnel mines, hidden under soil, should be used. The Russian border is quiet now, so modern mines should be available."

"Yes, that makes sense. What else?"

"Add more, better trained guards and divide the security force into two separate units, Sir. One section should be assigned to perimeter patrols and the other section will be used as interior guards."

Otomo smirked. "Put your proposals into effect immediately. Now, about Sergeant Takahashi. Losing a loyal, dedicated officer like you is bad enough. Why should I relinquish your equally loyal, dedicated assistant?" he asked with slow sarcasm.

"Sir, when Sergeant Takahashi and I complete the new

training of your expanded guard force, he and I will be the most disliked men here. If Sergeant Takahashi is left here alone, he'll become an infectious source of animosity. Some *Kempetai* will be loyal to him and others will resent his strict rule. Such dissension in the ranks might undo the improvements."

Colonel Otomo chuckled, "You will never know how much amusement you provide me."

Mystified by Otomo's attitude, Tomi added, "The caliber of your *Kempetai* should be raised."

"Why? Has anyone ever escaped from here?"

"No, Sir. But the remote possibility of escape can be eliminated by upgrading personnel as a prevention. Many *Kempetai* commanders retain the best men for themselves and we get what is available from a personnel pool that may sometimes be mediocre. But the Otomo Unit deserves the best, toughest guards who are now serving in elite Tokyo units. I know of such men by reputation. Your personnel requisitions, which have the highest priority, can specifically ask for individuals by name. Thus, Sergeant Takahashi and I will make certain that Pingfang Castle is escape-proof. I vow this upon the honor of my ancestors."

Otomo smiled smugly. "How did you come up with such novel suggestions? If I didn't know better, I'd say you had planned such an escape."

Tomi grinned as if being complimented. "I tried to think like a bored guard with a predawn erection who has the key to a dormitory filled with maidens. It's the same awareness that enabled us to improve fire prevention of your record storage."

"I had intended to reject your proposals, but prevention ... hmm. Begin at once!"

"Yes, Sir. And Sergeant Takahashi?"

"His transfer is conditional upon three things: my satisfaction with his replacement, the upgrading of guards and a marked improvement in security."

Tomi vowed, "I will work day and night until your objectives are achieved." Otomo's laughter followed him out.

***

Takahashi had preceded Tomi to Pingfang, and they greeted each other as brothers. Tomi told him how he planned to avenge Taiko's torture-rapes and his effort to get Takahashi transferred from Unit 731. Instead of gratitude, Takahashi scolded, "Why jeopardize yourself by trying to get me out? You and your *Samurai* loyalty! You don't understand how we peasants survive under the heels of the highborn. We are safest when ignored. Otomo will be suspicious now that you revealed Ruth's escape route. You've lost your mind as well as your finger!"

"Takahashi, the closer the lie is to the truth, the easier it is to believe. I'll get those two bastards transferred here. But yes, Otomo did behave like the fox who ate the pet rabbit. Almost as if he were playing an unknown prank on me. No matter. I'll have my vengeance, and you and I will leave this hell hole together."

Takahashi sighed disagreement, but dutifully prepared personnel requisitions. They cobbled a severe training program and an expanded *Kempetai* unit. Takahashi asked, "When the two Tokyo dogs get here, how do we kill them? What about defective protective suits?"

"Accidents raise suspicion. We set the trap and their own cruel natures will spring it shut. They don't know that I know who they are. They will get promotions with the transfer and secretly gloat over my ignorance. It's up to you to keep them away from me. Put them on the pregnancy project. Confide that, despite standing orders, the senior non-com on night duty often takes sexual comfort from the women during his inspection rounds. Stress that it's a privilege forbidden to lower ranks. They won't doubt you."

"Then I discover them in the act and arrest them?"

"No. They enjoy hurting women. I'll suggest to the project scientist that he have the logs routinely examined every morning for semen and bruises. Arrange to put the two on the same shift after our departure. They will be caught after we're back in Tokyo.

"About our replacements, do you have any candidates in mind? There are many bright officers at the depot eager for my job, but excellent senior non-coms are rare. We need someone who will impress Colonel Otomo as much as you have."

Takahashi chuckled, "The answer is in front of you, Tomi.

You're increasing the *Kempetai* by 40%, making the unit almost as big as an infantry company! You can upgrade our positions. Have a captain replace you and a second lieutenant replace me. Unlike you, most officers confuse rank with competency. Colonel Otomo will view the higher ranking replacements as proof of improvement." Takahashi briskly rubbed his nose and frowned, "But what if the bastards don't take the bait? Your chance for revenge will be lost forever."

"They are sadists with power over defenseless women. They will act according to their nature. That will destroy them."

"You are a dangerous enemy."

Tomi grunted, "You haven't met my mother."

When Takahashi and Tomi left Pingfang 60 days later, the improvements were complete. The higher-ranking officer replacements and additional guard force pleased Colonel Otomo. The two brutes would assume night shift duty the following month. Tomi felt no guilt because the women involved were doomed, no matter what happened.

Takahashi learned that Ruth's family had disappeared shortly after her escape. He sighed as the train left Harbin. "They are probably across the Russian border. I'll never see her again."

Tomi wondered which of them suffered the worst curse: never to see one's love again, or to see a loved one suffer the rest of her life?

CHAPTER ELEVEN

The sight of *Shinju Minato*, Pearl Harbor, inspired Tomi's first poem since Nanking:

> *America's sword*
> *Pointed at Nippon's bare throat*
> *Glitters dire menace.*

Only 90 days ago, the Yankee Pacific Fleet sailed to Honolulu from San Diego to intimidate Japan. Once a sleepy Navy coaling station, Pearl Harbor was a fortified island bristling with warships, hundreds of bombers and pursuit planes and several infantry divisions, as well as countless fuel, munitions and supply depots. Its dry docks were big enough to cradle battleships. Indestructible Pearl Harbor was designed to thwart Japan's destiny.

Tomi leaned over the rusty rail as the old freighter slowly moved past endless clusters of white oil storage tanks. He remembered General Tojo's tirade over the embargo: "80% of our oil comes from the Yankee giant. Now they halt oil, steel and scrap iron shipments and freeze our assets. We have no choice but war!"

Tomi had boarded the filthy tramp steamer in Port Arthur, posing as a fireworks salesman calling on wholesalers in Honolulu. He was to claim that his face scars and missing finger resulted from a fireworks accident. Because Tomi's photo had been printed in newspapers, he grew a wispy moustache and wore awkward eyeglasses.

General Tojo's instructions to Tomi were uncharacteristically vague. "We have more than enough spies who report the obvious. You are said to have a fresh eye. Look for the unusual."

Tomi respected Tojo. One of his staff meetings was worth a month elsewhere. Tojo's total recall put Tomi's to shame. While others fumbled with calendars, Tojo knew the day of the week for any date of the next ten years. When he commanded two brigades in Manchuria, he once introduced 124 of his officers, each by name and unit, without error. A tyrant to underlings, Tojo's keen intellect earned him the Emperor's trust.

Yet it was not General Tojo, but Tomi's uncle-by-marriage who best explained Japan's accelerated race toward war. "Thank the gods ten thousand times a thousand for the European war!" General Suzuki had said during their last dinner before Tomi left for Hawaii.

"Germany's amazing victory over the French, English and the Dutch will enable us to capture their southeast Asian colonies. After we attack the U.S. Navy, our German and Italian allies will declare war on America. The new timetable has Palace blessing." He added wistfully, "Some of us who sought three more years of preparation must obey. Even Tojo wishes for more time."

"Why wait three years, Uncle?"

"The Americans threaten us, but they have not mobilized. For political reasons, they remain on a peacetime economy, while we need much more time to consolidate the resources of Southeast Asia, especially oil. But our Navy believes we must start the war by destroying America's Pacific Fleet at Pearl Harbor because it threatens our extended shipping lanes. They assume the Yankees will be stunned and beg for a quick peace. I hope the navy's confidence isn't just impatience in disguise."

Several top admirals who openly opposed war with America backed off when others threatened to resign. The Japanese trinity of duty, hierarchy and harmony trumped common sense.

"I thought the Imperial General Staff prefers action sooner rather than later, Uncle," Tomi gently countered, remembering General Tojo's rage over the Yankee oil embargo.

"Dear Nephew," Suzuki chided, "Astute men in Japan and America have known for years that the Pacific isn't big enough for both nations. We need Asia's raw materials, and the Americans jealously guard their historic trade interests. 'Pacific' may mean 'peace' in *Eigo*, but it is where we will have to fight.

"Too much war preparation is wasteful; too little is disaster," General Suzuki droned as he glided into another of his annoying lectures. "Three decades ago, astute preparation enabled the Imperial Navy to destroy the Russian Czar's armada and army because they were at the end of a long supply line. We had better ships, better leadership, a brilliant surprise attack, and the short supply line. When we attack Hawaii, we will be the ones with longer, exposed supply lines."

Tomi looked at Pearl Harbor's modern facilities and was nagged by General Suzuki's assumption: "... only if we severely damage America's Pacific Fleet." How can Japan cripple an invincible force of nine battleships, three aircraft carriers, seven light and heavy cruisers, seventeen destroyers, three sub tenders and countless smaller craft and submarines? The two huge tank farms Tomi just passed contained 4,500,000 barrels of oil and aviation gasoline -- a six-month supply. Yankees swim in oil while Japan rations its supply.

After checking into a dingy hotel near the waterfront, Tomi went for a walk. His was the only hotel for blocks without lines of American military men patiently waiting outside lobby doors guarded by burly American military police. Tomi immediately recognized the familiar sight of men lined up for *ianfu*, comfort women. The civilian hotels had become American brothels for their servicemen. Military sex comfort was the same everywhere. When American soldiers and sailors were assigned new posts, they needed brothels until they met girlfriends. The long waiting lines confirmed to Tomi that the Americans had recently reinforced their garrisons and the fleet.

Honolulu was as commercial as Tokyo's *Ginza*, crammed with bars, nightclubs, restaurants, hotels, souvenir shops and movie theaters. The men in khaki and white uniforms were round-eyes, but the civilian population consisted of every hue, color and eye shape. They were Asians, but not a pure race of human beings, like the Japanese.

His first American meal was bad fish, overpriced, overcooked and overaged. He wandered into a newsreel theater and paid an exorbitant U.S. 10-cent admission. A Japanese first class private who made the U.S. equivalent of $2.07 a month couldn't afford to live here. Then again, an American army private received $21 a month, about the same as Tomi's officer pay. America was rich, yet they embargoed and threatened *Nippon*.

The Movietone Newsreel featured Europe's war. Tokyo newspapers were filled with pro-German stories and photographs of England's devastation by Luftwaffe bomber raids, a prelude to Hitler's cross-Channel invasion. This American cinema showed canny British propaganda: mass destruction of civilian homes mixed with footage of cheerful civilians going about their daily activities, as if the air raids could destroy buildings but not the admirable people's spirit.

Tomi was thankful that Tokyo, with its crowded miles of wood and paper screen houses, would never become an air raid target. Japan's leaders were too intelligent to allow that to happen. The newsreel showed fat-as-Chinese-dumplings barrage balloons streaming steel cables over London's skyline. The next scene showed grinning Englishmen with the neatly severed wing of a German bomber that had flown into a balloon cable. There were images of blazing anti-aircraft guns and workers frantically digging through rubble. The British message was clear: The island nation had high morale and remained undefeated, despite heavy German bombing.

***

On his first sales call the next morning, Tomi stuttered through a rehearsed speech and failed miserably. The arrogant purchasing agent, a tall *gaijin*, refused to buy, but Tomi managed to get decent orders from the next two firms. Everyone was patient with his thick-accented English, and Tomi enjoyed the art of persuading someone to purchase goods. Of course, his fireworks sold for a pittance, because they were cheaply produced by Chinese slave laborers in an Army factory.

It was late when he made his final sales call of the day, at a small firm located in Honolulu's old warehouse district. A beautiful receptionist greeted him in *Eigo*. When Tomi handed her his business card, she read his alias, '*Tsurumi Koji*' and she replied in conversational Japanese, "Please be seated." Without bowing, she went into an office.

The furniture was neat and her typewriter was modern. It was a modest, prosperous company. The tall beauty led him to her employer, Misokushi. Ruddy-faced and middle-aged, he politely asked Tomi in Japanese, "Would you prefer to converse in *Eigo* or *Nihongo*?"

His eyes widened when Tomi's reply, "Japanese, please" was accompanied with a crisp military bow. A *machigai*, mistake!

"So it shall be. Tsurumi-San. May this one have the honor of admiring your honorable employer's commercial catalogue please?" He spoke in the high honorific form that confirmed the military officer's bow had not gone unnoticed. When Tomi handed him the thick catalog and price sheet, the man deliberately stared at Tomi's finger stump.

"Please be so kind as to inform this one of your terms and delivery schedule."

"Sixty days net and freight. If you need the shipment quickly, I will be happy to cable your order." Tomi wrote quickly as Misokushi read items selected from a typed list. The order was generous. When they were done, he asked if Tomi liked American food and they laughed over Tomi's awful fish dinner. He invited Tomi to have dinner at his home. Impromptu invitations were never made to a stranger in Japan.

That evening Tomi was greeted by Misokushi's receptionist in his western-style home. She smiled and said she was his daughter, Michiko. In equal-to-equal conversational Japanese, she told him, "Keep your shoes on, please; this is an American *Nisei* home. My grandfather came here to work as a laborer in the pineapple fields. The Honolulu Fireworks Company is the result of grandfather's back-breaking work and thrift. He was an original founder of the Hawaiian-Japanese Benevolent Society and a trustee of the Japanese Hospital."

Michiko's beauty, poise and casual sense of equality was off-putting. She was Japanese, but her facial expressions were American, open and candid. Nothing was hidden. She spoke in a rich, full voice instead of the artificial, high-pitched female tone demanded of women back home.

"I've never been to Japan. Father went back once with Grandfather's ashes," Michiko said. "Frankly, from what I hear about the treatment of Japanese women, I don't intend to visit." She sounded like Tomi's unpatriotic wife. Was the Japanese spirit so easy to shed?

The excellent fish dinner, served by an elderly mixed-race servant, was marred only by *gaijin* metal utensils. After dinner, Michiko excused herself. She had a date with her fiance'. The men relaxed on the screened porch. Misokushi said, "Robert is a very fine lad from a good family. He's *gaijin*. They met at the university and plan to marry next year."

Tomi didn't know how to respond to such abysmal news. He sipped his plum brandy.

"There is plenty of racial prejudice in this polyglot paradise, but things are slowly changing for the better. Besides, it is her decision, not mine."

What kind of Japanese father allowed his daughter decide whom she married? And to a *gaijin*? In a less polite tone, he asked Tomi, "First time out of Japan?"

"Yes. Forgive me, Misokushi-San. I hope I haven't inadvertently offended you with my ignorance. I am new to sales and new to Hawaii."

"You aren't new to some things." He raised his trigger finger and pointed to his face. "Army?"

Carefully, Tomi gave his rehearsed excuse, "I had a year in the Reserves before I got a job in the plant. Actually, my scars are from a fireworks accident."

Misokushi's flat "Ah so," was disbelief expressed politely. "Did you know that Japanese peasants were brought here on three-year contracts to work in the sugar cane fields after America's Civil War? The *dekasegi,* Japanese emigrants, were treated almost as harshly as the black ex-slaves of American missionaries and their rich, land-owning descendants

"Despite all that, some stayed and the Japanese community grew, fed by many waves of poor immigrants." He smiled. "And we've been here ever since, joining the native Hawaiians, Americans, Samoans, Portugese, Korean, Chinese, Indo-Chinese and everyone else."

The thought of so many different races sharing the island chain was dizzying. How can such a mongrel people do anything well? Tomi thanked the gods that he was of a pure race.

"At the risk of being an insensitive host, Tsurumi-San, I will make a political observation shared by our entire *Nisei* community. We are worried about the strained Japanese-American relations. It is clear to us that militarism in Japan is the same as the German and Italian versions. War jitters make everybody crazy. Nonetheless, we are loyal American citizens. Even though we Japanese-Americans suffered humiliation in the past, we cherish our economic and political freedom. We are much better off here than we would be had we been born in your homeland." He stared at Tomi. "Michiko's children and grandchildren will enjoy the benefits of both races in a land where hard work is rewarded by economic, if not social equality."

Tomi responded with intended coldness. "It's late. May I impose upon you to telephone a taxi for me? I thank you for your gracious hospitality. You've been most kind."

Misokushi reacted with superior-to-inferior bluntness. "Tell your superior officers back in Tokyo that we *Nisei* are loyal Americans. Understand? Goodnight."

That night, Tomi writhed like a speared eel in the soft, lumpy hotel bed. Misokushi knew he wasn't a salesman. Would he report Tomi to the American military police? Tomi concluded Misokushi was simply a businessman who wanted peace and prosperity to raise mixed-race grandchildren and sell fireworks. He was an idealist living a false dream, but Tomi wished him well.

The next morning, Tomi rented an Indian motorcycle for an outrageous amount. The bike lacked a windshield and he was forced to waste 3 more American dollars, almost the equivalent of Sergeant Takahashi's monthly pay, to buy goggles. How did poor people exist here? But unlike Tokyo, he saw no beggars and even stray dogs looked well-fed.

Downtown Honolulu was crowded with autos and weekend shoppers. By the time he became familiar with the awkward gear shift on the side of the gas tank and the oversized foot accelerator pedal, he joined the steady traffic stream. He passed the Naval District Headquarters main gate, where a pair of Marine sentries stood at attention. Were all Americans this alert?

On the open road, he crawled in low gear behind a slow line

of concrete mixer trucks. They finally turned off the highway through two pillars that advertised in bold *Eigo* letters the Hickam Air Corps Base entrance. Heavy building construction made Tomi wonder if they were reinforcing defenses.

He halted at a nearby station to top off the gas tank. Waiting his turn for the single pump, he heard the attendant brag to a customer, "Wait 'til they finish the new officers' club; we'll get lots more business from the base."

Japan and America were poised for war, yet the Yankees constructed a huge officers' club for pleasure instead of adding fortifications? Tomi was certain he had misunderstood.

He was approaching the north end of Pearl Harbor when a loud horn blared impatiently behind him. It was a khaki-colored Chevrolet open truck filled with stern-faced military policemen. His heart pounded as he edged to the side of the road. The *Nisei* traitor Misokushi must have reported him to the American *Kempetai!* Did they shoot spies in peacetime?

The truck passed and an arm popped out the assistant driver's side. Instead of the expected signal to halt, Tomi got a friendly wave of thanks and the truck raced ahead on the 2-lane asphalt highway. He pulled off the road and removed his goggles to wipe sweat, grime and a splattered bug from his face with a trembling hand.

When the military strode Tokyo's crowded avenues and streets, everyone, including police, fearfully deferred to the uniform. In Hawaii, the military presence blended in without special privileges. Civilians ignored the soldiers and sailors except in the crude hotel-brothels and bar areas. The servicemen, clad in bright civilian shirts and easily identified by short haircuts, were polite to civilians. Clearly, the military had a lower social status than at home. Hawaii, perhaps all of America, was topsy-turvy.

After a half hour of easy riding, he spotted a dirt road that led up the mountain. It took concentration and arm strength to keep the front tire out of deep ruts. Tomi was rewarded with a bare spot near the top with a harbor view. He killed the engine, lowered the kickstand and went to the cliff edge. His aching buttocks were forgotten as he gazed down at the anchored fleet in the startling blue water. The U.S. armada looked more like slate-grey toys on an ultramarine blue carpet than the steel fist of America's anti-Japan policy. He unbuttoned his fly and urinated down the cliff, toward the Yankee fleet below. The childish gesture made him feel patriotic.

Through a white cloud bank, the morning sun flickered on large white numerals on the sharp bows of destroyers. The battleships and heavy cruisers, their huge cannon barrels aligned, were moored 2-abreast in a long row. The only movement on the placid water was made by tiny launches, like water bugs, skittering between the anchored monsters. He followed the thin wake of one of them as it pulled alongside an aircraft carrier, its flight deck crammed with aircraft.

The peaceful sight was unlike the grainy newsreel films of bomb-wracked London. Shouldn't the Americans have a sky full of balloons over Pearl Harbor? Easily manufactured, barrage balloons were rubberized woven fabric bags of flammable hydrogen. Aloft for up to two weeks and fixed to stationary cable winches, they prevented aircraft from making low altitude attacks and precision bombing runs. Were the Americans so strong that they spurned passive defenses?

Tomi mounted his bike and went downhill. If an unqualified person like Tomi saw the obvious, then, he reasoned, experienced American commanders must have highly developed plans to thwart air attacks. Yet, Japan could not retreat from China as America demanded. General Suzuki had said, "If we obey Yankee demands, our expensive war preparations become a wasted investment, and Japan would be plunged into another depression. Such a thing must not happen."

Riding past pineapple fields, Tomi saw the familiar wide Japanese straw hats worn by peasants of both sexes. In Japan the lowborn and their children would remain field workers with hoes in their hands forever, but as Misokushi proved, a peasant's son can become a successful businessman and his daughter the college-educated wife of a *gaijin* in two generations. If mainland America was like Hawaii, then the lowest immigrant could carve out a prosperous future for his children. But where was the harmony and hierarchy necessary for a stable, obedient society?

He sped along the mountainous eastern spine of the island

past a blur of villages with unpronounceable names: Kahuku, Laie, Hauula, Kahana, Waiahole, Lanikai, Walmanalo. The magnificent Diamond Head view on Oahu's southern tip failed to cheer because he had seen nothing with his 'fresh eye.'

Back at the hotel, he had no appetite and fell asleep to the sounds of boisterous, drunken sailors and soldiers enjoying the rough neighborhood. All Tomi could celebrate was his sunburned face and saddle-weary bottom.

***

The next day was *Nichiyoobi*, Sunday. Tomi arose early, refused the disgusting coffee and spit out the single bite from a sickeningly sweet round pastry with a hole in its center. He pushed the motorcycle out of the hotel's storage shed and sped through the deserted downtown and residential neighborhoods before slowly passing Schofield Barracks at mid-island.

Further up the island, he saw groups of players on a golf course. He rode past a country club that resembled a Hollywood movie mansion. Eight blue-colored staff sedans in the circular driveway were decorated with front bumper placards that displayed the one and two big silver stars of Navy admirals. Perhaps it was an early morning naval conference.

Past the driveway, he impulsively turned onto a gravel side road that led to the rear of the country club. Dozens of military staff sedans were parked in neat rows in the wide lot. He dismounted, lowered the stand and knelt beside the motorcycle's rear wheel, pretending to examine the drive chain. Most of the cars had the distinctive humpback feature of new Ford sedans, but none had those placards with stars. He should not have stopped. He had risked discovery for nothing.

"Havin' trouble?" asked a thin sailor holding a thick mug of steaming coffee.

"No, Sir. Check chain."

"Don't sir me, buddy, I'm only seaman second," he said with a friendly grin.

"So sorry."

He remained kneeling, hoping the sailor would go away

before Tomi was arrested for being so near an important military conference.

"Wait a sec. I got a rag. Your chain got too much grease."

"Thank you," Tomi grunted, silently cursing the helpful *gaijin*. If Tomi sped away before he returned, he might raise alarm. He had to act calmly.

"Here," the sailor said when he returned from a nearby sedan with a clean cloth.

Tomi cleaned grit off the sprocket wheel and excess grease from the chain. He stood up, folded the rag clean side out, and returned it. He said in a careful accent, "Thank you very much," and remembered not to bow.

"You work here?"

"Aaah, cousin. Him on bike I take to work."

"Had a 1936 Indian like this back home. Same red paint job, but yours is in better shape. Paid 15 bucks for mine, a fuckin' wreck. Musta been 10th hand." Tomi smiled, not understanding one word in four. What did he want?

After an uncomfortable silence, the sailor asked, "Kin I take a quick spin?"

What was spin? His voice was deferential and he looked longingly at Tomi's motorcycle. Does he want to ride it? Tomi took a chance. "OK."

"Hold this," the sailor said and handed back the cloth in one hand and the white mug filled with heavily creamed coffee in the other. He mounted the motorcycle and said, "Drink the joe if ya want. It's fresh and us drivers git all we want." He pulled the bike off the stand, removed Tomi's goggles hanging from the gear shift knob and put them on. A single kick from his seated position started the warm engine. He grinned, pulling away slowly and smoothly.

A fat, balding *gaijin* kicked open the kitchen screen door, dumped something from a pot into an overfilled garbage can and stared at Tomi. "Whaddafuck ya doin? Stealin' our mug?"

"Sorry, Sir. Mistah Seaman Secon Navy man-driva borrow moto bike. This cup driva." He smiled politely.

The scowling *gaijin* grabbed the mug, spilling coffee. He examined Tomi. A big red-veined nose was not the ugliest of the man's features. His stained apron and rudeness indicated very low status. Tomi stared back, expecting him to drop his impolite gaze.

"What kinda slant are ya? Chink? Ya don't talk local."

"Yes, Sir. Japanese."

"Your lucky day, Mister Moto. Shit-ass helper's a no-show on the busiest fuggin' Sunday inna month. Wanna fill in? Two bucks fer the day, and eats."

Tomi didn't understand his strangely accented *Eigo* but the hostile look of expectation and sentence inflection was a question. He was trapped. "OK," he said and grinned to hide confusion.

"Well, whatcha waitin' fer?" He went inside. Obviously Tomi was expected to follow. How would he get his motorcycle back? If he didn't obey, he'd attract attention. Tomi put the folded rag on a garbage can lid and followed.

The brightly lit kitchen was hot with the aroma of roasting pork and Tomi's empty stomach cramped. The ugly man walked past a row of black ranges to a long conveyer belt on rollers. Midpoint on the belt was a steel tunnel with open ends covered by hanging strips of moldy canvas. At one end was a work area with a dirty sink and a reeking garbage can surrounded by stacks of wire crates filled with dirty dishes. The food on the plates looked as hard as the filthy concrete floor.

Tomi used the *gaijin* negative and shook his head from side to side when asked, "Ever work one a these?

"Christ! I shoulda got a fuggin nigger stead of a gook." He impatiently pointed to an electrical junction box with a handle. "Juice's here. Hose here." He tossed Tomi a filthy blue and white striped apron. "Git your yellow ass movin, Mr. Moto! Gotta have dishes fer lunch." He slammed the mug down on the belt, and disappeared around a corner.

Tomi could not escape until his motorcycle was returned. He was safe as long as he worked to please *mittomonai*, 'Ugly.'

The apron was as filthy on one side as the other. Tomi shrugged, tied it on and threw the switch. The belt moved noisily, stirring up obnoxious smells. He glanced at a temperature gauge on top of the steel tunnel. The water was so lukewarm that he didn't have to do the math from Fahrenheit to centigrade. The ugly one demanded haste but Tomi noticed the machinery required a loader at his end and a retriever at the other. Not caring that his fingernails were black with motorcycle grease, he scratched at the food-encrusted plates. The greasy streaks were unaffected by the tepid water of the hose. Tomi smiled. He had returned to germ warfare. This time against the U.S. Pacific Fleet.

He found a scraping brush on the floor and worked faster. When he had the first load ready, he lifted the wire crate of dishes onto the moving belt and ran to the other end. The crate entered the tunnel, where one ring of nozzles sprayed soapy water and another rinsed the plates. Tomi checked the dishes in the crate.

He glanced around to make sure no one was watching him and picked off stubborn bits of old food. He put the first crate of half-clean dishes on the floor and returned to the loading end. Steam belched out of the box and his hose spray got very hot. He regretted that fewer American admirals would get food poisoning. He scraped, sprayed and loaded 3 crates of dishes at a time. When the crates of clean dishes reached the other end, he cut the power and ran back to offload them.

Why hadn't the manufacturer installed on-off switches at both ends? Probably to save money. So two workers were needed instead of one. Builders of Japanese tanks and U.S. dishwashing machinery had something in common: bad design.

The sailor who had borrowed his motorcycle appeared. "Thanks for the ride," he said, handing Tomi the key. "I parked next to the can where you left my rag. Goggles on the handlebar. Hey, I thought you didn't work here?"

"Cousin sick. Me take job," Tomi said with a grin. It was as easy to lie in *Eigo* as in *Nihongo*.

"Here's money for gas," said the sailor as he pressed a 5-cent coin in his palm. Tomi grinned and returned to work after increasing the belt's speed. Two hours later, the still-hot clean dishes were drying in neat stacks of wire crates. Tomi's low-caste supervisor must have been watching, because he returned when the final crate was clean.

"Finished? I'll be a sonuvabitch! OK, Mr. Moto, now ya work the line with me. Ya do the fuggin' swimmin' pool," he said, handing Tomi a ladle. Tomi wondered how he could dig a swimming pool with it. He ordered Tomi to unload the almost-clean plates onto a large preparation table. Tomi saw food particles on some plates, but no one cared.

One cook sliced and another forked huge slabs of ham onto the plates. Tomi's boss neatly plopped a large mound of mashed potatoes next to the ham and showed Tomi how to depress the bottom of a ladle filled with hot brown gravy into the potatoes. Then, with a twist of the wrist, the mashed potato crater was filled with brown gravy. Tomi made his first swimmin' pool.

They worked silently and swiftly. Negro waiters in white coats quickly shuttled the filled plates to the tables. Snapshot glimpses through the double swinging doors revealed distinguished-looking men in outlandish golfing attire. None wore gold-braided blue uniforms. All held drinks, and were relaxed and smiling. Why not? The admirals commanded a modern fleet in fortified Pearl Harbor with all the fuel they needed. The oil-rich Americans had gathered for pleasure, not for war.

The high-ranking officers dined as the kitchen crew sliced hot apple pies and put them on small plates. Tomi's task was to slap a big square of bright yellow cheese on each slice. Despite not having eaten all day, he dared not sneak a mouthful.

When the Negro waiters retrieved the dinner plates and served dessert and coffee, Tomi returned to his dishwashing. This time was easier because the food was soft. As he scraped and sprayed plates, he gulped down half-eaten pieces of leftover ham, cheese and soft buttered rolls. The amount of wasted food astonished Tomi. A village could be fed with what he tossed into the garbage can. He continued to work until all the dishes were washed and stacked. After carefully cleaning his work station, he reported to the ugly *gaijin*.

"I'm Fred," the low-caste grinned, exposing crooked, discolored teeth. "Ye'r a good worker, Mr. Moto. Fuggin' second shift will be here soon. We eat with them. I'll pay ya now."

"Thank you."

"Free next Sunday?"

Free? Did he mean *tada*, gratis? *Jiyuu na*, liberated? *Hanasu*, let go free? *Eigo* was a stupid language that confused more than communicated. Tomi grinned as if he understood.

"Fuggin' schedule change caught us with our pants down.

Fleet's comin' in every fuggin' Sunday, startin' today. The brass'll be here Sundays fer golf 'n a wet lunch, lucky bastards. 8 o'clock sharp next Sunday, Mr. Moto?"

"Yes, Sir. Moto free. Sunday sharp," Tomi said, dimly comprehending the crazy dialect. He wondered why he was called Mr. Moto. He shoved two crumpled dollars into Tomi's hand. Next Sunday, when Tomi was back in sane and rational Tokyo, Ugly Fred would wash dirty dishes by himself.

Tomi's overstuffed stomach and head were churning as he returned to downtown Honolulu. Before leaving Tokyo, Tomi had been told the U.S. Fleet routinely steamed out of Pearl Harbor every other Wednesday for seven days of exercises, and some officers and men got two weekends off a month.

If Tomi understood Ugly Fred correctly, the main warships increased their time at sea, but returned to port every Sunday to allow the officers to play golf. Yankee arrogance was as amazing as the amount of food they wasted.

The two U.S. dollars Tomi earned for a day of washing dishes was more than he made in three days as a First Lieutenant. Making money was easy for Americans. But could they be defeated?

CHAPTER TWELVE

The Navy's new bombers trained here because the secret naval base at Kagoshima Bay uncannily resembled Pearl Harbor. Closer to Shanghai than to Tokyo, the Kyushu Island's locals spoke an odd dialect. This was because Chinese and Korean fishermen, explorers and traders had established colonies here in pre-history.

Three hundred years ago, the Catholic saint, Francis Xavier, arrived here from China and unsuccessfully tried to convert Japan. More importantly, Kagoshima was where Japan first copied the West's guns and cannon. Now Japanese trained at Kagoshima with weapons superior to the *gaijins*. The wheel of history had turned in *Nippon*'s favor.

A formation of bombers, their *taiyoo*, red sun, insignias on their wings and fuselages, were vivid in the morning light as they swept low over swaying palm trees. In perfect unison, the four bombers dropped dummy torpedoes and zoomed away. Almost instantly, four white splashes became four straight wakes that converged on a slow-moving ship. Then, four thuds, spaced apart, indicated hits.

Lieutenant Kiga and Tomi followed the action; Tomi with binoculars and Kiga with a telescope. "The ideal airplane, the ideal Pearl Harbor torpedo and the ideal training harbor," the one-eyed Army pilot chortled. He was a colorful character who hid his intelligence but not his vast knowledge behind humor that was absent among most naval officers.

Tomi barely listened as Kiga babbled technical data. "Our B5N2 bomber is superior to the Yankees' Douglas TBD torpedo bomber. Both were designed in 1935 and both were low-wing, carrier-based planes with 3-man crews. Our aircraft has more horsepower, speed, range, maneuverability and bomb load; and is both a high-level and torpedo bomber. It carries the world's best aerial torpedo, and the Pearl Harbor vanes make it perfect."

The jargon was gibberish to Tomi, who disliked airplanes. But Kiga's reference to the torpedo adapted for the Pearl Harbor attack was a source of pride to every officer entrusted with the secret. Japanese experts adapted a modern weapon with a 5,400-year-old invention: plywood. Over 1,000 years before they built pyramids, the Egyptians glued thin wood sheets or strips together, making them stronger than solid wood of equal thickness.

Pearl Harbor's depth ranged between 40 and 50 feet. A torpedo launched from a plane usually plunged 60 feet below the surface before it stabilized and started running. Standard torpedoes would end up in the shallow harbor bottom. But the special plywood vanes, or fins, on the torpedoes enabled them to begin their lethal runs after a 12-foot plunge below the surface.

"Admiral Yamamoto must be very pleased," Tomi said politely.

"Right now he and his staff are celebrating the Spaghetti vs. Crumpet Battle of Taranto."

Vaguely, Tomi recalled reading about Taranto, where British Navy torpedo planes sank three Italian battleships a month ago in a fortified anchorage at the heel of the Italian boot.

"Why celebrate a defeat suffered by our *Itarijin* allies?"

Kiga sighed dramatically at Tomi's dullness. "If obsolete British bi-planes made of canvas and baling wire sank modern battleships of the Italian fleet, imagine what our torpedo bombers will do against the unsuspecting Yankees, now that we've solved the shallow depth problem!"

Tomi remembered the empty sky of Oahu Island during his motorcycle tour that Sunday morning a year ago. "Were the Taranto defenses not adequate?"

"First class," Kiga said. "The Italians had 600 anti-aircraft guns of all calibers. Despite that, the British destroyed the pride of the Italian Navy. Lost only two of their 20 Swordfish planes. The surprise attack ends Italy's control of the Mediterranean!"

"Any barrage balloons over the harbor?"

"You're balloon-happy, Tomi," he said, and lifted his black patch to rub the empty eye socket. Kiga was a decorated ace who had shot down 6 Chinese planes, including a Flying Tiger P-40 piloted by a Yankee. His flying career ended when he lost his left eye during a training accident.

"The Italians had only 30 of their 90 balloons aloft because of a hydrogen gas shortage. The lead British pilot later reported that his wing missed a balloon cable by inches."

"How did our intelligence get so many details so soon?"

"Our liaison officers questioned the Italians and read all their reports, including a few secret documents. Dumb Yankees never bothered to send naval observers."

"Surely the Pearl Harbor command realizes the significance of the Taranto attack?"

"Apparently not. Yankees are incomprehensible. They threatened us, yet they have three or four aircraft carriers in the Pacific, compared to our six. And they still haven't rigged anti-torpedo nets or barrage balloons at Pearl Harbor! We overestimated them as much as they now underestimate us."

Training in Kagoshima Bay was conducted 7 days a week, while American officers played golf on weekends. When the bombing exercise ended, flocks of seabirds resumed diving for fish. Tomi joked, "Those birds aim as well as torpedoes. Too bad we can't fill birds with explosives and train them to dive-bomb the American Navy."

A shadow crossed Kiga's face as if Tomi had said something inappropriate. The next morning Tomi was called into a staff conference. It was his first meeting with Rear Admiral Onishi, who had read Tomi's report after last year's Hawaii trip. His brief mention of the absence of barrage balloons and military inactivity on Sundays had stirred a high-level debate. Tomi was unaware that some planners had argued for Wednesday, December 10th as 'X-Day' because the dark moon phase was ideal for a surprise night attack. Admiral Onishi used Tomi's Hawaiian report to opt for early Sunday morning, December 7 as 'X-Day.'

Admiral Onishi invited Tomi to sit at the long conference table with his staff. Out of place in his drab Army uniform and low rank, Tomi hoped his medals looked impressive.

Admiral Onishi, a 50-year-old career officer, had a down-turned mouth and thrusting jaw on a puffy face that gave him a misleading belligerent look. He was one of Japan's foremost aviation pioneers and a popular poet. Unlike General Tojo and Admiral Yamamoto, he didn't engage in the high level debate about going to war with America. Instead, he concentrated on training aviators at Kagoshima Bay for the surprise attack.

"First Lieutenant Tomigawa, we have all read your report. Now we wish to hear your personal impressions of military activity at Pearl Harbor on Sundays," Admiral Onishi said with a slight smile. "Please include any small details that were omitted from your report."

Tomi was prepared for such an unusual open-ended discussion. "Sirs, this humble one apologizes for superficial opinions gathered during a hasty one-week visit last year. I am not an expert or a trained intelligence agent, and my limited observations are probably outdated. But I was told to look for small details. What impressed me was what I did not see. The Sunday morning silence of Honolulu was like the thick quiet after a Hokkaido snowstorm. There was a near-total absence of civilian or military noise on the roads and in the sky."

He remembered the sounds of drunken soldiers and sailors fighting outside his hotel on Saturday night, when the *gaijin* bed made sleep impossible. "It is my worthless opinion that the lower ranks carouse on Saturday nights and sleep late Sunday mornings, when many flag officers play golf.

"You mentioned sky. No aircraft?" A naval captain asked.

"I was indoors Sunday, Sir, but heard no aircraft engine noise in the morning. The day before, I saw a few small planes, but no formations. I could not tell if they were patrol flights."

"Your report specifically mentioned the absence of barrage balloons over Pearl Harbor. What made you think of that?" Admiral Onishi asked.

When Tomi had returned from Hawaii, the first thing he did after shaving off the silly moustache was to study military balloons. Many of the early studies were authored by Admiral Onishi, who had gone aloft in many observation balloons in France during the Great War and returned home to command Japan's first balloon unit.

"Sir, after seeing a civilian newsreel in Honolulu about the effectiveness of barrage balloons in the heaviest London air raids, it didn't make sense that the Americans weren't using them over their fleet anchorage." Several officers openly grinned satisfaction. They knew the British Royal Air Force Balloon Command had more than 2,300 balloons floating over London, forcing German bombers to release their loads from 10,000 feet with far less accuracy.

"Are you a barrage balloon expert?" a commander asked.

"No, Sir. I am only an Infantry officer who reads a little." But Tomi knew that a balloon cost 13,000 yen, a fraction of the cost of the German airplanes they impaired or destroyed.

Admiral Onishi asked, "Have you thought about the inexplicable absence of barrage balloons over Pearl Harbor, Ford Island, Wheeler, Henderson and Hickam Fields?" The Admiral wanted Tomi to support his own well-researched opinions. Tomi recalled the swinging doors of the country club kitchen and his glimpses of admirals in golf knickers and colorful plaid socks.

"Sir, perhaps it is another instance of Yankee overconfidence. This unworthy one's opinion is based on the briefest of glances of their admirals at a Sunday morning social gathering."

Admiral Onishi dismissed Tomi with orders to join him at the airfield.

Three hours later, Tomi was in a tiny wicker basket that oscillated wildly beneath an observation balloon. Airsick and dizzy, he fought not to vomit on Admiral Onishi. The balloon was attached by a single rope held by the ground crew far below. If Tomi's willpower was weaker than his nausea, he'd be known throughout the military as that airsick junior officer who threw up on the immaculate white uniform of Japan's top naval aviation officer. It would cost him his job on General Tojo's staff.

"Wonderful, *neh*?" Admiral Onishi said, taking a deep breath. "I was younger than you the first time. It was a French balloon in 1918. Now I go up at least once a week. It refreshes me."

He aimed his binoculars at an aircraft formation above them. "Unlike torpedo runs, horizontal bombing is inaccurate. From 9,700 feet, I estimate that even with this training, one, perhaps two out of every five bombs may miss the stationary battleships. We'll attack with ten formations of five carrier bombers, each to hit

'Battleship Row.' But high level bombing is the only way to hit the inside ships when moored two- abreast."

They watched the formation drop bombloads on anchored rafts in the bay. He smiled. "Our standard 551-pound bombs can't dent their battleship armor. A smart young naval officer gave us the idea of turning our armor-piercing naval shells into special Pearl Harbor bombs."

Tomi nodded, hoping his cold sweat wasn't obvious.

"Speaking of notions, where did you get the notion of diving birds carrying explosives?"

Despite the Admiral's casual manner, Tomi immediately knew this was why he had been invited into the admiral's swinging basket. He silently cursed Kiga for informing on him.

"It was a foolish thought, Sir," Tomi said lamely. "After First Lieutenant Kiga and I watched the torpedo bombers practice, I noticed how accurate the diving birds were in hitting fish targets."

Crammed together in the wicker basket, the admiral's hanging binoculars pressed Tomi. Admiral Onishi frowned and demanded, "The idea. Who told you?"

Fear replaced Tomi's nausea. He didn't know how to answer. It had been such a vague, casual idea. Tomi realized he needed a more plausible, logical answer than the truth.

"Honorable Admiral Onishi," he began, "this humble one was so impressed by the ingenuity and accuracy of torpedo plywood vanes that I merely took that concept to diving sea birds."

His stern gaze swung from Tomi to the horizon. "Those diving birds are marbled murrelets. Small and chunky, but what attackers! Their short beaks rip into every fish they aim for. Murrelets are Nature's perfect dive bomber.

"If Americans have anti-torpedo nets to foil our special Pearl Harbor torpedoes, our dive bombers and level bombers will get them. If the Yankees put up barrage balloons, we will lose many planes, but we will still get through. Hopefully, our midget submarines will sink a ship in the narrow harbor entrance to bottle up their fleet. Tell me, young man, given your short stay among them, how do you think they'll react to our surprise attack?"

Tomi parroted the safe response. "After the American Fleet

is rendered impotent and we capture the Philippines, they will sue for peace, as did the Russians after we sank their fleet."

The admiral snorted disbelief. "One of their aircraft carriers is called 'Hornet.' What if the Americans get as angry as hornets, refuse a peace treaty and continue fighting?"

"I'm sorry, Sir. I don't know."

"Don't apologize. No one else has that answer, either." He leaned over the basket and waved for the ground crew to haul them down. He mumbled to himself, "Then I must train thousands of human murrelets to crash dive into their ships."

Tomi didn't understand, but the words weren't for him to hear.

CHAPTER THIRTEEN
TOKYO, APRIL 1942

The stench was familiar. Only pride prevented Tomi from pressing a wet handkerchief against his nose like the sullen civilians who glared at him. Their lack of respect was understandable. The military had failed to protect the schoolchildren.

Mothers and fathers gagged as they shuffled like undecided shoppers along the neat row of charred and mangled bodies. They couldn't identify their own children among the lumps dragged from the smouldering rubble of the middle school.

Sorrow for the dead children was not as great as the collective shame of everyone in uniform who had failed the Emperor. Tomi did his job of estimating casualty totals; adding up the military's disgrace.

The national shame began hours ago. A low-flying airplane had startled the midday crowd, but the unthinkable didn't register until they heard bombs exploding. Worse, the Yankee bomber roared low over the God Emperor's Palace, then dumped its munitions on the crowded Shinbashi Railway Station.

Tomi and the other paper warriors were among the last to sift truth from wildly conflicting rumors that roiled Headquarters. Before dawn, the Navy Ministry had received a radio message from the ship, *Nitto Maru*: "Enemy contact. Bearing due west. Aircraft carrier, cruiser and escorts. Hit by salvos. Sinking. Long live the Emperor." Then silence. Other picket ships and fishing boats confirmed the warning before they joined the *Nitto Maru* on the sea bottom.

The American force was 660 miles away, headed toward Japan at 20 knots in heavy seas. The admirals in Tokyo, smugly aware of the limited range of the U.S. Navy's carrier-based planes down to the last drop of gasoline, planned to intercept the enemy in plenty of time before they were within flying range of Honshu.

Home Fleet warships steamed out of port and, as a precaution, anti-aircraft batteries were alerted and pursuit squadrons armed and fueled, ready to scramble. It was decided not to alarm the public, since the action would be out at sea.

Unexpectedly, the Yankee bombers were sighted over Tokyo at noon. Air Defense was doubly surprised when each of the 16 bombers flew in a different direction and altitude to individual targets, instead of using orthodox bomber formation.

Somehow, the cunning enemy had done the impossible. They launched land-based B-25's from an aircraft carrier. Tokyo Air Defense failed to down a single bomber, despite anti-aircraft fire and fighter plane patrols on high alert. Luck favored the sneaky Americans. By accident, one errant bomb hit a camouflaged fuel tank farm in north Tokyo. The precious oil was turned into black smoke that stained the clear blue sky.

Not trusting the reports of panicked civilians, junior staff officers were sent to assess the damage and casualties. Tomi was assigned to one of the wrecked schools, while a less fortunate comrade waded through piles of bodies at a bombed military hospital. The enemy had hit scattered targets in Yokohama, Osaka and Kobe. An airplane plant and an aircraft carrier under construction at Yokosuka Naval Base were superficially damaged.

Some of the 50 dead and 252 injured were children. But the worst damage was done by an insolent Yankee pilot who violated the celestial space over the God-Emperor's Palace. The brazen insult proved Japan was not safe from Yankees, despite their Pearl Harbor losses and Japan's many land victories.

After releasing their bombs, the enemy planes continued west until they ran out of fuel and crash-landed in China's Chekiang and Kiagsu provinces. Despite a massive manhunt, Japanese troops and their Chinese collaborators captured only 8 airmen. The twin-engine 'Mitchell' bombers carried 5-man crews. The *Kempetai* estimated Chinese partisans had helped 70 or more U.S. Army airmen reach safety.

Saving the 70 Americans cost China more than 250,000 men, women and children who were slaughtered on orders personally signed by The God Emperor. The captured Americans pilots were treated as criminals. The *Kempetai* tortured them long after they had been drained of military secrets.

"It is more complicated than loss of face," One-Eyed Kiga whispered when Tomi asked him about it. Unlike Tomi, Kiga had attended enough high-level discussions to know.

"The punishment was an Imperial decision. The God-Emperor had secretly offered the United States an immediate cease-fire through neutral embassies. Our only condition for a peace treaty was to retain the U.S. territories we captured. After all, the Yankees grabbed Cuba, the Philippines and Puerto Rico after they had deliberately provoked a short war with Spain.

"But America rejected our peace offer. The Emperor was furious. Yankees who were anti-war isolationists before Pearl Harbor now support war in both the Pacific and in Europe! How can rational minds anticipate the insanity of fanatics? We have no choice but to continue fighting. And the enraged U.S. has ample resources for a two-front war."

"And the future?"

"Less than encouraging."

Kiga's single eye swivelled to the only decoration in his cubicle, the regulation wall portrait of *Showa Sama Hirohito*. "Can it be that we, the masters of tactics, miscalculated our grand strategy?" he mumbled.

Kiga's honesty prompted Tomi to ask the question that poisoned his sleep. "If that is so, why did the God-Emperor order the massacre of 250,000 civilians in Chekiang? How does another Nanking massacre aid our legitimate cause?"

Kiga's eye blinked exasperation. "Killing gooks now is better than having 250,000 Japanese die in future Yankee air raids. The Emperor used mass executions to discourage other Chinese provinces from letting the Americans build airfields to bomb us. The Yankees missed a golden opportunity to hurt us the first time. We don't want them to try again."

"What missed opportunity? The entire nation was dishonored and shocked by the raid!"

"No. It was a botched, hasty operation that missed vital military targets. The dumb bastards lost all their planes. They ran out of fuel because they launched prematurely after the Hornet was spotted by our picket boats."

He whispered, "Few know this, but the Royal Court wanted all eight American fliers executed."

"Good! They murdered children."

"Those schools were no more targets than the oil tank farm. The middle school you inspected was one of many accidental hits. A frightened Yankee jettisoned his bomb load to gain speed when he spotted a pursuit plane." Kiga fingered his eye socket again.

"It's complicated, Tomi. Early in the China Incident, I flew escort for Prince Higashikuni's planned air raids on schools and hospitals. We broke the gooks' morale with those terror raids. General Tojo alluded to those attacks when he pleaded for the Yankees' lives. Tojo, aware that the Americans might retaliate, reminded the Palace that we have no law calling for the execution of captured enemy fliers. Tojo said that our own bomber pilots, including the *Showa Sama's* own uncle, Prince Higashikuni, might someday be held accountable. Because the prince was one of many of the Emperor's relatives with war service in China, Tojo thought he was protecting the Royal Family. The Imperial Wish was compromised: three American airmen, including one made insane from torture, will be executed. The others get life sentences."

Tomi gasped, "Tojo-Sama had to haggle like a fish peddler?"

"Nothing is as it appears. The Americans think General Tojo is an all-powerful military dictator like Hitler, Stalin or Mussolini. In truth, Tojo has to bargain and compromise like a slippery politician to carry out his policies. There are conflicting opinions on how to run the war, including your Uncle Suzuki's. The God Emperor is now so displeased with Tojo that he gave the army and navy leaders latitude almost free of Tojo's control. Despite his fierce loyalty to the throne, the longer the war lasts, the weaker Tojo becomes."

Tomi pondered Kiga's words. Japan's strategy was fatally flawed, because the enemy's nature had been woefully underestimated. And the Imperial Palace encouraged the war leaders to squabble among themselves. The sneak raid on Japan came from the carrier Admiral Onishi had mentioned at

Kagashima. He had predicted that if the Americans got as angry as hornets, they would fight until they won, no matter what the cost in blood or how long it took.

***

It was difficult to push through the patriotic crowds that gathered daily in the plaza facing the Imperial Palace. The one puny American air raid hadn't dampened the war spirit. Everyone was giddy with the string of rapid conquests of the *gaijin* Pacific colonies. Tomi and Takahashi watched the sophisticated city folk bow low from the waist, and rural peasants on their knees with arms outstretched, foreheads pressed hard against the concrete.

"Foolish ones," Takahashi muttered after checking to make sure no one heard him. With unconcealed bitterness, he told Tomi, "Years ago, my father borrowed train fare from the money lender to come here with his Sendai cronies to pay homage on the Emperor's birthday, which is in the same month as his. The trip ruined us. We didn't have money to buy seed that Spring. My younger sister was contracted to a local brothel and I had to join the Army. Father still babbles about how being here was his greatest honor." He shook his head and said, "I'm as patriotic as the next man, but ... " Tomi hadn't known about the sister.

Earlier in the day, Takahashi had telephoned Tomi from his *Kempetai* unit and requested a meeting as soon as possible. No reason was given or expected with open phone calls. Perhaps Takahashi's problem would be offset by Tomi's good news that they were about to reunite.

Tomi took his glum sergeant to a restaurant rarely frequented by the military and asked for a private screened nook. They drank to each other's health. With usual politeness, the reason for the sudden meeting was delayed. Raucous noise from the dining crowd masked their voices.

"Good news, Tomi began, refilling Takahashi's, sake cup as befitted an honored friend. "You're permanently assigned to my office. Next week you'll be a fat-ass desk soldier like me, fighting the war from a chair. It's better than duty in the *Kempetai* Tokyo records section."

Takahashi nodded without gratitude.

"What's worrying you? Bad news from home?"

Takahashi whispered, "Haruo, *neh*? Remember him, the Unit 731 non-com? He's the one who took over my unofficial business. He sends me money payments and bits of Harbin gossip in hand delivered letters. I got some news from him yesterday."

Takahashi had developed into an imaginative, discreet black marketeer who delivered as promised, and unlike some officers, wasn't overly greedy. Given wartime controls on civilian goods, he was deeply involved in the booming black market, but it never interfered with his duties.

"Haruo wrote to me about the *Kempetai* sergeants you had transferred to Unit 731. One ruined a pregnancy study with his cock and the other tried to cover up for his comrade. Otomo was outraged. They became logs, and died slowly and badly."

The sadists who had ruined Taiko finally got what they deserved. Tomi grinned and raised his sake cup. Takahashi averted his eyes.

"What's wrong?"

"I don't know how to tell you this except in my blunt peasant way. I read the two sergeants' files and found a curious entry. So I checked the files of their daily reports when they guarded the Honorable Lady Tomigawa during her house arrest."

Grim-faced Takahashi's Sendai accent thickened. "I am sorry, Tomi, but the records show that the Lady Tomigawa and her servant volunteered to be informants. They gave evidence against your family friend, the general who died during interrogation. That's how Otomo knew of your spy assignment when we arrived at Unit 731. It was a fucking trap."

Tomi didn't remember paying the check or the taxi home. He burst into his mother's bedroom, boots on.

"You -- a *Kempetai* informer? You had General Hashimoto tortured and killed. You entrapped me with a false spy mission knowing I'd be caught and Taiko destroyed! *Miko*, witch!"

Her startled expression smoothed and she said in a loud, calm voice, "Taiko, come in here and remove my son's boots. His manners have fled him."

Kneeling at his feet, Taiko's little hands trembled as she

struggled to remove his boots from tensed, stubborn feet. She didn't look up for help. As she left, he was surprised at his sex stirring. Both females were she-devils who used love as a weapon against him.

Through clenched teeth Tomi roared, "Are you a whore? You betrayed Honorable Father's memory with a lover you destroyed. Still unsatisfied, you betrayed me. Wicked shame!"

Scorn deepened her voice. "My shame is having a fool for a son! You know nothing, yet bellow in blind ignorance. Unlike you, I don't allow myself the luxury of venting emotions. May you never have to make the awful choices I faced. Sit down if you want the ugly truth!"

He sank to his knees, sensing the quick distance between his hand and sword handle. His mother stared at his hovering fingers.

"The *Kempetai* ordered Taiko to eavesdrop on me during General Hashimoto's visits. Had she refused, her family would have become comfort women and slave laborers. In despair, she came to me.

"If I was suspected of being among Hashimoto's plotters, then so were you. You would have been killed in some dank prison cell and the public informed that you fell in a minor skirmish somewhere. Their main quarry was General Hashimoto. That meant he was already doomed.

"I went to the *Kempetai* and pretended to be unaware of Taiko's spying. I expressed patriotic outrage that Hashimoto had voiced treasonous opinions to me. My acting convinced them. The house arrest was a failed attempt to snare any unknown conspirators who might contact me. As it turned out, they got little from me that they didn't already know."

"You betrayed your lover to save yourself!"

"No! I did it for you. Your bloodline must not disappear from history like so many others. My ancestors and the brave Tomigawas have as much right to be in the Royal Court as those who lead *Nippon* to disaster. Our ancestors require your survival. The painful truth is that friend and foe are temporary labels in our evil world of shifting loyalties."

"Crazy witch, what the hell are you talking about?"

"Time and politics make allies enemies and enemies allies.

When I was your age, America was our friend. Today America is the arch-enemy. If you survive to my age, perhaps America may be Japan's friend again. Survival and self-interest cause nations and people to do the unthinkable."

She shut her eyes and her lips twitched, as if tasting bad memories. "Like Taiko, I will perform disgusting acts if that is the price for keeping you alive. It is my fate for birthing only one son, who courts death where ever he goes."

"What of Tomigawa honor?"

Her eyes grew wide. *"Kara no ponchie!* You hollow caricature!" she spat. Tomi blinked and released the tightly-held scabbard to wipe her wet hate off his face.

"I debased myself to keep you alive and you whine about honor? There is no honor if you die without heirs. Find honor in breeding the next generation of Tomigawas! Failing that, poor Taiko's sacrifice and mine will have been in vain."

"So! Was Taiko brutalized or was that another of your crafty witch lies?"

"A partial lie. One sergeant was a family man, but the other one fancied Taiko and gave her the choice of submitting to him every night or Taiko's younger sister becoming a comfort woman. Powerless, I told her to comply and she caught incurable syphilis from the swine. To protect you from venereal disease, I had her tell you that she had been damaged by the rapes."

"You play God with our lives and sacrificed Taiko!" He pounded his fists against the tatami mat, wishing it were his Mother's face.

She grabbed his ear and viciously twisted it. Pain cut his anger. "Look at me!" she ordered. "If that syphilitic brute had demanded sex from me, I would have done exactly what Taiko did. Survival of the Tomigawas is worth any price!"

Her words were daggers. He stood up. Lady Tomigawa slowly sank to the mat. Like a witch, her life force shriveled and she became the dried husk of a tiny, old woman in a suddenly-oversized kimono.

A muffled voice came from within the heap of collapsed silk. "Survival outranks honor, my son. Only foolish warriors sick with the poison of pride think otherwise. Death is the coward's escape.

True courage is remaining alive despite shame and dishonor. You lack this pragmatism.

"Since I am at fault for not birthing another, wiser son, I had to keep the only one alive any way I could. You, who live because of our degradation, cannot judge us. You can only beg our forgiveness, either here or in the next world. We will be waiting once you understand that our love for you made us willing victims."

Like the moon, her face slowly appeared from behind wide sleeves into Tomi's hateful stare. His mother and Taiko's willingness to use their sex for his survival enraged him.

Tomi imagined drawing his sword and uttering the executioner's words, *"Anata no kubi. sarasu!* Your neck, expose it!" As if reading his murderous thoughts, his mother bent her head to the mat, offering him a target framed by the silk kimono collar.

Without her burning eyes on him, Tomi was able to speak. "I find honor in doing my duty while you wallow in plots that destroy the innocent. It is you who must beg forgiveness; first from Honorable Father's spirit then from his son. Farewell, Lady Tomigawa."

***

Unexpectedly, Admiral Onishi had assigned Tomi to one of his top secret projects. Takahashi and Tomi worked long hours, 7 days a week. Tomi scolded Takahashi into taking much-needed sleep at the non-com barracks. Takahashi felt guilty that Tomi worked longer, unaware that his superior wanted to avoid a few hours of Nanking nightmare-filled sleep in the officers' quarters.

Twice a month Tomi went to the Suzuki Compound on overnight leave. The household routine was different now that Uncle Suzuki was on the war production council. Suzuki, proud his nephew was a favorite of General Tojo and Admiral Onishi, no longer pressed for details or gossip.

The Suzuki's Taiko enjoyed Tomi's visits, comprised of dull sex and stimulating quarrels. Despite the loveless marriage, he respected Taiko's intellect. They often quarreled over politics, but Tomi knew better than to voice unpatriotic thoughts. After sex one night, Taiko sat upright and asked, "How can we win if the

Allies refuse to sign a peace treaty?"

Tomi ignored her and pretended to sleep. "You heard me! What happens next?"

"Ask your uncle," he grunted. "He's the industrialist general; I'm just a captain at a desk."

"What's the end game?" She shook his shoulder. Tomi slowly rolled on his back to stare up at her wide face. The lantern turned her small eyes into two *hashibudoo*, raisins. He knew she wouldn't let him alone until they had a mental intercourse as selfish and unsatisfying as her coupling. Tomi was trapped with an intelligent wife filled with discontent; a strong person who lusted to debate contrary opinions about politics, war, superiority of European culture, and the restrictions forced on women.

He spoke cautiously as if to her uncle, "Unless we defeat our enemies at sea, they won't let us keep their colonies. Despite our many land victories, we are forced to defend extended shipping lanes from constant American attacks on our cargo ships. Now our navy is stretched thin."

He recited the pipe dream of optimism, "If we can bloody their noses in a few naval battles, we'll negotiate a treaty. Either way, we keep some captured colonies."

She fired back. "What if our navy can't defeat their navy?" Tomi suspected she knew more than he did because of her many private talks with General Suzuki.

"Our German allies are preparing wonder weapons that will decide the war. Our biggest battleships fire shells much farther than America's warships. Everyone, including the Americans, knows Japan wants a decisive sea battle to force them to the peace table." Thinking of his own secret work, he added, "Perhaps we need a Japanese wonder weapon."

Unimpressed, she asked, "Does anyone analyze population numbers?"

"What?"

"Is there a world almanac at Imperial Headquarters?"

"What's a worarmanac?" He was annoyed by her glib ability to use *gaijin* "L" words.

"The annual book of facts with population numbers. I read the last edition before the *Kempetai* removed *Eigo* language books from the university library, and ..."

Tomi interrupted, "Everyone knows America has 150 million people to our 90 million. So what?"

She snorted derisively. "The American population has a much higher percentage of military age men than we do. It's as if we are fighting a country with a population more than twice ours."

He blustered past her startling information. "So what? Even when we're outnumbered in land battles, we outmaneuver and beat the Americans and their allies."

"Tomi, we caught them unprepared once. Now they're ready for us. You mentioned a stalemate. If there's a lengthy battle of attrition, we'll run out of young men before they do."

"Why your interest in population statistics, Taiko?

"The Europeans had a Hundred Year War. What if this conflict lasts a generation? I don't want my child sacrificed in a long war."

Tomi was about to retort, "Before fretting about such matters, first become a mother," when she said, "I'm finally pregnant. Goodnight."

Ignoring his surprise, she rolled over and soon her breathing became full-throttled snores. Tomi wondered how to tell his mother without apologizing. His wife's loud snoring held the answer. She would inform Lady Tomigawa and he would keep his pride intact. Let his mother come to him, grateful for the heir for whom she had debased herself and ruined his Taiko.

He waited impatiently for dawn, when he would pray at the household shrine for a warrior son. Unwanted questions expanded his headache. If his secret intercontinental project failed, what would happen to his son? Far worse than Japan without a Tomigawa would be a Tomigawa without a Japan.

CHAPTER FOURTEEN
TOKYO, MARCH 1943

The gods half-answered Tomi's fervent prayers. He had a healthy son, but as the child grew stronger, Japan weakened. Following the Midway naval defeat, the enemy island-hopped across the Pacific Ocean toward Japan. To stave off disaster, the military desperately worked on new weapons -- some rational, some grandiose. One-Eyed Kiga and Tomi headed two such programs.

Tomi's assignment was to make war on America's civilians. Japan's earlier attacks on mainland America had failed. A small patrol submarine fired a few cannon shells at a California oil refinery as President Roosevelt gave a radio speech. Later, two bombing sorties were made by a light seaplane carried in a submarine's watertight deck hangar. Combined, they caused less than $500 damage, but motivated the Yankees to strengthen their coastal defenses.

Japan's German allies talked of fantastic rockets and inter-continental bombers, but the super weapons were years away from operational. Kiga's and Tomi's secret projects grew to such importance that Admiral Onishi gave a briefing to the *shoguns* of the war production council.

"Captain Tomigawa, tell our distinguished guests about your *keikikyuu*, balloon program," Admiral Onishi ordered. Actually, the program had been Onishi's idea. If the wonder weapon succeeded, the Admiral would get the credit; if it failed, Tomi would get the blame.

Tomi's presentation was first because Uncle-by-marriage Suzuki headed the visiting delegation. Takahashi had thoroughly rehearsed Tomi into a straightforward, fact-filled presentation that Admiral Onishi preferred. Tomi stood by the easel while

Takahashi displayed a map of the vast Pacific territory under Japanese control: from Dutch East Indies in the south to Manchuria in the North; from Wake Island in mid-Pacific to the Burma-India border in the West. The newly-conquered empire looked massive, but everyone in the room knew of its fragility.

Tomi began. "The task is to take the war across the Pacific Ocean to the North American continent. Consider the enormous distance to the enemy's well-defended western coast. How do we deliver destruction that will break the spirit of American civilians and force them to sign a peace treaty? The answer is found in *shizen*, nature. The physical universe."

Takahashi put up a meteorological chart as Tomi continued, "The earth's rotation causes prevailing winds to flow across the Pacific from east to west, from Japan to North America. There are stronger air currents flowing westward at 30,000 feet. Our meteorologists describe them as rivers of fast moving air."

Takahashi displayed a photo of a Japanese weather balloon. Tomi said, "This is the weapon Admiral Onishi calls *Kaze soshite Kaji.* 'Wind and Fire.' The Wind will deliver the Fire."

The high-ranking guests, including Suzuki, leaned forward as Admiral Onishi, who carried an odd-shaped case, joined Tomi. Takahashi displayed an illustration of a round balloon covered with a tight fishing net from which hung a large capsule.

In a dramatic voice, Admiral Onishi interjected, "Imagine, honorable gentlemen, an unmanned weapon that requires no fuel or critical war materials. The Wind Ship measures 32 feet in diameter and is filled with easily-available hydrogen. The primary load is a combination of explosive and incendiary devices, designed to ignite forest fires along the western coast of America."

A fleet admiral interrupted, "Pardon me. But with a heavy load, how is proper altitude maintained given the temperature swings of night and day?"

"We use an altitude-triggering device that jettisons incremental portions of ballast from small sandbags. These are released one by one whenever the Wind Ship drops below the desired 30,000-foot cruising altitude. By the time the balloon drops all 32 sandbags, it should be over North America, where it will automatically drop its incendiary devices.

"When the Americans discover the balloons, won't they shoot them down?" someone asked.

"We think not. There's another explosive charge that destroys the balloon after the incendiary bombs are dropped. No one will know the existence of the balloons -- only their results. Given the unregulated nature of the American press, we will soon know the Wind Ship's effectiveness through newspaper stories of the forest fires. Captain Tomigawa, describe the two versions of the weapon."

Tomi recited, "Type A, the Army version, will be launched from Japan. The balloon, made of 600 pieces of mulberry paper pasted together, forms a leak-proof container. The capsule contains 5 incendiary bombs, one anti-personnel bomb and a self-destructive device. It is designed to set fire to America's large forested expanses around its cities, factories and farms.

"Type B will be launched at sea by Navy ships or submarines. This version is made of rubberized silk and carries a telemetry radio to track flight path, wind direction and speed. This data will enable us to launch when conditions are ideal."

Admiral Onishi removed a celluloid packet of green liquid from his case. "And this, gentlemen, is my own little surprise, a super-secret prototype of Type C. In addition to the usual explosive devices, Type C will carry chemical weapons manufactured by Special Unit 731."

General Suzuki saw Tomi's surprised expression. Onishi said, "Several biological solutions have been successfully tested. They will spread contagious diseases among humans or livestock when the Wind Ships reach North America."

A general stood and demanded, "What's this? Who gave you permission? Otomo's damn germs don't have General Staff approval! The enemy's poison gas stockpiles are bigger and more powerful! The Yankees are working on a major secret program about which we have scant information. We suspect it's either poison gas or germ warfare. If we start a plague in their homeland, they'll retaliate! With our population density and the enemy's geographic advantage, we'll lose far more than we'll gain. Many of our troops still carry those leaky gas masks made in 1935. Even the new ones can't compare to the Yankee's. I will not ..."

General Suzuki smoothly interrupted, "With profound apologies, Honorable General Takeda, we've heard only one of Admiral Onishi's two secret projects. Given our busy schedule, perhaps we should hear about the Admiral's other project. Then we will discuss our conclusions in private."

Admiral Onishi smiled at Tomi. "During the siege of Nanking, Captain Tomigawa singlehandedly attacked and routed superior Chinese units and captured valuable information. I am impressed by the Marbled Murralet, a sea bird that dives for fish with great accuracy. Why can't we dive into enemy fleets the same way that Captain Tomigawa attacked? Only this time it will be a brave pilot in a diving airplane."

A nod from Admiral Onishi brought Captain Kiga to the table. Kiga's black eye patch and glittering medals were impressive. His solitary eye casually absorbed admiring looks. "Ancient tradition calls for officers to lead attacks and when necessary, sacrifice themselves for victory. In the sky, we will duplicate *Bushido*, the Way of the Warrior.

"All here know the Americans build ships and airplanes quickly in fantastic numbers to challenge the Imperial Navy in our home waters. This must not happen, no matter what the cost.

"We in military aviation propose our own version of the *Samurai* who sacrifices himself by charging into an enemy horde. We will form special attack units, composed of volunteer pilots, who will crash their explosive-filled planes into enemy ships. When the enemy fleet assembles for an invasion, the special attack units will have a wealth of easy-to-hit targets. One plane may or may not sink a capital warship, but it will seriously damage its capability by crashing into the bridge.

"Unlike the British Royal Navy carriers with steel flight decks, the Americans still use wooden decks. A single special attack plane can destroy a Yankee carrier's deck. One airplane can nullify or destroy many enemy squadrons in one blow."

A professorial-looking civilian asked, "I'm told the American carriers bristle with anti-aircraft guns. Won't the plane be shot down before it can crash dive into a ship?"

"The divine mission planes will dive out of the sun and many will hit their targets."

The skeptical civilian pressed, "Will you have enough volunteer pilots for such missions?"

"I have interviewed a number of pilots whom I know personally. Three out of every four of our best, most experienced pilots will volunteer. New pilots will be trained as replacements."

Tomi had an unspoken thought: If elite pilots were used in the initial suicide crashes, their inexperienced replacements would be inferior. The quality of airmanship would decrease with each suicide dive. Sea birds lived to make the next dive, suicide pilots didn't. Americans built ships faster than Japan sank them. Tomi expected a *shogun* to ask about this flaw, but no one did.

***

Newly-promoted Major Tomigawa and Senior Sergeant Takahashi spent their waking hours in a windowless closet barely big enough for their desks. Covering the east-facing wall was Suzuki's gift, an enormous framed photograph of the Emperor astride a large white horse, reviewing troops. Lord Suzuki had explained. "Its size reminds your superiors that your Uncle is now a noble in the House of Peers, but your tiny office avoids envy."

Like all paper warriors, they started and ended long days of drudgery with ceremonial bows before the Emperor's photograph. Takahashi handled the routine paper work, leaving Tomi free to attend the Army's intensive English language course 3 afternoons a week, as well as time to visit the restricted library, where he searched in vain for stories about west coast forest fires in American news publications.

After the germ warfare proposal was cancelled for fear of retaliation, Tomi had supervised the launching of thousands of Fire and Wind ships over the Pacific during the American dry season. He suspected that the wily Yankees had censored the stories, but without proof of success, his program was cancelled.

Tomi saw the wide gap between Japan's propaganda and factual reports found in foreign periodicals. The Americans, once thought to be a timid race, wasted tens of thousands of men in suicidal assaults against Japan's heavily-fortified Pacific islands. The fanatical enemy took few prisoners and Japanese losses were huge. Magazine photos showed the Japanese dead in gory detail.

Like a giant, the unstoppable Yankees used the islands as blood-soaked stepping stones, coming ever closer to Japan. Takahashi looked at a map of the empire and snorted. "We are half the fucking size we were only two years ago!"

Tomi nodded. "Shrunken glory. Once I was told the Pacific Ocean would be called 'the Lake of Japan.' If this continues, we won't have a fish pond left."

Submarine and air attacks destroyed so many Japanese cargo ships that food supplies from Japan's colonies dwindled. Even small fishing boats were targets. Food, fuel and consumer goods were tightly rationed. Takahashi and other black market operators supplied the rich with scarce food, but everyone grew thinner. The very young, the sick and the aged died first.

During Tomi's nightly drinking binges with fellow officers, he learned many truths. A Navy commander said, "The Navy sends us out on stupid missions. We make it easy for the Yankee fleets to destroy us because our admirals repeat the same tactical mistakes."

A newly-assigned captain added, "I compile top secret casualty statistics. We lost 65,000 men in the Philippines' Leyte Gulf and the Americans lost only 4,000. In the next major battle, we killed 15,000 Yankees; but it cost us 256,000 men. The total kill ratio now is 16 Japanese for every American! In manpower and territory, we are losing at an ever-faster rate." He drew deep on his cigaret and exhaled a smoky whisper of despair, "Nothing left for us except to lose the war."

General Suzuki had told Tomi that the Americans had 3 times as many ships, guns, tanks and airplanes as everything Japan had produced since 1918. Defeat was inevitable. Whispered truths became public knowledge with the fall of Okinawa, the island as sacred as Honshu. Many civilians wore white, the color of mourning, for the 110,000 Japanese soldiers and seamen killed defending Okinawa. The Americans lost 12,500 men, huge by their standards, small compared to Japan's losses. 75,000 civilians perished on Okinawa. Entire families committed suicide, holding hands as they jumped from high cliffs onto rocks below. The Japanese Command had warned the Okinawa population that the

Yankees would rape women and children, then kill them.

Japanese soldiers who fought from the mouths of caves were buried alive by American bulldozers. Another Yankee tactic was to pour barrels of aviation fuel into the caves, turning the brave defenders into flaming lanterns, just as General Nakajima's special 'Nanking oil' had done to Chinese prisoners. When Okinawa fell, spies reported there were few atrocities by Yankees and that civilians had not been deliberately harmed. Instead, the invaders gave civilians and prisoners food and medical treatment. This news was kept from the public.

***

The only bright spot was Sergeant Takahashi's promotion to *Jun-I*, Warrant Officer, thanks to General Suzuki's influence and Takahashi's keen abilities, both on duty and in the black market. They celebrated by getting drunk at a modest geisha house.

"Tomi, I am not worthy to have you as my friend. I owe everything to you."

"Nonsense. You saved my neck more times than I did yours. I got the credit for your ideas, so shut up and drink."

Takahashi slapped his chest and bellowed, "Me, second-son of a starving Sendai farmer, am now a fucking officer! It's too much for my uneducated mind to handle." He sobbed, "I don't deserve your friendship."

"Takahashi. It is I who am not worthy of you."

Takahashi stood and pulled Tomi up by his arm. Although shorter, his solid muscular peasant's body was stronger. "Don't say that. I'm not worthy of you, not the other fucking way around!"

"Don't contradict me, Takahashi," Tomi slurred.

They shoved each other and knocked over bottles and cups. Spilled sake darkened the mat. A geisha supervisor rushed in and scolded them, making Tomi pay for the damages.

Outside the tavern, they giggled. Their faces were crimson-hued from drink, exertion and the two red lanterns swinging wildly in the wind. Takahashi hugged Tomi and bawled, "We're two tiny farts in a typhoon. What's going to happen to us? We've been a team since Nanking, but when the war is over, we'll separate. I miss you already."

"Takahashi, I swear by my ancestors that we will remain a team forever."

"Bullshit! Like all *Samurai* you'll forget your promise when you sober up in the morning."

"You drunken Sendai farmer! No wonder we're losing the war. You're an officer and don't know that it's already tomorrow!"

Two hours later, Tomi and Takahashi were at their desks. Tomi raised his tea cup. "To our team in war and beyond."

Takahashi groaned, "Yeah, but what kind of beyond?"

Civilian and military morale plummeted as the Yankees got closer. On March 9, 1945 Tomi and Takahashi ignored the daily air raid siren wails as they rushed to complete an inspirational but awkward presentation titled 'The Renaming of Defeated America.' Behind schedule, they decided not to go to the air raid shelter because their modern concrete and steel building was so close to the Imperial Palace. The Americans carefully avoided bombing the Imperial Palace and nearby office buildings, believing that if they killed the Emperor, the fanatical Japanese would not stop fighting until the last man, woman and child fell.

Takahashi and Tomi carefully lettered display cards with the characters for Washington, D.C.'s new name after the Yankees surrender: 'The Emperor's New Possession.' Suddenly, the entire building shuddered. Black ink dribbled off the brushes and blotted the cards. The large photograph clattered to a sharp angle as if horse and rider were diving to the floor below.

"Earthquake!" Tomi shouted, then remembered the air raid sirens. They ran to the nearest stairwell and froze before a west-facing window. It was as if the sun had poured its molten core upon Tokyo in curtains of brilliant orange, red and yellow flames, sweeping across the miles of homes. Overhead, geysers of black, grey and white plumes shot hundreds of feet into the sky. A vast armada of B-29 bombers dropped tons of incendiaries and explosives on Tokyo's fragile wood, bamboo and paper dwellings.

In less than two hours, 100,000 men, women and children were burned alive in the hellish firestorm, the biggest raid of the war. A full year before the Pearl Harbor attack, the Yankees had invented the M-69 gasoline-gel incendiary bomb specifically designed for the wood and paper homes of Japan.

Tomi stood at the warm window pane, certain his son, mother and Taiko were dead. Takahashi pulled his arm, "Come on, Tomi! Got to help those poor people."

Wondering if the Emperor's Palace had finally been hit, Tomi ran through long corridors to an eastern window. He was relieved that the sacred grounds beyond the tranquil moat were unscathed.

"The Emperor is safe, dammit!" Takahashi panted in frustration. "Let's go! People are burning."

When they reached street level, they were hit with the roaring noise, unbelievable heat and stench of human flesh and hair. Tomi's Nanking nightmare had arrived in Tokyo. They wandered helplessly among the crowds of dazed, moaning survivors in the dense smoke and heat.

Tomi noticed a small child in a colorful kimono in the smoky haze. In shocked bewilderment, she stood too close to a doorway, which glowed cherry red from the fire within.

The child's kimono started to smoulder. Tomi stretched out his arms and ran to her, yelling over the fiery roar. "Little girl! Little girl! Come here, quickly!" He was so close that he saw the disheveled hairs of her black bangs, her little forehead, her round, doll-like face and a sooty smudge on a pink cheek.

Startled by Tomi's appearance, she cried, "Mother!" Her tiny white stockinged feet flickered like little rabbits as she ran back into the flames. Framed by the blazing doorway, her bright yellow kimono with its red flower pattern turned into a bright torch. Tomi tried to reach her but a solid fist of heat hit him backward. Her shrill, steady scream of agony ended after he fell.

It was Tomi's fault. He was a tall demon who had chased a frightened child back into the fire. Takahashi lifted him and slapped at his smouldering uniform, not understanding that Tomi required the hot pain to punish him for having turned a girl-child into a bright lantern.

Takahashi and Tomi herded survivors into groups and waited for medical help or death, whichever came first. They learned not to touch the burned ones, whose skin came off like melted wax.

In a single-room schoolhouse that somehow escaped the firestorm, they searched for survivors but found piles of children's bodies. All appeared to be sleeping. They had suffocated from the firestorm, which had consumed all the oxygen. Tomi prayed that his baby son, mother and his Taiko had died the same way and not in screaming pain. Both men remembered the Nanking girls' school torture scene and the German Nazi who cried, 'Why? Why?'at the horror.

When rescue teams finally organized the triage of the dying, the doomed and the survivors, Tomi and Takahashi found a creek and splashed dirty water over themselves, rinsing off the worst of the clinging stench. Sitting on the muddy bank, Tomi said, "I'm going home, knowing what I will find."

Takahashi offered to accompany him, but Tomi refused. "I will see you tomorrow or the day after ... depending. Thank you, my brother."

Tokyo stank like Nanking as he headed toward his mother's house. Shuffling past miles of smoking ruins and ignoring dazed victims, The memory of the girl-child's final scream forced him to compose a *haiku*:

> *The enemy's fire*
> *Sharpens its fangs on the screams*
> *Of Tokyo's children.*

He gave a passing rickshaw puller 4 times the usual fare to carry him through the smouldering fire and debris-strewn route to his former home. He slumped in the wide seat and the puller's steady pace lulled him into an exhausted stupor. The rickshaw's 2 large wheels jolted over a trolley track switch, awakening him. The lack of destruction surprised him.

His boyhood neighborhood was untouched, but he feared his loved ones had suffocated. He ran into the house he hadn't visited since the terrible quarrel. Lady Tomigawa looked up from her desk in startled happiness. "I was just writing you, my son."

He winced when she touched him.

"You're burned!"

"I'm ashamed of my rotten behavior. Please forgive me."

"Never mind that nonsense. We both made mistakes."

He looked around for Taiko. His mother answered his silent

question. "Your honorable wife and son are unharmed. The Suzuki's sent a messenger. Their compound escaped the firestorm, as did this neighborhood. Only the gods know why. My Taiko is aiding survivors. The block wardens enlisted neighborhood servants for rescue work during the emergency."

She gently dabbed a soothing salve on his burns as he gulped cold tea. She gave him a 'charity-to-strangers' bowl filled with a rice cake and tea for the rickshaw runner squatting on the curb. The skinny man blessed Tomi with good luck that was undeserved.

He got back in the rickshaw and gave the puller directions to the Suzuki compound.

When he greeted his wife, she snapped, "Don't you dare wake up my son from his nap! And clean yourself before Honorable Uncle sees you in such an unpresentable condition."

He glanced down at his singed, muddy and torn uniform. His wife left the room and he entered the nursery, nodding a silent greeting to the bowing nursemaid. His sleeping son looked more like General Suzuki than Tomi. *May your life be a better one than mine, my son,* he thought and kissed him gently.

Two servants carrying clean clothes followed Tomi into the bath shed. They peeled off his uniform and gently sponged off the sooty grime that held the scent of burning death. Finally clean, Tomi climbed into the hot water and sat perfectly still. The intense heat on his painful burns reminded him of the girl-child.

For the next 140 days and nights, the sirens wailed and antique fire alarms, steel rims hanging on chains, resonated with frantic hammer blows. Unopposed, waves of B-29's continuously carpet-bombed an already destroyed Tokyo and the 5 other major cities of the Sacred Home Islands. The vengeful Americans were mutilating a corpse. When all major targets were charred rubble, the Yankee bombsights turned to the remaining 58 secondary cities and towns. Another 150,000 civilians died.

In a stuffy underground bunker, Tomi waited to present his proposed Japanese names for conquered American cities that were to be part of a morale improvement program ordered by hardline leaders. An elderly naval officer pontificated, "The Imperial Palace plans a mass *Kamikaze* attack that will destroy most of the American fleet. Ships that survive the air attacks will be sunk by our midget suicide submarines. Their losses will be enormous."

"Quite so!" a highly-decorated general added, "We have issued millions of bamboo spears to the civilian population. They will impale the half-drowned invaders who crawl ashore like gasping fish! Then we'll resume the offensive. The demoralized Yankees will be forced to sue for peace."

Tomi noted that the patriotic fervor increased as the war grew worse. Denial was woven into the Japanese character as a survival mechanism. Far more dangerous were younger zealots, who planned mass suicide infantry attacks on the invaders. Despite defeat and devastation, the die-hards were intoxicated with the spirit of *Bushido*, not caring how many millions of civilians would perish.

Tomi's suggested American city names were rejected. The only decision made was that, upon Japan's eventual victory, the U.S.A. would be changed to 'Colony of Inferior Rank.'

Tomi almost symphathized with the fanatics. Everyone preferred to dwell on a glorious death rather than live in an unthinkable future.

CHAPTER FIFTEEN
TOKYO, 1945

Takahashi ravenously devoured the contents of his *bentoo,* lunch box: a small scoop of brown rice, two withered radishes and a thin slice of pickle. Despite his hunger, Tomi claimed he was too hung-over to eat and gave his lunch to Takahashi. Tonight Tomi was to feast with Lord Suzuki, who would spout starvation statistics through mouthfuls of delicacies.

The Army-issue desk calendar read *Shichigatsu, Showa Neiju* the 6th month of the 20th year of the God Emperor's reign. The Yankee naval blockade was squeezing the calories out of the Japanese like a monstrous snake. Even Takahashi's black market no longer had food to sell, only tobacco and occupation loot. Allied prisoners, doing hard labor on 800 calories a day, died in droves.

Few knew that the *shidooryoku,* national leadership, was not starving, thanks to secret food deliveries to their homes. The Suzuki family compound had an abundance of sake and almost enough food. Tomi's baby son received all that he needed to survive, and Lady Tomigawa was sent an occasional food packet. The lucky few ate less, but didn't starve like so many others.

The famished majority were unaware that the government had secret warehouses from which the elite received rice, sake, dried fish, sugar, canned vegetables and fruit; and infrequently, tinned mutton and beef captured during early victories. Officials told each other that they must remain healthy and strong in order to make wise decisions in difficult times.

Hunger forced families to scour the countryside, trading family heirlooms for a few fresh vegetables or a knotted scarf containing a bulge of unpolished rice grains. Lowly farmer-peasants, ignored and disdained by city dwellers during the

Depression, now enjoyed fawning respect.

Tokyo had no fat people and few happy ones. The only non-alcoholic gaiety came from uniformed troops of pale-faced schoolchildren marching in step, cheerfully singing about victory over the enemy. Their little arms and legs, swinging in patriotic rhythm, were disfigured by the round, open red sores of malnutrition.

Civilians died either from starvation in a slow, silent spiral; or wet and loudly, coughing up blood from tuberculosis-infected lungs. The quickest mercy was to be roasted alive by Yankee fire bombs. Japan's soldiers, fighting last-ditch battles, frantically worried about their families at home. Death was unpredictable but bureaucracy was constant. Tomi performed meaningless paperwork for generals whose only duty was to decide when to issue the final 'fight unto death' order to the entire nation.

The only happy face that Tomi saw was in the *benjo*, toilet. Latrine Orderly Kogaki constantly beamed over his good fortune. Not only did he attend the personal needs of high ranking officers and celebrity-heroes like Tomi, but he also got free tobacco for storing Takahashi's black market cigarets. Takahashi explained, "The latrine is perfect for transactions. Everyone goes there."

The emaciated Kokagi chain-smoked as he cheerfully cleaned and polished the row of porcelain floor holes. When someone entered his latrine, Kokagi snapped to attention like a proud drill instructor in front of his perfect line of gleaming white oval targets, over which the generals squatted for their bowel movements.

"Tomi, do you know what's perplexing about Kokagi?" Takahashi asked as he licked moist traces from the bottom of his lunch box. "Our happy latrine-man is in the ideal position to observe that our well-fed leaders enjoy regularity while the rest of us have lost ours. This proves what I have long suspected: no matter what happens, generals are always full of shit."

He grew serious. "Unlike Kokagi, I know what's going on, Tomi, including the secret rations delivered to fat leaders' homes. If we live through this war, I will repay you a thousandfold for every grain of rice you have given me."

Tokyo no longer existed. The Army building where they

worked stood out like a lonely exclamation mark on the flattened landscape. It was one of the few undamaged structures close to the sacrosanct Palace. Most of the city was reduced to crazy heaps of jagged grey concrete, twisted steel, broken bricks and miles of charred wood.

Unopposed waves of B-29's trailed white contrails across the blue sky, each dropping 5,000 pounds of fire bombs. The silver giant bombers were 25,000 feet above the blackened corpses of all sizes. The grief-stricken could not point with certainty to where their family homes once stood. Japan was destroyed, but disorder offended the living as they continued their daily routines. After every raid, the debris-choked streets were cleared for survivors to shuffle to their assigned tasks.

At the end of long workdays, Tomi moved with the silent, haggard crowds in the summer heat, which cooked shattered concrete and unreachable human fragments into an obnoxious smell that soaked into uniforms, ragged civilian suits and women's shapeless, dark 'war' pants. It was unpatriotic to wear colorful kimonos in public.

Drab and exhausted, the Japanese encased themselves in a gloomy denial of reality. The government's glib lies and exhortations that poured from radio, newspapers and patriotic rallies were still believed by many ... a necessity that enabled people to endure yet another day. There was no alternative.

Tomi pondered how a once-proud Japan would cope with the impending defeat. Only Uncle Suzuki had the answers as he continued to exercise power from his unscathed compound guarded by hard-eyed men.

As the war worsened, his private dinners with Tomi quickened to an obligatory weekly ritual that began by sharing the hot tub in steamy silence. This night was no different.

Unlike most men, Lord Suzuki didn't gossip when he soaked in the luxurious bathhouse, his retreat from misery, starvation and death. Only slurps of sake and burps of contentment broke the steamy silence.

After the soak, they donned kimonos of rare quilted silk and ate a grand dinner. Many courses had more calories than Latrine Orderly Kokagi's family consumed in a week; or a beaten Yankee

POW was given in three. Lord Suzuki usually chewed and talked at the same time. Tonight he ate without preaching, and Tomi was grateful but wary. There was always a Suzuki surprise.

The servants were dismissed and they retired to his private study for more sake and conversation, blanketed by loud music. Lord Suzuki tapped one finger to the complexity of Bach's Fantasia in C Minor. "Did you know Bach was denied a coveted organist's position at a Hamburg church after he wrote Fantasia? He had a big family to feed and needed the job. It was one of his bitterest disappointments," Suzuki said without his usual preamble.

His fixed stare through the monocle signaled that an important point was being made. Tomi bobbed his head as a student should. "But Bach, genius that he was, survived to become immortal. Great nations, like great men, suffer setbacks. But ... ?"

Tomi voiced the response expected of the solitary student of the Suzuki Academy of Power:" ... But a great nation endures for eventual success?"

Suzuki nodded. "Did you know the Germans, perhaps Bach's ancestors, practiced cannibalism a few centuries earlier?" Tomi knew this odd fact was the spear-tip of a sake-drenched lesson. Tomi's wife claimed Japanese men pretended drunkenness to communicate because only then could they express unconventional thoughts or criticism without fear of penalty or loss of face.

Drunk or sober, Suzuki lectured only when his Victrola phonograph blared classical music from a speaker shaped like a morning glory blossom. Suzuki trusted no one, least of all his servants and guards. The blanket of music was his defense against the *Kempetai's* network of ears. The degree of Suzuki's dangerous candor was determined by the selection from his library of one-sided Victor Red Seal records. If he played Bach or Beethoven, Japan and Suzuki had had a bad day, and Tomi would hear whispered harangues about the blind fools in the reshuffled military government. The cheerful Rossini overtures hadn't been played since the devastating naval defeat at Midway.

When the steel spring inside the polished walnut phonograph cabinet lost kinetic energy and slowed the music to a dirge, Suzuki stopped talking. Tomi jumped up and gently lifted the arm of the needle from the groove without scratching the record. He cranked the wooden handle of the expensive machine, put the needle back in the record groove and waited for music to fill the room before he asked, "Cannibalism in Germany?"

"Yes. Hansel and Gretel. A fairy tale based upon true stories of stray children who were slaughtered for food by starving German peasants during 15th and 16th century wars."

Like Tomi's nasty wife, her uncle was able to pronounce the troublesome *gaijin* "L." Twisting the tongue so crookedly was another family trait. Tomi wondered if his son would have it.

"In defeat, a starving person will do anything to survive. Food replaces money. Hungry people can't eat bank accounts. Paper money is only good for ass-wiping," Suzuki sniffed and inserted another cigaret into his yellowed ivory holder. He stared at the white cylinder tightly packed with aromatic Virginia tobacco. "Cigarets become money too. You don't smoke, so you can't understand that life without tobacco is torture. People will pay any price for tobacco." He snapped open his Ronson lighter, taken from a long-dead American marine.

"Uncle, how much time do we have left?"

Before responding, Lord Suzuki pulled a blue silk handkerchief from his wide kimono sleeve and patted sweat from his face, skirting the monocle. "You ask when will we be defeated, not if. Times change and so must we." He filled his lungs with American smoke. "You get the same reports that I do. You read Yankee magazines in the restricted library. And you probably have learned the truth by talking to battle survivors."

He weaved and steadied himself. "Japan is a mortally wounded *Samurai* warrior. No arrows remain in our quiver and we grasp a broken sword that's as useless as a limp cock. We are surrounded by blood-thirsty enemies who hate our skin color and seek revenge for having humbled them in earlier battles. *Bushido* heritage demands that we fight to the death or commit suicide to show the Yankees we don't fear death." He hissed with contempt. "All that is fucking nonsense!"

Tomi's headache returned as Suzuki continued. "Some middle-ranking officers threaten to assassinate the royal advisors and kidnap *Showa Sama* if the court fails to order the nation to fight to the death. The fools are as blindly arrogant as those who received the Emperor's permission to attack Pearl Harbor."

He waved his hand, cigaret smoke trailing the motion. "Those die-hards have issued orders that all prisoners of war be executed! My connections and I have sent secret messages advising all field commanders to ignore the order." He carefully placed his cigaret holder down before slamming his fist into an open palm. "Times have changed!"

Tomi smelled fear and tobacco when he bent forward to hear Suzuki's whisper. "Why are your scientist friends at Unit 731 still using Yankee prisoners for vivisection and medical experiments? Why do we still torture and kill *gaijin* POW's? If we're not careful, we'll all be put to death as war criminals! It's going to happen in Germany. Then we'll be next!"

His eyes flicked around the room. "If the Americans learn about all of the 'Matters Best Left Unsaid,' they'll hang every war leader in Japan!"

"Uncle, what about the Emperor?

Switching to formal court language, Suzuki intoned, "The *Showa Sama* is safe. A monumental task has been accomplished. This humble one was honored to personally receive the Royal Wish. Official records were cleansed of delicate matters that involved members of the Royal Family. The expunging was done under this one's earnest supervision."

Tomi was impressed that his mentor had performed such a crucial task for the Godhead.

Suzuki returned to ordinary language. "Not an easy task to destroy nearly eight years of war evidence in a fortnight. But we learned from the mistakes of our defeated Nazi allies, who recorded everything. We erased most of the Imperial connection with 'Matters Best Left Unsaid.' And we will always deny that such things ever happened.

"Why should we compound our miserable defeat with flawed mythology and false heroics? We are a modern, competent nation led by very good minds. Japan has to survive and create a new future in a world not of our own choosing."

Suzuki's words echoed Lady Tomigawa's when she had

entreated Tomi to live like a coward and continue the bloodline. Now Lord Suzuki expected Japan to do the same. "We will become a despised, shit-eating penal colony. The Yankees will be our harsh masters for two, maybe three generations. The *gaijin* will inflict the same humiliations upon us that we did to the Chinese, Koreans, Filipinos and the other gooks we conquered."

Tomi pictured his infant son being tossed into the air and caught on a Yankee bayonet for sport. People buried alive in mass graves. An orgy of rapes. Would Japan become another Nanking?

Suzuki used his cigaret holder as a red-tipped dagger aimed at Tomi. "Survival is our new national mission, regardless of how despicable our lives will be as Yankee slaves! The *Showa Sama's* Imperial Wish is for Japan to survive this disaster!"

Headache forgotten, Tomi blurted, "The God-Emperor wants us to stop fighting now?"

"Not that simple. Obeying an Imperial Wish, a few of us are secretly working out surrender terms with the Yankees through a neutral embassy. Hopefully, they won't find much evidence of 'Matters Best Left Unsaid.' The Yankees and British hint that they will allow the Emperor to remain on the throne despite their earlier unconditional surrender nonsense.

"Meanwhile, we must oppose those who want to arm our women and children with bamboo spears for suicide attacks against the Yankees. At the appropriate time, the Emperor will agree to a surrender swiftly and without warning. The die-hards won't have time to organize resistance."

"But what about those who will die in the meantime? Our forces must stand down now."

Suzuki scolded, "What is more important? Saving lives or having the Yankees' guarantee that the Emperor remain on the throne? Surely that's worth a million lives."

Tomi shouted, "*Hai!*" over Bach. Every Japanese would gladly give up his life to assure the *Showa Sama's* continuity. Without him, there was no Japan.

"Fortunately, Nephew, the enemy doesn't want another Okinawa bloodbath any more than we do. Resisting an invasion of the Home Islands would result in useless carnage for both sides. The Americans realize the value of the Emperor, a good bureaucracy, a disciplined national police force and a docile population after a surrender. The Americans need our institutions and ruling class to keep the fanatics from turning Japan into a slaughterhouse. A peaceful occupation is in both our interests ... even if a few must pay the ultimate price as war criminals."

Suzuki removed a sheaf of papers from a red and black antique cabinet. "Enough about the politics of defeat. We must discuss the survival of Suzuki Industries. When surrender comes in a few months, bank accounts, currency and bonds will be worthless. For more than a year I've been converting my fortune into assets that are safely hidden in warehouses guarded by trusted employees and their families in small villages and remote hamlets. Big cities will soon be too dangerous. Here are itemized lists and maps of our farms, employee homes and warehouses on the Home Islands. The maps show locations of buried caches of gold, jewelry, U.S. dollars, pounds and other currencies."

Tomi glanced through the maps and accounting sheets, amazed at the total wealth.

Suzuki smiled without humor. "The enemy will search here and find nothing. Let them confiscate worthless bank accounts and securities! The real wealth is elsewhere. Memorize and return these papers to me tomorrow morning before you leave the compound.

"I share the secret with you, but not the hidden wealth. If, and only if, I am dead and you are the sole male survivor of the Suzuki-Tomigawa family, then you become temporary steward of the Suzuki assets, but you are never the owner. Understand?"

Tomi bowed agreement.

"However, if I remain alive, even as a war criminal in prison with a life sentence, on peril of your neck, remove nothing! The hidden assets belong to the Suzuki clan, not to you. Even if you must sleep in the gutter, don't take a single sen! When Tomyuko reaches adulthood, you will turn over control of Suzuki Industries to your son. He is my successor of the Suzuki clan, not you."

Tomi understood what he should have realized years ago. Suzuki and his niece intended to change his son's name from Tomigawa to Suzuki. He vowed silently that would never happen.

Sensing Tomi's anger, Suzuki growled, "Should you act

contrary to my instructions, be aware that I have some official reports of your illustrious 'Matters Best Left Unsaid' career. They bear your signature and personal chop, evidence of your work at Unit 731; how you spread plague germs among the Russians; and yes, even back in the old days when you participated in the Nanking Days of Shame."

He sighed dramatically. "These incriminating papers could land in the hands of a vengeful Yankee prosecutor. Then the Americans, Chinese and Russians would all fight for the honor of hanging you."

As Suzuki's protégé, Tomi was not surprised by the blackmail threat. "What if a Yankee tortures or tricks me into revealing the secret caches as I did to the old Chinese priest?"

"Die before you are captured. My niece has memorized the secret locations. Should you and I both join our ancestors, your wife will prepare Tomyuko for Suzuki leadership."

Now that Tomi had produced a son, the clan's wealth had more value than Tomi's life.

"One last point, Nephew. The Americans will intensify their bombing raids to pressure us as we negotiate to retain the Emperor and secure amnesty for the Royal Family. I want your wife, son, and Lady Tomigawa to go to our rural estate in Nagasaki for their safety."

"But Uncle, shouldn't they go to your property in Hiroshima? It's much closer. The Yankees have barely touched Hiroshima. It has no major troop concentrations or war factories. The Mitsubishi Ordnance Works is in Nagasaki."

General Suzuki stormed, "Now you're an air raid expert? I've already made arrangements. Such crucial decisions are mine to make, not yours. The family goes to Nagasaki!"

"Sir! The honorable general can order me to die and I will obey; but you cannot order the Tomigawas to do your bidding."

"Enough! My niece has agreed to take her son to Nagasaki. If you want Lady Tomigawa to go to Hiroshima, so be it."

Without another word, Tomi left the study with the secret maps. His sake-fed anger cooled as he changed from the borrowed kimono to his uniform. By the time Tomi staggered across the compound to his house, he wondered if Suzuki was right. Perhaps

Tomi's son would be safer in Nagasaki. Tomi stumbled into his darkened house, knowing that his wife had not waited up for him as a dutiful wife would have done.

The next morning, Tomi was in Suzuki's study. He bowed and returned the maps and files. "Honorable Lord, I have memorized the contents and vow to obey your instructions to the letter."

Suzuki smiled, "Thank you, Nephew. I am as pleased with your familial obedience as I am with your memory. Tell me, is your hangover as bad as mine? I got so drunk I don't recall you leaving."

Tomi forced a laugh. "Yes, Uncle. My headache tells me that I had more than enough of your delicious sake. It was such a pleasant evening that I too am hazy about my departure. In case I was too drunk to thank you, please accept my appreciation for your abundant hospitality."

***

Lady Tomigawa did not take the news of leaving Tokyo gracefully. "Mother, Suzuki has arranged for you and Taiko to move into one of his estates in Hiroshima for your safety. He believes the air raids in Tokyo will get worse, if such a thing is possible."

"Will I be joining Tomyuko and your wife?"

"They go to Nagasaki. He wanted you to go with them, but I believe Hiroshima is safer."

"So? You openly disagreed with a lord of the realm?" She snorted in disgust. "Will you never learn? What difference does it make, except to your silly pride? Did it ever occur to you that I want to be with my grandson, no matter where? Thanks to your stubbornness, now I must go to Hiroshima so that you save face. I shall miss Tomyuko beyond words, but at least I won't have to be with that insufferable wife of yours."

"I am sorry, Mother. I made a hasty decision. Please accept my apology."

"You behave like a vain *Samurai*. Such stupidity has ruined Japan. What will a proud warrior like you do after defeat? Do you have any idea of what you will become?"

Tomi pondered her question and said, "Once I thought that being a warrior was everything. Then I discovered that each success made me more discontented and unhappy. The more I succeeded, the less I became. Now, Mother, I know what I am not."

"Then there is hope for you," she snapped. He looked up, expecting forgiveness. But her eyes were as hard as when she had negotiated the marriage dowry. Tonelessly, she said, "Your shock was Nanking. Mine was nearly 22 years ago after the Great Earthquake destroyed two-thirds of Tokyo and almost all of Yokohama.

"Hirohito was Regent for his crazy, ailing father. Since the Prime Minister had just died, Hirohito was in complete control and answered to no one. He survived that Saturday afternoon because he was in Tokyo's first earthquake-proof building, built on Palace grounds. At the height of the ensuing firestorm, frightened crowds rushed across the moat bridge to the Imperial grounds, seeking safety. Police and palace guards turned the crowd away, forcing them back toward the inferno that had been ignited by lunchtime charcoal fires in demolished houses.

"Ancient folklore claimed a gigantic catfish, son of the Sun Goddess, sleeps at the bottom of the ocean. If the person on the throne displeases him, he will awaken and thrash around, causing earthquakes. According to legend, the only way to appease the catfish god is for the Emperor to relinquish his throne to another.

"We Japanese are superstitious, and Hirohito knew the public would blame him and not his insane father. Hirohito feared another relative would be named Emperor. He needed a scapegoat.

"Your beloved *Showa Sama* appointed a martial law commandant, and within days, the Palace-sponsored patriotic societies and the *Kempetai* were spreading rumors that Koreans, Communists and Socialists had offended the giant catfish god. Thugs and vigilantes hunted down everyone in Tokyo who spoke with an accent. 4,000 Koreans were dragged from their slums and publicly beheaded. *Kempetai* used the unrest to arrest political troublemakers and their families."

Uncomfortable with her treasonous talk, Tomi asked, "Where did you learn this?"

"Your Honorable Father told me about the Palace politics and I witnessed the street executions of Koreans. There's more. Is the truth too uncomfortable for you?

"The *Kempetai* killed several political prisoners in their cells on Hirohito's orders. There was a scandal when word of the Imperial involvement leaked out. It's difficult for you to grasp this, Tomi, but Japan was once a free society before Hirohito installed his own government. All the brave political leaders and newspaper editors who expressed outrage were later assassinated, arrested or intimidated. Hirohito, whose ancestors probably included Korean nobles, had thousands of innocent Koreans murdered as scapegoats to assure his ascension to the throne!"

"What about Honorable Father? Did he share your ... your feelings about the Throne?"

"Of course. Why else do you think he was selected to commit suicide? For generations both of our families have lived outside the royal circle because of our dual ancient claims to the throne. If only the strands of history had twisted differently ... "

"But our family has always been loyal warriors."

"In every war and revolt, the Tomigawas had to prove they were twice as loyal, twice as brave and twice as suicidal as anybody else. It's the price we paid for having purer noble blood than that ambitious man whom you revere as Emperor."

They sat in silence until he quietly asked, "Is everything I believe in false?"

"Japan is true! Only a few leaders are false. Our family is good, not evil. And so are you."

"We are defeated. What good is left in this world?"

"The Japanese people are good. You must help them."

"What can I do? I am nothing. Despite your words, Mother, In my heart I still revere *Showa Sama*! I can't help it."

She sighed wearily. "You are your father's son. Like him, you will die honoring your Emperor. But you are my son too! Survive and prosper because of the contradiction, not despite it." Dry-eyed, she handed Tomi a handkerchief to wipe his tears.

"Your Honorable Father and I cried in this very room the night he left to commit suicide for his Emperor. I have no tears left for you, Tomi. All I ask is that you honor both of us by remembering you come from both of us.

She reached across and gently touched his face. "You'll have to find your own way. I forgive you for acting like a fool; it's in your blood. Survive and learn to live as a historical contradiction. I will go to Hiroshima with Taiko."

Before he left, Tomi knelt before the small shrine in the garden and talked to the spirits of Honorable Father and the old priest of Nanking. His questions met with silence.

***

General Suzuki and Tomi took their families to the partially bombed Tokyo railroad station on August 1st. Lady Tomigawa and his Taiko would get off the train in Hiroshima, while the Suzuki's Taiko and Tomi's son continued south to the Nagasaki ferry boat.

Mother stared intently at Tomi as if memorizing his face. "Remember my words and my love."

Dropping all formality, Tomi hugged her. He glanced over her shoulder at his beloved Taiko, who lowered her head. He exchanged bows with his wife. Tomi lifted his smiling son, Tomyuko, and kissed him. "Until we see each other again, my Tomichan."

***

Five days later, Tomi was in his office when someone yelled, "A super bomb has destroyed Hiroshima! Everyone is dead!"

When he regained consciousness, Tomi staggered to the *benjo* and shoved a startled Kikagi away from the dirty latrine he was cleaning. Tomi retched and curled around the messy hole. Tomi saw Kogaki's canvas shoes and heard him say in a nicotine-tainted gust of concern, "Major Tomigawa! Are you poisoned?"

The poison was in his decision, which killed the two women he loved, along with some 140,000 others who died with them in the instant fireball. The Nanking priest had warned him that he would be cursed.

Three days later, Tomi returned to duty to find Takahashi

weeping bitterly. Tomi assumed that the Takahashi family in Sendai had been killed in an air raid. When Tomi tried to comfort him, Takahashi silently handed Tomi a two-sentence teletyped message. The words didn't register. He blinked in disbelief, then slowly read them again. The Yankees had dropped a second super bomb on Nagasaki. No one in Japan knew the main target had been another city obscured in industrial smog. The B-29 pilot had decided to drop the atomic bomb on less-important Nagasaki.

Tomi didn't feel the hypodermic needle. His son, mother and Taiko were holding hands with the little girl in white stockings as they burned. They begged him to help but he couldn't enter the flaming doorway. He was unaware that their endless screams came from his own throat.

Tomi resisted a return to reality, but Takahashi forced fed him and bullied him into shaving and bathing. Takahashi had removed his revolver and sword but he didn't care. He wasn't sufficiently alive to consider suicide.

Breaking tradition, the God-Emperor spoke directly to the Japanese people on August 15, 1945. In a pre-recorded radio speech, he ordered his subjects to "bear the unbearable." The Great Pacific War was over. But it too late for Tomi.

CHAPTER SIXTEEN
OCCUPIED JAPAN AUGUST 1945

In the stale swelter of summer, swarms of Yankee combat troops arrived with the Surrender. Japan's disarmed warriors in 'demobilization suits' -- uniforms with insignias ripped off – obeyed Emperor Hirohito's edict and behaved like defeated gooks.

Like bewildered creatures suddenly caged, the Japanese tried to assess their strange captivity, but the U.S. Army confused them. Instead of expressing contempt for gooks with bayonet and boot as Japan had done, the *gaijin* were gruff but good-natured. The Americans shared food and candy with begging children and shy women. The few Jap-hating Yankees punched and slapped no harder than a Japanese sergeant would.

Remembering the Japanese Army's own brutal policy of mass rapes and forcing females to be sex slaves in comfort women brothels, Tokyo's occupation-appointed civil government urged lower-class girls and war widows to offer themselves to Yankees.

The unspoken purpose was to protect upper-class maidens from dishonor and foreign sperm contamination. Notices urged unattached females to enlist in one of the new brothel organizations, including the 'Special Comfort Facilities Association' and the 'Recreation & Amusement Association.' A patriotic recruiting rally was even held near the Palace moat. In designated brothel districts, the Yankees overpaid their favorite prostitutes, to the consternation of the poorer Japanese clients.

Although the official brothels, often operated by *Yakuza* crime clans, would continue for seven months, women of many classes enjoyed a new freedom from restrictions. Japan had lost more than 1.25 million men, and the surplus of lonely women were attracted to young Yankees with money and food. A lucky few found genuine, lasting romance.

Yankees bargained genially for sex instead of taking it, as the Japanese soldiers had done. The price was a candy bar or cigarets. Demobilized Japanese veterans silently glowered as the mixed-race couples fondled and kissed in public. Loss of ancient traditions were part of defeat.

Non-suicidal repeats of Puccini's 'Madam Butterfly' were common as Yankees were shipped home for discharge, leaving behind broken-hearted *koibitos*, who would find new lovers among replacement troops. Venereal disease -- both Yankee and Japanese varieties -- blossomed into epidemic proportions among the careless.

Learning their new role as gooks, the Japanese came to regard Americans as oversized, spoiled children intent upon enjoying themselves. They only turned nasty when *okoru*, 'pissed-off' or mean-drunk. On the other hand, the American Military Police were quick to hit when Japanese inadvertently disobeyed because of the language barrier. But even then, MPs treated Japanese veterans no worse than they did their own soldiers who were unruly.

In this strange landscape of servile gooks and occupiers, Tomi met Takahashi in an alley off the *Ginza*, where streetwalkers and thugs from the crime clans did business with occupation troops. Takahashi nodded calmly when Tomi told him that Lord Suzuki had been arrested and was in Sugamo Prison as a Class A war criminal.

"You're probably on the next arrest order, Tomi. Get the hell out of Tokyo now!"

"I don't care. Besides, I have no money and no place to go. The Americans confiscated everything. All I have is what I am wearing." Tomi didn't need to mention Suzuki's vast hidden wealth because everyone, except the dense Yankee officials, knew that wealthy families and corporations had buried their wealth.

"Go hide at my folks' farm in Sendai. I've been writing them about you for years."

"How about you? Aren't you coming?"

"No, Tomi. There are big fortunes to be made here. The *Americanjin*, from generals to privates, are eager to deal in the black market. The dumb bastards want to sell us everything except their guns, uniforms and jeeps. It's a gold mine and I'm setting up an organization."

"You'll be arrested! All it takes is a *Kempetai* record or someone informing on you in exchange for a job with the Occupation Army."

"I'm a nobody. Besides, my *Yakuzi* pals will protect me. You are different. Too much hero publicity. Tokyo is dangerous for you, not me. I have enough cash on me for train fare, but nothing else. Here, take it. When you get to Sendai, change your name."

"Absolutely not! I will never deny my heritage."

"*Samurai* crap," he sighed. "Get out of Tokyo now!"

***

Sweating, dirty and weak from hunger, Tomi stood with other silent veterans, tightly packed in a wobbly pre-war railroad coach with its seats removed to increase capacity. They swayed in hungry, smelly unison as the usual 8-hour trip from Tokyo to Sendai crawled into its 14th tortuous hour because of frequent stops on the bomb-damaged track. No one had food or water but they knew they were the lucky ones who survived the war.

At Fukushima, Tomi separated from the throng who filed off the train to empty their bladders, stretch aching backs and beg for food. A troop train of Yankees, riding in first-class coaches with plush seats, was halted at the station platform. Tomi noticed these American soldiers were different from the tough, lean, older-looking combat troops who had first entered Tokyo. These troops must be replacements going to Sendai and points north. They wore the same steel helmets and carried rifles, bayonets and battle packs, but their cartridge belts were flat instead of bulging with ammo. Tomi guessed they were green troops, not to be trusted with live ammo. They behaved more like schoolboys on holiday than disciplined soldiers.

These Yankees must have disembarked from a troopship and immediately transferred to the train. Tomi mused that Japan was so weak that raw recruits were masters of a once-mighty military empire. Every Japanese veteran on the crowded train platform was a superior soldier to the soft Yankee babies who gawked at the veterans as if they were monkeys at a zoo.

Women on the platform averted their eyes when the Americans unbuttoned their khaki pants and waved their penises through the open train windows. They yelled, *"Pom-pom! Pom-pom! Skibbie! Skibbie!* Fuck! Fuck!" There were no officers or non-coms in sight to keep order.

An old crone, her thin body lost in a frayed, oversized kimono, squatted near the troop train.

"Skibbie?" she repeated, then made a 'no' motion toward her lap and a 'yes' motion to her gaping, toothless mouth. Like many elderly, she looked mentally unhinged from starvation, the bombings or both. The Americans clapped and whooped. Her bawdy, harmless humor matched their teenaged vulgarity. The rowdy soldiers gestured for her to come closer.

Like a friendly, hungry dog, the old woman smiled and hobbled over, lacking only a wagging tail. A soldier tossed her a combat ration biscuit. She picked it off the ground and bowed thanks. The thick round cracker easily withstood the old woman's toothless gumming. She hobbled away to find water to soften the yellow-brown hardness.

Tomi's growling stomach reminded him that yesterday he had eaten a single scoop of dirty brown rice at a charity kitchen, and nothing the day before. Tomi refused to beg food from the Yankees, but hunger betrayed him. Reluctantly, he went to the same train window. A grinning thin soldier with grotesque blue eyes and large white teeth offered Tomi two round crackers stuck together with a layer of white paste. Tomi hesitated and the American moved it toward his own mouth and made loud lip-smacking sounds. Gut-wrenching stomach cramps doubled Tomi over. The soldiers laughed at Tomi's contorted response to the eating pantomime.

Tomi couldn't help himself. He unbent and accepted the offered food. He had eaten captured enemy combat rations before, but never two crackers with paste between. He thought this must be the American *sandoitchi*, sandwich.

"Eat, gook, eat," the soldier urged. Tomi tried to bite an edge, but ravenous hunger made him devour it whole. His mouth was so dry, the food stuck in his throat. He couldn't chew, swallow or cough it up. He bobbed his head like a crane gulping a big frog. Gagging, he forced the stubborn cracker down, but his mouth was filled with an offensive, medicinal taste.

The American laughed as if Tomi were a circus clown who had done something funny. Other soldiers stuffed their genitalia back into their trousers and pointed to Tomi. Why was he being ridiculed? He heard a new English word 'prokit,' along with the usual 'gook' and 'fuckin' Jap.'

The blue-eyed *gaijin* showed Tomi a small aluminum tube, unbuttoned his pants and pretended to insert it into his penis hole. Laughing, he aimed the tube at Tomi and squirted whitish cream out of the needle-like opening. It dribbled down the outside of the coach. The soldiers howled even louder when Tomi's face registered comprehension and disgust.

He had eaten venereal disease medicine. They had killed his family and now this. He wished he had eaten poison. Other Japanese veterans were as baffled as Tomi, but the railroad workers in somber, dark uniforms looked away in embarrassment. They were familiar with the common prank that America's child-soldiers played on starving gooks.

He heard his mother's voice. "Survival is the only honor you have left." To keep from vomiting, Tomi imagined his sword hacking off the Yankee's arms and legs; 5 cuts for each leg and 3 for each arm joint; 16 strokes in all. He felt blade cutting through bone. When the *gaijin*'s ugly blue-eyed head screamed for mercy, Tomi would split the torso.

The fantasy ended. Tomi was *obutsu*, filth, a nonhuman humiliated by the victors. He couldn't bear to remind himself that he had done far worse, starting with Nanking and beyond. Yes. He would survive, but he had to take revenge upon an enemy he was forbidden to hurt. In frustration, he glanced about. Two Japanese black marketeers with thick rolls of yen were buying cigarets from the Americans at the coach nearest the steam locomotive.

Tomi pulled out his almost-worthless small change in sen bills. A hundred sen equaled one yen. Both were paper currency, but sen bills were smaller. Would the newly-arrived Yankees know this? Could Tomi trick them as they had tricked him?

He went to the farthest coach, where he wouldn't be

recognized as the gook who ate venereal disease cream. He waved his roll of sen and asked, "Tobacco? Tobacco? Me got much money for tobacco."

An American with a freckled face held up a carton of cigarets and waved him over. "Hey, gook, over here! How fuckin' muchee?" Tomi didn't understand the words but knew the big oaf wanted to haggle. He showed half his roll of sen and raised two fingers.

"No fuckin' way!" the American snarled. His three sausage-thick fingers signified 300. Shaking his head in mock disappointment, Tomi looked down at the rails, then raised two fingers and a finger across another finger to signify 250.

"Fuck you, gook. 300! I know the goin' price."

"OK GI-San." Tomi said and reluctantly held up the entire roll. The American tried to grab the money without handing over the cigarets. Tomi lost his temper and without thinking, snapped to attention and barked at the fool, "No trick, Private! You trade honest. Now!"

Even a half-trained recruit knew a superior officer's command voice. The American obediently handed Tomi the carton and accepted the roll of Sen. Tomi nodded curtly and turned around before he shoved the sharp-edged carton under his belt and tunic. Tomi walked away, praying the train would leave before one of Japan's occupiers knew that he had been cheated.

Behind a deserted shed, Tomi carefully peeled back the small end of the white and gold colored carton and removed one pack of cigarets. The ornate gold label read: 'Chesterfield.' He removed the cellophane and silver paper wrapper to lift out a single cigaret. The aroma was fragrant with wealth. Tomi neatly re-wrapped the pack of cigarets and returned it to the carton, hidden against his concave stomach.

Even before he saw the hot grill cart in front of Fukushima Station, he smelled its delectable scent of baby chicks, split and impaled on skewers, sizzling over the charcoal brazier. Four to a skewer. The cart peddler's grey-stubble beard widened to a smile when he saw the offered cigaret. He handed Tomi a full skewer.

Tomi bit into the hot morsels, not caring that he burned his lips and tongue. He crunched the fragile bones and licked the skewer. It was the finest meal of his life.

The train whistle hooted and Tomi ran back to the coach and squeezed into the press of veterans. Unlike them, he carried a precious secret. He could outwit the enemy.

***

His Nanking interpreter no longer taunted him in the constant nightmare. Instead, Chen Ta cried big tears that splattered the Nanking wall chart. "Why are the numbers of the dead painted in grey ash and bone instead of red ink?" Tomi asked.

"That's all that's left of the children burned alive in air raids, including your own son. You *Jih-pan kuei-tzu*, Japanese devil," Chen Ta sobbed, using the Chinese curse.

"I'm truly sorry for the evil we caused. Please forgive me, Chen Ta. Why do I smell hay and shit instead of roasted human flesh? Is this Nanking or Tokyo?" The ghost wept.

In the predawn darkness, Tomi awoke to soft plops of heavy raindrops on the thatched roof. He shifted to ease the pain in his lower spine and breathed through his mouth. He didn't mind sleeping next to the ox, but the pervasive stench of aging human excreta was awful.

Japanese farmers collected and stored 'night soil' in giant vats outside their huts to use as nitrogen-rich fertilizer for the rice paddies. But the stinking reality of the Takahashi farm in Sendai was better than awaiting the gallows of Sugamo Prison.

Fully awake, Tomi sat up. Shit stank no worse than his destiny. He silently prayed to *Kannon*, the Buddhist Goddess of Mercy, for the spirits of his beloved son, Mother and Taiko. He heard the Takahashi family stir; simple farmers who lived to see another sunrise while his own loved ones were floating dust.

After sharing hot tea, cold rice and pickles with the family, Tomi politely volunteered to help Elder Takahashi with his night soil collection rounds of household latrines. The old man reluctantly agreed, torn between his son's debt to Tomi and the ancient peasant wisdom that any dealings with *Samurai* always led to trouble.

He hitched the *ushi*, ox, to the honey wagon, a two-wheeled cart loaded with two rows of three tall barrels each, and began the weekly route. The ox slowly plodded past rows of small wood houses, all dull brown look-alikes, and stopped at the right place without a command.

Elder Takahashi loudly announced his presence to the housewife and, after much bowing, carefully dipped excreta from the customer's indoor latrine hole with a long-handled wooden scoop. Without spilling a drop, he transferred each load into the open top of the black, elegantly-shaped barrel, which was gracefully tapered at both ends. He bowed, and with ritual politeness, thanked the housewife for her family's contribution to the next rice harvest.

Takahashi and his ox moved in the unending circle of back-breaking rural life: collect shit in the honey wagon; plow and plant rice seedlings; fertilize and harvest. Consumed rice grains passed through human gut and the resulting shit was collected to fertilize the next crop. It was an unchanging cycle that had begun 4,000 years ago in China.

Tomi was a disaster as a honey dipper. He gagged and lost his breakfast, a double offense when so many starved. Takahashi pretended not to notice. "Here's our next stop. A tragic shame! Lost her only child in an air raid only weeks before the war ended. Her pilot husband was killed earlier."

The attractive young *yamome*, widow who responded to Takahashi's polite call resembled Tomi's beloved Taiko. She gazed overlong at the handsome stranger in the officer's demobilization suit and led him to the indoor latrine. Sexually aroused, Tomi tried to hide his erection and dribbled shit across the tatami. She reacted with full-throated vehemence. Tomi bowed and apologized. Startled by his upper-class Tokyo accent, she clamped a hand over her mouth and slid the door closed. He had stained her home and destroyed the possibility of companionship.

After he deposited the widow's night soil into the barrel, Tomi begged Takahashi's forgiveness with the lowest of bows. Red-faced with anger, the old man returned a slight bow and took the long handled dipper from Tomi's hands. Elder Takahashi was gruff. "Tomigawa-Sama, our family owes you much for protecting my son through the long war and raising him to an exulted rank. Even my ox was bought with the increased Army pay he sent home. Please do not take offense from my blunt words, but your talents do not fit here. Your destiny is elsewhere. I am an ignorant farmer, but this I know: the eagle cannot swim like a turtle any more than a turtle can fly like the eagle."

He scratched his stubbled chin and squinted westward. "We are halfway to Sendai City. Perhaps you'd prefer to go to town and find something more worthy of an eagle?" This was a direct order, one that a royal chamberlain could not have given with greater finesse.

Tomi bowed and thanked him for his sage advice and walked three miles to town. His dismissal as the assistant shit-dipper on a six-barrel honey wagon proved that he lacked the crudest of civilian skills. How was he to survive in a Japan that no longer needed warriors?

Sendai was a heap of rubble, but traffic was heavy on the few cleared streets. Tomi waited at the main intersection with a large crowd. Even when a wide gap opened in the lumbering line of heavy U.S. Army trucks and speedy jeeps, the crowd stood in place, warily looking at a distant trolley speeding downhill from the north.

"Why isn't the crowd moving?" Tomi asked a man in a tattered uniform.

"New here, are you? The electric trolley must pass first. The ancient relic has no brakes. Several old people and reckless veterans have been run over. Imagine living through the Great Pacific War and air raids, only to be sliced in half by an old trolley!"

The trolley careened noisily down the sloping street, gained momentum and clattered past the crowd. It slowly lost speed and rolled to a stop where the broad avenue flattened. Shaken passengers got off to walk among the ruins, survivors of another brakeless ride.

Tomi had reached the other side of the intersection when a voice behind him boomed, "Second Lieutenant Tomigawa!" He turned slowly, prepared to be arrested. Instead, a short, bandy-legged stranger snapped to attention and saluted. Tomi suspected the man knew him from the Nanking or Unit 731.

Tomi made a careful, neutral bow.

"Lieutenant! Don't you remember me?"

"Please forgive me, I do not. Besides, one does not call another by rank these days."

"Yes, Sir, Tomigawa-Sama. You've gotten so skinny I hardly recognized you, but one cannot hide tallness and face scars. Speaking of scars, Sir, look at the tip of my nose. Remember?" The little stranger laughed and pointed to an indent on his wide peasant nose.

Despite the heat, he wore his demobilization suit, an infantryman's cold weather uniform, complete with big winter boots. He was sweating, but in 4 months he'd be comfortable and Tomi would freeze in his thin summer uniform. He speed-talked in the slurred *Miyagino* accent. "The Ooooh Ahg pig farm, when you called me cockroach?" Tomi gestured a negative.

"I'm Sato! 'Bear' Harada slapped me for dropping my rifle; then you marked my nose with the bayonet. Best lesson of my life! I survived the war because of you."

Tomi remembered the clumsy young recruit and the gang rapes in the filthy pig sty. He remembered the naked Chinese woman standing in front of Sato with his bayonet stuck in her ribs.

To Tomi, she had never been the fabled Ooooh Ahg, the Crippled Chimpanzee of Nanking, an early legend among veterans. She was the first and most remembered of his many executions. Tomi wondered if her girl-child had survived.

"Why thank me?"

"You saved my life many times, Lieutenant ... um, Sir. Your harsh lesson inspired me to become skilled with the bayonet. I was among the best in the 2nd Sendai Infantry Division." Sato looked around to see if any Yankee soldiers were nearby. One had to be careful not to be overheard by *Nisei*, second-generation Japanese-American soldiers.

He whispered, "I stuck dozens of sleeping Yankees in their foxholes on Guadalcanal. The *gaijin* howled and bawled like babies. Each time, I imitated your strokes at the pig farm. I got a medal, Order of the Kite, Second Class, for saving my company commander. Both of us were badly wounded. When he was taken off Guadalcanal in a supply submarine, I went with him. We were among the few survivors of that miserable, fucking island. After I recovered, I became a bayonet instructor here in Sendai. I'm in your debt for the rest of my life."

"You are much too kind, Sato. I only did my duty. And I was less than kind to you during The Bear's patrol. You became a bayonet hero and teacher of steel because of your own excellent warrior spirit. You, not I, are responsible for your achievements. Please accept my congratulations." Tomi bowed as if Sato was the superior.

Surprised, Sato stumbled over unfamiliar formal words. "Sir! It is not proper that this unworthy one be favored by a great *Samurai* hero. For years I've boasted to many now-dead comrades about how I was your student on that fateful day."

Energized by an impulse, Sato snapped to attention. "Sir, would you give this unworthy one the profound honor of sharing a meal?"

Tomi hesitated, not knowing if Sato had enough money. In a voice hoarse with emotion, Sato pressed, "Sir, it is important to me. Please be my guest."

"It is I who am honored to dine with a brave, decorated warrior who fought well."

Sato tried to grow a foot taller. People stared when he shouted, "*Sho-I* Tomigawa, the famed hero, praises me!" Embarrassed by his own outburst, he said in a low tone, "Come, Lieutenant, sorry – I mean Tomigawa-San. We'll celebrate this lucky meeting."

He pointed to a small building made of new lumber at the northeast corner of the intersection. "Tomi-Sama, we will eat at the first restaurant opened in Sendai since the war."

"Has rebuilding started already?"

"Interesting story, Sir. A fucking *Shinajin*, Chinese gook, told the occupiers that he was brought here as a slave laborer and convinced the Yankees to let him set up a *soban* shop as personal reparation. Actually, the clever whore's son was one of our collaborators, but no one dares inform on him. He's got connections. Shen Sung-jen would be shot if he returned to China. None of our businessmen has the guts to ask the Yankees for permission."

The tiny restaurant, its walls still weeping the aromatic resin of newly-cut pine, was empty save for a sullen policeman eating in a corner instead of directing traffic at the dangerous intersection. Sato and Tomi were served bowls of noodles from a huge steaming pot by a thin man with badly decayed teeth who spoke unaccented Japanese. The enterprising Shen Sung-jen's intent stare at Tomi revealed him to be a face memorizer and perhaps an informer. They sat and slurped thick, heavy noodles floating in a hot, fatty broth made of dog meat.

"Delicious, Sato! Can't remember the last time I had such tasty noodles." Sato giggled with pride and motioned to the Chinese proprietor, who hurried to heat small bottles of sake.

"It is against the law for the Chinese gook to sell sake, but ..." Sato whispered.

Shen bowed to the blue-uniformed policeman and gave him a *koh* of sake as a bribe before he served them. Sato would pay for the policeman's sake. Defeat had plunged orderly Japan into a chaos as uncontrollable as Sendai's ancient brakeless trolley.

"*Kanpai!*" they toasted each other. Addressing Tomi in the reverent form, Sato said, "This humble one never expected to see the heroic Tomigawa-Sama again, let alone here," It was the polite, indirect way of asking how Tomi came to Sendai.

"Please Sato, call me Tomi. Thank you for your generosity. Like so many these days, I have no family and own nothing except my demobilization suit. I'm staying at the farm of my comrade's father just east of here. But they can't keep feeding someone who's worthless as a farmer or honey-dipper. I've got to find work, any kind of work."

Tomi rubbed his hand across the plank table and sniffed the sticky fresh pine tar on his fingers. It was the scent of life. "I have a peculiar urge to do something useful. How stupid of me to be ambitious in a time of no opportunities." Tomi forced a laugh to dilute the pity in Sato's dark eyes. "You have no idea how wonderful this is. Thank you, Sato, for restoring my spirits. Now I'm a happy man ready to face Sendai City's trolley."

Sato aimed his flat round face at the ceiling and laughed, exposing his strong stained teeth in the light of the single naked bulb hanging from a wire. He flicked his eyes at the police officer and pursed his lips. Tomi understood and silently chased the final noodle with his chopsticks.

Giving Shen a grander title than deserved, Sato called out, "*Shujin-San*, honorable host, tea please." When the Chinese collaborator brought it, they slurped without talking until the policeman belched, ignored Shen's bow and left without paying.

Sato whispered, "Forgive this impertinent question, Lieutenant, oops, Tomi. Is your name on the war criminal list?"

"No, Sato. Not even 'C' Category," Tomi lied. "I worked in a tiny clerical office. No record of Matters Best Left Unsaid."

Both men silently remembered Nanking. To break the mood, Tomi added, "Actually, much of my time was spent at the Army's English Language School."

Sato's look of amazement resembled a Kabuki actor. "You speak English and perhaps read it?" Tomi nodded.

"I'm assistant crew chief in the gook troop, the Japanese who work for the American Army. I'm at the old 2nd Infantry Division's garrison at *Tsutsujigaoka*. The Yankees call it 'Campu Fowrer.' We can use an *Eigo*-speaker, but the pay is modest."

Sato explained that Sendai, indeed all of Miyagi Prefecture, was ruled from 'Campu Fowrer' by the U.S. Army 9th Corps' Provost Marshal, his Military Police and the Japanese Police, some of whom were *Kempetai* veterans.

Two days later, Tomi was in the gook troop, working at the same place where his father had served as an officer before the Great Pacific War. Tomi read and re-read the *Eigo* typewritten on his crisp new work paper: 'Tomigawa Tomoyki. Japanese National employee assigned to the 622nd Military Police Company, U.S. Army 9th Corps, 8th Army, Camp Fowler, Sendai, Miyagi Prefecture.'

Scrawled by an uneducated hand at the bottom of the document were his duties: latrine orderly, water boiler stoker and substitute barracks-cleaner. It was his passport to a future.

CHAPTER SEVENTEEN
SENDAI, JANUARY 1946

Tomi was on his knees, scrubbing stubborn shit spots inside a toilet when he heard "*Oi! Hotsy mizu, hayaku!* Hey! Hot fucking water! Hubba-hubba!" from the shower room.

He raced to the massive white shape with a donkey cock who stood inside a cone of shower water. Tomi bowed. "*Hai!*"

The naked GI bellowed louder. "Hotsy fucking *mizu, Ima!*"

The soap-lathered Yankee's eyes were squeezed tight, but Tomi bowed again and shouted "Hotsy *mizu* now. Yes, Sir! *Atsui mizu ima.* Hot water now!" The GI and Tomi both used the patois of Occupied Japan, a bastard mix of crude GI slang and ungrammatical simple Japanese.

Tomi ran into the winter night, his bare feet in *getas*, open wooden clogs, in foot-deep snow. Cold bit his feet. The boiler shed was around the far outside end of the latrine, where Tomi had already banked the fire for the night. The Yankee was taking a late night shower after being with his *koibito,* girlfriend.

When the Japanese Imperial Army had occupied the dark wooden barracks of *Tsutsujigaoka,* a crew of laborers did what Tomi now did alone. He tended the coal-fed hot water boiler and kept toilets and old wooden floors spotlessly clean despite bad Yankee aim. The tired joke among latrine orderlies was: "The Americans dropped so many bombs on us because of their aim is so terrible. The round-eyes can't even piss straight."

He placed a few coal nuggets into the maw, as if spooning precious medicine into a sick child's mouth. He thought of his son, consumed by the atomic fire. The boiler gauge needle slowly wiggled up to an extravagant temperature.

Next to food and cigarets, coal was gold in Sendai. Unlike temperate Tokyo, northern Honshu was hammered by Arctic winds that howled across the Sea of Japan from the Manchurian Plain. The less fuel Tomi's inefficient boiler ate, the more coal he could steal. But it was impossible to coax more heat from the old latrine boiler.

Tomi's fellow workers begged him for tiny bits of coal to smuggle out of camp. To a shivering family, each lump stretched their limited charcoal supply. Following a poor rice harvest, the first winters of the Occupation were the coldest in a decade.

Convoys loaded with men and war material from America had been replaced by ships carrying Army supplies, as well as food to keep Japan from starvation. The cargoes included coal for Army cook stoves and furnaces.

The only time Tomi didn't shiver uncontrollably was in the overheated barracks latrine and boiler room. If he couldn't steal coal to barter for scarce winter clothing to replace his thin summer uniform, he would die of pneumonia or the tuberculosis epidemic raging in Japan.

To get the coal, he had to increase the boiler's efficiency by removing the thick crust that clogged the water tubes. But where could he get acid? He pictured Camp Fowler's layout. Like most Imperial Army posts, it duplicated a Prussian Army garrison; a quadrangle of barracks around a large parade ground. Its tenants were the 622nd Military Police Company's barracks on one side, and a heavy construction engineer battalion barracks on the another; plus officers' quarters, motor pools, mess halls and a medical dispensary in an enclosed square.

The Yankees did a curious thing in the center of the parade ground. They bordered the tall flagpole with a plot of grass enclosed by a white picket fence. Dwarfed by the huge red, white and blue garrison flag that fluttered overhead stood a waist-high, 37-millimeter Japanese cannon. The occupiers turned it into an outlandish lawn ornament by painting it white with bright red wooden spokes. A horse had pulled the Model 94 Infantry rapid-fire artillery piece in battles from Shanghai up the Yangtze to Nanking and beyond. Now it was a garish trophy.

During the short lunch break the next day, Tomi sat next to a cadaverous MP motor pool worker who had spent the war tending the engines of a minesweeper that never left Tokyo Bay.

"Yoshida-San, what do you do with old batteries?"

Chewing his rice to make it last longer, Yoshida mumbled, "Dead batteries are tossed in a pile outside the motor pool. They end up as trash. Why does *Sekitan-San,* Mr. Coal, ask?"

"I need acid from batteries to clean boiler tubing."

"No difficulty, Mr. Coal. I'll even loan you a funnel and a carrying can if ..." Yoshida trailed off his words as he pretended to swallow an imaginary last grain of brown rice from his chopsticks.

He grinned when Tomi said, "In return, permit me to give you two pieces of coal."

At the end of his shift, Tomi crunched through deep ice and snow in open wooden clogs. It was worse than walking in bare feet. He couldn't feel his toes and feared frost bite. A warmly-shod GI approached and Tomi had to step aside into a deep snowdrift to let him pass. Tomi's courtesy and low bow were ignored.

He ran past the parked jeeps, weapons carriers and trucks, their stiff brown canvas topped with caps of snow, into a garage lined with dimly-lit repair bays. This was his first time here. He inhaled the thick odor of lubricating grease and metal mixed with sharp-edged fumes of gasoline as a long-forgotten perfume of his youth.

Yoshida was hunched over a work bench. As Tomi approached, a Yankee military policeman burst through a narrow side door. Startled, Tomi snapped to guilt-stiff attention. Only authorized gooks were permitted in the garage. Tomi could lose his job for being here.

The MP, dressed for patrol duty in an open jeep, wore a thick woolen overcoat with a wide, turned-up collar. Only his *gaijin* nose was exposed to Sendai's bitter winter. The white 'MP' painted on his helmet was duplicated on a black arm band, symbols of the American *Kempetai.* The web belt around his waist sagged with gear. On his right hip was a heavy-caliber automatic pistol in a leather holster. A wooden club and a canvas pouch filled with several ammunition clips was attached on the other side, along with a flashlight and first aid pouch. Despite his youth, the MP looked *tsuyoi,* powerful.

Tomi's bare feet ached as he stared at the MP's thick,

rubberized leather and canvas boots into which his sharply-creased olive drab trousers were tucked.

Yoshida looked worried when the American said, "No heat in my jeep. Fix it hubba hubba or give me another." Both men went outside. Tomi trailed behind. Yoshida and the Yankee unfastened the jeep hood and rested it against the windshield. The MP stepped backward. Anyone who knew motors would have stepped forward.

Yoshida blustered, "I fix-u jeep-u hubba-hubba. No sweat-u." His upper half disappeared over the dark engine. He unscrewed the fly nut and removed the air filter from the carburetor top with a flourish. He carefully placed the circular piece on the frozen ground, as if that were a crucial first step of repair. He returned to the engine, ignored the thermostat and stared at the radiator as if waiting for the solution to appear.

Yoshida said in Japanese to Tomi, "There are many jeep-u, but none with the MP markings. My fucking motor pool sergeant just drove out with the last one to visit his whore. I can lubricate and do simple repairs, but I don't know shit about heaters."

Courtesy forbade a *Nihonjin* to deny a superior's request because face would be lost by both men; one for asking the impossible and the other for not doing it. The polite response was, "Yes Sir. I will look to it now." Out of respect for the MP, Yoshida was bound by courtesy to promise a repair that he could not do. This cultural difference made GI's think all gooks were liars.

Tomi knew what would happen. Angry about freezing in an unheated jeep for 8 hours, the MP would tell his superiors that the motor pool gook had lied to him about fixing the heater. Yoshida would get in trouble and Tomi fired for being in the motor pool without authorization. Tomi did a clumsy dance on his freezing feet. He decided silence was his worst option. Besides, how different were jeeps from old sedans?

Tomi faced Yoshida's grease-stained skinny bottom and bowed. "Pardon me, Yoshida-San, May I seek your wise advice? Is it not true that the engine heat exits from the manifold? And is there not a pipe from the manifold to carry heat through the engine firewall out beneath the dashboard? Or perhaps the radiator thermostat is defective and should be removed?"

-242-

"Huh?" Yoshida exclaimed as he reappeared from the engine compartment." Start fiddling if you know anything at all and bluff if you don't. Please help me, Mr. Coal!"

Tomi replaced Yoshida over the fender. In the darkness, he touched the hot cast iron engine block and cried, "*itai*, ouch!" The Yankee aimed his flashlight at Tomi's hands.

"Thank you, Sir. Prease keep frashright this way."

Tomi gazed at the jeep engine and saw America's mechanical soul. His fingertips felt form and he knew the function. Even the battery bracket was solid steel. The wires and cables were heavy gauge, and the looped handle of the oil dip stick was twice as thick as any he had ever seen. The Yankees wasted steel as they did hot water. Tomi chided himself. How could he, a gook who cleaned filthy latrines, criticize America's automakers? They were the world's best,and must have excellent reasons for what they did.

Tomi knew the jeep from intelligence reports. Only 5-feet-wide and 11- feet- long, it carried a half ton of cargo through mud, snow and up steep mountains, thanks to a powerful engine and 4-wheel drive. Only America possessed such a combat workhorse.

"Mr. Coal!" Yoshida called impatiently. "Find the trouble?"

Startled, Tomi croaked, "A moment, please, Yoshida-San."

The Yankee's wavering light beam revealed that a crude, flanged pipe on the cast-iron manifold had separated from a ragged hole in the jeep's firewall. Probably installed by gooks or their Yankee bosses, the engine got the heat instead of the driver.

"The problem is a pipe, Yoshida." Tomi guessed the jeep had been shipped to Japan from a South Pacific island. That would explain the temporary heating rig. Sensing that he'd soon have a warm jeep, the Yankee whistled a merry tune.

"Yoshida, this can be fixed in a few moments. All we need are tape, wire and a roll of asbestos. I'll get them if you tell me where."

"Quicker if I do it," Yoshida said. He told the GI, "Jeep-u OK *ima*, now," and walked toward the garage, arms outstretched like a ballerina as he stepped over deep ice-covered tire ruts. Tomi shoved the loose pipe end through its hole and bowed to the Yankee, who wasted his flashlight batteries by illuminating his warm boots instead of switching off the light.

Embarrassed by how he mispronounced "L," Tomi said in slow English, "You are most porite, Sir. Thank you for your kindness with frashright."

The soldier interrupted his whistling long enough to answer in a passable Northern Honshu accent. "*Doo itashmashite.* You are welcome."

"Ah so! You speak Japanese very good," Tomi said. It was polite to compliment *gaijin* who had memorized a few words; like giving a nut to a parrot for mimicking a human.

"*Iie. Watakushi wa oroka na seito.* No, I am just a stupid student," the MP responded, and his bulk of multi-layered clothing, weapons, ammunition and leather tilted forward into a bow at the proper level. Amazing! The MP knew bowing etiquette and used the formal personal pronoun. Except for a POW about to be executed, he was the first Yankee who had bowed to Tomi.

"Please, if I may be so impolite, Honorable Sir. How did you learn to speak our language so quickly? Did you study in school?" Tomi asked in *Nihongo.*

The MP waved his stiff palm in front of his nose, the proper negative gesture, and said, "I speak only phrases I've picked up." He lapsed into *Eigo.* "MP's give orders to Japanese, but we cannot converse." He added in *Nihongo,* "My ear is dumber than my tongue, but I try to learn." Tomi politely hid his astonishment and bowed again.

Yoshida returned with enough wire, tape and insulation to fix six jeeps. Tomi ducked his head into the engine compartment and the MP aimed his flashlight on Tomi's numb hands as he whistled the same bouncy tune again.

When Tomi had wired the connected pipe in place and taped asbestos around its length, he asked Yoshida to start the engine. Tomi enjoyed the deep roar as he studied the unfamiliar carburetor, its open throat sucking in the cold air. His face was bathed in the breeze of the whirring radiator fan, which carried the rich odor of rubber and oil cooking in hot metal.

Tomi heard a symphony of automotive logic and electrical timing, as perfect as a Bach concerto. The continuous storm of exploding gasoline and air mixture moved pistons up and down inside oil-slicked cylinders to the precise beat of electrical sparks.

A Buddhist, Tomi knew that mystical paradox and factual scientific thought were equal paths to Ultimate Truth. He knew that Right Mindfulness and the Right View existed within the jeep's mechanical perfection, just as it did with the Sung dragons of the Nanking priest.

The clatter of the jeep's worn valves disturbed his silent prayer. The careless Yankees had failed to perform proper maintenance. Tomi could only rev up the engine by gently turning the idle screw on the carburetor. The higher RPMs would cause overheating next summer, but both the jeep and Tomi would survive the winter. He nested and screwed on the air filter.

Reluctantly, he returned to the cold Sendai night. He lowered and locked the hood, then snapped to attention. He bowed military-style to the MP and Yoshida, and gave the good news: "Yoshida-San! As you ordered, the jeep-u heater is repaired. Thank you, Yoshida-San for supervising me."

Yoshida smiled and answered, "No sweat-u, Tomi. You my *ichiban* good-u boy. *Jootoo.* You good-u gook workah."

"OK guys, knock it off. I'm late for patrol. *Domo arigatoo gozaimasu,* thank you very much." The MP climbed into the canvas driver's seat and needlessly gunned the racing motor. He took off one olive drab glove and felt the heat beneath the dashboard.

"*Jootoo*! Superior!" the MP grinned. He shifted into first gear, moved a few yards then braked. "Sorry. Almost forgot," he said politely and gave two cigarets to Yoshida. The jeep moved away, crunching ice-covered ruts.

Yoshida handed Tomi the cigarets. "I didn't know you were a mechanic! And you speak good English. Mr. Coal, you are full of pleasant surprises."

"The cigarets are yours, Yoshida. I was lucky. The jeep is much like the trucks Henry Ford sent us after the Earthquake. That MP acts like a human being, not like the rest of his kind."

"Not bad for a *gaijin*, that one. He has a kind stomach. I hear they call him 'Peri' or 'Perry.'"

"Perry? Like *perapera,* fluent? How ironic for a MP who tells me in *Nihongo* that he's a poor student of our language."

Tomi gave Yoshida a package of small lumps wrapped in a

torn sheet of 'Stars And Stripes,' the Yankee newspaper. Tomi collected discarded newspapers from wet latrine floors and dried them to read and improve his English. Instead of squatting briefly over a sanitary hole, the baffling *gaijin* sat for long periods of time reading or talking to each other. They ate too much, then wasted so much time shitting. When did they find time to fight the war?

Unwrapping the crumpled newspaper, Yoshida said, "I heard that Mr. Coal is a man of honor. You give me four lumps of coal after we agreed on two."

"I am grateful for the acid, Yoshida. I am in your debt."

Yoshida was doubly pleased when Tomi did all the work. He unscrewed the caps of cells and tilted the discarded batteries over a wide metal can. Working in the dark, he splashed acid on his numb hands. He rubbed snow on the burns and kept working.

Yoshida brought him a jar of clear petroleum jelly to smear over the burns. When Tomi thanked him, Yoshida asked, "May I ask how a *Samurai* hero is also a skilled mechanic?"

"I love cars. My father had a Model T Ford and taught me how it worked. Later, I spent much time at the Academy motor pool." Tomi waved a burned hand at the parking area filled with long lines of olive green Jeeps, weapons carriers and heavy trucks. "Compare these marvels to our underpowered vehicles."

Yoshida soberly replied, "When one sees firsthand the Yankees' firepower and horsepower, it is remarkable that we lasted so long. It's a tribute to the Japanese spirit."

Tomi didn't voice his thought: *No! Why did we foolishly wake up the sleeping giant?*

Yoshida spat toward the American vehicles and said, "As you can see, I need help. I work hard, but the Yankees get pissed off-u with me. They are lazy and spend their time getting sex while I'm stuck with the work. I know Navy steam-driven engines, but not these damn gasoline things, so I bluff. If I can get permission, would you like to work here part time in addition to your regular job?" Yoshida bowed his head. "And if I get the job for you, may I humbly ask for two lumps of coal a week? My youngest daughter has tuberculosis and our cold house is bad for her."

"I am so sorry about your daughter. Even if you can't get me the extra work, I'll give you coal as often as I can without obligation."

"But what about your own needs? You can trade coal for food, a coat, women, whatever."

"Allow me the honor of helping your daughter."

Tomi carried the heavy can of acid past the painted cannon to the boiler shed. He rested and warmed up until the MP midnight patrol went off duty and bedded down. After the fire died, he drained water from the boiler and replaced it with clear battery acid to dissolve the mineral crust inside the tubes. He drained the acid before it ate through the thin tubing. Chemical fumes grabbed his throat as he tilted buckets of hot liquid and clumps of dark, calcified minerals into the snowbank.

He flushed out the tubing several times until only clean water showed. He started a fire and the temperature needle inched up faster than before. When it inched to the boiling point, he adjusted the valve and ran into the latrine and shower room. The barracks were silent. He walked across the sodden duckboards and opened a shower faucet. He put his hand in the torrent of hot water, stinging his acid burns. Yes! Water gushed, hotter and faster.

"Much hot water for MP's of Campu-Fowrer. Much, coar ... No! Much coal for me," he quietly said aloud, practicing the "L" sound that echoed in the shower.

"I sound just rike gooks. I will rearn – no! I will ra, la, le, learn to pronounce Engrish, English, rike, like Americans." He forced his tongue to curl back up against the roof of his mouth in an unnatural position to pronounce 'L,' one of the two *gaijin* letters absent from the Japanese alphabet. The other letter. 'V,' was for a few crossover words like *vaiorin*, violin.

"Camp Fowler! Camp Fowler!" he said, trying to pronounce the "L" correctly. Tomi returned to the boiler room, banked the fire and sat close to the heat. He was exhausted and hadn't eaten since noon. Although it meant no food until tomorrow, Tomi decided not to hike several miles to the Takahashi farm.

He reviewed the night's events with a vague sense that something important had happened that wasn't yet shaped into thought. Why did he feel so hopeful? He tried to think like Lord Suzuki who turned complex historical trends into practical ideas.

Most Americans don't hate the Japanese. They were forgiving.

His mind raced like a jeep engine. Sex aside, there was something more to the winner-loser status. Perry, the polite military policeman who was trying to learn Japanese, was a clue. Throughout history the slave often influenced the master. The Gauls mixed with their cruel Roman rulers and the Anglo-Saxons melded with Norman overlords, both in language and culture. Surely the best example of all was how the Chinese absorbed their Manchurian invaders, making them more Chinese than the Chinese themselves. All it took was time.

Tomi undressed and draped his wet summer breeches over a pipe to dry. He wiggled his toes in the heat. Europeans and Asians were different races. Could they mix well? Who knew? Lord Suzuki would have replied, "Who cares?" All that mattered was the dynamic of the current relationship."

That's the missing thought Tomi groped for: Relationship. "*Niisan! Otooto!*" Tomi yelled. In the cramped English language, there was only one word for brother. But in Japan, the difference between the status and power of a *niisan*, older brother, and an *otooto*, younger brother, was sufficiently significant to have separate nouns.

Given its American character, the Occupation made the Japanese their younger brothers. The Japanese, in turn, adapted quickly to their junior role. The *gaijin* older brothers are teaching the younger brothers their alien ways. Tomi had a wild thought. Perhaps the Japanese might become the Americans of Asia.

Tomi laughed and shook his head, too exhausted to expand upon such a big thought. He pulled a flattened cardboard box from behind a pipe and placed it on the floor. He took several copies from his neat pile of old Stars And Stripes, and used them as a blanket. He curled up, knees close to his chin, and pressed himself into the tiny, warm space between boiler and shed door. He smiled as he hummed the melody that MP Perry whistled.

"Da-da-da-da, Doo-doo-doo." Years would pass before Tomi learned the name of the tune: 'Let's Remember Pearl Harbor.'

CHAPTER EIGHTEEN

On the night before Christmas Eve, the U.S. Army hung seven Class A war leaders from the busy Sugamo Prison scaffold. All had been convicted of war crimes, but the Japanese public knew the real reason was that they had lost the Great Pacific War.

Six were as guilty as Tomi for war crimes, but not General Matsui. The warrior-scholar had braved royal disfavor and tried to prevent the months of rapes and massacres that began on that miserable Nanking dawn, 11 years and 9 days before.

Sixteen others, including Lord Suzuki, were serving life sentences, while many others had shorter prison terms. The Americans pretended the brutal policies had not originated in the Imperial Palace, and Hirohito remained on the throne.

No longer a hated and feared enemy, Japan was America's unsinkable aircraft carrier anchored next to the Asian heartland, where Communism spread like a fast cancer. Americans released their Japanese POWs around the former empire and shipped them home; unlike the Soviets, who still held thousands of Japanese POW's in Siberian prison camps.

The executions in Tokyo's Sugamo Prison were a death parade in quick time, paced one to two minutes apart, starting with General Doihara, head of the notorious POW and civilian internee camps in Malaya, Sumatra, Java and Borneo.

Next was ex-Prime Minister Tojo, whom the Americans mistakenly regarded as Japan's arch war criminal, though others in the Palace had continued the war at a horrific cost of life. Tojo had resigned when Saipan fell in July, 1944. After the Surrender, when the American military police arrived at Tojo's house to arrest him, he shot himself in the chest but had missed his heart.

The Americans nursed him back to health for his execution.

General Muto, who had implemented the Emperor's punishment policies of conquered populations, was next to hang.

Then, the prison guards half-lifted tiny General Matsui to the gallows. He was number four, the bad luck number. Wasted by tuberculosis, Matsui wasn't heavy enough for the noose to snap his neck when he dropped through the trap door. Thrashing violently, Matsui slowly strangled in agony until the executioner, an Army master sergeant, ran beneath the gallows, grabbed the unlucky general's soiled legs and yanked down hard. Nine long minutes passed before executions resumed.

The final three to die were General Itagaki, responsible for starving and killing POWs in Southeast Asia; ex-premier Hirota, chief planner of military expansion; and General Kimura, under whose command Allied POWs and civilians had been tortured, starved and executed.

The seven warm corpses were stuffed into floppy G.I. body bags and loaded in a 'meat wagon,' an Army ambulance in the prison yard. Not trusting the Tokyo crematorium staff, a military police convoy took the bodies to the Yokohama Municipal Crematorium. Some said the charred bones and ash were scattered in the bay, while others claimed that patriotic crematory workers secretly saved handfuls of ashes and bone for grieving families.

Emperor Hirohito's only punishment was having to publicly declare that he was a human being, and not a god. With the exception of Prince Konoye, who committed suicide the night before he was to report to Sugamo Prison, none of the other royal family members involved in the war were arrested by the Americans. Relieved to still have an Emperor, albeit a mortal one, Japan pragmatically accepted the executions as the victors' right, and life went on.

On the commoners' side of the Imperial Moat, in the towering *Daiichi* Building carefully left untouched by B-29 bombers, was *MacArthur-Sama,* Supreme Commander of Allied Powers. General MacArthur ruled Japan with paternalistic respect to a once-fierce enemy who fully cooperated in a remarkably peaceful occupation. He gave Japan a new constitution that forbade war and permitted women to vote. Tomi's wife would have approved.

***

Tomi, now a full-time motor pool gook, followed the proceedings of the International Military Tribunal for the Far East in clean Stars & Stripes newspapers instead of piss-sodden ones lifted off latrine floors. Perry, his MP friend, provided him with other newspapers and magazines.

None of the published accounts mentioned Colonel Otomo, commandant at Unit 731, whose war crimes were evident. Gradually, Tomi pieced together the truth from *uwasa*, rumors. Otomo and his top aides had fled to Tokyo when the Soviet Army invaded Manchuria in the war's closing days. The Russians captured technicians at Unit 731, but wily Otomo had not only destroyed the official records, but had also hidden a duplicate library of complete data in Tokyo.

The Cold War made Otomo's research data priceless. The Americans regarded Otomo as the world's expert on anthrax, smallpox and other plague weapons. No one mentioned the untold thousands of humans who suffered from his research.

Fearing the Soviets had captured germ warfare experts at Unit 731, the Americans quickly struck a deal with Otomo that was similar to those made with key Nazi rocket scientists. Otomo exchanged his exclusive knowledge for freedom. As a bonus, he proved to the Americans that the Soviet Union had only captured low-ranking technicians. The sole reminder of Unit 731's scientific horrors was the crematorium's twin chimneys.

Because Otomo got blanket immunity for all Unit 731 personnel, and records of Tomi's other war crimes were hidden by Lord Suzuki, Tomi was alive to mourn General Matsui, the man who had tried to prevent the Rape of Nanking.

Tomi was more sad than angry that America preached justice, but acted with cynicism. The Yankees had atomized his son, mother, his only love and his wife, but Tomi knew the real murderers were the ambitious Palace leaders who had stupidly led Japan to war.

As the Cold War worsened, the Occupation softened.

Yankees, paying for cheap sex and servants with their black market profits, treated the courteous, hardworking Japanese as their little brothers, and encouraged local industries. There were even rumors that many war criminals, including Lord Suzuki, might get reduced sentences.

Tomi was too busy at the Camp Fowler motor pool to pay attention to the increased tension between the Soviets and the West. He was a rarity, a skilled mechanic who spoke English. He also schemed as he observed the Army's wasteful practices.

"When do you sleep, Tomi?" Yoshida asked as he scanned the motor pool status board, which showed that Tomi had changed oil and lubricated 4 trucks, 3 weapon carriers and 6 jeeps during the night. The GI mechanics were nursing hangovers in the mess hall over coffee and cigarets.

"Even with your help, we are still behind, and that snotty officer insists that a vehicle must be redlined if it's not serviced per the maintenance schedule.

Tomi had been waiting for this. "Yoshida, why don't we just check the dipstick levels and change oil every other time? We'll skip every other grease job, too. I'll fake entries on the status board and you can do crucial repairs instead of unnecessary maintenance."

"But the Yankees keep track of petroleum products. They're worth a lot on the black market. If oil and grease usage drops, they'll get suspicious and we'll be fired or arrested."

"Not if I remove the unused oil and grease at the same time the old stuff is discarded."

"The engines will get ruined without the scheduled maintenance."

Tomi waved a negative hand. "Let me show you how the Yankee mind works. Please go to spare parts and get replacement choke cables from a jeep, a weapons carrier and a truck."

When Yoshida returned, Tomi laid the 3 cables on the floor. "Each cable is listed as a different part, Yoshida, but you see they are identical except for length. Why do the Yankees spend extra money manufacturing, shipping and maintaining inventories of 3 replacement cables instead of shipping one long size that can later be cut into the desired length?"

"What does this have to do with oil and grease?"

"It's American waste, Yoshida. Yankees are so rich they don't think about waste or excessive safety margins. The Detroit engineers probably instruct the Army to replace the oil and filter often, because they designed parts for the worst possible combat situations. But our jeeps and trucks travel on roads, not on dusty battlegrounds. MP oil doesn't need to be changed that often. Same goes for lubricating grease points."

Yoshida gave a disapproving hiss, and Tomi talked faster with an edge of authority in his politeness. "Yoshida-San. If you allow your obedient subordinate to work the night shift, I'll handle everything. I'll wipe clean each engine filter, oil filler cap, oil pan plug and grease point so that every engine looks serviced. I will dispose of the new unused oil along with the old."

Yoshida blinked indecision and scratched his rump. Hating himself, Tomi pointedly asked, "How is your daughter?"

"Not good. The TB is worse. We can't afford those Army sulpha pills on the black market."

"I'll give you extra cash to buy her medicine after I sell the unused oil. I'll start working on it tonight. Good! It's settled."

The following day, when Perry came in for his patrol jeep, Tomi took him aside and speaking Japanese to flatter him, said, "My friend, I need a big favor that carries risk."

"So? How may I assist you, Tomi-San?"

Tomi switched to *Eigo* because Perry's vocabulary was limited. "Do you know Moore, who drives the waste truck to the dump?"

"Yeah. That redneck owes me 5 bucks from a crap game."

"*Subarashii!* Splendid! Perry, if you ask him to tend to a small matter for me, I will pay his debt and his brothel visits. Do you mind helping me?"

Perry whispered in Japanese, "Black market complications?"

"No sweat, Perry. Only risk is Moore. Can he be trusted?"

"No. But I'll figure a way to sew him up."

"Sew him up? As with a needle?"

"Slang, Tomi. It means I'll handle him."

The plan worked smoothly. On his way to the Army dumping ground with a truckload of used oil in barrels, Moore stopped at a garage Tomi had rented near a brothel. While Moore got prepaid sexual comfort, Sato vigorously hand-pumped new oil out of chalk-marked drums. Sato refilled the barrels with a mixture of old oil and water before Moore returned.

Tomi sold the fresh, top-grade Texas oil to eager local trucking companies. Even after he had paid Yoshida, Sato, the brothel, garage rent and a bribe to the policemen at the corner sentry box, Tomi cleared several thousand yen a month.

Tomi worried that Moore was the weak link. He might get greedy and threaten to expose Tomi unless he got a huge bribe. Perry grinned. "I already handled it. Moore regularly gets mail from his wife, preacher and a couple of the church elders. I got their names and addresses and showed him a letter I'd written for the brothel owner, who demanded payment for Moore's weekly visits. I even described his sex habits, so his wife knows the letter isn't phony. That redneck will behave."

"Perry, you've done me an even greater favor than I asked for! How can I repay you?"

Perry looked down at his polished paratrooper boots that MPs wear instead of the dull combat boots of common soldiers. "You are my *yuujin*, friend. When I need a favor, I'll ask."

After several months of steady profits, Tomi searched for other Yankee waste that could be turned into money. Tomi watched MPs at the mess hall pile food on their aluminum trays, and after eating their fill, scrape large amounts of food into garbage cans. Outside Camp Fowler, a small band of war orphans, widows, crippled veterans and homeless squabbled over the dumped food waste before a bulldozer buried it.

Remembering that Americans like the direct approach, Tomi was given verbal permission from a non-com to haul away the food waste instead of burying it.

Tomi used his black market cash to make a down payment on a nearby pig farm that he had asked Takahashi's father to select for him. Elder Takahashi agreed to supervise the operation and despite his objections, Tomi insisted on giving him a decent salary and a percentage of the profits.

"Feeding swine GI food is a fine idea, Tomi-Sama. They will grow fat quickly. But mark my words, you will regret using cripples and frail widows to do the work. Why use inexperienced castoffs? You're making my job as boss harder than necessary."

"Takahashi, your reluctance is understandable, but I am taking food out of the mouths of these unfortunates who pick through the garbage cans. Two or three frail widows, youngsters and veterans with missing limbs can do the job of an able-bodied man. I don't pay them much,and they don't eat much. You turn the farmhouse into a dormitory for all of them."

"Crazy! Farm plots are tended by families, not castoffs! It has always been this way."

Tomi said gruffly, "Well, these people are my farm family. Please treat them with respect."

Elder Takahashi was unhappy, but obeyed. Every evening his ragtag crew hauled discarded food from the mess hall to the pig farm in push carts and Takahashi's ox wagon. They carefully separated the mess into three piles -- edible food for their own meals, choice bits to peddle on the street for their pocket money, and slops for the *buta*, pigs. Tomi had gotten the idea from his recurring Nanking nightmares about Oooh Ahg's pig farm.

When Tomi ambitiously tried to get more food waste from other Army mess halls, he was thwarted. "Talk to Mazaki, head of the Sendai *Yakuza*," a friendly gook mess hall worker advised in a hushed voice.

Tomi resolved to keep his temper in check as he climbed the steep steps to an office over a newly-constructed pachinko pinball arcade in Sendai City. He disliked the *Yakuza* cutthroats, who had often supplied comfort women for Japanese army brothels by kidnaping and extortion. Now the enterprising outlaws flourished in the crazy, new semi-democracy. Despite the Occupation authorities' tough policies, the *Yakuza* infiltrated government and the economy with money made on the black market, buying Army supplies from thieving officers and soldiers.

Two *wakashu*, toughs, who called themselves the clan chief's children, guarded the door. Tomi gave his name, apologized for coming unannounced and requested to see Mazaki-San. "You wait," one said with a sneer. His look-alike partner glared with suspicion.

A deep voice bellowed, "Tomigawa! Get in here!"

The *oyabun,* clan father, a strong-featured man not quite the size of a Sumo wrestler, filled the small room. The man who stood next to Mazaki was the Chinese noodle shop owner. Tomi tried to recall his name.

Mazaki ignored Tomi's bow. "Why haven't you paid respects before now? You're not a hero now; you're a fucking pig farmer." His eyes glittered as he watched Tomi for a reaction.

Insults were the usual opening when faced with an unknown swordsman. Such crudeness was an act. Tomi used equal-to-equal casual politeness and calmly replied, "Had I known you wished to see me, I would have visited long before now."

"Think you're the clever one, do you? I've been watching your little oil deal for months." His voice rose as his outrage bloomed. "Now you want to grab all the mess halls' waste food! I let a pigmy like you alone because my trucking company clients need oil. But you take advantage of my kindness by sneaking into my territory."

The policemen and brothel owner must have alerted Mazaki as soon as Tomi had bribed them. Mazaki was greedy and powerful; but never kind. Tomi knew he was lying about the reason for not stopping the oil deal. Tomi had intruded into his territory, so why had he waited until Tomi's unasked-for visit to complain?

Mazaki's impoliteness showed that he didn't fear Tomi personally. What then? He suspected that Tomi had MP friends, but didn't know their rank or power. Mazaki's fear of pissing-off an MP officer was Tomi's only weapon. He knew better than to ask to be left alone. That would be a sign of weakness.

"As you say, Mazaki-San, We are small, modest businessmen." Tomi stressed the formal pronoun. "We didn't intend to compete with anyone. My honorable superiors do not seek unnecessary complications unless they are forced to act."

Like an inept swordsman, the Chinese noodle shop owner moved hastily. He broke his silence, giving Tomi the perfect opening when he said, "He's bluffing, *Oyaban.* No one in the gook troop has that kind of official connections. This lying cocksucker was a latrine orderly until a few months ago. I remember him – a starving scarecrow who begged a free meal in my restaurant."

Tomi raised his hand, wiggling the stump of his missing

finger. "Giving bad advice to your wise and all-knowing superior will cost you a finger, Shen."

When a *Yakuza* gang member offended or caused his boss to lose face, the underling would beg forgiveness by cutting off the tip of his own finger and send it, gift-wrapped, to his crime clan father. Many gang members had missing finger joints because of the practice called *yubitsume*.

Tomi continued the attack without making Mazaki lose face. "Shen Sung-jen!" Tomi snarled his name like a curse. "I think your noodle shop needs MP protection. A patrol jeep will park in front of your place for 15 minutes each day for 4 days starting tomorrow. If you're lucky, not every Yankee MP will piss on your front door."

Shen looked sick, and Mazaki was impressed that Tomi's unknown patrons had the power to direct MP patrols. Shen would quickly lose both business and face when word got out that the MP's were angry with him.

Tomi bowed slightly. "Mazaki, I profoundly apologize for being the unwitting cause of Shen's awkwardness. I assure you that we seek to avoid any future misunderstandings that might necessitate military police presence at other business establishments. Such actions would not serve my masters or you in the long term."

"Yes, Tomigawa-San, I agree," he said grudgingly.

Tomi bowed lower a second time. "My profound thanks for your guidance. We will heed your excellent advice and not to approach any other Yankee mess halls. Our hungry hogs will dine only on military police delicacies from Camp Fowler."

"So be it, Tomigawa-San. Perhaps I'll help you again in the future."

They ignored the downcast Shen, who now had to choose which hand would donate a fingertip. Mazaki stood and exchanged equal bows of farewell with Tomi. Outside on the busy street crowded with shoppers, Tomi's confidence sagged. He could have asked Perry to park at the noodle shop for a few days, but the bluff was only a skirmish. Mazaki would eventually learn the truth – that Tomi lacked connections. The *Yakuza* had too much power to be thwarted for long.

***

Elder Takahashi was in Tokyo visiting his son when Tomi was ordered to report to the camp facilities officer, Captain Hammel. The gook troop called him *Akai Inu*, Red Dog, because of his red hair. Like some rear-echelon officers, he displayed war souvenirs on his desk that hinted of a combat record as empty as his Japanese artillery shell paperweight.

"I'm combining all camp waste hauling into a single contract: food waste, rubbish, septic tank contents -- the works. Several Japs have already submitted bids. I heard you have an informal deal for hauling MP mess hall garbage, so I'm including you. But if you don't get the contract, you'll be part of the upcoming force reduction. For your sake, you'd better have the low bid."

"Captain Hammel, Sir, what is force reduction?"

"Job cuts. We're eliminating some gook troop jobs. The mess hall gooks will be replaced by GIs on KP duty. The motor pool will lose a couple of jobs, too." He barely hid a smirk, which puzzled Tomi, considering he had never met the officer before.

The MP motor pool wasn't Red Dog's jurisdiction, but he could fire any Japanese national in camp. Tomi would have to submit the lowest bid or lose everything, including his job.

Food waste was the only legal profit in the new contract. Sorting, hauling and disposing of rubbish and latrine wastes weren't profitable tasks. It was not a good move, but Tomi had no choice. Everything he had was at risk. The pig farm was heavily-mortgaged and the 12 people in his farm family depended upon it. Without Tomi's motor pool job and black market sideline, their rice bowls would be empty.

Two days later, Tomi reluctantly submitted a rock-bottom bid and won the contract.

Elder Takahashi returned to the pig farm in time for Tomi's weekly dinner with his adopted family. His satisfied expression showed that he had made his ceremonial bow across the Imperial Moat in the direction of his beloved Emperor, as well as visited his successful son.

"Tomigawa, my son sends his former officer deep respect and regards. He's delighted that things go well with you. He thanks

-258-

you for buying my train ticket." Takahashi's mood abruptly darkened when he heard about the new contract. "So? What will we do with all that GI shit?"

"Your honey wagon gave me the idea, Takahashi. We'll sell the GI night soil to farmers as a rich fertilizer to make rice harvests bigger," Tomi said.

"Every honey dipper knows that G.I. shit is no good!" Takahashi snorted. "The fucking Yankees wipe their asses with tons of paper. Damn stuff doesn't dissolve like our paper. It suffocates newly-planted rice shoots and cannot be used as fertilizer." He hurled his worst insult at Tomi."City dwellers, humph!"

Elder Takahashi chided Tomi in front of his family, but loss of face was Tomi's least worry. Because of his stupidity, he would drown in a sea of useless *gaijin* turds. He was ruined.

"I'll contact Younger Son in Tokyo, Takahashi said. "Perhaps his clan will loan us money until you figure a way to get out of the cursed contract. If not, everything is lost."

"No! A loan would be a mistake. I won't be the drowning man who drags his friend down. If I fail to perform the contract, I'll be fired and unable to repay a loan."

The muttered profanities of Elder Takahashi almost drowned out the soft voice of Kasahara, the one-legged veteran. "I heard that Americans don't use night soil for fertilizer. They sanitize the turds in factories before dumping them into rivers and lakes."

"Yankee turd factories?" Tomi asked in disbelief.

"Well, like a factory. Giant mixing blades pulverize the stuff into a sewage soup."

Old Widow Mori stood and bowed from the waist in the traditional way, remaining in that position as a woman's silent request for permission to speak to a male superior.

Tomi sighed, "Honorable Widow Mori. Please stand up straight and say what's on your mind without asking my permission every time. The old ways are unnecessary here."

As usual, she stubbornly ignored Tomi's words and remained frozen in her bow, reducing her 4-foot height in half. "Tomigawa-Sama. This humble one apologizes for the impolite interruption.

Forgive me, for I am but a mere woman, ignorant and old. Is it not possible that something like a giant hair comb can remove the shit paper by moving back and forth in the vat?' She unbent to wave her gnarled hands back and forth with the melodic smooth grace of a geisha. Everyone stared in wonder at both her perfect dance gesture and brilliant suggestion.

Kasahara chortled, "I made bunks for our troops in the Okinawa caves. Get me the right kind of wood and nails and I'll build you Widow Mori's giant comb."

"Wait! I'm the only able-bodied man here and I don't have time to run this farm, plus push a silly fucking contraption back and forth in a honey vat," Elder Takahashi complained.

Tomi ignored him and turned to Kashahara. " If I get you metal tubing for the teeth, can you embed them firmly in a wooden frame with a handle, like a giant rake?" Jeep canvas tops were supported by 'V' struts that the motor pool had in excess.

"Put a long cross bar on each handle and make them two-person rakes that we all can use," 60-year-old Moto added. "I'm as able-bodied as you, Takahashi. Just ask the widows about me." Everyone laughed because Moto was the farming hamlet's bull. After a long day's labor, despite shrapnel wounds, he happily coupled with any lonely widow who was in the mood.

"Kasahara," the Elder Takahashi said grudgingly, "while you're at it, make a couple of small rakes for the children to comb the *gaijin* shit paper off the tines of the big rakes. We'll mix the paper in with the slops. A hog's gut isn't as delicate as a rice shoot. But Tomi-San, my ox can't haul tons of GI shit."

"Civilian trucks sit idle at night. The trucking firms will be happy to make extra money. I'll get a special curfew pass from Captain Hammel. We'll honey-dip the stuff into empty oil barrels and wash out the truck beds after finishing our night runs."

Everyone raised their tea cups to toast future success. Even Elder Takahashi smiled.

***

Tomi's idea failed. The truck owners nervously claimed that their vehicles weren't strong enough to handle the loads, an obvious lie to signal Tomi they had been ordered not to cooperate. When Hammel refused to give him a curfew pass, Tomi knew he had walked into a trap. Mazaki was waiting for Tomi to drown in shit; then he'd take over.

Tomi had to neutralize the *Yakuza* and somehow get Captain Hammel to grant him a curfew pass. To counterattack, intelligence was needed. How did the *Yakuza* control Hammel? Tomi pictured the false war souvenir on his desk and guessed it was male ego, which meant sex.

He called Michio, the oldest, smartest orphan on the farm. "Here's money to buy a sturdy used bicycle. During the day, follow Hammel's jeep whenever he leaves camp, but doesn't head toward the Dependents' Compound, where his wife and daughter live."

After a week of false starts and losing the speeding jeep, the lad finally tailed Hammel to a private home, where a beautiful woman welcomed him. Michio giggled as he repeated the neighborhood gossip. "The pretty one is Shen's woman. At noon when Shen is busy cooking noodles, she is softening the red-head *gaijin*'s noodle."

Tomi guessed Mazaki had made Shen donate his woman instead of a fingertip. Tomi told Perry that Hammel's main bribe was use of Shen's woman, but confessed he had no idea how to deal with a corrupt American officer.

Perry grinned. "No sweat. All you need is evidence to bluff the dumb jerk."

Michio learned to use Perry's borrowed camera and photographed Hammel's white skin glowing like a lighthouse beacon under, over and in between Shen's woman. Tomi praised Michio. "Your diligence may save us. I'm indebted to you."

That night, Tomi's nightmare was replaced by visions of Chen's woman. He had been womanless too long.

Mazaki had to be defanged first or the blackmailed officer would run to Mazaki, who would get Tomi fired, or worse, hurt the farm family. Tomi's timing had to be perfect. He needed the help of his good friend, now a *Yakuza* black market operator.

"Elder Takahashi, here's train fare for tonight's Tokyo Express. Please hand deliver this letter to your honorable son and feel free to explain our urgent plight in your own words."

"I don't like this, Tomi," Elder Takahashi objected. "Makazi is too powerful. My son's career will be ruined by this vain attempt. You ask too much of him."

"I respect your wisdom and experience, Takahashi-San. But I'm confident my former Warrant Officer will succeed without any difficulty."

Inwardly, Tomi wasn't sure he could evade the trap. If the Tokyo Clan did give him immunity from Mazaki, Tomi's debt to the *Yakuza* might be large. Tomi might be the cricket who escaped the wok only to land in the pot.

Thirty days later, there was still no response from the Tokyo *Yakuza*. Tomi's spirits fell whenever he watched hungry GIs lined up at mess halls or the latrines. Camp Fowler's septic tanks were fast filling to capacity. The sea of GI shit would swamp him.

"Mushi Mushi! Hello, are you there, Tomigawa-San?" It was Sugita, owner of the biggest trucking firm, calling on the motor pool's Japanese phone.

"If you still need my trucks and drivers, they are available now. There's one problem. You offered us generous terms for your night hauling, but, ah, certain other parties want a 20% *zei*, tax. This is not our doing!"

"I understand your situation, Sugita. The tax isn't a problem. I'll call you when we're ready for the first night run. Thank you very much for your cooperation."

Takahashi's *Yakuza* boss in Tokyo had reached Mazaki. The tax Mazaki demanded from the Sendai truckers was to save face. Tomi was happy to pay, because it would keep Mazaki away and drastically limit the Tokyo clan's claim on Tomi, since they would get half the tax.

Now it was time for Perry's trick. Tomi picked up the motor pool field telephone next to the local phone. When the Signal Corps switchboard operator answered, Tomi demanded in an authoritative command voice, "Put Captain Hammel on the line." Perry had made Tomi practice until his "L" was perfect.

"Captain Hammel? We have orders to interview you about your Mazaki dealings. Would you prefer to do it in your office or here?"

"What? Who ... who is this? Are you C.I.D.?"

Every enlisted man and officer in Japan, including MPs, feared the Army's Criminal Investigation Division, whose agents wore uniforms without rank insignia.

"The Mazaki case is high priority. I'm sending one of my best undercover agents, a Nisei from Hawaii, to see you. He'll be there in five minutes. It would be best if you cooperate and extend him every courtesy. Do not warn Mazaki! Got it?"

Tomi cleaned his greasy hands with gasoline but didn't change out of work clothes. When he walked unannounced into Captain Hammel's office and closed the door, Hammel stood, hand gripping his spent shell paperweight. "What the fuck you doing here? Get the hell out!"

"There must be some mistake. Major Yarnell told me that you would be cooperative. You'd better call him, Sir. He'll be mighty upset. Perhaps we should go to headquarters."

"No, no. Won't be necessary." Hammel breathed hard and blinked in disbelief. "You are a C.I.D. Nisei, and not a gook? Jesus, you're good! Sure fooled me." Tomi grinned and shrugged, American-style. The C.I.D. had many Japanese-American agents.

"Under no circumstances, Captain Hammel, is my identity to be revealed to anyone. That includes your fellow officers, your superiors and your wife. If my identity becomes known, you will be held personally responsible by higher command. Do you understand, Sir?"

Hammel nodded and sank into his chair. Tomi slipped the photographs out of a manila envelope and spread them on his desk.

"Oh dear God. This is awful! My wife ... "

"You were sucked into a *Yakuza* ring that peddles stolen U.S. Army property. We've had them under surveillance for months, but your affair with Shen's woman might complicate our investigation. However, we have no reason to embarrass you or your family, Sir."

Hammel's face beamed with hope. "I'll do whatever I can to help the C.I.D."

"Thank you, Sir."

Tomi pulled out a pad of blank MP arrest forms, another Perry touch. "How did you meet Mazaki? When and where did he instruct you to offer me that silly combination contract? What favors were exchanged, other than your visits to Shen's house?"

Tomi printed the candid replies in English and added several Japanese characters.

"Sign the report. I'll witness it." Tomi boldly added his own name, rank and serial number, First Lieutenant Thomas Tomigawa, 02202927, glanced at the wristwatch with the olive drab band that Perry had loaned him, and wrote down the military time and date.

"The Miyagi Prefecture *Yakuza* are part of a much bigger gang. This has the personal attention of our Tokyo brass. My orders are to remain under cover and gather more evidence. To do my investigation without Mazaki getting wise, he's got to think that I'm just a two-bit crook with a couple of MP officers as silent partners. You tell Mazaki that in exchange for my truck curfew passes, I gave you a bribe. To prevent a double cross, I threatened to tell your wife that you share pussy with that Chinaman – who, by the way, was a Japanese Army collaborator during the war. So you'd better stop visiting her, Sir."

Tomi then dangled a reward. "What's your date of rank?" Hammel's sheepish response indicated that he was long past due for promotion and would be discharged in the post-war downsizing. "Obviously I haven't authority to make promises, but if this investigation ends well, your cooperation will be noted in my reports. Should be helpful when you come up for review."

Tomi gathered up the photos like a spilled deck of playing cards. "These are yours. The negatives are locked in our confidential files. Now you'd better give me night curfew passes for ten, no, make that fifteen vehicles. Makazi has to think that I'm just a gook rival."

Tomi held out his hand and Hammel shook it vigorously. "Oh, by the way, Yoshida in the MP motor pool and Sato, the assistant supervisor, are my paid informers. Make certain they are not in that force reduction or the shit will hit the fan at C.I.D."

"Absolutely! You can count on me to keep your guys in the gook troop."

Following Perry's coaching, Tomi stepped back and gave Hammel a snappy Yankee salute. The return salute, crisp and correct, showed that Tomi temporarily owned the grateful buffoon. Red Dog Hammel would probably be shipped back to the States without ever knowing the truth.

Mazaki's attempt was a valuable lesson. Tomi could not risk his fragile business and those who depended on him on the whims of undependable Yankees or *Yakuza* favors. He needed to build a solid business that could not be easily destroyed.

CHAPTER NINETEEN
SENDAI, JUNE 1949

Yoshida and his wife tearfully selected small bones from their 11-year-old daughter's cremated remains, in accordance with Shinto-Buddhist tradition. Tomi never told them that greed, as well as tuberculosis, killed Michiko. Her American wonder medicine had been diluted by *Yakuza* black marketeers to double profits.

GIs stole the sulfa pills used to cure venereal disease and sold them to the *Yakuza,* who peddled half-strength crushed powder to desperate families. Tomi hadn't found out until it was too late.

Tomi joined the Yoshidas and their surviving daughter to pray. Buddhists knew death wasn't an end, but only a change -- one step closer to Enlightenment. But Tomi nursed a helpless rage about children who needlessly died because of black market greed.

Tomi imagined the old head priest of Nanking scolding him, "Do not waste precious time cursing evil." The priest chanted the ancient Chinese motto: "Think. Organize. Do good." Tomi worried that hearing voices was a sure sign of madness.

Yoshida carried his daughter's ashes in a box hanging from a white silk strap around his neck. His wife, daughter and Tomi followed. Tomi selfishly brooded about his own sanity instead of Yoshida's loss.

Michiko's ashes rested at the Yoshida household altar, where too few friends and neighbors came to light incense sticks and pray. The Yoshidas' home had become *densensei no uchi,* a contaminated house, because of the tuberculosis. Perry, Sato and Tomi visited often to make up for the lack of mourners. On the important 34th evening of mourning, Tomi visited the Yoshida home by himself. Perry and Sato were on night shift. In the morning, Yoshida would take his daughter's bones and ashes to the cemetery.

Tomi prayed for Michiko's spirit by lighting a special incense stick that lasted all night. Tomi's eyes were closed when someone knelt next to him, and a rich feminine scent stirred his groin. Tomi peeked, but couldn't see her face. The somber, dark kimono was that of a mature woman, but her perfumed scent was maiden-fresh. Tomi left the altar bewitched.

"Tomi, may I introduce Yamamoto Yoshiko?" Yoshida's wife said. "Miss Yamamoto was Michiko's favorite teacher. She spent many hours with Michiko, giving her lessons and playing games during her illness."

Michiko's teacher was the same Chinese gangster's woman who had been secretly photographed pleasuring Captain Red Dog Hammel. Tomi returned her bow, remembering the images of her erotic skills and shaven cleft. How did she end up a *Yakuza* slut?

"What subjects do you teach, Miss Yamamoto?" Tomi asked.

"I no longer teach. Many of my pupils died in the raids and it's too heartbreaking to go back. Now I live alone and study," she replied in a soft upper class accent. Yoshiko meant 'good child,' but she had been neither good nor child-like when Michio photographed her softening Red Dog Hammel's noodle.

"She's too modest," Yoshida bragged. "Our Miss Yamamoto writes stories -- you know, novels. Someday she will be famous -- perhaps another Murasaki Shikibu."

"Ah so, Yamamoto Yoshiko," Tomi teased, "you would modernize the world's oldest novel? The courtesan who wrote 'Tales of the Genji' understood men of power and how arrogance could destroy them. A cautionary tale for us today."

"Well said, Tomi," Yoshida chortled.

Remembering photos of her playing tunes on Hammel's flute of obnoxious white flesh, Tomi asked, "Does your talent include playing any musical instruments?"

"Regrettably no, but with a good master, I learn quickly." Her stare made Tomi hard. She wanted him as much as he wanted her.

They left together and were silent as he followed her inside her small house. "Welcome to my humble home, Tomi. I was startled when I heard your name. Shen often told me how much he hates you. You seemed to recognize me too. How can that be?"

Tomi wondered if she was sex-bait in a trap set by Mazaki.

"You were pointed out as Shen's woman some time ago."

"No longer. I discharged a family debt. Now, as you can see, I'm alone ... and lonesome."

Tomi knew he should leave, but his *chimpo* disagreed. They hurriedly disrobed and Tomi was soon enveloped in her warmth. Like a summer storm, it ended suddenly. After a few thrusts, he filled her with several years of waiting sperm.

Wiping herself in front of him without modesty, she tilted her beautiful head and coyly smiled, "How long have you been without a woman?"

"Longer than you've been without a man." Tomi embraced her, determined to be slow and deliberate this time. But his *chimpo* refused to harden, despite her skill at playing his flute. He could only see Red Dog Hammel's dead-white skin and Shen's rotting teeth. After more half-hearted fumbling, they gave up. He walked home feeling melancholy and empty.

A few days later, Yoshida suggested, "Perhaps a seashore picnic at Matsushima would cheer up my wife. How about coming with us Sunday? Yamamoto Yoshiko said she'd be delighted to join us. She said she likes you."

"I appreciate your invitation, but that person is not for me. It's too complicated to explain."

Fifteen days later the *fukuzatsu*, complication revealed itself when Tomi urinated. Yoshiko had given Tomi a gift.

The pain and dripping stopped after he took a course of full-strength sulfa pills, which Perry had gotten him. But months later, the symptoms returned, worse than before.

Japanese doctors are notoriously blunt. "Gonococcus," the Tohoku University doctor said as he held up the microscope glass slide like a trophy butterfly. "An interesting specimen. Neisseria gonorrhoeae is a common bacterium spread by Yankees. But your infection is a rare combination of Neisseria and 'China's Revenge,' a nastier venereal disease our boys often got from comfort women during the war. There is no cure for this virulent strain. Sulpha controls symptoms, but the disease is permanent. To prevent infecting others, always wear a condom."

"But what about children?"

"Too late for that. You're sterile."

Tomi walked out the dark brick entrance of the university into the morning rain. He had destroyed his family heritage with a venereal disease born of military conquest: Japan in China and America in Japan. Tomi knew it was fitting punishment for a paper warrior and war criminal turned grease monkey and oil thief.

Tomi debated whether to step in front of the old brakeless trolley or sit on the railroad tracks and await the Tokyo Express. He decided on the more reliable express. But first he must kill Mazaki, Shen and Yoshiko. By midnight the world would be rid of two *Yakuzas*, the diseased whore and Tomi, the idiot who destroyed his heritage with a too-quick fuck.

Sudden paralysis hit him as he walked past a Buddhist Temple. Only his outstretched hands prevented a fall. He couldn't bend his knees. The damned doctor should have warned him about this symptom. Walking on his hands and feet with rump in the air, he moved through the mud of the temple courtyard and felt like Ooooh Agh, the Crippled Chimpanzee of Nanking.

He clutched the ritual water basin to catch his breath. His fear of a stroke ended when the numbness faded. He washed his filthy hands, stood erect and staggered into the deserted temple.

Lacking the traditional fruit or flowers, Tomi filled the plate with all his pocket money. He lit an incense stick with trembling hand and bowed three times to Buddha's statue. Tomi told the spirits of his son, mother, beloved Taiko, Yoshida's Michiko, his wife and the old Nanking priest that he would soon join them all.

Tomi chanted the ancient words: *"Namotassa Bhagavato Arahato Sammaa Samuddhassa.* Honor the Lord, the Blessed, the Perfect, the Supreme Enlightenment."

His heartbeat slowed and a drowsy calmness filled him as he chanted: "I take refuge in the Buddha. I take refuge in the Doctrine. I take refuge in the Community of Participants."

His prayed to earn merit; to purify and advance him toward *Nirvana,* Liberation and Enlightenment. But Tomi was an unworthy, diseased fool. Within his head, he heard the old Nanking priest ask sadly, "Why have you forgotten your family?"

"Weren't you paying attention?" Tomi snapped. "I prayed to all and even included you."

"Your other family."

"I have no family. All were killed by atomic bombs."

"You are confused because you dwell within your own woes. The others need you."

"Others?"

"Twelve whom you lead and many others destined to join you. They are your future"

"What others?" Tomi asked aloud, but the echo in the deserted temple mocked him. Tomi fled the temple to escape his venereal hallucinations. Outside, he expected daylight but found dusk. How did he lose a full day? Fearing madness, he hobbled home and fell into bed.

He slept around the clock and awoke marveling that, for the first time in 9 years, he hadn't suffered the Nanking nightmare. Late for work, he joined the crowd at the narrow bridge over the railroad tracks, where he had planned to die. But what would happen to his grimy misfits, who tended his swine and strained paper from GI night soil? The crippled veterans, unwanted widows and castoff orphans would suffer in Japan's cruel society. Were they diligent workers because Tomi had raised them up from dirty scavengers? No, they had earned their self-respect.

Tomi needed his farm family's hard work, enthusiasm and ideas as much as they needed him. The only way he could live with his diseased self was to remain worthy of them. He was jostled as he walked slowly across the bridge, still deep in thought.

Four years ago, Sendai was a rubble-strewn monument to failed militarism. Now it mirrored the impatient dawning of a new nation – one that had to deny its worst war sins as it arose from the greyness of defeat. Commercial success was Japan's new obsession. Why else did Lord Buddha and the Shinto gods grant Japan's survivors a second chance after millions of loved ones perished? Tomi refused to believe that his loved ones died while others lived because of random chance in an oblivious universe. There was a reason why he was still alive.

The *Nihonjin*'s drive to succeed was not fully understood by their American masters. Tomi mulled over a new truth: stripped of its military myth, reborn Japan needed to be more than a cheap copy of the flawed American people, who preached an idealism imperfectly practiced. Having lost a generation of men to war, Japan had to avoid blindly aping the affluent, confused U.S. culture. Japan had to select only those ideas and technologies that fit its own national character. To survive the Yankees' force-fed contradictions, the Japanese must re-invent themselves as a new breed of economic creature.

Tomi was startled to find himself at Camp Fowler's gate. He had dreamt grandiose concepts when he should have concentrated on his immediate survival. Tomi showed his gook troop pass to the bored GI guard and turned left toward the MP motor pool, source of his black market profits envied by predators. Sooner or later, a *Yakuza* or corrupt Yankee officer would squeeze him out. Tomi remembered the old priest's sing-song advice in Mandarin Chinese: "Think. Organize. Do good." He would think. He would organize. But Tomi wasn't sure about doing good. He was the last of a long line of warriors headed toward extinction.

***

"Why fuck a dried-up old woman?" Widow Mori complained. "When I cried out, the barbarian stuck his tongue down my throat. No warning, nothing. He never gave me a chance to take him in the right way. No, he just pushed in ... and let me tell you, it wasn't that far. I've had better in my day. He had to be blind drunk to grab me instead of all those lonely women who would have been happy to have him. No, I'm not hurt, but see how he dirtied my best kimono?"

Little Widow Mori was angry when Tomi sent for the local midwife, the hamlet's unofficial nurse. Despite his protests, Mori jumped out of bed and from a bowed position, proceeded to scold him. "Must you invite the whole world in to witness my shame? You are making matters worse. The gossips will claim I encouraged him, then complain because I was not yet satisfied. Oh, Tomi-Sama, the embarrassment you cause me! If only I hadn't stopped to pee."

Last night Widow Mori had squatted on her way home. A

drunken G.I. appeared out of the dark, pushed her on her back and raped her. Afterwards, the GI fell into the ground level vat of night soil. Drenched in shit, he dribbled a trail leading back to camp.

After examination, the midwife said, "Mori is a tough farm woman who birthed many children. She's uninjured but the *gaijin* may have given her venereal disease. I'll watch her."

Tomi ran to Camp Fowler, where he breathlessly told the startled guard, "Please telephone the MP Charge of Quarters. Have him inform Staff Sergeant Perry that Tomigawa of the motor pool is at the gate. It's urgent."

Widow Mori and Perry enjoyed a special relationship, much to everyone's amusement on the farm. When she wasn't telling him obscene jokes and teaching him rustic curse words, she acted like a Japanese mother and matchmaker. "Perry," she childed. "Don't be a butterfly boy. It is undignified for an important non-commissioned officer to sleep with second-hand blossoms. You need a good girl. It is much better."

"Find me one exactly like you, and I will happily settle down," Perry promised. She had been returning from a meeting with a virgin candidate's family when she was attacked.

"Are you positive she's not hurt? Poor little thing. I'll make that bastard suffer before he goes up on charges," Perry vowed.

Unlike the Japanese Army's official policy of permitting mass rape, torture, kidnap and murder of civilians in conquered lands, the U.S. Army's punishment for rape was 10 to 20 years in prison. To avoid publicity, the Army often charged a rapist with several lesser crimes.

Perry quickly identified the rapist as Technician 5th Grade Harold Boyle. The transport supply clerk had returned to barracks drenched in shit. Instead of making an immediate arrest, Perry had T/5 Boyle followed after he finished duty. A patrol reported that Boyle had joined the long line at the Army Prophylactic Station, across the intersection from Shen's noodle shop. Tomi posed as an interpreter and rode in the back of Perry's jeep.

"Boyle must not have used a condom or prokit last night," Perry said. "Now he's afraid of catching the clap, the rotten son of a bitch!"

No," Tomi said. "It's good news for Widow Mori. He wouldn't

bother if he has a dose."

GIs weren't permitted to leave camp without condoms and small needle tubes of prophylactic cream. Most GIs preferred the less messy and more effective liquid antiseptics at the Pro Station. Tomi ruefully wished he had had a condom or needle tube of cream after he left the shaven cleft of Shen's woman.

Sendai's back streets crawled with *yami no onnas*, 'angels of the night,' who serviced soldiers for cigarets, candy or yen. Experienced *Yakuza* whores insisted upon condoms, but homeless girls and desperate war widows with hungry children allowed reckless soldiers to go bareback. The resulting venereal contagion spread among American troops at a speed that Colonel Otomo's scientists would have envied.

Perry parked his jeep across the trolley tracks and watched the rapist in the waiting line of soldiers. Boyle was scrawny and short. Acne marred an otherwise ordinary face. When Boyle finally reached the Pro Station entrance, Perry got out of the jeep, removed his night stick from his web belt and sauntered past the waiting GIs. Tomi followed Perry inside.

Boyle was hunched over a long urinal trough, about to insert a glass medicine dropper filled with purple prophylactic fluid into his penis. Perry reached around and rapped Boyle's cock with the night stick. The skinny rapist howled in pain and writhed on the floor. Tomi wished Perry had waited another moment; then Boyle's shaft would have been filled with sharp glass shards.

Resisting arrest and trying to escape!" Perry yelled, kicking the fallen soldier in the stomach. Boyle folded up his knees and Perry swung his night stick hard across both kneecaps in a swordsman-like stroke.

The Pro Station medic who rushed to help the screaming soldier recoiled when Perry warned, "Keep away! This guy's a psycho. He may have a knife!"

Perry and Tomi dragged Boyle across the street, his pale penis still hanging out the unbuttoned olive drab fly. The line of soldiers watched fearfully as Tomi shoved the sobbing Boyle in the backseat, where Perry handcuffed him to a bracket. They bounced over the trolley tracks at high speed toward the police station. Boyle cried, "I'm hurtin' real bad."

"Just love taps, you fucking sad sack! You don't know what hurt is. Speak any gook?"

"No," he groaned.

The police station was divided between Military Police and Japanese Police. A young, serious MP desk sergeant, his automatic pistol in a non-authorized leather shoulder holster, nodded at Perry's orders. "Goldie, you never saw this one. Nothing goes in the log. Taking him to the other side. Call me if the lieutenant shows up or a patrol needs assistance."

Japanese policemen pretended not to notice as Boyle was dragged toward an empty cell used for interrogating their civilian prisoners. The cell stank of unpleasant things, old and new. Perry instructed Tomi in Japanese, "We've got about two hours. Avoid hitting his nose, mouth or eyes. No broken bones. There's a knotted towel in that water bucket. Swing the soaked towel like a club on the kidneys. Hurts like hell without leaving marks or cuts."

Grabbing a fistful of hair, Perry violently shook Boyle's head. The whiplash would damage the neck muscles without bruising. "The old lady you raped last night? She's dead."

"Can't be! I didn't rape her. The gook wanted a fuck."

"Bullshit! The dead woman was way too old to screw. She coulda' been your grandmother."

"I didn't know she was an old mama-san 'til after."

"How'd you kill her? Choke her to death? Jap police are examining the body and those guys are thorough. You're facin' a murder charge, fellah." Like all good policemen, Perry was a convincing actor. No wonder he had gotten several promotions despite his youth.

"I didn't kill her. She was alive. Honest to God!"

"You're gonna spend the rest of your miserable life at Fort Leavenworth, where creeps who rape and murder old women get special treatment. Guards will look the other way when all the animals gang-bang you. You'll need a new asshole after welcome week. Then they'll knock out your front teeth and you'll be on your knees, making lots of new friends."

"I didn't do nothin'. Honest! I was stinkin' drunk. I didn't pay attention to the gook 'til she squatted down and showed she wanted fucked. What are my folks gonna think?"

"Cut your bitchin'. Full name? " Perry asked, taking out his arrest form pad.

"Boyle, Harold L. Engineers."

"What's your M.O.S.?"

Boyle said, "Clerk, but I'm doin' a supply sergeant's job, truck equipment and tools."

In Japanese, Perry said, "His job is a wondrous surprise, Tomi. Do you think we can use him instead of merely beating and arresting the fool?"

"Then everyone will gain, especially Widow Mori."

"Gently, gently catches the monkey." Perry drawled in a parody of Tomi's Tokyo accent.

"Boyle, you draftee or Regular?

"Drafted. Only three months to go. Oh jeez, what'll I tell my folks?"

"Maybe I can give you a break. But you gotta do exactly what I say. Take my pen and pad and write exactly what I tell you. Got it, soldier?"

Boyle furiously wrote in a schoolboy's bad scrawl as Perry dictated slowly: "Last night I got drunk and beat up and raped an old woman on the farm road behind Camp Fowler. Then I fell in a big vat of shit. I hurt both my kneecaps and groin. That's g-r-o-i-n. After duty today, I went to the Pro Station. Instead of using blue liquid, I goofed and squirted in alcohol. It burned inside my penis. No, Boyle, not with a 'u.' Lemme spell it for you: p-e-n-i-s. I made a fuss and the MP's came. They found stolen tools in my pack that I was going to sell on the black market. The MPs did not threaten or use force on me. I make this statement of my own free will."

Perry read the confession by the dim overhead bulb. "OK. Sign your name and then print below it 'T/5 Harold L. Boyle' and your serial number. Leave room for me to witness and date it."

Boyle protested, "But Sergeant, I ain't no thief! Never stole a thing. All I sell the gooks are my cigarets, same as everybody."

"Look kid, I didn't ask you to confess to killing the old mama-san. This way, you're only charged with theft; unless you prefer 20 years in prison for murder.

Boyle looked like an obedient dog awaiting his master's next command. Perry folded the paper to fit inside his jacket pocket.

"Where you from?"

"Clairton. That's in Pennsylvania, Sergeant."

"I know that, kid. I'm from Pittsburgh, right next door." Perry shook his head, "It's a damn shame that a guy from Western Pennsylvania has to go to prison. If I had my way, you wouldn't even be charged with stealin' government property, let alone raping and killin' some old lady. I know it was the booze."

"Honest, Sarge, I didn't mean to hurt her."

"I believe you, Harold. Maybe there's a way out. If you re-up for a 3-year hitch, I might get the Provost Marshal to waive all charges. Then you'd be free and clear."

"No way! I ain't Regular Army. I'm goin' to trade school. Gonna be a telephone lineman."

"Listen up, Harold. The Army is hard up for trained people. That's how come you're doin' a sergeant's job. The only way I can get you off the hook is to tell the brass that you want to enlist. You get a third stripe, have stateside leave to see your folks, then return here to your cushy job. Hell, with your sergeant's pay you could save lotsa dough. In 36 months, you're a rich civvie, drivin' a brand new car to trade school."

"I ... I don't know. It's a big decision. Gotta think about it."

"Think about what?" Perry shouted. "You better think about doin' hard time for murder and rape. Once I'm outta this cell I gotta start paperwork. Then it's too late."

Perry gently pushed Boyle against the bars. "Why should I stick my neck out for a jerk too dumb to know a good deal?"

"Wait! Please wait! I'm sorry, Sergeant. I'm hurt and ain't thinkin' straight. I'll sign up for a Regular Army hitch if that's the only way. Yeah. Sure. I'll do it."

Perry pointed his thumb at Tomi, "Whoa! Not so fast. This here gook works in the MP motor pool and understands English. He's some kinda big shot from the dead mamma-san's village. Mayor or something. He saw you last night and identified you."

Boyle and Tomi were both startled by Perry's introduction. Tomi returned Boyle's curious stare with hatred. Tomi wanted the scum to suffer. Boyle's excuse for raping Widow Mori was that she was a gook; the same racial prejudice as the Rape of Nanking. Tomi's old sins made him want to hurt Boyle for his new one.

Perry saw Tomi's expression and stepped between them. "Harold, you've got to convince this pissed-off gook mayor that you're sorry. You gotta apologize for raping and murdering the village mama-san. If you don't, he'll file charges with the police here. Then I can't help you."

"Honest. I'm sorry. I didn't hurt her. It's a mistake," Boyle chattered to Tomi.

"You've gotta pay the dead woman's family compensation," Perry added.

"Compensation? What's that?"

"Japs ain't like us Pennsylvania white folk, Harold. You gotta give them plenty of cash so they can save face. It's some kinda gook pride thing. The money proves how sorry you really are. Enough dough and the village won't squawk to the Army or police. Remember, there's a dead rape victim out there that needs a whole lot of explainin'."

"But Sergeant, I ain't got no money."

"Look, kid, there's more than one way to skin a cat. "You admitted sellin' stuff on the black market. So? That's how you get money to pay the murdered gook's kin."

"*Tabun*, maybe," Tomi hissed through his teeth. "Mamma-San famiry get cash and other thing. G.I. truck stuff mo' better. Famiry buy ox then everyone OK."

"How much?" Perry demanded and Tomi squinted at the ceiling of the cell, then counted fingers, "*Tabun*, 3,000."

"Yen?"

"Occupation script. Mama-San got big famiry."

"No fucking way! You ain't goin' to take advantage of Harold just because the old woman croaked after he fucked her. 500 in U.S. script is tops!"

Tomi looked dejected and mumbled, "Maybe 800 OK. But want now. No wait. Need much GI 'quipment too."

"But I ain't got nothin'," Boyle whimpered.

"No sweat. I'll cash in some of my War Bonds to pay off this greedy fuckin' gook for you. You pay me back with stuff from your supply inventory."

"Jeez! How can I pay back that much?"

"Use your head, Harold! You slip this gook tools and stuff

once a month, then he'll peddle it on the market and give me some of what he makes, 'til your loan is paid. Just switch some inventory to the lost 'n broke list. You'll have it made in the shade."

Low cunning replaced Boyle's fear. "The re-enlisting part kinda' makes sense but the black market is big trouble for me and a good deal for you, Sarge."

Perry sighed, "This ain't Clairton, Pennsyl-fucking-tucky, and you don't know shit. I gotta convince my captain and the Japanese police that you're innocent, but gooks saw you fuckin' the dead woman. GIs saw you drippin' shit into camp. Guys in your own outfit will testify at your court martial. You're as good as convicted right now unless I lie like a sumbitch."

Perry put his hand on Boyle's shoulder. "I'm trying to keep you outta that prison. You don't wanna know the awful things they do inside to young meat like you for the next 20 years."

Boyle pressed his face into the bars and sobbed. Tomi said, "Maybe, I be witness. Say you not same GI I see at farm?"

"Hey! What a helluva idea! With me doin' the report and this gook as your witness, you're off the hook. But you owe this gook your virgin asshole, front teeth and freedom. Now you stay here while I get a statement from this gook before he changes his mind."

Perry slammed the cell door hard from the outside and locked it. "A most profound sound," he said in Japanese and snapped off the cell light. "He'll cook in the dark until my shift is over, then I'll drive him back to camp."

"Well done, Perry. Widow Mori gets a generous nest egg and we have a new source for tools. But after he pays back your loan, I want to give him 30, maybe 40 dollars a month."

"Why, Tomi? We've got the little shit sewed up tight."

"A steady salary makes him a guilty accomplice. It assures his future silence."

Perry grasped for the correct words, *"Shizuka no joshu?"*

"Exactly. Our silent junior partner. Thanks to your clever acting, the U.S. Army retains a qualified supply sergeant for three years and we expand into vehicle repair. All because Widow Mori was sexually violated and stripped of dignity. We can't undo evil but we'll give her enough money to buy a house, plus a steady income so she can enjoy what's closest to her heart."

"What's that?"

"You, or rather, your obedience as her almost-son. She emotionally adopted you a while ago. If you really want to ease her shame, make her the happiest woman in Sendai by obeying her wish that you stop being a butterfly-boy with city women. Widow Mori is from the old school. You must allow her to select a virgin bride for you, just as she did for her dead sons. Did you know that she's been talking to Yoshida about his other daughter for you."

"I barely know the girl! What about you? What the hell do you sacrifice? How about a wife for you too?"

Tomi laughed and said in English, "Tough shit! Widow Mori adopted you, not me."

"So I'm trapped just like that jerk Boyle."

Choosing his words carefully, Tomi answered seriously, "Not trapped, but not free choice either. You and Widow Mori have a different relationship. It's more than you two sharing the same sense of humor. She's proud of you -- not just for your promotions and police exploits, but for how well you speak Japanese. She believes it is her duty to pick the right woman for you. If she doesn't, she will have failed you. It's about love and family obligations. You are her Japanese son, Perry."

CHAPTER TWENTY
SENDAI AND TOKYO, JANUARY 1950

Perry, Yoshida, Sato and Tomi munched peanuts and gulped Fuji beer from bottles twice the size and potency of diluted Army-issue beer. It was late, and the silence of the cavernous garage echoed the pistol shots of random burps. Tomi's partners, sitting on his narrow Army cot, lined up their empties on the oil-soaked dirt floor of his combination office-home. Perry called it a drunken company directors' meeting.

Tomi leaned back and, American-style, rested his feet on the battered desktop, careful not to touch the open ledger that was the reason for celebration. It had been was their best month ever.

"What's the score? I lost count," Sato slurred.

Yoshida tried to focus on the bottles. "Perry had four, but you're drunker on three."

"Well then, it's a tie. *Kanpai!*"

Afraid they'd get too tipsy before he made his announcement, Tomi said, "My friends, things are going well, but we need to make changes. Our revenue is enough to get us a bank loan for a diesel repair shop and buy more farmland before prices get too high. But the bank insists we incorporate. So here's my idea: Each of you will get shares equal to 15% ownership." He said it in both languages to make sure they understood.

"No way!" Perry protested in English. "The business is yours. I'm only here when I'm off duty. I don't deserve squat."

Sato asked, "I'm confused. What is a squat?"

"*Rei.* Zero. Nothing," Perry translated.

"I also don't want this squat," Sato proclaimed. "Don't shame me by giving me more than I deserve. You work and live here like a monk. My job is easy compared to yours. I refuse to take your hard-earned profits." For emphasis, he yelled at Tomi in English,

"No squat!"

Yoshida smiled. "Ah, Mr. Coal hasn't changed from the old days. He still gives more than what is asked. Sorry, Tomi, we refuse to accept more lumps of coal than we deserve."

"But it's only fair."

Everyone worked longer hours than they had in the gook troop. Yoshida helped with paperwork, Sato was shop foreman, and Tomi handled customer sales. Perry took care of the Army black market deals. His MP protection kept the *Yakuza* away.

"Without you, I'd have nothing. You must take more!"

They mocked him by waving negative hands in front of their noses in comic exaggeration, and laughed when Tomi cursed. He should have waited until they were drunker.

Yoshida, the oldest and wisest, suggested, "To show you proper respect without diminishing ours, we each will accept no more than 5% ownership."

Perry added, "Yes, and Tomi retains the right to buy back our shares. Ownership always remains with him."

"But what about our mechanics? Don't they deserve more than this squat?" Sato asked.

Red-faced with shame, Tomi stood and bowed an apology to Sato. "Thank you for reminding me about that which I must never forget. Another 5% of my shares will go into an employees' retirement fund, which includes the farm family." All agreed.

Perry drained his fifth bottle, burped and said in Japanese, "I wish to make a shop proposal with deep apologies because, at times, I may not be the most skilled of craftsmen."

Sato, Yoshida and Tomi giggled, then burst out laughing. Everybody prayed when Perry picked up a tool. He couldn't turn a screw without ruining the head, or tighten a bolt without stripping the threads. He was *kikai no hakuchi*, a mechanical moron. But the gods give balance. Perry was very bright and did sums on the abacas as fast as anyone. His Miyagi accent was near-perfect, even though he refused to speak the slower, preferred Tokyo accent.

Perry and Tomi conversed in a reversal of each other's language. Tomi now spoke *Eigo* as bluntly as a brash, slangy Yankee, while Perry was politely indirect in Japanese.

"OK Perry, let's have it."

"Japan has many old trucks in need of repairs. Should we not expand to fill this need?"

"Yeah? Supply sergeants who peddle parts don't grow on trees," Tomi countered in English.

Sato asked, "Parts grow on trees?" Tomi repeated his reply in Japanese. Sato scratched his head. "*Eigo* is a crazy fucking language!"

Perry ignored him. "Our man Boyle tells me he has a cousin, a First Cavalry sergeant in Tokyo, who wants the same arrangement down there. We'd have to set up a shop. Should we refuse, he'll find someone else, probably *Yakuza*."

"Boyle openly bragged about his black market deal? If the C.I.D. finds out, we're screwed!"

"Yes, that was my second reaction," Perry continued in *Nihongo*. "My first was to shoot the fool. But Boyle is more worried about us than we are about him. If I'm caught, I lose my stripes and get 6 months in the stockade, while Boyle thinks he faces a long stretch in Fort Leavenworth. He claims he can trust him."

"Tell me about Boyle's relative. Is he also a jack-off?"

"Yes. Sergeant Moore is Regular Army, but a person without honor. His wife and children are in the States. He calls her a spendthrift bitch, and keeps extending his overseas duty. His Japanese pillow partner threatens to ditch him for a young officer if he doesn't set her up in a nice Tokyo apartment like her girlfriends have. The love-struck fool is desperate."

"What will this Tokyo sad sack do for us?"

"Everything. He's in charge of replacement parts for everything from forklifts to battle tanks; staff sedans, jeeps, trucks, weapons carriers, bulldozers and tractors."

"So? You want us to be the Tokyo Tank Turret and Tread Repair Company?" Tomi quipped in Japanese as he wiggled his finger stump. "I've had an experience with a tank."

"Moore bragged that he can falsify paperwork so that much of what he sells us will come directly off freighters at Yokohama, still packed in original grease."

"Is that possible? What about the risks?"

Perry seemed to sober up before he continued in

Japanese. "Yes. Moore can do it. Occupation personnel turnover is so constant that there are too few experienced people. Supervision and oversight are weak. There's much laxity. Troop strength is drastically cut, yet material still pours in from inflated old requisitions drawn on surplus stateside stockpiles. So secretly diverting some of it isn't difficult."

"How does our local parts pimp fit in?"

"Boyle wants to be the go-between for double his monthly bribe, but we don't need him. Let's run Tokyo separately. But we can give Boyle a nice raise for his tip."

Sato asked, "Can the Tokyo GI who grows automotive parts on trees provide proper tools and big equipment for a new shop?"

Perry pulled a paper from his pocket. "For starters, he can give us ten complete sets of mechanics' tool kits, body work jigs, three heavy hydraulic jacks, a steel plate press and straightener, two truck engine chain hoists, valve grinders, the standard bench equipment, and three electric welding sets that, unfortunately, lack local adapters."

"No sweat-u," Sato said. "I rewire hubba hubba."

"Moore will deliver the parts we order, cash on delivery. He's so anxious that he'll include, free of charge, a complete library of Army manuals for everything that has wheels, treads or steel tracks. I suppose a shelf of Sherman tank repair manuals might impress some of our customers."

"Cash on delivery? Do we have enough to do it?" Yoshida asked. "Tokyo will be damn expensive with rent, utilities, salaries, shop fixtures, furniture, sales expenses and big-time bribes. We'll spend money like drunken GIs before we see one yen of profit."

Tomi shared his doubts, but an offer like this dropped from the sky once in a lifetime.

"So we charge more," Perry said glibly.

To avoid a debate, Tomi asked, "Who goes to Tokyo?"

"Oh no! It has to be you, Tomi, at least at the start, along with Sato part time in the shop," Perry countered. "I'll handle Boyle's supply, accounting and some administration. Yoshida can add sales and customer contacts to his responsibilities. But he'll need an assistant."

Yoshida said, "Young Michio will make a good number two. He's smart, hardworking and eager to learn. Tomi, you did me a big favor transferring Michio here from the farm."

Actually, Michio had asked Tomi about working in the shop, and Tomi agreed, grateful for the orphan's photographs of Captain Hammel with Chen's woman.

Perry clapped Sato's shoulder. "You, my drunk friend, will be sleeping on the Tokyo overnight train for a while. You must run the shops here and in Tokyo until Tomi finds a trustworthy southerner to take over. How about three days a week in each shop? Set up another parts repair benches. It's a money-maker."

Tomi's mechanics were trained to replace whole systems and components instead of wasting time struggling to repair parts in inaccessible places.

Tomi objected. "Not so fast, Perry. I'm not sure I'm ready for Tokyo."

"Takahashi's son is your old comrade, not ours. Do you think he'd ask his *Yakuza* clan for permission to move into their territory for anyone else but you?"

"Squeezing into the tight Tokyo business community won't be easy. Connections are to Tokyo what water is to a fish." Tomi was quoting his uncle, who was in prison. Tomi had wanted to visit him but wasn't emotionally ready to go home.

"We'll ask our customers to brag about us to Tokyo trucking owners," Yoshida suggested. Tomi nodded slow approval and drained his bottle of beer. As usual, unexpected events drove his future instead of careful planning.

***

Tokyo's scars of war and emotional scabs of defeat were barely apparent. Tomi compared cosmopolitan Tokyo to Sendai's rural countryside, where families struggled to fill their modest rice bowls in unending drudgery. Tomi realized that he had been living in a time capsule filled with his old Tokyo ghosts. Now he wanted to be part of this unstoppable, reborn city, fueled by the easy prosperity of military occupation.

Dominating the busy *Ginza* shopping district was the

venerable *Takarazuka Gekijo,* where GIs were entertained with U.S.O. stage shows. It had been renamed the Ernie Pyle Theater after the popular war correspondent who was killed by a Japanese sniper a few days before the fighting ended. This irony was lost amid the babble of milling crowds of former foes who ignored old hates for new profits and pleasures. Outside the nearby Army post exchange, GIs openly sold their weekly rations of cigarets to *Yakuza* black marketeers for yen that were, in turn spent on sex, sake and souvenirs.

In front of the British Commonwealth Service Club, soldiers of every hue and race -- English, Australians, New Zealanders, Canadians, Hindus, Sikhs, Gurkhas, Kenyans, and South Africans -- haggled with brazen streetwalkers and peddlers. Though underpaid by American standards, these victors were also free-spending tourists who fed Tokyo's prosperity and spiraling inflation.

On the crowded streets, military vehicles mingled with new Japanese buses and trucks that were twice as big and powerful as the dinky pre-war models that Tomi repaired in Sendai. The Occupation authorities had encouraged the major corporations like Mitsubishi, Minsei and Nihon to build well-designed diesel vehicles that were efficient and dependable. The heavy traffic blared a warning that worried Tomi: soon there would be far fewer old trucks for him to repair.

The few available rickshaw pullers refused to carry him, preferring the lavish-tipping GIs. A traffic policeman directed him to a bus stop. He must not be late for his Sugamo Prison visit.

***

"Ah, jail transforms little pleasures into grand ones," Lord Suzuki said, exhaling a cloud of cigaret smoke. They were in a sparse visitors' room, guarded by bored GIs who looked as if they were selected for size, not vigilance.

Suzuki was delighted with Tomi's lavish gift of cigarets, fresh fruit and tinned delicacies. Between languid puffs, he grilled Tomi about his truck repair business. Finally satisfied, he stared at Tomi. "You are thinner, but there's something else."

"I'm older." Tomi laughed. "And so are you."

"Exactly what an American would say!" Suzuki exclaimed, slapping his hand on his thigh. "No human being would reply so directly. You have learned the *gaijin* bad manners along with their language. Your face wears that silly Yankee openness. I bet you sometimes dream in *Eigo!*"

Tomi pleaded guilty, and Suzuki preened like a rooster through the wire screen that separated them.

"Are you well treated by the guards?"

"Yes. Just the other day I played Boo and caught one."

"Boo?"

"I'm still spry enough to brace my back and legs against the narrow cell walls and climb up to the ceiling. There, I perched like a mountain climber and waited for the new guard to make his rounds. When he saw the empty cell, he panicked. I jumped down and yelled, 'Boo!' Last year, I made a guard wet his pants. Everyone got a big laugh out of it, especially our regular guards. One must create innocent surprises to offset the monotony of routine. It's the worst part of being in here for both inmates and guards."

"How do you keep busy, Uncle?"

"I write, study, exercise, read piles of newspapers and do crafts. I find basket weaving comforting, but my more talented colleagues make toys and art objects out of paper and wood. They give them to the guards as presents."

"I'm glad that everyone has good relations with the guards."

"It's not bad, considering the false war crimes they charged us with. The first few years were uncomfortable and the food is still bland. It matters not. I won't be here much longer."

"What do you mean?" said Tomi, fearing his uncle had a terminal illness.

"Class A prisoners will be released soon. No one will serve a life sentence, thanks to the Cold War," he boasted.

"Wonderful! I'm so happy for you. You'll be surprised at how everything has changed."

"I know what's happening outside better than you. When the prison gates open, the leadership clique will march out. We are Japan's new heroes, ready to resume command!"

"You mean the Americans will allow it?"

"Allow it? The Yankees desperately need us now. We'll dig up our hidden assets and get back to business. We have maintained our political connections, and a few of my fellow prisoners will seek high office. Ah, the delicious revenge of watching the Occupation rulers fervently kiss the ass of a war criminal when he becomes a cabinet minister. I shall enjoy that very much."

"I had no idea."

"Think, Nephew! Land battles of armies, artillery and tanks locked in combat are as obsolete as knights on horseback. Future wars will be fought by dropping atomic bombs, and the Yankee airbases here are only minutes away from the heartland of Red China and Soviet Asia. Japan is the U.S.A.'s strategic jewel, its anti-communist client state. This requires an experienced, proven leadership in our new democracy. Don't worry, we'll extract a steep price for this cooperation, and America will gladly pay. We've had preliminary talks about a peace treaty to end the Occupation, but that's a few years away."

He scrutinized Tomi. "You never touched the Suzuki assets, even when you were desperate. That pleases me, my Americanized nephew. I trained you well. Tell me about your new Tokyo garage plans. Need money?"

"Ten service bays would be ideal, but we will have to settle for five."

"We? Who else is involved?"

Tomi described his unlikely partners; a young MP staff sergeant who spoke fluent Japanese; a former Nanking soldier who got him his gook troop job, and his Camp Fowler motor pool boss. Suzuki nodded when he mentioned their shares. Unmentioned but obvious to Suzuki was Tomi's unwitting partner-supplier, the U.S. Army.

"That warrant officer of yours. I've forgotten his name. Is he in Sendai with you?

Tomi didn't directly answer his question, but used the deliberate flat tone that carried deep meaning. "I am to be Takahashi's guest for dinner this evening at his establishment. It will be our first reunion since I left Tokyo. He is now a person of, ah, certain influence."

"Ah so. And his business place is … where?"

Tomi named the notorious entertainment district controlled by *Yakuza*.

Suzuki nodded, "Never borrow money from your ex-comrade, or you will end up working for his masters. By all means, ask him for small favors and yes, do many small favors for him, including hiring at least one person whom he will recommend. That person is a spy. By knowing his identity, you can defend your secrets and avoid problems. Despite all that you've done for him, Takahashi cannot be loyal to you. He has sworn a blood oath of obedience to his *Oyabun*. Not even friendship comes before that."

"After all we've been through together, I thought I was immune from the typical *Yakuza* takeover. I planned to ask him for a big loan tonight. Thank you for the timely warning."

Suzuki's eyes glinted with satisfaction. He reveled in correctly analyzing a situation with scant information. Prison and age hadn't reduced his ability to see around dark corners. Tomi expected a lecture and this time he welcomed it.

"In addition to new wealth, insatiable greed and crude manners, your friend's *Yakuza* clan has *kankei,* connections. Even women can vote in free elections now, but the *Yakuza* buys elected politicians just as corporations and banks have always done. It's the same as the U.S. I call it the Democracy of Dollars. Everyone's money is equal."

He talked candidly, unafraid of being overheard. Tomi thought this was a very strange prison.

"Your warrant officer's masters now wield more power than the royal throne, which, for better or worse, is demoted to performing traditional rituals. Our occupiers rest their *gaijin* asses on Japan's four-legged stool: industry, banking, senior civil service and the *Yakuza*. The day isn't far off when the *Yakuza* will buy political parties as easily as we do. I'd advise you to stay out of their clutches. It is like dancing with a hungry bear."

Tomi was again the ignorant junior officer being lectured by his all-knowing superior. But this time, Tomi needed to know how to survive in this strange new Tokyo. Suzuki had accused Tomi of acting like an impolite American, so he used that blunt weapon.

"Uncle, how and where can I get a big credit line to open my second repair operation?"

Suzuki blinked away shock, then smiled at confirmation of Tomi's *gaijin* lack of manners. He enjoyed proof of his astuteness as much as his tobacco. He whispered the name of a bank.

"Enjoy a friendly reunion with your wartime comrade tonight. But don't accept his money, even when he presses you. You neither want nor need it. Tomorrow at noon, you will be expected at the bank's executive offices. The senior vice president will introduce you to several colleagues. They will invite you to the Bankers Club for a private luncheon meeting."

Suzuki peered through the mesh screen at Tomi's only suit, threadbare and pre-war. "Nephew, your apparel is barely adequate for Sugamo Prison," he sneered. "Tomorrow, please wear a decent suit, shirt and tie." He glanced at his own U.S. Army prison garb and smiled, "Consider this one time you don't use me as your example. During lunch, a banker will casually ask about your plans. Be brief, because he doesn't give a damn how you reply. He only wants to know how much you need to borrow. Ask for no less than 20 times as much as you need. Invest the excess in something else, perhaps real estate. It doesn't matter. In these inflationary times, only the stupid save cash, while the shrewd borrow and repay loans later with cheaper money. Understand?"

Tomi nodded, wondering where to invest the excess capital. In Tokyo, Sendai or both?

"The bigger the loan, the more prestige you have. It's a matter of face for them and me. The loan will be quickly granted at the lowest interest rate. When you ask for more capital later -- and you damn well better or I'll be quite angry -- the bank will grant it."

"Thank you, Uncle. Words cannot express my profound gratitude. As always, I am indebted to you." Tomi bowed and wondered how a war prisoner could contact his banker before tomorrow's meeting. Lord Suzuki's couriers must be well-bribed prison staff.

Suzuki ejected the butt from his American cigaret holder

and replaced it with a fresh one. He said casually, "The bank also will handle the paperwork to transfer 10% of your corporate shares to Suzuki Industries as collateral. Is that satisfactory?"

"Most satisfactory, Uncle. I am honored." He bowed again. Tomi knew that after the loan was eventually repaid, the shares would not be returned. Suzuki Industries, which was one of the bank's owners, was his newest shareholder at no cost to itself. Tomi had gained another partner. It was not unlike a *Yakuza* takeover, but with superior connections, status and table manners. Actually, it was a bargain, considering all the new contacts and business opportunities Suzuki Industries would provide. This is how Japan always did business.

***

An overweight Takahashi and Tomi toasted each other at dinner and reminisced about the old days. Joviality masked their scrutiny. Tomi could not see the bright son of a humble farmer within the girth of his expensive silk suit and flesh that reeked of cologne. He had no idea what Takahashi thought of him.

In the old days, *Samurai* flaunted their power by lopping off the head of a peasant who failed to bow sufficiently low. Takahashi used anger as his sword. His servants cringed in open terror. He did this to impress Tomi, but only embarrassed him.

Takahashi had all of his fingertips, indicating keen career skills, and his thick rings flashed prosperity. He bragged that this expensive hospitality house was only one of many he owned, and broadly hinted of other major enterprises. Takahashi's only complaint was that his father refused to move to Tokyo, where he could live like a rich man, bask in his son's success and bow toward the Emperor's Palace as often as he liked.

"It's your fault, Tomi. Honorable Father loves managing your ever-expanding farming operation. He says that never in our family's history has so much farmland been under a Takahashi's personal control. He brags that you're one of the biggest landowners in Miyagi Prefecture and that he's your manager-partner. He calls you many things; the least praiseworthy is 'most generous nobleman.' Yeah, I guess you are a rarity for your class."

Takahashi seemed unaware of the envy that laced his words.

Tomi ignored the insult and raised his sake cup. "My old comrade and friend. I am forever in the debt of your honorable family, who gave me shelter and food as they would their own flesh and blood during the bad times. I can never repay their hospitality."

Using the vulgar 'Hey!' in a fake Miyagino accent, Tomi complained, "Your father fired me from my first civilian job after I dribbled night soil on a customer's floor. He said I was the world's worst honey dipper and banished me to Sendai City to seek my fortune."

"Best fucking advice you ever got!" This time, their laughter was sincere. During the lavish dinner they exchanged well-remembered war experiences but omitted 'Matters Best Left Unsaid,' an important etiquette in Occupied Japan even when *gaijin* were not present.

Tomi was curious about the fate of Ruth, the Chinese-Jewish woman, but since she wasn't mentioned, he could not ask. Takahashi was not the same person who had crept through the Unit 731 mine field to help his pregnant lover escape.

During the war, Takahashi's black market dealings benefitted their unit. Now he used his remarkable intelligence and cunning in a crime clan. His transformation shocked Tomi, who ignored the fact that he, too, was engaged in theft and criminal conspiracy.

A tough-looking bodyguard with two missing fingertips entered and whispered in his employer's ear. Takahashi said, "I have to go out for a while but in the meantime ...." He yelled and four beautiful girls entered the room and bowed. He selected one and said, "Take this one. Relax and we'll meet for drinks when I return."

Tomi's skilled companion would report to Takahashi that his friend insisted on wearing a condom each time, uncommon for clients of this expensive place. Takahashi would know that Tomi had Shen's disease. The bath, massage and sexual acrobatics exhausted Tomi. He was awakened from a deep sleep by the soft, imperative words, *Oyabun* awaits you."

His mission evidently successful, Takahashi celebrated by

getting sloppy drunk on vast amounts of Santori scotch. Tomi slowly sipped sake and watched.

"You're too fucking thin, Tomi. Not wasting away from a venereal disease, are you? Gotta watch where you stick your *chimpo* these days." Takahashi's eyes lacked the compassion that they once had. Obviously news of Tomi's incurable clap evoked no sympathy.

"Just too much work and skipping meals. The business keeps me busy."

"Yeah, you mentioned something about opening a shop here. You're gonna need buckets of yen that you don't have. Don't worry, I'm rich. Whatever you need, you'll have."

"Thank you, my friend. I appreciate your generosity, but money isn't a problem."

Takahashi's bleary face showed open surprise. How did he know that Tomi lacked funds? Was there a *Yakuza* informer in Tomi's group? Takahashi's father didn't have access to Tomi's secret ledgers, so who else could it be?

"Don't need money? That's a big surprise. You wanna operate here like in Sendai?"

Tomi belched politely and sipped in silence. He was afraid to reveal too much.

"Tomi, you tricky *Samurai*. You got big-time MP connections down here too?"

"No, just a few officers who are kind enough to help me out," Tomi lied. "But I wouldn't start here without first discussing it with you, and hopefully get your associates' approval. That's the main reason I'm here, my friend. I need your help."

The fiction of having top brass partners would make sense to the *Yakuza*. No one knew everything, and Tomi was a tiny operator. Many Yankee officers and high-ranking civilians in Japan and Germany returned home rich from shady deals.

Tomi said, "Your associates' approval of my insignificant business is foremost. Then I'll need to find a shop in a good location. The real estate market is crazy. So I ask you, my Miyagi-born friend, help me find the right place in the city of my birth."

"Ya look 'round yet?" he slurred.

The best lies were folded around truth. "I just arrived

today. A site outside of Tokyo proper will do, somewhere with a decent road network, which means near a big army base." Tomi paused, furrowed his brow with obvious guile. "I just had a thought. What about Saitama Prefecture? Aren't Zama and Camp Drake there?"

Zama was the replacement center for newly-arrived GIs and sprawling Camp Drake was the First Cavalry Division's main base. Takahashi would think that Tomi's fictitious generals were stationed at one or both installations.

"Wha? Those suburbs ain't worth shit. I've been looking around for ya. Found the perfect place between Tokyo and Yokohama. You can handle both markets at once."

Tomi had not mentioned his plans to Elder Takahashi, yet his son knew of the expansion even before Tomi had left Sendai. Who was the spy?

"I'd rather have a shop for Tokyo business and maybe later, open a Yokohama shop. I have enough to finance both start-ups." Tomi silently blessed Uncle Suzuki for keeping him from ending up with the *Yakuza* as his controlling partner.

Takahashi showed his obvious disappointment. "My real estate agent will take you around tomorrow afternoon. You can use my car and driver."

"Thank you Takahashi, but I have a luncheon date at the Banker's Club. Will the following day be satisfactory?"

Takahashi was drunk enough to show that he was impressed. Few *Yakuza oyabun* dined at the exclusive old money club in Tokyo; at least not yet.

"That reminds me. Do you know where I can buy a business suit, shirt and tie early tomorrow? What store would you recommend for fast service?"

"Loan you one of my Italian-made suits. Oops, forgot that I've grown and you haven't." His laugh turned into a cough. Tomi looked away as he tried to spit in a napkin and missed.

"Stay here tonight and enjoy a couple of my girls. They'll measure you, and after breakfast, a banker's blue suit will be ready. Fancy shirt, tie and shoes too. This ain't poor little Sendai."

"Wonderful! Thank you so much. I was concerned about that," Tomi said, knowing that several women would work through the night while he cavorted with a Takahashi whore. "I also need your advice about hiring a bright senior clerk to handle my sales administration."

"Sure. But what 'bout the rest? Ya know, mechanics, accountants, purchasing and inventory clerks, whole goddam staff. I have lots of experienced people lined up for you."

"Thank you, Takahashi, but as with our mechanics, we must do our own training as we operate in a non-Japanese way. It's easier to instruct a fresh young person than undo old ways. But having a bright assistant that you recommend will help me find my way around. Tokyo is almost a foreign city to me."

When they stood and bowed goodnight, Takahashi startled Tomi by asking in a sober voice, "Your uncle, Lord Suzuki. I assume you visited him today?"

Surprised by the sudden change, Tomi admitted he had.

Takahashi continued in the same quiet, respectful tone. "Please convey to the Honorable Lord my deepest respects, and tell him that I, like his nephew, look forward with profound happiness to his release. It cannot happen quickly enough, because the nation needs him. Perhaps he will honor my establishment by permitting me to host a dinner party celebrating his forthcoming freedom. I assure you it will be in the finest taste and decorum."

Shocked by the formal invitation, Tomi bowed low and said, "I will convey your most gracious invitation to him at the earliest opportunity, friend Takahashi-Sama, and with pride."

There was no smell of scotch on his breath when he clasped Tomi on the shoulder affectionately. "My dearest friend, you have no idea how sincerely pleased I am that your uncle is in a position to help you. I am delighted with your good fortune." He bowed again and left with a purposeful stride.

Takahashi had been guzzling cold tea from a Scotch bottle to feign drunkenness, but the two women kept Tomi too busy to dwell on Takahashi's motives for his act.

The next day, Tomi left the pleasure palace dressed like a successful businessman.

***

The day after the bankers' meeting, Tomi masked his anger at the outrageous high rent for the shop selected by Takahashi's beaming real estate agent. But if Tomi refused, Takahashi's clan wouldn't permit him to operate. The overcharge was the *Yakuza's* tax for doing business. In a few months, Tomi would buy the building, knowing that he'd again pay too much. But if inflation continued, the building would still be a worthwhile investment.

The spacious shop had a concrete floor and secure storage for black market parts. There was vacant land on either side for expansion. The building was on a main road, a short walk from the railroad station for workers. The bonus was a second floor office for his spartan living quarters, and room for a strong safe to keep secrets from Takahashi's in-house spy. Reluctantly, Tomi had to admit that the *Yakuza* had found the ideal place for him. On balance, it was worth it.

During the train ride home, Tomi stared out the window and pondered why Takahashi had deliberately revealed that he had begun the location search before Tomi left Sendai. And why did he admit surprise that Tomi didn't need a loan?

Tomi realized that Takahashi had risked everything to tell him about the Sendai spy without violating his *Yakuza* oath of obedience. Like a brother, he was genuinely relieved that Tomi hadn't fallen into the *Yakuza* money trap.

Takahashi had acted like a crude gangster, but inside he was more a man of honor than Tomi. Takahashi had walked through a *Yakuza* minefield to help Tomi while remaining loyal to his masters. Tomi looked at his reflection in the train window, but didn't like what he saw ... a self-centered, ambitious snob dressed in Takahashi's gift, an expensive, custom-made suit. Besides, the shoes hurt.

CHAPTER TWENTY ONE
Yokosuka, November 1950

Two sleek destroyers herded a convoy of wallowing troopships and armed freighters toward open sea as fishing trawlers on the reverse course outraced a squall to shore. The grey scene begged a *haiku*, but Tomi's bloodshot eyes saw only men headed toward separate destinies. The American replacements on the troopships would soon face death in the freezing foxholes of Korea, while the fishermen would be enjoying the warmth of their wives, delighted about the price of fish in Japan's soaring prosperity.

The white wakes of warships and bobbing boats creased the dark blue heave in patterns as unpredictable as last night, when Tomi once again met the ghost of his 'Matters Best Left Unsaid' past. No matter how much he drank and fucked, the shame would cling like the random splatters of gull droppings on the pier, where his new wealth came ashore.

Tomi inhaled sea air spiced with diesel fumes, fish waste and rotting wood, then returned to the unloading. When the huge crane swung a mangled tank out of a ship and dropped it onto one of his flatbed trucks, the noise that hammered Tomi's hangover was the clang of profit.

The Sherman and Sheridan tanks, still stinking of gore and gunpowder, were rough nuggets of the gold mine Lord Suzuki had given Tomi after he and other war criminals were freed from prison. Suzuki, remembering Tomi's heavy repair equipment, had somehow secured a lavish contract to patch badly-needed U.S. Army tanks damaged by North Korean attackers.

Hurt by heavy casualties in yet another war that began with a surprise attack, the retreating Americans bought tons of replacement supplies from Japanese firms, including Suzuki

Industries, because they were cheaper and faster than material shipped from the States. The Japanese called the Korean War 'The Gift from the Gods,' and welcomed the invasion of pleasure-seeking American soldiers. Japan was the military staging base, supply depot, aircraft carrier, whorehouse, recreation rear area and souvenir shop for a bitter war that raged 150 miles off its western coast.

Through the haze of his hangover, Tomi reviewed the events of the previous evening's party celebrating Suzuki's freedom.

"This time we are on the right side of history," Lord Suzuki had croaked. "Let others bleed as we count capital instead of casualties!" Tomi had hosted last night's party celebrating Suzuki's release from Sugamo Prison at Takahashi's plush hotel, no longer a brothel now that Yankee generals, admirals and Washington V.I.P.s grunted their way through the lengthy menu of fleshy pleasures. Takahashi had quipped that the *Yakuza* prostitutes achieved what the old Imperial General Staff could not do: bring the U.S. military-political leadership to its knees.

Lord Suzuki had invited 20 of his closest friends who ruled Japan through interlocking directorships, connections, secret deals and *wairo*, bribes. All were cordial to Tomi, who felt like a junior officer among the generals guiding Japan to a prosperous future. Over a sumptuous dinner, the executives, politicians and senior civil servants cheerfully gossiped, haggled and pledged each other new favors before the heavy drinking and sex began.

In addition to Takahashi's hostesses, there were lovely movie stars and entertainers eager to give potential sponsors samples of their pillow skills. The women, glamorous in American-style cocktail dresses and formal gowns, led the powerful to well-appointed rooms off the banquet area. Celebrity geishas in kimonos played classical instruments, sang, recited poems and easily matched wits with Japan's keenest minds, as the men recuperated between women.

Tomi watched Japan's *shoguns* enjoy themselves and he prayed for a long war. How many battle tanks, trucks and jeeps would he have to repair to pay this evening's sex bill? He told

Takahashi his concern and was laughed off. "Don't be naive, Tomi. My associates will profit hugely from the political contacts made here tonight. I have gained much face. You have done me an enormous favor. There is no bill. I should be paying you!"

Tomi's relief faded when Lord Suzuki waved them over to greet a latecomer. "I'm sure you and Takahashi-San remember my dear friend and colleague."

After an impolite pause, and so not to shame Suzuki, Tomi reluctantly bowed low to his former Unit 731 commander. "Honorable Doctor Otomo," Tomi murmured. He was surprised at how unchanged the scientist looked.

Otomo addressed them as inferiors. "Ah, Tomigawa and Takahashi. I see your extraordinary luck continues. Long ago I forgave you for foolishly risking your necks to help that Chinese Jewess escape. I overlooked your prank because she didn't get far and I needed you two. My *joodan*, joke," he giggled at his two-language pun, "was that you never knew. You forgot the lesson I taught you at our first meeting: Rule Number One. Never lie to Doctor Otomo."

Takahashi looked as if a sword had penetrated his belly. Tomi led him away and overheard Otomo telling a puzzled Lord Suzuki about Takahashi's 'love log.'

Tomi guided the dazed Takahashi through the crowd to his office. He feared Takahashi would kill Otomo with his barehands, but he underestimated Takahashi's discipline.

"That *kikai na koto*, monstrosity, soils humanity," Takahashi said without emotion. "Go back to your guests, Tomi. I'm OK." He picked up the telephone as Tomi left.

Lord Suzuki interrupted Tomi's apology about Ruth's escape attempt, "Your flaw of idealism must please the gods, because somehow you manage to avoid the many disasters you so recklessly court," he scolded. "No more ancient history! Doctor Otomo is important to us at this critical time. Go and make your peace with him immediately!" Tomi bowed and obeyed.

"Your uncle has stomach cancer," Otomo said calmly, taking a flute of champagne from a tray. Ignoring Tomi's shock, he took a noiseless sip and led Tomi to a vacant room that stank of thick perfume and recent sex. "He hides it well, but his cancer is extremely painful. Lord Suzuki wishes to remain mentally alert to the end, but will require heavy sedation. In four months or less, he will be gone."

Tomi tried to speak but instead sobbed, not caring that Otomo stared at him with cold, clinical interest. Why had the beast-scientist been chosen as the messenger? Uncle always had reasons for everything he did. Tomi regained control when the reason came to him. Lord Suzuki wanted him to absorb the news before they discussed the future without emotion.

Otomo delivered another surprise. "Lord Suzuki intends to name both of us to his board of directors. You, as possible heir-apparent, and me for many reasons, not the least of which is my high standing in American military circles. Lord Suzuki made me prove the power of my Washington connections by securing that Army tank contract for you. My influence brought you success and validated my U.S. Army standing to your Uncle's satisfaction."

It was an open secret that Otomo had exchanged his biological warfare data for immunity from war crimes prosecution. A consultant to the U.S. Army Chemical Warfare Branch after the surrender, he remained free while others were punished for lesser war crimes. His protectors had ignored his vivisections on tens of thousands of victims, including a few Yankee POWs.

"My Washington colleagues were disappointed when I failed to give them the name of the officer who deployed my bacteria weapon among Soviet troops in 1939. After all, it has been 11 years. I told them I heard a rumor that he was killed in the war."

If Otomo gave them Tomi's name, he'd lose the Army contract and perhaps worse. Silently, he waited for the blackmailer's price. Otomo set down the empty glass and delicately tapped his chest and stomach. "Europeans once believed the heart was the seat of emotion and intellect, while we thought it was the belly. Ancient Egyptians thought it was the liver. How silly! It's here," tapping his high forehead. "Mankind's best brains are those who seek pure knowledge despite cheap morality and backward laws. We scientists shape modern times with penicillin, sulfa drugs, DDT and other advances. Surely the atomic bomb is the most extraordinary intellectual feat of all, because it reduces war to seconds instead of years."

Tomi's loved ones had disappeared at Hiroshima and Nagasaki in a flash of technological brilliance that Otomo revered. Tomi was getting rich because of Otomo's influence in Washington, the city Otomo had wanted to ravage with anthrax.

Sounding less like a scientist than a street hustler, Otomo said, "When I reviewed my research data before giving it to the Americans, I found a project I had once dismissed as insignificant. Belatedly, I recognized it as a major concept in developing polio and cancer vaccines. If I'm right, within a decade I will be revered as much as Fleming, Pasteur and the Curies for the secret inside my head. Think of the enormous profits! Parents will pay any price to save their children from the crippling disease, and cancer patients will gladly sell their souls. But the Suzuki board of directors knows little of science. Lacking vision, they will balk at the start-up costs, high risks and years of research. I need your support when I put my proposal to the board. They will listen to you."

The grandiosity offended Tomi, but Otomo was a careerist who wouldn't risk his reputation on a fantasy. Otomo was blackmailing Tomi for a greater good. If he did have a secret path to curing polio or cancer, it would be under the dying Lord Suzuki's patronage.

"Otomo, if I am honored with a seat on the board and, if Suzuki Industries benefits from your medical discovery, you will have my support. Now please excuse me, I must see my Uncle."

Lord Suzuki waved off Tomi's grim concern. "A fantastic party! We'll talk this weekend. Don't look so damn sad. Get a fresh movie starlet to make you happy." Suzuki rejoined the cluster of elder statesmen around Japan's number one *geisha*. Tomi was grateful that he didn't have to pay her $1,000 fee for a few hours of witty conversation. Tomi tried to follow his dying mentor's advice, but the film stars were occupied. He settled for two seductive hostesses, but his gloom withstood their gymnastics and his drinking.

The next morning, when he arrived at the wind-swept pier, he was hung over and short-tempered with his employees. Both he and they were grateful when driving rain halted the unloading. Water would dilute the gore inside the tanks and give Tomi a chance to visit Yoshida at a nearby hospital. Tomi should have gone sooner, but he was annoyed that Yoshida had deserted him for a greater loyalty.

A neat red disc of blood blossomed on Yoshida's white bandaged stump, which resembled Japan's national flag, 'Circle of the Sun.' Yoshida was woozy from pain killers, but he caught Tomi's stare. "Ugly, huh? I was grabbing a smoke on deck when we hit a stray mine. Blew me off the fantail. Crew went down, poor bastards. Yankees pulled me out of the drink." His thin face, naked without a cigaret, had aged.

"The wound is bleeding. I'll get the nurse."

"Nah! Supposed to drain. Got so many antibiotics in me that if I bottled my piss I could be a one-legged black market. Just bad luck to be on a suicide sweeper."

"A suicide sweeper?"

"Dumb Yankees' minesweepers are steel-hulled, so they attract magnetic mines. We had the shitty job of leading their invasion into Inchon Harbor with our old wooden minesweepers."

The groaning patients in Yoshida's crowded ward proved the lie of Japan's new made-in-America 'No War' constitution. The wounded were Japanese Navy and Marine veterans who sailed with and, in a few isolated instances, fought alongside the Yankees in Korea, an embarrassing fact that both nations hid. The 'Gift from the Gods' war had a bloody price tag.

In June, North Korean Communists, led by Soviet-built T-34 tanks, invaded South Korea, America's client nation. After wasting a full day in stunned disbelief, General MacArthur sent ill-equipped and poorly-led occupation units from Japan to stop the attack. Their World War II bazookas bounced off the Soviet tanks, and thousands of Americans were slaughtered in the hot summer of retreat. The Americans and South Koreans were pushed into a tight perimeter at Pusan, where they bravely stood their ground and died in greater numbers.

In September, well-equipped elite divisions from the States landed at Inchon Harbor behind the advancing North Koreans and tuned the tide of battle. The U.S. Navy, shrunk by peacetime budget cuts, used Japanese veterans to crew a few minesweepers and freighters. Tomi had just gotten the Army contract and needed Yoshida. But he had ignored Tomi's pleas to remain, and instead obeyed his former captain's request to return to the engine room of his old ship, a mine sweeper. Yoshida had survived the war because his skipper kept him in Tokyo Bay instead of the lethal South Pacific. Yoshida owed his captain *gimu*, an obligation.

A nurse brushed Tomi aside to give Yoshida a morphine shot. After a long silence he mumbled, "Toes on my missing leg still ache. The fish must have chewed my leg to the bone by now. Being a fucking cripple is odd, Mr. Coal."

The Japanese were repelled by physical defects of any kind and the country's many maimed veterans avoided social embarrassment by rarely appearing in public.

Tomi chattered with false cheer. "The new artificial limbs are fantastic. You'll be running around the shop floor just like the old days. Only your wife will know which is the good leg. Heal quickly. I need you. The Americans insist that we open another tank repair shop at Sasebo because it's the closest port to Korea. They're even giving us a free building and equipment.

"Here's my plan. Soon as you're able, take over the Yokohama shop and I'll run Tokyo. What do you think about bringing Michio down from Sendai to boss the Sasebo operation? Never thought that orphan from the pig farm would be so good at handling our real estate and truck repair shop. You trained him well."

Michio? Yeah, he'll do a fine job. Too fucking bad about his problem."

"What problem?"

"*Yakuza* forced him to spy on us. I had to talk him out of killing himself."

"Michio is their spy in Sendai?"

"He was blackmailed."

"How?"

"Prefers men," Yoshida said, and drifted off without seeing Tomi's rage.

Tomi fired Michio, relieved that his secrets would now be safe from the *Yakuza*. Three weeks later Yoshida appeared in a wheelchair in Tomi's office. Surprised, Tomi congratulated him on his recovery. Yoshida snarled, "Shut the door."

Yoshida was ashen-faced. He panted, "When I roll out of here, either you will have rehired Michio or you'll never see me again!"

"What's this about, Yoshida? I'm confused."

"I'm the one who is confused about you!"

"What are you talking about?"

"Michio can't change who he is any more than I can dance."

"He is who he is. Worse, he spied on me," Tomi growled. "What's it got to do with you?"

Yoshida looked with disgust at the empty pant leg fastened with a safety pin. "Does having one leg make me a gook, an inferior? If Michio isn't a human being after all he's done for you, then you probably won't think of me as human either.

"He and I are human beings, not gooks! I don't want your fucking pity. When you fired Michio for being different, you punished me 'cause now I'm different too. You're an economic animal who cares nothing about those of us with the bad luck of being different! We called you 'Mr. Coal' out of admiration. You, the highborn war hero, never looked down on us. We called ourselves Team Tomi because we were equals. Hell, you included Perry, proving that even a *gaijin* can be a human being too. What happened to you?"

He clawed his shirt pocket and swore, "Fuck! Not smoking is as shitty as having my ass stuck in this damn wheelchair. Everything has turned rotten, including us."

"You mean that Michio is a ... a ..." Tomi's trailed off.

"A cripple? All I know is that he can't help who he is any more than I can walk." Yoshida growled without hiding tears. "The homosexual stuff is confusing. I've worked on ship engines that were exactly the same, but one required different maintenance than the other. Maybe people are made that way too. All I know is that Michio is the same person you were about to promote until I blabbed his secret. He didn't change, you did!"

To hide his rage, Tomi lowered his head. Yoshida was in pain and in shock. All this stupid emotion over a flower petal boy.

Any female could give Michio more pleasures than he got from men. His sexual sickness made no sense, unless as Yoshida claimed, it was his nature. If that were true, then he had no choice.

Tomi didn't want to lose Yoshida any more than he did Perry. It didn't matter that one was *gaijin* and the other a cripple. Tomi needed both of them. When Perry returned from Korea, he planned to join the team full-time. Was being a homosexual as permanent as being a *gaijin*? Tomi never thought about it before. Michio had been a superb employee who had yet to be replaced. He had been forced to spy to hide the truth from Tomi. Perhaps Yoshida was right. Team Tomi was a bunch of oddballs.

"Drink this," Tomi said gruffly, pouring hot tea out of his thermos.

" If this doesn't get me smoking again, nothing will."

"OK, here are my terms. Michio is back on the team if he vows to be discreet. And he cannot hire others like him. It's not a matter of who is or isn't a human being, it's about reputation. We will fail if customers suspect that we are a bouquet of flower petal boys."

Instead of being grateful, Yoshida replied, "You know Michio is discreet. However, my return to Team Tomi depends on your agreement to another idea I have."

Tomi had acceded to one demand and now Yoshida, acting like a sharp bargainer, was asking for another. He had somehow gained a new confidence since losing his leg. He was tougher than ever, yet caring. It would make him an even better manager. Tomi asked warily, "What now?"

"I want to hire qualified crippled veterans like myself. No preferential treatment. They must perform as well as or better than able-bodied men."

"You want our company to be a fucking freak circus?"

Yoshida shook his head in sad frustration. Tomi knew that Yoshida had never failed him, and if he promised cripples would do outstanding work, he would make it so. There were many skilled mechanics among the tens of thousands of crippled veterans. Tomi would get the best of the lot. But men without an arm or leg crawling inside a tank? It would be Yoshida's problem to make them perform. If not, they would be fired and Yoshida would stay. Tomi had nothing to lose.

"I agree to try it as an experiment. We will start with a few in your shop. I hold you responsible."

"So be it, Tomi. Now please call me a taxi. I don't feel so good. Wasn't supposed to sneak out of the hospital."

"I'll have someone drive you back. From now on, when you want to come here, call and I will send a car for you. The sooner you get fitted with a prosthetic leg, the better. Just between us old motor pool gooks, I don't manage the shop as well as you." They clasped hands Yankee-style. Yoshida spun his wheelchair around and left.

***

There were no tears when Lord Suzuki and Tomi discussed the future. "When my will is read, all will be shocked that you will not replace me. Surprised?

"No, Uncle, I'm relieved." Their discussions were blunt as time ran out. "We both know I haven't the zeal to lead Suzuki Industries as you did."

"Precisely. You'd do a decent job, but your true passion, like mine, is building your own company. But you must always continue to be on the board of directors. Your large stock inheritance requires your active participation and I know you will always vote as I would."

A low groan escaped his flaccid mouth. For once, he didn't protest when Tomi called in the doctors and nurses waiting in the hall. All had been handpicked by Doctor Otomo long before the scientist's corpse was fished out of the Imperial Moat the morning after the Suzuki's freedom party. Despite the long distance from Takahashi's hotel to the canal, there was no evidence of foul play and the police quickly dismissed the case as 'accidental drowning due to intoxication.' Scant newspaper space was given to the mishap or to Otomo's background. The *Yakuza* weren't alone in wanting Doctor Otomo quickly forgotten.

Tomi had had his technical people pour over Otomo's personal notes, but they found nothing remotely related to polio or cancer. If there had been a secret path to a cure, it died with the science monster of Unit 731. Or had Otomo lied?

The doctors and nurses eased Suzuki's agony with a shot. He insisted that Tomi stay with him, even when they changed his diapers. He was no longer embarrassed over his accelerating weakness, which brought the two men closer.

They resumed talking as if nothing happened. Tomi was unperturbed when Suzuki referred to himself in the past tense. "You can't patch tanks and jeeps forever. Your uncle's death gives you all the growth capital your little company needs for a few years. What will you do when this goldmine of a war ends?"

"I've been working on one of Perry's ideas. He wrote me from Korea while recovering from his wound. He suggests we produce a small automobile for the domestic market."

Suzuki grunted excitedly. "How big is the market for such a car? What about competition?"

"Honorable Uncle, Japan's car manufacturer executives are your personal friends, but, with respect, I think they are wrong. Why must we imitate the West's inferiority?"

For the first time in hours, Suzuki smiled. "Explain." Talking business made him forget pain.

"Detroit, especially Ford and Studebaker, have new, dramatic styles that look fine but are much the same under the sheet metal. The French and Italians have well-designed cars but require much maintenance. Germany's Volkswagen is mechanically superior, but its little air-cooled engine lacks horsepower and its unsynchronized gear box takes getting used to. Only the crazy English enjoy repairing their undependable cars every weekend."

"American cars give Japanese owners status," Suzuki retorted. "You'd gamble your uncle's inheritance on a weak market dominated by Detroit giants?" Suzuki asked with a cunning smile.

"Perry's bold idea requires a skirmish before we mount a full-scale attack."

"You spend too much time fixing broken tanks! Military strategy doesn't apply to cars."

Tomi was stubborn. "Motorcycles first, Honorable Uncle. Then, a tiny three-wheel car containing a motorcycle engine; then a bigger four-wheeler. The production is the same; only the scale differs. There's a domestic need for a quality motorcycle. I'll build a plant to produce 2-cylinder motorcycle engines that can easily be switched over to 4-cylinder engines for the home market."

"Dollars are better than yen, Nephew. You'd ignore the export markets?"

Tomi waved a negative hand. "The world regards Japanese products as cheap and unreliable because of our pre-war crap. This won't change overnight. I must first succeed in the domestic market. By the time I export, all flaws will be gone."

"And what is the tactical weakness in this ambitious scheme you and your *gaijin* friend have dreamed up?" Suzuki never trusted a man who was unaware of his own weaknesses.

"I'm not an engineer or production expert, but when I visited the big Japanese truck factories, their production lines reminded me of an old newsreel of Henry Ford's first plant. The smug engineers I met were like the dolts who designed my armored car in Nanking and the inferior tanks in the Great Pacific War. Damn things were obviously underpowered and unreliable. Japan may lack creative engineers and designers. Do I have to hire smarter Americans or Europeans?"

Lord Suzuki whispered, "It's not brains, it's culture. Get my briefcase from the desk." Every morning at dawn, General Suzuki's second-in-command personally delivered a case bulging with daily financial and production status reports to the dying *shogun*.

He leafed through the case. "Here it is. An American statistician, W. Edwards Deming, lectured before the Union of Japanese Scientists and Engineers last July. Made quite an impression. Before Dr. Otomo had his unfortunate accident, he sent me lecture notes, which are being published. Deming's subject was 'Statistical Control of Quality.' Take these notes home. We'll talk about it tomorrow morning."

Tomi would have to cancel several meetings. He took the packet and bowed. "Sleep well, Uncle. I'll see you for breakfast."

At home, Tomi's excitement grew after reading a few pages. The document was a blueprint of how Tomi could efficiently build motorcycles, automobiles or anything else.

All that Tomi accepted as wisdom was wrong, according

to the unconventional Professor Deming, who said the buyer, not the builder, was the ultimate judge of quality. Feedback from employees and customers was encouraged. Boiled down, his concept was: "Constantly improve product and service through innovation, worker education and research. Be alert for defective products and staff incompetence. Select suppliers for quality, not price. Improve production and service by consistently improving quality.

"Supervisors and employees must work together for better products and must not be afraid to report problems to management. Create a sense of teamwork and eliminate 'top-down' goals and slogans. Improve and explain. Let employees set their own goals. Eliminate numerical quotas because they don't stress quality. Management must listen to problems and suggestions to build teamwork and better workmanship. Use statistical quality control techniques so everyone strives for improved quality."

Deming was ignored by American industry, but not by Japan. His eight days of lectures created a revolution in manufacturing thought. Tomi had re-read the Deming notes for the fourth time when the telephone rang. By the time Tomi returned to the compound, Lord Suzuki had joined his astute blacksmith ancestors.

At daybreak, Suzuki's executive vice president arrived with the daily briefcase. He bowed deeply, offered condolences and presented it to Tomi, who bowed lower and formally handed it back as if it were a sword. The gesture told the executive that he, not Tomi, was the next leader.

Doctor Deming's blueprint enabled Tomi to create a new kind of company. For his new corporate symbol, Tomi selected a stylized version of the white pine leaf for the same reason Suzuki gave thirteen years ago -- it endured without decay. Tomi would build for the sake of building, because he too, had no successor.

CHAPTER TWENTY TWO
DEARBORN, MICHIGAN   JUNE 1954

"It's no secret. We perfume the pig, same as GM and the others," Falbot said when Tomi asked about next year's model.

Perry muttered, "Can't help you, Tomi. Must be new slang." Japanese businessmen never speak *Nihongo* in front of American hosts, but Perry was vain. Since marrying Yoshida's daughter, Noriko, Perry acted more Japanese than Tomi. He was proud to be the bilingual executive of a Japanese auto company, a status that far exceeded his steelworker family background.

"Please forgive my poor English," Tomi asked, "but what is perfume the pig?" Tomi had few illusions about American automakers, but the bankers insisted he tour Detroit, as many Japanese executives had done following the 1952 Peace Treaty.

Falbot smiled. "Your English is fine. Perfuming the pig is slapping chrome and flash on an existing model between the big design change years. We don't touch the skin, chassis or engine. Best way to goose sales without big bucks. We move the iron, the dealer profits from cherry trade-ins and the customer drives a new car. You'd do well to follow our example and start perfuming the pig in your small domestic market."

Perry glowered, upset that Detroit's smug executives treated them like the manufacturing midgets they were. When TomiCar started four years earlier, Japan was producing around 30,000 autos to the U.S.'s 8,000,000. Tomi suspected that towering American arrogance could be exploited.

Perry was impatient because they weren't selling cars in the U.S. When he left the Army to join TomiCar, Tomi belatedly discovered that his round-eyed friend didn't truly 'think' Japanese, despite his fluency. Yankee culture had permanently crippled his mind. Tomi's estimation of Perry was the same as Lord Suzuki's opinion had been of Tomi when he had been a young Imperial officer. Perry and his countrymen saw the world in black and white, and demanded instant solutions. Such lack of nuance and patience were flaws. Although he was truly fond of Perry and America, Tomi knew he had to exploit the strengths and weaknesses of both.

To show that he understood, Tomi smiled. It was difficult to stay current with the fluid, colorful slang. Tomi knew that 'moving iron' meant selling cars to avoid swollen inventories, and that a 'cherry trade-in' was a used car in pristine condition. Slang bared a society's attitudes.

The next evening, when Tomi's hotel elevator halted and four rowdy civilians wearing incongruous military caps entered, one peered down at Tomi's visitor name tag and sneered. "Hey guys. Here's a gook I musta missed on Okinawa. So fuckin' many of 'em, it was like shootin' squirrels." Tomi was reminded that many of tomorrow's car buyers were still yesterday's enemies. Tomi pretended he didn't understand. During the slow elevator ride to the lobby, Tomi blocked his humiliation and the smell of the sneering Yankee by retreating to his inside and dwelling on the slang expression, 'Like shootin' squirrels.'

Six years before the Pearl Harbor attack, animal lovers in Japan had introduced the North American squirrel. The cute beggars of food in public parks were thought to be superior to the shy Asian flying squirrels that hid in forests. The 'made in U.S.A.' squirrels brought spotted fever, ticks, lice and other diseases that quickly spread among humans and Japan's native creatures. Another grim joke by the gods of unintended consequences, who allowed starving people to be shot like squirrels on Okinawa.

In the lobby, Perry saw Tomi's dark look. "Something wrong at home? Is my Noriko OK?"

"What's wrong is here. The war still isn't over for some Americans." He told Perry about the elevator incident in hushed *Nihongo*.

Perry said, "I know that type. Fucker was probably a rear echelon jerk who never saw real combat -- phonies with itchy trigger fingers were a dime a dozen after the toughest fighting. All blowhards and braggarts."

"Almost nine years since the war, yet the hate remains. Perhaps it's too soon for us to enter the U.S. market."

"No! The Nazis killed millions of Jews, yet American Jews now buy Mercedes and Volkswagens just like everyone else. Germany supports Israel. Except for former POWs, who have damn good reasons to hate, and a few assholes, most Americans no longer regard Germany and Japan as enemies."

They took the last empty booth in the hotel bar which was rapidly filling up with executives, conventioneers wearing military caps and overly-friendly women in tight dresses. Tomi asked Perry about his afternoon. Tomi had visited a numbing row of executive offices, while Perry had gone on a factory tour, permitting him to do what he called 'shit house sleuthing.' When the Army Military Police belatedly cracked down on black market dealings, Perry went undercover, posing as a new replacement in units with high rates of theft. Perry gathered evidence by overhearing latrine conversations while pretending to read 'Stars & Stripes' with his pants around his ankles.

Perry said, "Told my company guide that I had the runs and spent time in restrooms listening to guys taking sports and numbers bets. Never saw so much goofing off on company time. Seems management doesn't care as long as quotas are met."

"How can a factory run without worker discipline?" Tomi blurted before recalling that Detroit auto workers had been forced to strike for bathroom breaks and pay increases. Before the war, one car company hired thugs to attack strikers with baseball bats.

Perry shrugged. "Everything is different here than back home. Heard a guy bitch about running out of engine mount bolts. Boss told him to use ordinary bolts until the right ones arrived. How many cars rolled out with weak engine mounts?"

"A supervisor put his quota above quality? Perhaps that was a rare isolated case."

"No way. Everyone knows somebody who got stuck with a fucking Monday morning lemon. I'll never forget my old man's 1939 Hudson sedan."

"What's a Monday morning lemon?"

"A car that leaves the factory with all kinds of problems. Some workers and inspectors are so hung over on Mondays or after holidays that mistakes are common."

"But surely the company fixes a factory defect for the customer?"

"No. The dealer sends the complaint to zone, who bounces it up to region. Those guys' bonuses are based on minimizing factory-related repairs. The buyer gets the runaround while making payments on a goddam lemon and the repair bills pile up. Drove my old man nuts! When his Hudson was in the shop, he'd bar-hop on the long uphill walk home from the mill. He was a mean drunk and gave Mom and us kids lots of pain." No wonder Perry, a tough kid from Pittsburgh, had re-invented himself in Japan.

"Ah, so. That explains what happened today. The plant manager I visited approved using automatic transmissions designed for another model due to a delivery delay. The manager bragged to me that by the time the transmissions started slipping, the odometers would be on their fourth digit. He ordered the affected cars to be spread among dealers in America's snowbelt and ordered extra transmission replacement parts for the profitable repairs. The service people were to tell dealers that it was the drivers' fault for spinning the drive wheels when they got stuck in deep snow. The plant manager probably thought I pulled the same production trick at TomiCar."

They ordered hamburgers and more beer. Tomi thought the world's most successful automakers were both bright and stupid. They generated big profits efficiently, yet ignored Dr. Deming's Law of Quality Control. *Deming-Sama* was Industrial Japan's guiding spirit of quality. No one in Detroit had even heard of him, so they worshiped quotas over quality. No wonder lemons slipped through and they sold 'perfumed pigs.'

Thanks to Dr. Deming's principles, the lowest TomiCar worker had the authority to stop the production line whenever he spotted a problem. Japanese employees worked harder and smarter because they were responsible for quality. In return, they enjoyed lifetime employment and job dignity. Japan made better cars because of Dr. Deming.

Even if Americans no longer hated their former enemy, the 'made in Japan' reputation for inferior products lingered. Tomi had to decide whether to invest in greater production line quality inspections or a modest warranty that covered rare factory defects. Either way was a gamble. Since Perry would be selling TomiCars in America, Tomi asked which quality route had the most appeal to Americans.

"TomiCar must offer both," Perry said through a mouthful of beef, onion, pickle and bun.

"Both?"

"Yes, production quality control plus a money-back guarantee. We'll prove our superiority by giving every buyer an iron-clad factory warranty. None of the horseshit Detroit gets away with."

"Can't be done with a low-priced car. We'll go broke."

"We're sure to go broke if we don't offer a quality car with a guarantee. Only way to prove TomiCar isn't pre-war crap."

Tomi growled like a master scolding a clumsy servant. "Don't try to make your sales task easier with extravagance! I'm overextended. You know I invested my uncle's inheritance in expanding the factory. You must sell cars in America without spending money I don't have."

The hurt on Perry's face revealed that Tomi had leaked too much inside anger. "Sorry. Okay, convince me."

A fast eater, Perry washed down the last bite of his food, and forgetting he wasn't in Japan, politely burped loudly. Startled patrons glared at him. Perry bobbed his head and droned, "*Watashi no tomodachi kookyuui*, my friend of superior rank." In case the old-fashioned title wasn't sufficient ass-kissing, he repeated Tomi's favorite quote from Confucius: "The path to genuineness is to choose what is good and cling to it." To hear ancient Chinese wisdom quoted in *Nihongo* by a *gaijin* in a noisy bar was odd. But everything about TomiCar was odd.

Perry used English to make his case. "U.S. car buyers are afraid of getting stuck with lemons. What are the odds, one lemon in 200? One in 500? Who can tell? Lemons happen because Detroit suffers from quality control lapses and poor labor-management relations."

"So! The buyers will be even more suspicious of our 'made in Japan' cars."

"No. It's a fantastic marketing opportunity. We will sell our cars with a money-back offer: 'If your TomiCar is a lemon, we'll repair it free of charge or buy it back from you.' TomiCar will stand out from all the other American and Japanese auto makers."

"I prefer outstanding profits."

Perry said patiently, "Thanks to Dr. Deming and you, TomiCar produces better quality cars than Detroit, so what are we risking? Take 5% less profit from our American sales and reserve it against complaints and the rare buy-back. Dealers will be delighted with the sales lift they'll get with our lemon ad campaign."

"What lemon ad campaign?"

"A Japanese responds to the direct question, 'Do you have lemons?' with 'Yes, we have no lemons.' But an English-speaker says, 'No. We have no lemons.' Tomi, please say, 'Yes, we have no lemons' in your worst gook troop accent."

After a long pause, the shame and misery of the former latrine orderly colored his utterance: "Yes, we have no remons at TomiCar."

"Use that same sad reluctance when you repeat it in our radio and TV ads. It shows how serious you are about TomiCar's quality. 'Yes, we have no lemons' and our money- back guarantee will convince otherwise dubious car buyers."

"That's crazy! We can't afford a guarantee, let alone a big advertising campaign, not to mention a training course for dealers' mechanics. No! We start small and grow gradually."

"If we start small, we stay small and the big competitors will devour us."

Tomi's half-eaten hamburger was cold and the beer flat. Perry sounded like a glib American salesman making his pitch as his tight fist released a finger for each point, "One, TomiCar is high quality. Two, our 'Yes, we have no lemons' money-back guarantee ads will get noticed. And three, we'll have a strong dealer network."

"There is no point three! Remember how reluctant the established Japanese dealers were?"

"I'll have hungry secondary dealers who can't get profitable franchises from the giants. No smug fat cat dealers."

"Will American banks give weak dealerships loans to buy an unknown car from Japan?"

"No. We will finance dealer inventories from our line of credit."

"What line of credit? Our bank won't finance such a risky scheme. Use the Japanese part of your brain, Perry! That which has never been done before must be wrong because it has never been done before, and thus remains unorthodox and undone."

"There's another source of credit. Takahashi's people."

This time Tomi was careful not to reveal his anger at Perry's foolishness. Tomi startled the waitress when he yelled, "Two double scotches on the rocks, please."

The expensive liquid that burned his gullet was as unfamiliar as his thoughts. Perry's wild 'remon' scheme forced Tomi to examine the *kitsune*, fox of his own ambition. Japan's mystical fox was wiser than humans because it knew hidden dreams and fears.

Tomi's inner fox told him that unless he took the big gamble, TomiCar would remain a fringe player vulnerable to failure. TomiCar's Japanese competitors were all high quality producers -- Honda, Yamaha, Toyota, Mitsubishi, Kawasaki, Nissan and Suzuki Motors. He called Suzuki Motors 'the other, bigger-but-unrelated-by-marriage Suzuki.' All of them, plus European car companies, would keep TomiCar out of the tough Detroit-dominated U.S. market. Perry was right: TomiCar must grab market share quickly because they weren't the only Japanese company with Dr. Deming's quality-oriented production.

If he went to Takahashi for funds, Tomi would become a *Yakuza* stooge. His disgusted bankers might even call in his current loans and Tomi would be deeper in debt to greedy racketeers eager to control legitimate businesses.

Tomi would rather fail than end up as powerless as a worn-out *Yakuza* prostitute. He thought about politicians who, upon gaining high office, managed to separate themselves from crime family obligations made early in their careers. A clever politician knew the *Yakuza* avoided any scandal that might trigger a public clamor against crime and corruption. Could Tomi turn TomiCar into a goldfish bowl so the publicity-shy crime clans would refrain from a brazen takeover?

Perry was silent as Tomi mulled. Chin nested on palm, Perry feared he had lost his argument. He moved his empty whiskey glass around the plastic table like an ice skater making the Arabic figure '8'. Tomi was feeling the scotch as he followed the wet tracing of '8', the Japanese lucky number.

It reminded Tomi of the famed Toyoda family who, after the war, changed the company name to Toyota because in the *Katakana* alphabet it took eight lucky strokes to spell 'Toyota.' Their superior quality cars were such a success that Toyota Motor Corp. Ltd. had recently formed a separate sales corporation to expand its overseas markets.

If Tomi used a big *Yakuza* loan to capitalize a separate U.S. public corporation, while keeping his Japanese manufacturing corporation separate and at arm's length from them, he'd have the goldfish bowl visibility needed to avoid a takeover. Tomi would also offer bargain-price shares to Perry's U.S. dealers and distributors. The *Yakuza* wouldn't dare take over an American corporation that sold TomiCars, given the U.S. Securities and Exchange Commission oversight.

But there was a major flaw: the *Yakuza's* loss of face. It would eventually become obvious to everyone that Tomi had outwitted the crime clan and he would be punished, perhaps in an 'accidental' drowning.

The only way to avoid *Yakuza* vengeance was for Tomi to lose face. Somehow, the world must think that Tomi was a sucker, outmaneuvered by the far more clever crime bosses. Negotiating through Takahashi, he would reluctantly agree to a staggering interest rate that would satisfy their monumental greed. Takahashi knew Tomi well enough to recognize the hidden stratagem, but hopefully his masters would not. It would be years before Tomi could restore his personal reputation, but by then TomiCar would have won its share of the American market, and the loan repaid many times over.

Tomi would endure a flood of disgraceful publicity as the 'gook troop latrine cleaner' and 'stupid Sendai pig farmer' whom the *Yakuza* loan sharks outwitted. He would be the high-born sucker that Japan's press loved to hate. The humiliation would be as bad as when he ate the venereal cream sandwich at the train station. But he had no choice.

Tomi scribbled numbers on damp paper napkins. Unlike the U.S. sales corporation supplying credit to dealers, the Japanese factory must build and export TomiCars without *Yakuza* money. He had to assemble domestic and export car models on the same line. Mixing the domestic model and the drastically different export model simultaneously had never been done before. His employees would have to work overtime without extra pay, and his suppliers had to accept promissary notes instead of cash.

He made several flawed financial assumptions before he was able to come up with a competitive U.S. car price and a slim profit margin, allowing for exorbitant interest payments. To make any profit, he had to gamble that the U.S. dollar would move up sharply against the yen. Tomi was building a flimsy house of cards with too many *moshi*, ifs.

"Perry, can you sell 5,000 cars a year in the U.S.?"

"Best I can do is 2,000 tops by Year Three or Four."

"You must sell 2,500 units in the introduction year and 5,000 by Year Two, or we lose everything." Tomi deliberately understated the far higher sales quantity needed for survival. It was too soon to tell Perry the truth.

"Sell 2,500 units in Year One? Impossible! What if there's another recession, or someone matches our warranty offer? What if I can't get enough dealers?"

"Do you believe in your plan or not? Sign up three times the dealerships you think you need. Have a TomiCar dealer in every small town in the U.S.

Perry protested, "I won't have time to train a staff! I'll have to set up the dealer network by myself. I'll be on the road for the entire first year. No sense bringing Noriko here to be alone in a foreign land. She's better off with her family." Unlike a Japanese husband, Perry hated being away from his wife.

"I'd like to fly back to Japan to see her once in a while, Tomi," he added ruefully.

Both knew Perry would be living out of a suitcase in shabby motels, eating greasy food and working 14 hour days, 7 days a week. Given Tomi's habit of demanding updates in around-the-clock phone calls. Perry wouldn't sleep much.

"Don't worry. I'll barter a few cars for airline tickets. You'll get home several times a year," Tomi lied, knowing Perry wouldn't have time to fly home, given the outrageous sales goals that would be heaped upon him.

"Thanks, Tomi. When I sell that 5,000th car by Year Three, I'm giving both of us Golden Remon awards." Tomi winced inwardly at such innocence. For Perry's plan to succeed, he would become its first victim.

"Every time a dealer makes his sales quota, he'll get a 'Golden Lemon Award' ... a gold-plated lemon presentation, with all his customers invited for free lemonade, lemon meringue pie and lemon drop candy." Perry gushed, "America's going to be 'lemon' conscious. Your face and fake gook 'remon' accent will be famous. How much of a guarantee can we afford? 36 months? 48?

Tomi ran out of cocktail napkins but knew his numbers. "Two years is all we can warranty. No tires or air conditioning. Only engine, transmission and drive train."

"Biggest market is California. Air conditioning's a must."

"OK. Air conditioning," Tomi mentally saddled Perry with another 800 cars in the hidden sales goal. "Why aren't you asking for consumer market research like Detroit uses?"

Perry shook his head. "Our quality level is far beyond the expectations of car buyers here, but if I ask, 'Would you buy a Japanese car?' the answer would be 'no'. We'll attract them with our money-back guarantee and surprise them with our quality."

Tomi's hidden sales targets would shock the trusting Perry, but Tomi had no guilt about misleading him. A wise general never tells a soldier the low odds for survival before a battle. Imaginative and loyal, Perry was indispensable. He was the *kamikazi* weapon in Tomi's U.S. invasion.

Unwary dealers would eagerly sign up for Perry's no–limit credit plan to bankroll their inventories, never expecting to be saddled with an unprecedented flood of unknown cars. With their showrooms and lots overflowing, the dealers would have no choice but to 'move iron' at lower profits, or face bankruptcy.

If Tomi's cynical 'stuffing' strategy and Perry's unorthodox marketing ideas worked, buyers would flock into stunned dealerships for 'no lemon' TomiCars. If not, Tomi would not be any worse off than if he had failed in slow motion.

Tomi hoped Perry and his marriage would survive the nearly impossible task of compressing six frenetic years into two. Tomi had a fleeting moment of shame as he looked at Perry and remembered the young MP who had asked motor pool gooks to fix his jeep heater on that freezing Sendai night. Perry, responsible for much of their success, had never failed him. But now he was about to sacrifice Perry, as well as himself.

EPILOGUE

The stooped figure in the Imperial Japanese Army uniform glared back at the full-length mirror and saw a vain old man, unhappy that his jowls sagged over the stiff collar. The 'Henry Ford of Japan' was hailed as a self-effacing genius after he insisted that TomiCar's success was due to the Japanese spirit of hard work. Such bullshit was tiresome.

He needed both arthritic hands to lift the solid gold lemon from its wood cradle on the desk. The inscription, 'Yes, we have no lemons,' carved in both the English and *Katakana* alphabets, had made Tomi a celebrity, and his company a legend.

Tomi had worked Perry and Yoshida to death. Perry had a heart attack at age 50, and Yoshida stroked out soon after he retired. Perry's widow, Noriko, hadn't spoken to Tomi since the funerals of her husband and father. Childless, Tomi doted on Perry's two sons, whom he had named as his heirs. But Noriko's silence was a deserved punishment. He returned the lemon to its base for the last time.

TomiCar was the result of his calculated ambition, just as the Rape of Nanking had been the calculated evil of his nation's ambition. The narrow field cap didn't fit on his thick white mane. Too much hair. Too much guilt. A lifetime of too much, too little, and all too fast.

The priceless Sung dragons Tomi had acquired at great cost were now rotated every six months among the world's most prestigious museums in a special exhibit free to the public. The old Nanking priest had been right: Tomi's life was long and bitter.

'The past is a bucket of ashes,' the poet Sandburg had written. Tomi's bucket brimmed with a shame that he must empty. The older he got, the more his war sins scalded. His sword and faded medals were real, but the uniform was a made-to-order fake for the man who had lost his honor at Nanking.

Japan still officially denied The Rape of Nanking and other war crimes, including its comfort women sex slave sins, despite mountains of evidence and countless witnesses. To deny monstrous evils was to repeat it. Japan had to admit its war guilt.

Tomi's boots stood erect like two brown and glossy exclamation marks from his ugly past. Vanity prevented him from getting a servant to help. Breathing short jagged bursts, he wrestled on the unyielding boots.

He called his driver, who was shocked to see his master in a uniform from the dim past. It was a short drive through the empty streets of central Tokyo to *Yasukuni Jinja*, the National Military Shrine. There, in predawn darkness, Tomi prayed to his family and the three million souls who perished in the Great Pacific War.

Hot tears escaped and splattered on the ground when he made a final bow. Making as crisp an about-face as his worn hips allowed, he tried to march back to his limousine with dignity, knowing that his stride resembled Charlie Chaplin's comical walk.

Tomi eased his aching spine into the soft leather rear seat and said, "Drive slowly." At a funereal pace, the limo glided toward the Imperial Palace moat.

His father had committed *seppuku* here, where the Imperial Japanese Army Club once stood. "Stop here, then return home. I won't need you again," Tomi instructed the puzzled chauffeur.

Staring at the departing *Taiko Daiyamondo*, the Taiko Diamond limousine, Tomi was proud that it outsold its inferior, the Rolls-Royce. Every TomiCar model carried a variation of the name 'Taiko.' There was the *Taichan*, the compact sedan; the *Terri-Taiko* sports coupe; the *Ichiban Taiko* luxury sedan; and the *Daiyamondo* limousine, which he thought of as 'Taiko's Tears.'

The glow of the limousine's distinctive taillights disappeared and Tomi sighed. No choice then, and none now. He must apologize for his nation's war crimes so that Japan might face its future with honesty, not denial. The plaza bordering the castle moat was empty. He thought of the distances of his life:

Almost a half mile from the Palace to the Shrine; less than a half mile from where the Military Academy stood. The distances between his beginning and end were half-assed fractions, not precise metrics. But his Japanese soul was whole.

He faced southeast. Behind the Imperial Palace outer wall of massive grey stone blocks stood the Emperor's Inner Palace. He bowed and silently screamed, *"Banzai!* Live ten thousand years!" – not for the man who dwelt within, but for Japan's hoped-for moral leadership.

Tomi reached into his uniform pocket for a white envelope, and placed it on the ground. Written on the envelope in bold, black strokes were the Japanese characters, *'Nippon wa shazai suru,* Japan acknowledges fault.'

A gentle breeze playfully wafted the envelope. He slipped off his Rolex to paperweight the fluttering document, which announced how his wealth would be used to fund a foundation for victims or their descendants of Japanese crimes during the Great Pacific War. Copies of the letter had already been sent to major news services around the world. Hopefully, his celebrity death would empty his bucket of shame. He prayed that all would heed the last sentence of his letter, written in Japanese and English:

If one person is despised as a gook, then we are all gooks. The world's future depends upon our mutual respect and compassion. We are all brothers and sisters.

He fumbled with the old-fashioned fly buttons to expose his belly. He inhaled bravely, but exhaled a whimper.

He gripped the family sword that would soon exist in a world without a Tomigawa. His first cut was weak, tentative. Tomi forced himself to fall upon the blade -- a bad decision -- clumsy and messy. Blood puddled the slab of Tokyo's unyielding concrete skin. As he slipped into final weariness, the old man wondered if humankind would be worthy of his pain.

There are courageous Japanese school teachers, writers, war veterans and others who champion the truth. But their political leaders continue to deny Japan's war crimes, cynically waiting for victims and witnesses to die off. Modern Japanese history textbooks are sugarcoated with 'spin' and falsehoods. Even Japan's rich Korean-Chinese cultural roots are disdained amid pseudo racial superiority. To deny the past is to be trapped in a quagmire of undigested history.

"By three things is the world sustained: by truth, by judgement and by peace."

–The Talmud

"...and some truths are best revealed as fiction."

– R.W.